W9-ALM-129

WITHDRAWN

738 DAYS

738 DAYS

STACEY KADE

A TOM DOHERTY ASSOCIATES BOOK

NEW YORK

This is a work of fiction. All of the characters, organizations, and events
portrayed in this novel are either products of the author's imagination
or are used fictitiously.

738 DAYS

Copyright © 2016 by Stacey Kade

All rights reserved.

A Forge Book
Published by Tom Doherty Associates, LLC
175 Fifth Avenue
New York, NY 10010

www.tor-forge.com

Forge® is a registered trademark of Tom Doherty Associates, LLC.

The Library of Congress Cataloging-in-Publication Data is available upon
request.

ISBN 978-0-7653-8040-1 (hardcover)
ISBN 978-0-7653-8041-8 (trade paperback)
ISBN 978-1-4668-7413-8 (e-book)

Our books may be purchased in bulk for promotional, educational, or
business use. Please contact your local bookseller or the Macmillan
Corporate and Premium Sales Department at 1-800-221-7945, extension 5442,
or by e-mail at MacmillanSpecialMarkets@macmillan.com.

First Edition: June 2016

Printed in the United States of America

10 9 8 7 6 5 4 3 2 1

To everyone who still believes in love, in spite of being bent and broken by this world. Don't give up.

ACKNOWLEDGMENTS

All writers have story ideas that intrigue them but won't likely ever see the light of day. Too weird. Too dark. Too scary to contemplate writing.

This is one of mine. And the joy of seeing the idea become a full-fledged book has been beyond measure! I owe so many people an enormous debt of gratitude for the realization of Amanda and Chase's story.

To Linnea Sinclair, my critique partner, who said, "Yes, write that one," when I dared bring up the idea. To my incredible agent, Suzie Townsend, whose unwavering confidence in and enthusiasm for this story gave me the confidence I needed to write it.

To my editor and my friend, Whitney Ross, who gave Amanda and Chase a home and a future beyond scribbled notes in my journal. Thank you! It has been so much fun working together to make this story come to life.

To everyone at Tor/Forge for being excited about this book. You guys are amazing! Thank you especially to Amy Stapp and Seth Lerner. (Seth, I *love* the cover!)

To everyone at New Leaf Literary & Media, especially Kathleen Ortiz, Jess Dallow, and Danielle Barthel.

To Brent Crawford for generously sharing his experiences with acting and being on set. (I took *huge* liberties with the information, so any mistakes are mine.)

To Sophie Jordan, who gave me the advice I desperately needed to write certain scenes in this book.

To those near and dear to me who listen patiently, force me to step away from my computer every once in a while, and/or provide yummy carbohydrates in mass quantities: my husband, Greg Klemstein; my sister, Susan Barnes; my parents, Steve and Judy Barnes; Age, Dana, and Quinn Tabion; Ed, Debbie, Lauren, and Eric Brown; Becky Douthitt; and Michael, Jessica, Grace, and Josh Barnes. I love you!

Also, Taylor Swift. I always write to music, and *1989* was on repeat while I wrote and revised this book. "You Are in Love" made me cry every time.

738 DAYS

PROLOGUE

Amanda Grace

Two years ago

Amanda. Wake up. Chase's voice is urgent in my ear.

I don't want to move. I know from experience that this hazy moment before full consciousness, before the pain kicks in, is the best it's going to get. As it is, I can already feel the rawness between my legs returning, the distant throb in my cheekbone growing sharper, and the taste of stale blood is getting stronger in my mouth.

He must have loosened another tooth last night. A molar, maybe; those are pretty much the only undamaged ones I have left.

Amanda, get up. Chase sounds commanding, but there's also panic, which he's trying to hide. *This is it. Our chance. Listen.*

The thump of heavy boots on the stairs to the basement makes my heart skitter in my chest, like an animal frantic to escape from behind my ribs. Just like usual.

But something else is different this time.

I listen more closely.

Two sets of footsteps, and then . . . voices.

"It sounds like it might be a circuit board. That means parts. Or maybe it's just a dirty sensor. I won't really know until I get into the furnace." This new voice is male as well, but it sounds older, out of breath, and vaguely annoyed.

Someone else is here. Someone besides Jakes.

The realization shoots electricity through my veins. In all the time I've been in this room—years, I think, but I'm not sure how many—no one has been in the house, let alone in the basement. The sole footfalls on the floor overhead have always been Jakes's distinct drag/shuffle.

Until today.

I open my eyes, realizing belatedly that my left eye isn't co-operating. It's swollen shut. But that doesn't matter. Someone else is *here*.

"Furnace is this way," Jakes says, his voice growing louder as he moves closer to the false wall that hides the entrance to my cell. His tone holds that sullen note I know too well, and everything in me recoils. He's in a bad mood.

My heart sinks. That's only going to make things so much worse later.

Not if you're gone, Chase says stubbornly. He's been here almost as long as I have, keeping me company, keeping me sane. He still believes that we'll get out one day. I can't afford to think like that. It hurts too much.

"You can fix it today, right?" Jakes demands.

"Don't know. Won't know until I have a look," the repair guy says, his irritation clear. I can picture Jakes shifting from foot to foot, his rage contained, but barely, by the constant motion. He is a control freak—and a violent sicko freak on top of it—but the control thing is huge. Letting someone else into his little kingdom has to be just pissing him off beyond all measure. And I would be the one to pay for it.

Another reason to get out of here now, Chase reminds me from where he's leaning against the opposite wall, the sole of his black motorcycle boot pressed flat against it. His posture is relaxed, but tension is thrumming through him. If he could shout for me, he would do it. But he can't, so he's stuck.

"Excuse me," the repair guy says to Jakes pointedly. The furnace is right outside my room. I see it every time Jakes comes in. And I can easily imagine Jakes in the way, standing guard in front of the section of the wall that opens to where I am.

Actually, I don't have to imagine it; the piece of drywall on hinges doesn't quite reach all the way to the floor, so when I turn my head, I can see their shadows moving in the inch-wide gap as Jakes reluctantly cedes his position.

After a moment, the repairman settles with a sigh in front of the furnace. The tools hanging on the false wall jingle slightly when he bumps it. He is *that* close.

The temptation to call out rises up in my chest, but it dies before any sound can emerge. Jakes is down here somewhere, too. If I make noise, try to ask for help, and Jakes hears me . . .

I close my one good eye as terror dries out my throat.

Amanda, you have to let this guy know that you're in here, Chase insists. I can feel his gaze boring into me, those dark blue eyes so familiar to me after months of staring at them. *Today is the day we've been waiting for. You may not get another chance.*

I can't. Jakes might hear me, I say. Leaving this horrible place, this cell decorated to look like a twisted version of a girl's room, feels like an impossible dream, one I gave up a long time ago. Focusing on survival takes all my effort. It seems so much safer in that moment to stay curled up on the mattress. *He'll kill me.*

He's going to kill you anyway, Amanda, Chase roars. *DO SOMETHING.*

Hot tears roll silently down my bruised face and into my hair as I slide off the mattress onto the floor, taking all the pink and frilly, ridiculous and hateful bedding with me. I can't scream; it's too much. I just can't. But maybe I can try something else.

The air out here is much colder, and the icy concrete beneath the thin pink polyester nightie that Jakes has given me to wear sends a shiver through me.

What if he just ignores me? What if he asks Jakes about me and he believes whatever Jakes tells him? I demand of Chase. *That could happen.*

But I'm moving, scooting across the floor. Chase nods encouragingly, his blond hair perfect as ever in the early morning light that seeps through the cracks in the boarded-up windows. *You have to try.*

The chain wrapped around my left wrist moves with me, the faint clink muffled by blue plastic wrapped around the links. Just like what you'd use if you'd chained a dog in your yard and didn't want to hear him moving around.

The chain is attached to a thick metal hook that's set into the concrete wall to my left. Normally the chain is long enough for me to reach the bathroom on the other side of the room—a mold-infested shower without a curtain, a chipped and broken sink, and a toilet that barely flushes.

But today my chain was barely long enough to let me turn over on the mattress.

Now I understand why Jakes shortened it so much last night and why last night's "visit" was so much worse. He *knew* someone was coming to the house this morning.

But he didn't dare warn me and give me a chance to plan.

I inch closer to the door, staying flat on my back, my heart fluttering in abject terror. I can't stand, can't walk; the noise of the movement might be enough to draw Jakes's attention. He has to be listening for any hint of rebellion from me. I'm just hoping he won't be *looking* for it.

Once I've reached as far as the chain will allow, I stretch out my right hand. The door and the gap beneath it are right there. So close. My fingers brush the rough, unfinished edge of drywall.

I can't reach, I tell Chase.

You can, he says without hesitation.

Yeah? Whose arm is it? I snap at him.

But he doesn't take offense, just watches me with that expectant look that won't let me off the hook.

Ignoring the shooting pain in my left shoulder, I lean as far forward as I can, putting all my weight against the band of metal on my wrist.

My left shoulder gives an agonizing pop, and I bite down hard on my lip to keep quiet, the blood seeping between my teeth and into my mouth. Then, with one last herculean effort, I thrust my free hand toward the gap.

My fingers fit through, barely, sliding into the slightly warmer air of freedom on the other side.

I freeze. That's it. All I can do. I'm terrified it won't be enough. I'm equally terrified that it'll be too much.

My whole body is quivering with fear, and I want nothing more than to pull my hand back and curl up in a defensive ball.

But I don't.

Chase crouches next to me. *You're okay. You're going to be okay. Just keep at it.*

I listen, waiting for Jakes's bellow of rage and the pounding footsteps toward my door. I'm ready to retreat and huddle into a protective position at an instant's notice.

But there's nothing. Just the off-tune humming from the repair guy and metal clinks and clanks as he opens up the furnace.

That's when I realize there might be something worse than not trying to be rescued: trying and failing.

I risk moving my fingers, scratching what's left of my dirty and bloodied nails against the paneling on the other side of the wall.

The quiet humming and metal clinking continue for a second;

then there's the sound of shifting fabric and a sharp inhale of breath. "What the—"

My lungs lock up, and I can't draw in any air. He *saw* me. Dizziness spirals over me, and white spots dance in my vision. If he calls to Jakes, I'm dead. He might be too.

But another beat of silence passes.

I take the risk of scratching harder, trying to communicate without words. *Help me.*

There's a louder clank then, and a small grunt of effort. Through the gap, I can see the repairman's shadow shifting, moving. He's standing up.

I snatch my hand back, clutching it to my chest, and my left shoulder throbs.

"I need a part from my truck," he says in a louder voice. To me? To Jakes? "I'll be right back."

No, no, no! Don't leave, I beg him silently. *You saw me! I'm here!*

He's going to come back. He's not going to leave you here, Chase promises. *He saw you.*

But Chase's absolute certainty enrages me. I tear my gaze away from the gap beneath the door/wall to glare at him. *How do you know? You're not out there. You're not even real!*

I regret the words as soon as I think them because, in that instant, my hard-won illusion pops like a bubble, and Chase is gone.

I'm alone again, with nothing but the tattered and torn poster of Chase Henry, the same one my sister Liza had in her room, hanging on the opposite wall. He's giving his best brooding smirk to one and all from the page, a single white feather drifting through the background behind him as a nod to the angelic character he plays. But it's flat, two-dimensional. He's not here.

As soon as the repairman's footsteps retreat up the stairs, Jakes comes to my door.

"Are you awake in there, Mandy?" he asks softly in that quiet slippery tone that makes my stomach turn. "He left so quickly.

Did you say something? I hope not. If he finds you, our special time will be over, and I don't want that. Do you?"

His nails scrape against the false wall outside like it's my skin, and trembling, I retch quietly, the bile bitter in my mouth.

It feels like forever, years, decades, centuries, but it's probably only about ten minutes before the doorbell rings, and Jakes curses under his breath and limps toward the stairs to let the repairman in again.

I curl into myself, shaking with quiet sobs. I don't have the strength to try again. And Chase isn't here to push me.

I'm done. It's over.

Except it's really not—the repair guy will eventually leave and Jakes will come back—and I want to die at the thought.

Above my head, a commotion suddenly breaks out: shouting, and running feet that pound the floor so hard that my ceiling shakes, raining bits of dirt on me.

The noise jerks me out of my misery and into panic. Anything unexpected is probably bad. My time here has taught me that too well. Instinct has me scrambling away from the door to huddle in the corner, near where my chain is attached.

I cover my ears with my hands as the chaos above continues, climaxing with a loud bang that I realize must be a gunshot.

Jakes killed the repairman.

I feel a flash of grief, but it's surmounted almost immediately by sheer panic. I'm next, no question.

I don't know how much time passes. It feels like seconds and hours, both. My first clue that someone is in the basement again is the jingle of the tools hanging on the false wall and the loud scrape of the door as it opens.

A scream is trapped in my throat, as always, and I'm pressing myself against the wall before I realize that it's not Jakes at the threshold.

Blond hair scraped back into a ponytail, a short snub nose, deep grooves inscribed between her brows, her mouth drawn into a tight line. It takes a moment for her features to arrange themselves into a face, one I don't recognize. I haven't seen anyone else in so long.

She's wearing a dark blue uniform with a heavy black vest. POLICE is printed in big white block letters across the front of the vest. The letters dance in front of my eyes, refusing to stay put.

"My name is Officer Beckstrom. We're here to help you," the woman says slowly. "Can you tell me your name?"

I shake my head violently. Jakes will be furious if I talk to her. A dim part of my brain registers that something unusual must have happened upstairs, if she's here and he's not. But I don't trust it.

Her brows draw together, pity written across her features, and for the first time in months, I wonder what I must look like. "He's dead," she says gently. "He can't hurt you anymore."

I just stare at her. Those words . . . that's impossible.

"The HVAC guy called 9-1-1 when he saw you," she says, when she sees my doubt. "Jakes ran when he saw us. He was going for a loaded shotgun in the back bedroom."

To kill me. He threatened it often enough. I shudder. Or maybe he thought he could hold them off.

I don't know which is right, and somehow that makes it harder to believe what she's saying. But clearly something has happened.

"He has the key," I manage to say eventually, my voice rusty with disuse. I lift my arm, showing her the chain and the padlock holding the metal band around my wrist. Thanks to my efforts to signal the repairman, fresh blood coats the dull surface, where the edges cut into my skin.

Her mouth tightens at the sight, but she nods and speaks into a radio attached to the shoulder of her vest.

Then she takes a few steps into the room, her gaze searching the corners before she turns her back on them and faces me.

"You're okay, you're okay," she says, approaching me with her hands out, like I'm an animal that might bolt.

She sounds so much like Chase that I look to his poster. But he's still just paper. And I miss him.

"Can you tell me your name?" she asks again when she's closer. She moves to kneel in front of me, and instinctively, I scoot away.

But this time, I answer her. "Amanda Grace."

Her eyes widen slightly. "Amanda Grace," she repeats slowly and with reverence, as if I've said something holy or wise. "We've been looking for you for a long time. We didn't think you were—" She cuts herself off with a grimace.

But I know what she was about to say—they didn't think I was still alive. I'm not upset. It's a reasonable assumption, and one that would have been proven correct, eventually. Even now, I'm not 100 percent sure that they were wrong. I don't feel alive. I don't feel . . . anything. Maybe I am dead, and this whole thing is just a hallucination, my afterlife.

My mouth wobbles on the verge of a hysterical laugh. My version of heaven is simply being rescued from this hellhole. It does make a certain kind of sense.

Another officer appears at the door to my room, which has now been open longer than any time since I've been here. He is younger than Officer Beckstrom. His gaze skates over me, the bruises on my face and the horrible stained and see-through nightgown, before skittering away, two bright spots of color rising on his already flushed face.

Steadfastly avoiding looking at me, he moves into the room just far enough to hand Officer Beckstrom a small, familiar brass key. Then he retreats, but not before I notice that his blue latex gloves are stained red on the fingertips.

Jakes's blood.

Jakes is really dead. That's the only way he would have given up that key. The only way he would have given me up. The revelation snaps through me like lightning, and suddenly, I'm crying without any memory of the tears starting.

Officer Beckstrom murmurs soothing words as she removes

the padlock quickly and efficiently and then the band around my wrist.

The chain drops to the floor with a definitive slap, and it is the single best sound I've ever heard.

In a matter of moments, Officer Beckstrom has a blanket wrapped around my shoulders and she's leading me to the door. Away from the room. Out of hell.

At the threshold, I glance back just once, looking to the poster on the wall, my only company, my only reminder of home for so long, and I send Chase one last message. *You were right. Today was the day. Thank you.*

But he remains silent and still, just ink and hope pressed into paper.

1

Amanda Grace

Present day

The closet in my bedroom at home is exactly sixty inches long and twenty-four inches wide. The floor is hardwood. Pine, I think.

It's not quite long enough for me to stretch out completely, about three inches short, but that's close enough. If I curl up on my side, I'll have plenty of room.

"Come on, Amanda," Mia shouts from downstairs, her voice carrying through my partially open bedroom door. "Let's go!"

"I'll be right there." I will my feet to move, to take me out the door and down the stairs, but I am, for the moment, frozen.

I have good days and bad days. And today is definitely one of the latter. Sample Sundays always are.

The third Sunday of every month, Logan's Grocery offers free bits of cheese, sausage, and burrito on toothpicks, and you'd think they were giving away hundred-dollar bills dipped in gold. The store is always swamped with people filling their carts and their mouths. I do all right during the week, when it's mostly the same faces over and over again, but Sample Sundays are the living embodiment of chaos. And it shreds the last nerve I have. Strangers everywhere, loud noises, unpredictable movements. That's pretty much the trifecta of crap that kicks my anxiety into high gear.

But staying home isn't an option, either. Or, at least, not one I'll allow myself to consider.

"Amma, stop staring at your closet!" Mia bellows. "It's fucking weird."

I grit my teeth. Sometimes having sisters, particularly ones who know you too well, really sucks.

"Mia," my mom snaps sharply. Then her voice drops to a murmur, and I can't hear her words but I recognize the pleading tone. I know exactly what she's saying. The same thing she's been saying for the last two years.

Give her more time. This is a coping mechanism . . .

Don't push . . . she's been through so much. There are bound to be issues.

We just need to try to understand . . .

"I don't care," Mia says defiantly at full volume. My younger sister has never lacked in confidence or lung power. She wants to be a singer or an actress or both. She's been a drama queen since birth; now she's just looking to go pro. "She's the one who freaks out if I go without her. It's her choice."

I close my eyes. That is—or was—true, unfortunately. One of the side effects of surviving the worst possible thing to happen to you is that you're left with this new awareness of the world. There's no control, no true safety; it's all random chance. Anything can happen at any time, to you, to the people you love. The world is full of sharp edges, just waiting to hurt you, one way or another.

The first day Mia went to work at Logan's, six months ago, no one told me. I had a panic attack when she didn't come home, and nothing my parents said could calm me down. It was a terrifying, helpless feeling, all this anxiety washing over me and not being able to stop it. I could understand what they were saying, that Mia was fine, that she would be home soon, but I couldn't stop the alarm shrieking in the back of my mind or the tiny voice that whispered they once thought I'd be home soon, too.

It's a little better now, especially since I started working at Logan's, too, and our schedules mostly overlap. Mr. Logan, the owner, has known my parents forever and hired me without hesitation. It's the epitome of pity employment, if there is such a thing. Still, being there, however difficult, feels more like a triumph than staying home, worrying and wondering.

"It's been two years," Mia complains. "How long do we have to live our lives around—"

"Mia! Can you shut up? I'm trying to study, and you're upsetting Mom." That's Liza, emerging from the den, no doubt with a scowl, and escalating this fight to twelve on a scale of one to ten. Mia and Liza have never gotten along; they are polar opposites. And with me in the middle but preoccupied and unable to keep the peace, it's only gotten worse.

"Butt out, Liza; no one asked you!" Mia shouts. "Amanda, if you're not down in ten seconds, I'm leaving without you."

"Mia, no, you can't," my mother pleads. "She worries about you."

Dr. Knaussen, my current shrink, thinks I lack "closure." I never saw Jakes taken into custody or even his sheet-wrapped remains. So my brain is still trying to protect me by keeping me afraid for myself and Mia, in particular. She's the same age I was when I was taken. The logic is not hard to follow, even if it's frustrating to live with.

That, however, does not explain why this lack of closure has presented itself as an obsession with my freaking closet. Then again, this is the same brain that produced Chase Henry as a "coping mechanism." I didn't even *like* his show when it was on, not after the first season, anyway.

"Mom, Amanda isn't your only kid!" Mia protests.

"I know it's difficult, but you might try not being a selfish brat for a day, Mia," Liza says.

"How is this my fault?" Mia demands in an outraged shriek. "I didn't even do anything! I'm just trying to go to work. "

"Girls, stop, please! Your dad—"

"Isn't here. Is *never* here," Mia says. "Nobody will say it, but it's true. And it's because of her."

A loud crack echoes through the foyer. Liza's hand across Mia's face, I'm sure. I can see it as clearly as if I'm standing right there.

The sound and the ensuing yelp of pain send a jolt through me. That never would have happened before. My family is imploding, and it's my fault. Two years have gone by, and I'm still stuck, still struggling.

I hurry into the hall outside my room and then start down the stairs. "I'm here. It's fine. I'm ready—let's go." I pat my pocket to make sure my plastic name badge is in there.

The three of them look up at me and freeze in place, as if they forgot I was here and able to hear them. My mom is in the middle, but her arms are tight at her sides, as if she doesn't know who to reach for, to comfort or reprimand. Liza and Mia are facing off, Liza with her arms folded across her chest and her chin tipped up defiantly and Mia holding her cheek, her mouth still an open circle of surprise and pain.

It strikes me again how incomplete they look—my mom without my dad, my sisters without me. And yet, there's this sense of weary soldiers in the same battle; they're in this misery together. They are a unit, somehow, formed in my absence, formed *by* my absence. And I'm on the other side of the divide, and I can't reach them, no matter what I do. I guess that makes sense. I was the one taken, but my abduction happened to them.

The argument dies, as if my presence has sucked all the oxygen out of the room. But it still smolders beneath the surface, ready to spring to life again with the faintest breath of encouragement.

"Whatever. I'll be outside." Mia, blinking back tears, spins around and pushes out through the screen door.

Liza's gaze sweeps over me from head to toe, taking in the long-sleeved flannel shirt that hides the scar around my left wrist and the loose-fit yoga pants that hide the rest of me. (So far no one at Logan's has said anything about my very lax adherence to the dress code. Again, I'm sure Mr. Logan has something to do with that.)

Liza's mouth pinches in, but she doesn't say anything. Of course not. She can barely look at me. "Are you okay?" she asks me politely. As if we didn't once share a bathtub and, according to disgusting family lore, apparently poop in unison.

"Yeah, I'm fine," I respond automatically. What else am I supposed to say?

Having established this fact, for whatever it's worth, Liza turns on her heel and returns to the den and her stacks of law school textbooks.

"Are you sure, baby?" my mom asks, wringing her hands. "You don't have to go. We can work on the next section of trigonometry. Help you catch up a little more."

"No, it's okay." My class graduated a little over a year ago, but I still have another six months of home-school high school ahead of me. I tried to go back, tried to reconnect, but my friends had all moved on, finding new friendships, becoming different people, really. Two years is a long time to be gone in high school. It's a long time no matter what, I guess.

One more Sunday of extra catch-up work isn't going to make a difference.

"She's going to work, Ma, not war. She'll be back in eight hours," Mia shouts from the porch. "So will I, if you care."

"I can drive you," my mom offers to me hopefully.

Mia gives a disgusted sigh and stomps down the steps and the path to the sidewalk without looking back. Her bright red hair, about ten shades brighter than my auburn and Liza's hint of highlights, flaps behind her like a warning flag.

"It's okay, Mom. Mia's right," I say. "We'll be back soon."

Any fear I might have had about venturing outside slides to the background as I rush out the door to catch up with Mia before she disappears around the hedge. Whatever might be happening just out of sight is always worse than whatever is in front of me.

The sky is a perfect seamless blue, a sharp contrast to the red and yellow leaves on the trees, and the late October sun is warm on my shoulders. Too warm for long sleeves, but I don't wear anything else these days. It's the kind of day where it feels impossible that anything bad could happen.

Which means I'm on extra-high alert. That's why, as soon as I clear the hedge, I notice the battered black car idling, motor loud and thrumming, on the other side of the street a few houses down, facing us.

Is that weird, out of place? I'm not sure. It's not a car I recognize.

"I don't need a babysitter, Amma," my sister says to me as soon as I reach her.

Apparently she sees no irony in addressing that statement to me using the nickname she gave me because she couldn't pronounce my name when she was, in fact, a baby.

"I know. It's not about that, Mia. It's me, not you." Which, by the way, is still the suckiest excuse in the book, even when it has nothing to do with rejection.

I steal another glance at the car. It's a Mustang, I think. The light off the windshield changes abruptly—the movement of someone inside or a passing reflection? I can't quite tell with the tinted windows.

My stomach grows tight, and the air feels too hot and thick to breathe. My brain produces a vision of the car roaring across the street and a man with a blurry and unidentifiable face pulling Mia inside, while I stand motionless on the sidewalk, unable to do anything.

I swallow hard, try to clear my mind and slow my breathing. Sometimes I can stave off the panic attacks if I catch them fast enough. It's like stopping a roller coaster right at the peak of the hill: a second or two too late and there's nothing to be done but ride it out.

The dumb part is, I've had enough therapy to know this isn't really about a strange car. It's about everything else, my fear about what might happen at the store, what might happen by just being out in the world. I'm fixating on the car simply because it's here, a symbol of all the unknowns that I can't control.

"I snuck out last night," Mia announces, kicking at the dead leaves littering the sidewalk. "Did you know that?"

The shock of her announcement jerks me out of my impending panic attack, dumping me firmly into the present. "No," I manage.

"Just a party at Sammy's, no big deal." She shrugs.

"Sammy who?" It clicks an instant after I ask. "Sammy Lareau?"

She gives me an odd look. "Yeah, Jude's brother."

"But Sammy's my age," I say. What I don't say: *Why is he holding parties that high school girls attend?* "What's he still doing here?"

"Throwing good parties?" She makes an impatient noise. "Who cares? The point is, Dad caught me coming back in. He's sleeping on the family room couch most nights, I guess, if you didn't know." She shoots an accusing glance at me.

Stung, I pause for a step. No, I didn't know that, but that's because someone would have to actually talk to me for that to happen. And my dad, much like Liza, doesn't seem to know what to say to me or even how to be in the same room with me for more than a few minutes.

"He woke Mom up. And when they both finished yelling at me for being 'irresponsible and foolish,' do you know the first thing Mom said to me?" Mia doesn't wait for me to try to guess. " 'What if Amanda had woken up and found you gone?' " She gives a bitter laugh. "It's like, 'Do whatever you want, Mia, as long as it doesn't affect Amanda.' But everything affects you."

The pure venom in her words burns like acid. This from my sister. The one who once followed me around everywhere, begging to be included in whatever I was doing because Liza was ignoring her, or pleading with me to play Don't Break the Ice because Liza had declared it to be babyish.

Like I want it to be this way? I want to shout. *Like I would ever choose to be afraid forever?* I set my teeth against the urge to grab Mia by the shoulders and shake her.

"It's not fair, you know?" she continues. "And I can't even get angry about it without looking like a shitty person. I mean, who gets mad at the girl who was . . . gone for two years?"

Gone. That's the polite euphemism everyone seems to prefer. Like I was on vacation or at sleep-away camp or something.

A fresh burst of frustration blooms in my chest, at Mia, my malfunctioning brain, and Jonathon Jakes for continuing to mess up my life even two years after his death.

But I keep my mouth shut. Because Mia's right. It's not fair. And if her yelling at me makes her look like a shitty person, then my being angry at the quality (or lack thereof) of my life "after" makes me look like an ungrateful one. I mean, I'm the "Miracle Girl," according to the newspapers; I survived. The two girls they dug up from Jakes's backyard were not so lucky.

So I understand a little better than Mia gives me credit for.

Not that I can say that. Not that I can say anything to make it better. We are all just . . . stuck.

Right as we pass the car, it revs up and pulls away from the curb.

I stop, every muscle in my body screaming with tension, my hands and feet tingling, and spots flashing in my vision.

But the vehicle moves past us without hesitation.

After a moment, Mia turns around, realizing that I'm no longer with her. When she sees me, her expression softens with pity, which I hate almost as much as, well, her hatred.

"Just because something bad happened once before doesn't mean it's going to happen again, Amma," she says, taking my arm and tugging me forward gently. She sounds weary and world-wise, older than sixteen. "Past performance is no guarantee of future events, right?" She waves her free hand in a breezy gesture.

I wonder if she knows she's quoting a stock fund commercial instead of some sage philosopher. That is very Mia. She's the ultimate mimic with little care for her source material.

But I just nod and take a breath, trying to force my lungs to accept oxygen by sheer force of will. That's easier than trying to explain, easier than pointing out the flaw in her logic and her false sense of security.

Because what has not yet occurred to Mia—or most people, in fact—is that if that concept is true, the reverse must also be.

In other words, just because yesterday went smoothly doesn't mean today isn't going to fly off the fucking rails when you least expect it.

But nobody wants to hear that from the Miracle Girl.

2

Chase Henry

Why do bad ideas always seem better the night before?

Just one more—come on, man. I'm still good enough to drive.

I know this great backroom poker game. Ten K minimum. We'll kill it.

She is giving you serious come-fuck-me eyes. You should totally get that.

Race you to the next intersection. Pussy brakes first.

I don't know, but I've had enough "night befores" to realize this is a trend, not a one-off kind of a thing. And somehow, I'm still agreeing to crap. Maybe *that's* the better thing to question.

The thick manila folder Elise thrust at me when I climbed in the car is heavy in my hands, and looking at it only makes me feel more uneasy. The labels across the front and the tab section are in all caps, screaming at me: AMANDA GRACE.

I shift uncomfortably in the seat, the leather upholstery creaking beneath me as I stretch my legs out, bracing myself as the driver takes another turn a little too fast. "You sure about this?" I ask Elise.

Her forehead pinched in annoyance, she looks up from her phone, where she's texting with one hand and holding on to the door's armrest with the other. The car service she hired to drive us from our hotel in Wescott, where we're filming, to nearby Springfield has taken her promise of a massive bonus for on-time arrival very seriously. Tires-screeching-around-corners seriously.

"That's so cute," Elise says, her expression smoothing out with a smile. "Your Texas comes through when you're anxious. I never noticed before."

I roll my eyes. "I'm not—"

"We should capitalize on that the next time you have an on-camera. Our target market will eat that up. Cowboys and shit." Before she's even finished her sentence, her gaze is glued to her phone again. "Just make sure it doesn't bleed through on set. Smitty is supposed to be from here. Wherever-the-fuck-this-is, Pennsylvania," she says dismissively.

Smitty is the reason we're here. My first role in over two years. It's a small part, the addict best friend of the lead, in a ridiculously small-budget independent film, *Coal City Nights*. Barely a week's worth of work, and I'm damn lucky it's mine. I only have it because Max Verlucci, the writer/director, was part of the writing staff on the first season of *Starlight*, and he wrote some awesome Brody-centric episodes that gave me a lot to work with. And it probably didn't hurt that Max left the show before things really went to crap. Still, I had to swear to him that I'd take it seriously and I wouldn't fuck around.

When you're on the verge of being homeless and another too-famous, too-soon statistic, it's pretty easy to make that promise and mean it.

Now that *Coal City* is getting industry buzz, thanks to the exploding popularity of the two leads, Jenna Davies and Adam

DiLaurentis, I'm even luckier to *still* be cast. I'm not exactly Hollywood's favorite son at the moment. Or anyone's favorite son, to be honest. You can screw up, yeah, but you've got to have the fame and talent to back it up. I cashed in credit that I didn't have yet, which only pissed people off. So now I'm trying to make a comeback. At twenty-four.

Jesus. Why doesn't anyone ever tell you that sometimes where you start is the best it's ever going to be?

But they don't. And then you spend the rest of your life doing anything and everything you can to get back. Including some shit that maybe you shouldn't.

"Elise . . ." I begin.

She lowers her phone with a sigh. "Chase," she says, mimicking me with more than a hint of impatience. "It's going to be great. There's a fine line between innovative media use and exploitation, and sometimes you've got to cut it closer than everybody else to rise above the noise."

I am not so sure about that. And my doubt must have shown through.

"Chase, either you control the media or the media controls you. It's that simple, sweetie," she says, as if she's speaking to the slow kid who keeps trying to put the square shape in the round hole. She sets her phone down just long enough to squeeze my thigh in what I'm sure is meant to be a sexy distraction or possibly reassurance but comes off more like a very familiar kind of condescension. *Keep quiet, pretty boy. Let the grown-ups do the thinking.*

Elise is only a couple of years older than me, but she's smart, Ivy League smart. And she definitely thinks she's smarter than me. She might be, but it's my life, a fact she doesn't always seem to recognize.

Her hand traces circles higher on my leg, which is, much to my irritation, actually working. My dick has zero conscience, apparently. It occurs to me, not for the first time, that sleeping with my publicist, even if it's only on a casual, we're-like-colleagues-with-benefits basis, was probably not a great choice. Another one of those brilliant "night before" decisions.

"Besides," Elise continues with a coy smile, "she's going to love it. I mean, who wouldn't love to have Chase Henry stop by for a visit?"

Actually, it seems that maybe there are a lot of people these days who wouldn't be so thrilled. At least, judging by the number of callbacks I'm not receiving.

Not that I can blame them, exactly. It's not as if I didn't help this train wreck along with my own stupidity. It's just so weird how fast things turn. Three years ago, maybe four, I was on the number-one show on television, setting new records for the network.

Now I'm here, in a car in the-middle-of-nowhere-Pennsylvania, heading to do possibly the best thing for my career but also maybe my worst thing as a human being, and I can't tell which one it is.

"I mean, God, you saved her life. She says it right there in black and white." Elise gestures at the file she prepared. Or, more likely, her overworked assistant, Nadia. Elise has very clear ambitions, and I seriously doubt that doing her own photocopying fits within that scope. "She's going to be thrilled to see her hero, and the exposure we get will be fantastic. It was the anniversary of her rescue a couple of weeks ago, and everyone's been trying to get an update without any success. I mean, she turned down *People*." Elise shakes her head with a tsk of disapproval. "It's a win-win. Stop worrying."

Reluctantly, I return my attention to the folder and the pages inside. Most of them are printouts from various websites, the relevant portions highlighted in yellow, as if Elise (or Nadia, acting on Elise's instructions) doesn't trust me to find it on my own.

Phrases leap out at me. "Abducted by her former bus driver . . ."

". . . two years in captivity . . ."

". . . Grace, dubbed the 'Miracle Girl,' released a statement saying she's just happy to be home."

". . . escaped when she signaled a furnace repairman . . ."

". . . credits a poster of actor Chase Henry (*Starlight*) with reminding her of home and keeping her focused on escaping the horrible conditions in Jakes's basement."

The *People* magazine cover, dated two years ago, is less discreet. "Chase Henry saved my life" is the pull quote on the front cover. Ironically, it is the one other time Amanda Grace and I have ever shared space—there's a small photo of me in the corner, a publicity shot of Brody scowling from the third season, with the line, "What Former *Starlight* Hunk Is Driving Dangerously Close to the Edge?"

That was the header for my second DUI.

I wonder if we sent something to Amanda. I cringe at the idea of a bouquet showing up at her door with some hideously inadequate note: *Sorry to hear about your abduction. Best, Chase.* But honestly, I have no idea what my team—well, my former team—might have done or not done.

I was a little self-involved back then. Okay, a lot self-involved; I was busy watching my career go down in flames like a meteor over Russia and developing a brand-new problem with alcohol.

But I remember hearing about Amanda and the poster, though only vaguely. Possibly as a talking point on *The Tonight Show* or something. God, I hope I didn't say anything stupid or shitty.

Amanda's picture on the *People* cover, a still from her interview with Diane Sawyer, looks familiar. She's young, probably eighteen at the time, only four or five years younger than me, and pretty with pale skin and reddish-brown hair pulled back in a bouncy ponytail. Her dark eyes are a surprising contrast. She looks a little too thin, but she's smiling, a perfect girl-next-door, volunteer-at-the-animal-shelter expression.

Elise's phone chimes with a text. "Excellent. They're on their way," she says. Her thumbs fly across the screen in reply.

"Who is?" I ask.

She waves her hand dismissively. "Amanda, to her job at the store."

Elise said "they," implying more than just Amanda, but I'm more focused on the implication of her words. "You had someone following her?"

"Of course not." Elise sounds offended. "I had someone watching her house."

I stare at her. "Jesus, Elise, you're stalking a former kidnapping victim?"

Elise leans over and catches my chin, forcing me to meet her gaze. "You are brilliant. I believe in you, Chase." Her green eyes are fierce and sparkling with emotion. "But you need this to go well. *We* need this to go well." She blinks quickly but not before I see the sheen of tears.

Elise took me on when George, my first publicist, dumped my ass into the general office client pool a few years ago. Which basically meant that I no longer had a publicist, even if that wasn't the official stance. Elise, once George's assistant, threw her chips in with mine to start her list when no one else would have me, and she's paid for it with George directing other would-be clients away from her, as punishment. She has almost as much at stake as I do.

And she's right. I need the publicity boost visiting Amanda will give me, especially if she agrees to the set visit Elise has arranged. The media will be all over it—they freaking adore the Miracle Girl—and I need to do something to bring myself back as a trending topic. Preferably something positive, or *seemingly* positive. I have an audition in a couple of weeks for second lead in the new Besson action/adventure flick, and I need that role. I need to at least be considered.

So, yeah, it's ghoulish, but at this point, I'm out of better options. My agent is currently pretending I don't exist, and my manager quit months ago. The money is gone, so are the cars and my condo. The credit card people are calling all the time. And they're about the only ones.

If I don't do something to save myself, I'll be back to shoveling manure on the family ranch in a couple of months. If I'm lucky.

But it's more than that, too. Acting is the only time I ever feel whole, connected to the world and in sync, doing what I'm supposed to be doing. The rest of the time, it's like I'm killing time and trying to blend in . . . badly. I'm most myself when I'm being someone else, weirdly enough. It's not just a job; it's part of who I am.

I need it. I don't know how to be me without it.

So, I have to do anything and everything I can to stop the downhill slide.

I nod in reluctant agreement, and Elise beams at me, any hint of tears vanishing. Then she kisses me quickly before tapping another message out on her phone.

Besides, Elise is right: Amanda will love it, the internet will devour it, and I'll get a chance to show myself off as the new-and-improved Chase Henry.

If my conscience is twinging a little, well, so what? Everybody's happy, and all's well that ends well.

Springfield doesn't look all that different from Wescott, where we're filming. Another small town with stone churches, old houses in bright colors with fancy woodwork, and trees shedding leaves in crazy shades of red and yellow.

But Max grew up in Wescott, and they were eager to welcome him home to film. I wonder, though, if that will still be the case once they actually see the movie. The script is good, excellent, even, but it definitely shows the darker, claustrophobic underbelly of growing up in a small community. Which is exactly why I wanted in. Smitty's "Westville" isn't anywhere near where

I grew up in Texas, but I know these characters, these people. And Smitty reminds me of Eric, my former cast-mate and friend.

The grocery store where Amanda works is not at all what I pictured. It's small, something locally owned. But judging by the sheer number of pickups and battered SUVs in the parking lot, I'm guessing it's just the closest place to buy food, rather than a political message (*Buy local!*) or a status symbol (*Organic only!*) to shop there. I might have been living in L.A. for too long.

We pull in and slow to a stop near the entrance, and Elise snarls at the sight of the paparazzi clustered at the corner of the building, smoking and talking to each other. "I told them to stay out of sight until we got here. They're going to fuck this up."

She turns to me. "Are you ready?"

No. "Yeah." I unbuckle my seat belt and tug my T-shirt down, more for the calming effect of doing something than the need for it.

"Just remember, keep smiling," Elise instructs, unbuckling her own belt and fishing inside her oversized bag for her wallet to pay the driver.

I nod grimly. I remember this part. When *Starlight* first took off, I had no idea. None of us did. Calista, who played Skye, and I were working nonstop on a studio set. When the network sent the two of us to the MTV Movie Awards as presenters, we opened the limo doors to find the crowd screaming our names. My first thought was that it must have been a publicity stunt, "fans" planted near the red carpet with signs that someone in the production department had made.

But no. I figured that out when Calista and I, with a collective WTF shrug, veered off toward the side to sign a few autographs. The crowd surged, and a few velvet ropes weren't keeping anyone back.

People don't realize how disconcerting it is to find yourself alone with an overexcited fan . . . or even worse, a group of them. It sounds awesome—girls screaming your name, shaking and fainting when you come close. But in reality, it's scary as hell. They don't see you as a person. You're not the guy who accidentally locked himself out of his hotel room because you're an idiot. (I left my key card in my pants from the night before.) Or the guy who drank so much that waking up in vomit was not an uncommon experience.

You are *more*—you are an icon, a symbol, and talking to them, trying to connect, is impossible because it violates their version of reality. They don't want Chase, the idiot, recovering alcoholic at twenty-four, the guy with a perpetual patch of dry skin at the corner of his mouth. They want Chase Henry, the perfect guy who always says and does the right thing.

But they'll take a piece of you—sometimes literally—as a substitute.

It's enough to make you run. Which, I know, comes off sounding like vintage ungrateful asshole, but that's not it. I have (or had) a career because of those fans. I owe them everything. But that doesn't make them any less terrifying in a group. The power of their want is heady, until you realize it's not for you, not the real you.

I wish I'd known all of that earlier. I might have done a better job of just thanking Robert De Niro for his work, instead of spitting enthusiasm all over him, literally and figuratively, that time I bumped into him in the Starbucks line.

I push open the car door and climb out. Immediately, the paparazzi stir themselves, pointing cameras in my direction and calling my name, with loud voices that manage to sound both bored and annoyed.

Habit has me hunching my shoulders and ducking my head until I hear Elise hiss behind me: "Chase. Smile."

I straighten up and attempt to affix a pleasant expression on my face, without looking directly at the cameras. This is supposed to seem natural, unplanned.

Through a gap in the white butcher's-paper advertisements covering the windows, I catch a glimpse of Amanda. Rather, the back and side of her, as she stands at a cash register, trying to scan an apparently stubborn head of lettuce. Having stared at pictures of her for the better part of an hour on the ride over here, she is immediately recognizable to me.

Her dark red hair is in a limp ponytail that brushes her shoulders. She seems shorter than I imagined, or maybe that's just because she's so thin. Too thin. The plaid flannel shirt she's wearing—in seventy-degree weather?—hangs from her narrow shoulders.

When she turns to speak to the customer, I get her full profile, and she doesn't look anything like the bright-eyed girl from the pictures, relieved to be home but uncomfortable with the cameras and attention.

She's paler than before, which I didn't think was possible, and it only highlights the deep purple shadows under her eyes. And when she speaks to the customer, her smile shakes at the edges.

This girl . . . she looks haunted.

Oh, fuck. Whatever has happened in the last two years since she got back, she is not better.

And I'm here to capitalize on it.

I stop walking.

"Chase," Elise says under her breath in warning.

For a second, I consider turning around. Just move past Elise, get in the car, and have the driver speed (and he most definitely would) back to Wescott and the hotel. I'll do my best as Smitty and maybe that'll be enough.

But it won't be. And I can't.

The clicking of the cameras is absurdly loud, reminding me that every second of this hesitation is being recorded for all of posterity. If I back out now, I'll still make headlines—the wrong kind. "Chase Henry Leaves Superfan 'Miracle Girl' in the Lurch" or some other crap. Even though Amanda's not expecting me, it won't matter. Someone, somewhere, will get a shot of her crying or looking overwhelmed (like she does right now, when facing that head of lettuce that is just not scanning) and it'll be everywhere.

Shit.

I swallow hard, bolster my fake smile, then move confidently toward the automatic doors.

I can do this. Nothing has changed, not really. She'll still be excited, probably. The media will still be happy to jump on it, maybe even happier with her noble but obviously suffering visage front and center.

And I've done worse.

Inside, the fluorescent lights flicker overhead, eliminating every shadow and any place to hide. Amanda's register is three down from the door. The twenty feet between us seems an impossible distance to cross and also not nearly enough.

Nobody pays me any attention. I'm just a guy if you don't recognize me, and the older couples and families in the checkout lanes at Logan's Grocery are not, as Elise would put it, my primary demographic. But a cluster of five or six guys, aiming cameras through the door and the windows, and shouting my name, causes a stir.

The customers stare and point at the photogs, but confusion is the primary emotion for the moment, rather than anger or defensiveness. Thankfully.

I put my head down and move toward Amanda's register.

I'm only one lane away from Amanda when one of the assholes outside decides to change things up.

"Amanda! Hey, Amanda! Over here," he calls through the open door.

She turns and her gaze catches the paparazzi first. The spark of irritation that flashes across her face adds new life to her expression, which gives me hope that this isn't going to be a total disaster. But she looks about inches away from flipping them off or calling the cops, neither of which would be good. I'm not entirely sure of the legality of them being quite this close to the store, although still not in it.

"Amanda, hey," I say quickly, stuffing my hands in my pockets because I don't know what else to do with them. My heart is beating too fast, and I can feel my nervousness written all over my face. Elise's plan is dependent on Amanda's enthusiasm bubbling up and smoothing over any weirdness, but this all just feels awkward and *wrong*.

Amanda glances at me for a split second and then back to the photographers, almost in dismissal.

Then I see it click. Her whole body stiffens.

You hear about people freezing in place, but I've never really seen it happen until now. It's like every muscle in her body decided to seize up all at once. Her hand on the register drawer contracts in a painful-looking claw, and then she's staring at me, her dark eyes huge in her whiter-than-white face.

It would be almost comical except for the sheer terror in her expression. Her mouth works as if she wants to scream, but no sound is coming out.

I feel the urge to look behind me for whatever is causing this reaction, but I already know.

Oh, no, no, no. I take another step toward her. "Amanda, I—" I try again, and my voice breaks with the strain to sound normal, unthreatening.

But she throws her hands up in defense, catching the open register drawer in the process. Coins spray out everywhere as she drops to the ground, crouching behind the wall of her register cubicle, and it's my turn to freeze.

I don't care how much research Elise (or Nadia) did on Amanda Grace, the Miracle Girl. Whatever I am, or more accurately, whatever Chase Henry is, to this girl, "hero" is definitely not it. Not even fucking close.

3

Amanda

Weird things sometimes trigger flashbacks.

Most of the time, the causes are obvious, expected even. The distinctive reek of stale cigarette smoke on someone's clothing; the bitter, metallic taste of blood in my mouth when I accidentally bite my cheek; a raspy male voice that sounds like Jakes's; ragged fingernails with dirt caked beneath them.

But other times, it's bizarre the connections my brain chooses to make. The first time Liza made bacon after I came home, I ended up on the bathroom floor in a cold sweat. I couldn't figure it out until I talked it through with my therapist at the time. Apparently, the bacon smelled too much like hot dogs, which I'd eaten daily in my basement cell. Sometimes warmed up, sometimes not. By the end, I could barely choke them down in either state. And evidently, cooking bacon had a similar enough scent to set off the memories.

I will live happily for the rest of my life never, ever laying eyes on another hot dog, but I miss bacon, damnit. One more thing taken from me.

So, in theory, there is nothing about arguing with Mrs. Cahill about the condition of her lettuce to trip a flashback. She wants half price because it's "too wilted," which is what she always says. It might help if she didn't put it in her cart first thing and then proceed to pile everything on top of it. Also, half price on a buck twenty-nine? Please.

I am vaguely aware of the commotion behind me, near the doors, but three hours into my shift, I'm basically numb, overwhelmed by the constant state of alertness. I hate Sample Sundays.

Then someone calls my name.

I turn to see photographers, paparazzi, leaning in through the doors and taking pictures through the windows.

Someone must be doing some kind of retrospective on my story for the anniversary, even though I'd said no to all the interview requests. Miracle Girl rises again. Great.

Just as I'm about to ask Andy, the nearest bag boy, to run and tell Mr. Logan, the owner, to call the cops on them, someone else says my name. Much closer. And the voice sounds so familiar.

I see the guy standing at the end of my lane, just a few feet away, his hands stuffed in his pockets. He's absurdly and out-of-place handsome, tall and blond with dark blue eyes, and watching me with a familiar look of concern.

The world tips sideways, and I can't breathe.

Chase Henry. Chase Henry is here.

The store windows behind him flicker out of existence, replaced by boarded-up windows and peeling green paint on concrete walls. I'm not in Logan's anymore—was I ever? Sometimes it's so hard to tell what's real and what my brain has created to help me survive—I'm back in the basement at Jonathon Jakes's house.

The air feels too thick, choking me every time I try to inhale.

The band around my wrist is warm from the heat of my skin and blood as the metal bites into my flesh. My body aches again, that bone-deep pain, with bruises and abuse. I want to scream, but my voice is trapped in my throat, like a bubble I can't force out. How did I get back here? I was out, wasn't I?

Chase looks alarmed, staring at me. Oh God, that can't be good. He's always the calm one.

He takes a step toward me. "Amanda, I—"

Overhead, the distinctive shuffle/thump of Jakes walking on the floor above makes bits of dirt and insulation rain down on my head.

The sound of Jakes, obviously alive and, if not well, certainly not dead, is like a punch to the gut.

No. No, no, no! He's supposed to be shot, in the ground. Gone.

You didn't really *believe that, did you?* The evil voice in my head is back, the one that keeps me awake at night by bringing up awful memories and all the things I should have done.

I drop to the floor, whimpering, my hands up in defense. I can't do this. Not again.

Then a flash of red moves through my vision. I blink, and Mia is suddenly in front of me, blocking most of my view of Chase. She's pushing at his shoulders, moving him away.

For a second, just a half moment, I'm confused. Mia was never in Jakes's basement; as often as he threatened it, it never happened. I *know* that.

And that's all it takes for reality to snap back into place.

The basement vanishes, and I'm on the floor in Logan's, in my register cubicle. My hands and feet are numb. Coins in all denominations lay scattered around me.

Slowly, sound trickles back in. I can hear the buzz of agitated voices, the beeping of a distant register, and my sister shouting at someone.

No more basement, no more Jakes. It's like living in *The Matrix.*

But one thing from that flashback is very real. Chase Henry.

I can see him over the wall. He's still here, walking backward, his hands up in defense against Mia, who's after him like a girl possessed.

"What the hell is wrong with you?" she screams, taking another swipe at him. "You just show up here? Don't you know? Get out!"

"I'm sorry," he says. "I didn't—"

His eyes lock with mine, and then he turns abruptly without another word and walks out. I feel the strangest twinge of something. Regret? It's fleeting, gone before I can identify it.

Andy kneels next to me at the entrance to my register cubicle, his eyes wide above his acne-scarred cheeks. "Are you okay?" He's careful to keep distance between us.

But it's not enough and too much at the same time. *I'm not safe. It's not safe here.* The words beat as a refrain in my head, keeping time with my racing heartbeat.

"I have to go. I have to . . . I just have to go." I push myself up to stand on shaking legs. I have to get out of here. Now. Everyone's staring at me, and that's not good, but it isn't enough to stop me.

I can feel the pressure hanging overhead, the sensation that something bad is going to break open and pour down over all of us. I don't even know what that bad thing is, but I can sense it, the same way you can feel a heavy July thunderstorm rolling in. And I can't fight it, not this time.

Logical, rational thought would indicate that this is just an anxiety attack. A natural reaction to my body offloading a crapton of adrenaline into my system, a system now customized and shaped after years of trauma to leap immediately to the flight-or-fight instinct at the first sign of trouble, imagined or not.

Knowing that should be enough. And maybe on another day, if I'd caught the anxiety train on the tracks at the top of the hill instead of the bottom, it might have been.

But true clinical anxiety gives zero fucks about logic and rational thought, and when I'm in the throes of it, neither do I.

I push past Andy and run.

"Amanda, wait!" Mia shouts after me, but I ignore her and the photographers and everyone and head to the back of the store. There's a delivery entrance through the storeroom. It opens up to a small employee parking lot. From there, if I cut around the side of the building, I can avoid the cameras and I'll be heading the right direction for home, which is only three blocks away.

Five minutes. Maybe less. Just keep it together. A few more minutes. You're okay.

But it's hard to accept that when the sky feels like a gaping maw preparing to spit some unknown form of disaster on your head.

Mia catches up with me as I reach the parking lot. "Amanda, stop! It's okay, please!"

But it's like I'm controlled by someone or something other than myself. I don't care what she says. My instinct is screaming "danger," and that's all that matters.

I shake my head at her, the most I can do, and keep moving.

She stays with me doggedly, a step behind, as I race home, and she's crying. But her ragged sobs are interspersed with strings of creative and furious epithets that only Mia would come up with ("son of a llama-licker motherfucker" might have been one insult or two—it was impossible to tell), which would have made me laugh under different circumstances.

When our house comes into sight, I put on an extra burst of speed up the path, onto the porch, and through the front door, which is standing open. I just need to be safe. I feel like a beating heart exposed without the protection of skin and bone.

"No, thank you, she's here now," my mom says into the phone, watching me from the doorway to the kitchen as I throw myself into the foyer like a marathon runner stretching for the finish line.

She hangs up on whoever called without even saying good-bye, her forehead pinched deeply with worry. "Amanda, are you okay?" She approaches me with her hands out, as if she means to hug me or hold me still, but then she hesitates. "What happened? Where's Mia?"

The panic roaring in my head dies down a little, as I attempt to catch my breath. It's better here, in familiar surroundings, but it's not enough. My legs are jelly from running and shaking with the desire to keep going. I can feel that jittery push inside me, the need to stay one step ahead of whatever is coming.

Standing there on the worn blue and white rug that used to serve as the ocean for our Barbies when Liza and I played years ago, I try to talk myself out of it. *I'm safe. Nothing is going to happen here. Mom is right here.*

But that itch, that undeniable sensation sending up the alarm, *Danger, danger, danger!* just won't let up.

"I'm sorry," I whisper to my mom, tears burning my eyes. I'm not sure if I'm crying for her or me or both of us. She wants so badly for me to finally get my life back. So do I.

"What?" She looks baffled. "Amanda, talk to me. Tell me—"

Behind me, Mia rips open the screen door and crashes into the foyer. Snatches of her breathless explanation drift upward as I pound up the stairs.

"Chase Henry . . . at the store . . . Amanda freaked out . . . hauled ass out of there . . . so going to be fired!" From Mia's plaintive wail on that last part, I'm pretty sure she's talking about her employment status, not mine.

I cross the threshold into my bedroom, my sanctuary, and close the door behind me. It's pretty much unchanged from when I was "gone." Dusty stuffed animals hold court on a shelf above my dresser with Mrs. Stuffykins as Queen. Old calendar pages featuring baby rabbits are plastered on the side of my desk. Photos torn out of *BOP* and *Seventeen* and campus pictures secretly cut from Liza's discarded college recruitment brochures ("Just because I don't want them anymore, Amanda, doesn't mean they're yours. God!") randomly decorate the walls, all at about the height of five feet. Eye level for me then and now. A rumpled pink flyer on my bulletin board advertises show choir tryouts my sophomore year. They took place two days after I vanished.

My mom offered to have it all cleaned up and repainted, to replace the curtains, the comforter, everything. But that triggered a colossal fight between my parents. Apparently, my dad read an article or talked to one of my many therapists (probably Dr. Leary, his favorite) and "drastic changes to the environment" were verboten for people like me. Whatever.

It's a shallow, suffocating kind of comfort, the sameness of my room. It's a memorial to the Amanda who was and who, I'm beginning to think, never will be again.

The closet beckons, offering a soothing dark corner, a door to draw shut on the world, eliminating all chance of being surprised, scared, or taken. Eliminating all chance of living, too.

I take a few steps deeper into my room to stand across from the partially open sliding door. Tags on my new clothes, purchased by my mother over the last year and a half, flutter in the breeze from the ceiling fan. I can't wear them, the clothes. They're all bright and happy, with snappy colors and stripes, crisp sleeves and hems. Some of them are even short-sleeved. More evidence of my mother's fierce—and possibly delusional—belief that I will, one day, be "okay."

I hate the reminder they provide of my weakness, my inability to progress past the point where fear controls my every decision.

I have plans, things I want to do with a future I once thought I would never have. But none of that matters if I can't get this under control.

"Amanda, are you going to hurt yourself?" my mom asks through my bedroom door, startling me. Her voice holds a forced sternness, and I can hear the quiver of uncertainty in it. Someone has told her to take this approach. "I need you to tell me what you're planning," she says.

"No, I'm fine," I manage. "I just need a minute."

Which is both true and not true. I am most definitely not fine, though I don't have any intention of taking pills or cutting my wrists or whatever this random expert has warned her of. I don't need to. I'm contemplating crawling into a closet to hide; what life is there to end?

"I'm calling Dr. Knaussen," she says, her footsteps fading away.

But I already know what Dr. Knaussen will say. She'll call it a setback—such a nice, tidy term to represent a messy spillage of emotions and chaos. Normal in the recovery process, expected even, when encountering a surprise trigger, like Chase-freaking-Henry at my job.

Why was he even here? Two years ago, after the television interview and all those articles where his name was thrown around, that would have made sense. But now?

It doesn't matter. If it weren't him, it would have been something else eventually. The fear is endless, and I can't seem to break free.

It takes only a few seconds to shove all my shoes down to the other end of the closet, making room for myself to the sound of my tears landing on the hardwood floor with quiet splats.

And the moment my back is tucked against the corner, miserable relief spreads through me, instantaneous and enormous, like a giant splinter removed from my whole body. I don't even have to pull the door closed. This time.

I press my fist to my mouth and scream silently against my skin.

Because this is not the setback Dr. Knaussen would like me to believe it is; that would imply forward progress at some point. It's been two years, and I've stalled out, seemingly for good. This is just my life. And I don't know what to do, how to make it better.

Even worse, I'm not sure it *can* be made better.

* * *

I wake, my neck stiff and aching. The room outside my closet is blue with twilight. I must have fallen asleep, though I don't remember dozing off.

My fingers clutch at my left wrist automatically, confirming that I'm still free. It's a compulsion, an OCD-like tic, to check my arm first thing, every time I wake up. It started when I was in the hospital and the nightmares were so vivid, I couldn't always tell what was real.

As always, my skin is bare but for the cuff of my shirt and the scar from the band that held my chain.

My face is sticky with dried tears, and my knees are aching from my cramped position.

Experimentally, I stretch my legs out toward the heap of shoes on the other end, the muscles releasing reluctantly in a sea of pins and needles.

In a fit of frustration, I kick at the offending pile of footwear. Hiding in the closet is just one step too far, moving from "pretty understandable response to trauma" to "batshit crazy."

Sighing, I tip my head back, the coolness of the drywall soothing through my hair.

". . . never would have happened, Claire, if you hadn't let her take that job."

I lift my head up. That's my dad's voice. My mom must have called him at his office. He sounds pissed. Crap.

"No," my mom says sharply, "it was the television interview that started all of this . . . but if you were more involved—"

"Don't blame me," Liza snaps. "Dr. Shapiro recommended it. And it worked exactly as planned . . . got the press off the front lawn. I didn't know they would run with the Chase Henry bullet point . . ."

Oh God. They're fighting again.

I lean sideways, peering out from the closet. My bedroom door is now open. Someone has been in to check on me. But there's no one here now.

The voices sound like they're coming from downstairs. The kitchen, probably.

"It's not my fault! Just because I wanted to get a job. Most parents would be thrilled!" That's definitely Mia. I can hear her clearly enough. People in the next county can hear her clearly enough.

I groan. I need to get down there, reassure them that I'm all right. But I don't feel any strong motivation to leave the safety of my homemade hidey-hole. The panic has passed, for the moment. My heartbeat has slowed into the range of normal, and the driving beat of impending doom has receded. Finally.

Then the doorbell rings. I hear hurrying footsteps, probably Mia's, then the distinctive creak of the front door opening. Another voice, one I don't recognize, speaks, the tone low and calm. Male, definitely, but I can't catch his words.

I sit up straighter. Who's here now? Maybe Mr. Logan from the store, checking on me? How embarrassing.

Reluctantly, I crawl out.

I stand up carefully in my room, my legs shaky and tingling from the lack of blood flow. Behind me, I can feel the closet's tentacles pulling at me, like the tar strands clinging to the bottom of our flip-flops in the parking lot for the community pool on all those hot August days.

But I make my way out of my room and into the hall, heading for the stairs, expecting to find my family gathered in the kitchen, or if there's a guest, maybe the living room.

Instead, in a repeat of earlier today, they're gathered at the base of the stairs in the foyer. Only this time, it's not just my mom and sisters, but my dad as well. And they're not facing off against each other, but standing in a single line of solidarity—Mia, Mom, Dad, and Liza—which is . . . unusual.

Then I see the only other person present.

Their seeming opponent—the mutual enemy that has drawn them all together—is one guy, standing with his back against the door, his head ducked down, the brighter gold bits in his dark blond hair glinting in the foyer light, and his hands stuffed into the pockets of his jeans.

Chase Henry.

My breath catches in my chest, and I wait for the panic bees to swarm up and start stinging.

But my insides are strangely calm. My heart does a quick little skip, but that's all. Instead, I feel that weird flicker of . . . what?

Connection, maybe. Which is ridiculous because this Chase Henry is not "my" Chase Henry, for lack of a better term. I know that.

He doesn't look as he did in the poster or my memory. He is taller than I imagined. I can't see much of his face, just the left side of his profile, which is mostly in shadow anyway, but he seems tired, older. There are lines by his mouth, as if he's been unhappy lately or spent a lot of time frowning.

He's wearing a battered work jacket over his T-shirt now. Nothing like the slick leather coat he wore in the poster and, therefore, in the room with me.

And yet, I can't shake that feeling of a link, a bond, when I look at him. And with it, the odd sensation of being able to breathe deeper, like part of me was somehow waiting for this and can now relax a little.

Also a completely ridiculous notion. But this one sort of makes sense, in a crazy way. Chase, my version of him, was my security blanket. I needed him, a representative of home and the hope I was too afraid to allow myself (again, according to therapists galore), so my brain created him.

The real Chase in the foyer below physically resembles the protector I created so I'm reacting to him in the same way.

As if sensing my scrutiny, Chase looks up at me, those familiar dark blue eyes taking me in.

The impulse to move away shoots through me and vanishes almost as quickly. I hold my ground, wrapping my fingers around the banister at the top of the stairs, staring down at him as he stares up at me. A long beat and then another passes.

"Why did you even let him in?" Liza demands of Mia loudly. She is leaning around my parents to glare at Mia. But there are bright pink spots of color in Liza's cheeks, just beneath the dark frames of her glasses. My normally unflappable sister is . . . flapped. Then again, she's the one who had Chase Henry on her bedroom wall for years.

"I wanted to hear what he had to say for himself." Mia lifts her chin defiantly.

"Mia," my dad says sharply.

"*Dad,*" she says in a mocking tone, knowing that he'll do absolutely nothing to scold her. She's always been his favorite.

"Shhh!" My mother stretches her arms out, one toward Mia and the other toward my dad, like a crossing guard. As if that would somehow stop the sound from carrying or end the argument.

Chase turns toward me slightly, catching my attention again. He pulls his hands from his pockets and holds them out in front of him, as if showing me that he means no harm. I appreciate the gesture, if nothing else.

"I shouldn't have just shown up like that today, at your work," he says slowly. "It was a stupid idea, and I'm sorry I scared you. I didn't think it through."

One by one, almost in order—Mia, my mom, my dad, and Liza—their heads snap around, their mouths falling open when they see me.

"Amanda, go back to your room," my dad says, avoiding my gaze. He can't look at me anymore. Not for long. "You don't have to listen to this."

"We should call the police," Liza says, even as she folds her arms across her chest and makes no move toward the phone.

"Amanda can decide for herself what she can handle," my mom says pointedly to my dad. "We just need to—"

"Oh, here we go again." Mia throws her hands up in the air. I ignore them all and focus on Chase. "Why are you here?"

Chase's mouth tightens, deepening the lines on either side of it. "I wanted to apologize personally. I didn't realize—"

"No, I mean, why now?" I ask. "Why come to Springfield?"

He takes a deep breath and rubs the back of his neck, then lets his hand fall to his side.

"I don't know how much you know about me," he says. "About what happened. The show I was on was cancelled a couple of years ago."

"Good riddance," Liza muttered. "Zombies?"

"It started falling apart, and I kind of got screwed up in the middle of all of it," Chase admits. "Made some mistakes, got into some trouble."

My dad straightens at that, seeming to loom larger, which is pretty impressive considering he already stands six foot five. About five inches taller than Chase, from the look of it.

"I'm clear of that now," Chase says quickly, red splotches appearing high on his cheekbones. "But I'm having issues with booking work. I love what I do, but my reputation is . . ." He sighs. "It doesn't matter. Someone I trusted suggested that the publicity from a photo op with Amanda and maybe a set visit for a few days on the movie we're filming over in Wescott—"

"Like one of those celebrity charity visits for sick kids?" Liza asks in disbelief.

"They're making a movie in Wescott?" Mia asks, perking up a little.

Chase doesn't seem to know who to respond to. "Uh, yeah, it's just a small independent . . ." He shakes his head. "It's not important. The point is, I was wrong to listen to that person. I was just . . ."

Desperate. He was desperate. I can see it written across his face and hear it in the gaps between his words. I recognize the expression, that feeling of your back against the wall, and not in the safe-in-the-closet kind of way.

"I was wrong," he finishes, his expression grim. "And I've fired her. So it won't happen again."

"You didn't think my daughter had been exploited enough?" my dad asks in that deceptively mild voice I recognize as the calm before the storm.

"Mark," my mom snaps. "Not in front of Amanda." She glances at me worriedly, as Mia gives a loud huff of exasperation, which is met with another glare from Liza.

I remember the five of us in the kitchen on a Sunday morning, my dad goofily dancing around with each of us in turn, while my mom made pancakes. Mia was little, maybe eight, and barely able to keep up, but she was laughing like a crazy person. Then we all were when my dad grabbed my mom, pulling her away from the griddle and scattering Bisquick everywhere as he spun her around like they were ballroom dancers.

Now, just a few years later, I am actively destroying my family, setting them against one another, without even trying.

"Yes, sir. That's why I wanted to apologize in person," Chase says to my dad wearily, with just a hint of defiance . . . and an accent? Does he have a drawl? I never imagined that. "It was a shit . . . it was a horrible idea. I don't know what I was thinking. I'm just going to go." But he pauses as he turns to the door and glances up at me.

"Amanda." He tips his head at me in a faint nod, his jaw tight. Then his hand is on the front door, pulling it open.

Most of the time, the *big* moments in life sneak up on you; it's only in hindsight that you recognize them as significant. When Jonathon Jakes asked me to help him look for his lost dog, my only concern at the moment was whether I could do it and still get home in time to beat Mia to the last cup of Easy Mac in the pantry. My conscience won that battle, to my eternal regret, and clearly, Mia got that cup of Easy Mac.

But this time, it's different. I can feel it, that discordant clanging inside of me. In a few seconds, maybe less, Chase Henry, the real version of my imagined security blanket, will walk out that door and down the steps, gone forever, and that just seems *wrong*. Powerfully wrong. If I don't do something right now, I know I'll regret it, even if I don't know why.

An instinct I don't fully understand pushes me to speak. I'm not even sure which words are coming out until I hear them, along with everyone else.

"The set visit. What if I want to go?"

4

Chase

The stunned silence that follows is crazy loud. No one so much as breathes. Then a refrigerator kicks on somewhere nearby, the faint hum the only clue that I haven't suddenly lost my hearing.

I turn and find Amanda's family frozen in place.

"What?" Mrs. Grace asks finally, her hand clutching at her throat, as if she can't quite breathe around the word.

"You're kidding, right?" The younger sister—Mia, I think—scoffs at Amanda. "Sometimes you can't even leave the house without talking yourself up to it."

I raise my eyebrows. The frustration and bitterness in Mia's voice would corrode a brand-new battery port. Little sister is pissed about something.

"Absolutely not," her dad thunders, and that's exactly what it sounds like: thunder. Loud and intimidating. He's a big dude.

"This isn't good," Amanda tries to explain. "You're fighting all the time, and none of this is getting any better. I need to do something—"

"I don't think that would be wise in terms of your recovery," the older sister says, her mouth pinched in disapproval.

And I don't think it's wise for me to be here anymore. I said what I needed to say, and clearly, this situation is way more complicated than anyone knew. Even now, there's a strange tension between Amanda and her family, with her on one side and the four of them on the other, like they're fighting an invisible war.

Definitely time to leave. I don't need this kind of trouble, no matter what Elise says. I'll find another way to get publicity. There has to be something I can do, some avenue I haven't tried yet.

The empty feeling in my gut suggests otherwise, especially considering the inevitable fallout from today's epic and well-documented fail at the grocery store, but I reach for the door again anyway.

"What if I want to go?" Amanda repeats defiantly, but her voice is softer this time, and something in it draws my gaze to her again.

She looks as frail as she did earlier today, her frame thin in her oversized clothes. But her dark eyes are bright with challenge and her face is flushed with color; in short, she appears way more alive than she did just a few hours ago, much more like the girl from the pictures in the file.

And now that girl is meeting my gaze, waiting expectantly.

That's when it clicks.

She's not asking them; she's asking *me*.

Oh, shit. My mouth falls open, but no words come out.

"I'll help you get the pictures you want," she says.

"Amanda, you can't!" her older sister bursts out.

"Honey." Mrs. Grace steps out of line with the rest of her family, like she might approach Amanda, but she stops well short of the stairs. "I know he might seem like a friend because of . . . what happened."

There's a collective flinch from everyone but Amanda.

"But," Mrs. Grace soldiers on, "he's a stranger. You don't know what his *intentions* are." She manages to convey every possible awful sexual connotation in one word.

I straighten up. "Hey, wait a minute." I'll admit to some messed-up priorities, but I'm not *that* guy.

Amanda tilts her head to the side. "Mom. I doubt it's any worse than anything that's already been done."

That sends a ripple of shock through them.

"Amanda Diana Grace!" Mrs. Grace is horrified.

"I mean, unless he plans to kill me, and I don't think that's the case." Amanda shifts her gaze to me. "Is it?"

"No!" I manage, but it comes out half-choked with surprise. Jesus.

"Good," she says simply.

"After everything we've been through, you're crazy if you think we're going to let this happen," her father says. "This is insane. You're . . ."

Insane. The word hangs in the air.

"It's our job to protect you, even when you won't protect yourself," he finishes. "You can't do this."

"I'm twenty," she reminds her father sadly. "Maybe you missed that while you were at the office or just avoiding me in general."

He rocks back, as if she slapped him, and then, his face white and his jaw clenched, he storms out of the foyer, heading deeper into the house.

"Amanda!" The older sister glares at her, before hurrying to follow their father.

Whoa. Amanda has sharp teeth. Good for her.

But then she turns her attention back to me. "Well?" she asks, and I can see the determination and vulnerability in her eyes. She's looking at me like she's out in the middle of an endless ocean and I'm the only land in sight.

Fuck.

No. Just say no, a panicked voice in my head says. *This has crazy mess written all over it in capital letters.*

But if I say no, I'm walking away from my best chance at getting what I need. The media would be all over Amanda visiting me on set, especially after the flameout earlier today.

I shift my weight uncomfortably. Damnit. None of this has gone as planned. Amanda is not the enthusiastic fan that Elise depicted, grateful for a couple of pictures and a short, carefully monitored visit, managed by a production assistant or publicist. My only job in that scenario would be to smile politely and act interested, maybe even eat lunch with her. But this, this is something else, trouble I can't afford, responsibility I don't want.

But when I open my mouth to say a politer version of that, something else comes out instead. "Bring a jacket," I say. "It's colder now."

Relief washes over Amanda's face, followed immediately by what looks like uncertainty. But then she squares her shoulders. "Five minutes," she promises and steps back from the railing, disappearing in the direction, presumably, of her room.

I grit my teeth. What have I done? This is definitely going to be one of those moments where, tomorrow, I'll be wondering what the hell I was thinking. Actually, I'm already wondering that, and yet I can't seem to bring myself to call out, "Sorry, never mind," and haul ass out of there.

Mrs. Grace hurries past me and up the stairs without so much as a glance in my direction.

"So, what movie?" Mia asks, folding her arms across her chest. Her resemblance to Amanda is unmistakable, but she's clearly younger, maybe just sixteen, and her chin and nose are more pointed, giving her a distinctly slyer appearance.

"What?"

"What movie are you filming in Wescott?" she elaborates slowly, as if I'm the stupid one for not understanding her abrupt conversation shift.

"Oh. It's this thing, *Coal City Nights*. Max Verlucci is—"

"Season One writer, yeah." She waves her hand dismissively. "I know. Liza has the whole *Starlight* series on DVD."

Liza? The older sister with the permanent I-sucked-a-lemon expression?

"The zombies were cool, but the narrative went to crap in the third season." Mia watches me, waiting for my reaction, and this somehow feels like a test.

"Yeah." What else am I supposed to say? She's right. Zombies on a show about a guardian angel in love with the girl he's supposed to protect made no sense.

"You know she's messed up," Mia says.

It takes me a second to process another of Mia's whip-fast topic changes. "Yeah, I'm kind of . . ." . . . *getting that.* It sounds too flip. So I just settle for repeating myself. "Yeah."

"This is a big chance she's taking, and she doesn't do that very often anymore," Mia says, eyeing me suspiciously, as though I've done something to trick Amanda into this.

"I . . . okay." It feels much too warm in here suddenly, and I flap my jacket back and forth, trying to cool off.

"So don't screw it up." She fidgets with her sleeve, picking off an invisible bit of lint. "It's not her fault, obviously, but she's right. Everyone's trying so hard, but it's not getting any better. Maybe we're making it worse—I don't know." She shrugs, the tight motion barely visible. "My dad wants to pretend it never happened, and my mom wants to make every second about Amanda getting better. And if one of them is right, the other one has to be wrong. It's kind of hellish." She pauses, staring down at some unknown point on the floor, and she seems younger, smaller than before. "It would be nice not to be trapped in the middle of that, just for a while."

Shit. "Listen, uh, Mia? What do you think—"

Amanda reappears at the top of the stairs, struggling into a black zip-up fleece, a canvas bag dangling from one arm.

That was fast. Was it even five minutes? How is this happening so quickly? I swallow loudly.

"How will we reach you?" Mrs. Grace, wringing her hands, follows Amanda down the stairs.

"I have my cell phone."

"Amanda, please don't do this. You're not ready. Dr. Knaussen—"

"Dr. Knaussen can call me, too. I'll check in with her just like usual." Amanda sounds confident, but her hand is trembling as she moves it along the railing in her descent. She catches me watching and tightens her grip, steadying it.

"But small steps, Amanda—" Mrs. Grace persists.

"Aren't cutting it, Mom." Amanda stops at the bottom of the stairs and turns to face her mother. "I'm not making any progress that way, not anymore. And I want to have a life some-day," she says in a softer voice, a quiet plea for understanding. "Besides, you're the one who keeps saying I should do whatever I feel like I'm ready to do."

Except I'm not entirely sure Amanda's all that ready. As soon as I pull the door open and step out of the way to let her lead, she freezes up, like someone terrified of heights balancing on the edge of the high dive.

I can feel the tension behind me from Mia, from Mrs. Grace, who are both, undoubtedly, watching this play out.

Maybe this'll be over before it even begins. I'm not sure how I feel about that. Relieved, I think. A sign from the universe that it wasn't meant to be, as my agent used to say. You know, before he stopped taking my calls. "Is everything—"

"Fine. It's fine," Amanda says shortly, tugging her bag up higher on her shoulder, and then, with a deep breath that seems more appropriate for someone about to face a ravenous and rabid grizzly bear, she pushes forward and out the door.

Oh yeah, she's definitely not ready. And neither am I.

This is such a bad idea.

5

Amanda

I just left the house. To stay with a stranger. Overnight.

My chest constricts painfully at the thought.

Behind me, the screen door slams shut, and I can hear the sound of Chase's footsteps on the porch steps and then behind me on the path to the driveway. Is it possible for footsteps to sound reluctant and/or resigned? Because if so, his do.

I inhale through my nose and exhale slowly through my mouth, trying to count, four in and eight out, and do both the breathing and counting quietly enough so as not to attract even more attention. The truth is, I don't have time to freak out right now because I'm pretty sure I've got about thirty seconds before Chase finds a polite excuse to back out. I need to think this through and come up with a way to convince him this is still a good idea.

But it's hard to think when my skin is buzzing. The sun is

down, and it's really getting dark now, the automatic porch lights providing the only illumination. On a bad day, this is usually when my anxiety kicks into high gear, for some reason. Combine that with the unpredictability that comes with being outside—branches moving in the wind like arms reaching out for me and dead leaves skittering at my feet like small crabbed creatures—and I should be a wreck.

Except this doesn't feel exactly like one of my tsunami waves of anxiety or even the start of a panic attack. This is more like I'm plugged in, connected in some weird way. Like I've taken a leap over the edge of a cliff, and I'm enjoying the fall, for the moment. I'm hyperaware of everything, the scrape of my shoes on the concrete, the faint ticking of the engine cooling in the car on the driveway, the birds chirping and fluttering as they settle in for the night.

A hand lands solidly on my shoulder, and my heart catapults into my throat. I jerk away violently, tipping myself off balance and nearly landing backward in one of the evergreen bushes that line the sidewalk.

Chase jumps back from me, his face almost comical in shock. I'm not sure who is more surprised. "Sorry!" he says, his hands up as if he's under arrest. The light from the porch catches on the car keys in his palm, making them gleam. "I just thought . . . your bag." He tips his head toward the bag that's now hanging from my wrist, the bottom of it dragging on the ground.

Oh. Yeah. I want to close my eyes in defeat. That makes more sense than some random attacker sprinting up between us and grabbing me, which, of course, is what my brain signaled.

Again, there's very little space between stimulus and panic for rational thought. "Sorry," I say, straightening up and pulling my bag onto my shoulder.

"No, I'm sorry," Chase says quickly. He looks toward my house, as if expecting someone to come charging out. He might not be wrong. "I should have realized—"

"No, it's okay. It's just . . . I'm a little jumpy. When people touch me unexpectedly," I say, fumbling for the words that will make this not weird. It's not uncommon for rape survivors to have trouble with being touched, but most people just don't think it through. Touch is human instinct, an attempt to comfort, even.

A pained expression crosses Chase's face, and he takes a step back, as if I'm a ticking emotional time bomb and might explode in messy tears and gibbering nonsense right then and there.

Really? I'm the one who lived through it, but he can't stand to hear me reference it, even obliquely? God. He's not "my" Chase, and that is so screamingly obvious. But I suppose that's better than if he were like the people who are eager to hear every detail. There are definitely those, too.

Still, all my awkward damage is fully on display, and I can feel panic bubbling up in my throat. In a second, Chase isn't even going to bother with the polite excuse.

As if he can read my mind, he takes a deep breath and says, "Listen . . ."

"Look, I know this is crazy," I say, cutting him off. "Or weird or both. You don't know me, I don't know you. And this is obviously not what you were expecting when you came here . . ." Shit, I'm babbling. *Stop babbling.* "But I have a reason, a good reason for asking to come along."

He raises his eyebrows expectantly.

I'm tempted to ask him if he minds waiting to hear said reason until we're in the car on the way to Wescott. I can feel time, and my summoned-from-nowhere courage, slipping away. I would bet my life that my mother is standing at the picture window in the living room, watching us, waiting for me to retreat and fly back into the house.

Suddenly, I can see myself walking past Chase, up the stairs, into the house, and to my room, where I lie down again on the floor of my closet and just stay there forever, living on that pile of discarded shoes.

"You need help. You said so," I blurt out.

He stiffens. "That's not exactly what I said."

Good, Amanda, way to put him on the defensive.

"No, I didn't mean . . ." I take a deep breath and start over, borrowing his words. "I don't know how much you know about what happened to me." I pause.

He nods slowly. Someone did research for him. But clearly not enough.

"Obviously, I'm having some trouble getting back to normal. I mean, I'm doing okay. I have a therapist and everything, and it's not like I'm suicidal or anything." I force a laugh, but his eyes go wide.

Clearly that thought had not entered his mind until I put it there.

"But I'm stuck. And I need to find some way to fight through. And I thought . . ." I pause, trying to find the right words, ones that will explain without scaring him away. "When I was in that place," I say carefully, "I had only one link to home. There was a poster on the wall. My sister had the same one. Chase Henry as Brody Taylor. The one with the black leather jacket and the collar . . ." I catch myself tugging at my fleece to demonstrate, as if he needs the reminder, and stop, feeling my face heat up.

Chase's mouth twitches with a faint smile. "The angry librarian?" he asks.

"Huh?" I ask, confused.

He tips his head toward the house, and I realize he's describing Liza. Perfectly, actually.

And that makes me relax enough to laugh, a little giddy. "Yeah, that's her. She was so in love with you." The words come out in the same teasing tone I used to use with Liza herself whenever she would drag me in to watch *Starlight* with her and then stand six inches away from the screen so as not to miss so much as a micro-blink from "Brody Taylor."

Chase ducks his head, his hand rubbing the back of his neck, and it's hard to tell with his face in shadow, but it looks like he's blushing. And that causes a weird pinch in my stomach.

"The glasses are fake." The words pop out of my mouth, and I have no idea why. "She only needs them for reading, but she wears them all the time to make people take her more seriously. Law student and whatever."

He nods solemnly. "I see."

What the hell is wrong with me? I'm stuck in babble mode. "Anyway," I say, struggling to refocus on my point. "The poster. It was a link to home, and apparently, according to, like, every therapist in the world, I needed an outlet, a coping mechanism or whatever. So my brain sort of made one, I guess." This all sounds so crazy. Crap.

"And it looked like you," I make myself continue. "Gave me the courage to keep hoping, and the strength to keep fighting." I'm caught for a second in the memory of "my" Chase whispering in my ear that last morning, pushing me to reach out, literally, to catch the furnace repairman's attention. "Saved my life, actually."

The real Chase looks taken aback.

"It wasn't *you*," I say quickly. "I know that. It's this psychological equivalency thing."

"But you think I can help you," he says, sounding doubtful.

"Not you, exactly." I'm struggling to explain something that seemed so clear in my head just a few minutes ago.

The screen door opens with a distant creak. "Amanda, is everything okay?" my mom calls out into the night.

I'm running out of time. Sheer surprise and my momentum are the only things that kept my family from mounting a stronger argument, and they're regrouping—I'm sure of it. "Yes, everything's fine, Mom. We're just working out some details."

"You should come back inside. We can talk about it some more," she says, and though the shrubbery is hiding her from view, I can easily picture her rubbing her arms up and down, like it's winter and freezing out here.

I ignore my mom and turn my attention back to Chase. "It's who you represent in my head. It's like . . ." I search my mind to come up with something that will make sense of the weird leaps and turns my brain made. "Is there someone you're close to? Someone in your family or . . ."

He shifts a little, shoving his hands into his pockets again. "My grandfather."

"Okay, is there a smell that reminds you of him?" God, if he says something like "farts" or "pork rinds," this is so not going to work. But I'm in it too far now to back off.

He nods reluctantly. "Pipe smoke. He used to smoke a pipe."

"So, when you smell that, um, smoke or tobacco, it reminds you of him, how you feel when he's around . . . or how you felt?" I'm not sure if Chase's grandfather is still alive, and the voice in the back of my head is screaming, *You're messing this up!*

"Yeah," Chase says after a moment.

Wow, how very talkative Mr. Henry is. Maybe it's a good thing he has someone to script his lines for him. "Okay, it's like that. Seeing you reminds me of the Chase in my head. Gives me that extra push to be strong. And I . . . I kind of need that right now."

Said out loud, it sounds ridiculously juvenile and fantasy-like. Of course the real person would have no bearing on a situation that existed only in my head. And we are total strangers. What on earth gave me the idea that this would work?

"I have plans," I blurt out. "I want to go to college, get my degree in psychology, art therapy, maybe. But I can't, not when I'm like this. And when you explained why you were really here, I thought there could be a mutual benefit." My face is hot with embarrassment.

"How do you know this won't make things worse?" Chase asks with a deep frown. "Like today."

I must have really freaked him out at the store. "That wasn't you, exactly. I get flashbacks sometimes, triggered by various and random things. It's PTSD, like what soldiers have?" I hesitate, but I figure I might as well be honest. "And I can't guarantee that won't happen again. But it won't be because of you. I was . . . taken off guard today—that's all."

He stays silent for a long moment. Too long. I can't read his expression.

"Please," I say, holding steady against the urge to squirm. I hate begging. Hate the empty, cored-out feeling it creates in my middle, but I don't have a choice here. And when I hear the porch door squeak shut, I know my mom has gone in to get my dad. Time's up.

Chase stares at a point over my head, his mouth tightening. "All right," he says finally. "But we can skip the photo ops. That was just—"

"No," I say. "Definitely not. That's what you need, right?" The only thing keeping this from being a complete Amanda Grace freak show is that he's getting something out of it, too. I am clinging to that with everything I've got. But he does maybe have a small point. "If we can schedule something, though, rather than them creeping up on me, that would probably be better."

He flinches. "I am so—"

I cut off his apology. "It's fine. It'll be fine. It's just a few days, right?" I sound confident enough I almost believe me.

Chase nods.

"Obviously, if it doesn't work out, I've got plenty of people who'll be happy to come get me." And shout, *What were you thinking?* the entire sixty miles back home.

Chase is frowning at me again, and I realize suddenly I'm not sure who I'm trying to convince. He's already agreed.

I hold out my hand. "So, we have a deal."

He pulls his hand from his pocket but hesitates before touching me. He meets my gaze squarely. "Okay?" he asks.

That he remembers to ask—granted, it was only like two minutes ago that it first came up, but still—sends a weird little flutter through me. "Yeah," I say, "it's just when I don't see it coming." Which isn't exactly true. I tense up, even at the most casual contact, unless I'm really distracted. But that doesn't happen nearly often enough.

I steel myself for the brush of his skin against mine. But he takes my hand in his in one quick motion and shakes it firmly, with no attempt to linger and zero bone crushing. His palm is dry, and his touch is kind of . . . pleasant.

"Deal," he says, releasing my hand immediately. Then he steps around me and leads the way to the car, letting me follow at my own pace with no worries about anyone behind me.

Huh. One thing I'll give the real Chase Henry: he's a quick learner. Not maybe as fast as "my" Chase, but that version lived in my head. This Chase probably deserves a little more credit for figuring out as much as he has.

Or maybe he's just as eager to get out of here as I am.

6

Chase

I'm going to hell for this.

I'm pretty sure I was headed that direction anyway, but now? There's no question.

Chase Henry Mroczek, latest designee for the lowest circle of fiery damnation, where all people who do crazy-stupid things for fame go. Not that it's fame I'm after, exactly.

I buckle my seat belt—it takes two tries to click, stupid rental car—as Amanda, who already has her belt in place, pushes her bag into the backseat through the gap between us.

"Everything—" I cut myself off from asking her, yet again, in one more way, if she's all right. "Ready to go?" I ask instead.

She nods, tugging her sleeves down over her wrists and using her fingertips to hold the cuffs in place.

God, there's nothing more awkward than being trapped in a car with a complete stranger. Except maybe being trapped with someone who sort of knows you, or knows a version of you. And in this case, that's both of us, I suppose. Amanda knows "Chase Henry," the public persona, and whatever idea she has of me in her head. And I've got pretty much the same thing for her.

Worst first-date-that-is-not-a-date ever.

I fumble getting the car into reverse. The gearshift has a weird notch cut out between park and reverse. Who's the genius responsible for that? If it's not a standard H stick shift, do we really need to get fancy for a fucking rental car?

The silence on Amanda's side of the car is deafening. "Sorry, it's a rental," I mumble. "Elise . . . my, uh, former publicist took the car and the driver." I'm lucky she bothered to drop me off at the local Hertz. When Elise commits to an idea, she really commits.

Amanda lifts her shoulder. "It's fine. Better than I could do."

"Not used to shitty cars?" I ask, trying to make a joke.

"No license," she says.

Duh, Chase, because when she was sixteen, she wasn't exactly in driver's ed, and driving lessons probably weren't her first priority these days.

"Sorry," I mutter. I can't seem to speak more than ten words to her without shoving half my leg down my throat.

"It's okay," she says, her gaze fixed forward.

I move my arm to brace my hand against the passenger-side headrest, standard position for reversing out of a driveway, but I catch the almost imperceptible flinch from Amanda.

Shit. Right.

I snatch my arm back, though that makes me feel lopsided and dangerously close to taking out one of the millions of evergreens that line their property with my side of the car.

Add to that my absolute certainty that Amanda's huge father is going to come barreling out after us at any second, and we're lucky to make it out to the street without damage.

But we do, and the road is silent and still. No photographers. No angry dads. So that's something, at least.

"Are you warm enough?" I ask after a few minutes, hoping for something to do, to say. I could drag out adjusting the temperature into a few conversational exchanges.

"I'm fine," Amanda says.

Guess not.

I tap my fingers on the wheel. Can I turn on the radio? Or would she consider that rude? I have no idea. We're in this together . . . sort of, but not really.

The only sounds in the car are the distinct non-purring of the engine and the rush of the tire treads on the road, and every second of silence that ticks by just makes me more and more uncomfortable. The next sixty miles are going to be brutal. No, forget that. The next twenty-four hours. That's probably the quickest turnaround that I can manage while still getting what I need out of this mess.

"Can you, uh, talk to me?" Amanda asks, her voice sounding strangely small.

"What?" I ask, startled. Looking over, I find her clutching tight to the armrest as if we're speeding along at ninety instead of a very sedate, and legal, forty-five miles an hour. We haven't even made it to the freeway yet.

"Just talk to me," she says again. In the blue glow of passing streetlights, she seems paler than earlier, her forehead pinched with effort.

"Is something—"

"I haven't been more than a few miles from my house in a long time, and I'm kind of having a hard time thinking about anything else right now, so can you please just talk about something?" she asks, enunciating each word with precision. "Anything," she adds, with a hint of temper, before I can ask. "The economy, who really slept with who on *Starlight,* or whatever. Just words, please."

"Okay, okay," I say quickly. But it feels more complicated than that. Like navigating a conversational minefield. Are there certain topics that act as triggers for her? I won't talk about *Starlight*, not that kind of stuff, anyway. But if I bring up anything I know about her, is it a reminder that I, along with most of the country, have details about her life that we normally wouldn't?

"Chase," she says through gritted teeth.

"What did 'we' talk about before?" I ask and immediately want to kick myself. Talk about reminders. I set off the minefield without even taking a step.

But Amanda gives a strangled laugh. "You were a figment of my imagination and not exactly a sparkling conversationalist."

"So not much different than reality," I mutter. I'm great with crowds or in front of a camera. But one-on-one, as a person, I kind of suck at it. I always have. Probably one of the reasons I feel more comfortable being someone else.

She lets out a slow, controlled breath, her feet jouncing on the floorboards with anxious energy, then inhales with that same deliberate effort. Obviously some kind of calming technique. "How about this? I'll ask you questions," she says.

"Yes, I can do that," I say, relieved. Press junkets. I'm used to those. Nothing but questions. Usually the same ones over and over again. Only this time, of course, there's no list of off-the-table topics.

"Brothers and sisters?" Amanda asks, hitting one of the forbidden topics on her first try.

But refusing to answer feels stingy, considering what I'm asking her to do. "One brother, younger. Aidan. He's . . ." I pause and do a quick calculation in my head, and then I have to double-check because it doesn't seem possible.

The memory of his small, pale, scared face peeking out between the banister spindles is so clear in my mind. But I haven't seen him since the night I left six years ago.

Which means the kindergartner I left behind, the one who

followed me around everywhere, who begged for boots like mine, who watched silently from above as everything went down that night, is practically a teenager now. Probably sullen as hell and secretive, if I was any example.

"He's twelve," I say finally. I wonder if Layla stopped sending me the notes and the pictures he drew for me or if Aidan stopped creating them for me.

"Hometown?" Amanda asks quietly.

I wrestle my thoughts away from Aidan and my family to answer her question. "Tillman, Texas. It's a speck on the map, like a smudge on your screen. A few thousand people. Way more cows."

"Most disgusting thing you've ever seen."

A memory immediately leaps to mind, one I haven't thought about in years. It's like her questions have cracked open a dark closet in my mind where I've shoved everything from my life before.

I half-laugh, half-groan, remembering the smell, the warmth, and the splattering sound, all equally gross and exponentially terrible in combination. My grandfather's booming laugh had echoed through the whole barn when he saw me. "I can't . . . give me a second to think."

"No, no censoring," she says. "Let's hear it. I'm intrigued."

And when I glance away from the road to her, she does seem to be sitting up straighter, her grip on the armrest not quite as punishing.

"Okay." I sigh. "Let's just say it involves being in the wrong place at the wrong time and a cow with too much grass."

She frowns, and I realize that the daughter of an engineer and a former preschool teacher is not going to understand what that means.

"Too much grass in a cow's diet has really nasty digestive consequences. Usually, uh, explosive consequences. And if you happen to be bent down nearby, mucking out the barn . . ." I shrug, feeling my face grow hot. Why, exactly, did I bring up diarrhea in this conversation?

Amanda twists in her seat to face me, her eyes bright with amusement in the dashboard lights and her mouth open in disbelief. "Seriously?"

I raise my eyebrows. "You think I'd make that up?"

She shudders. "I hope not. Did it get on you?"

"No way to really avoid that. The ears were the worst, though. So many places for it to get to."

"That *is* disgusting!" She's laughing, but she sounds delighted, more impressed than grossed out, as if she's ranked my answer against the others she's gotten for that question and I've come out ahead. "What were you doing that close to the business end of a cow?"

"Occupational hazard. It's the family business." It was, anyway.

She tips her head to one side, and I'm bracing myself for a series of questions along that line.

But Amanda Grace is a natural interviewer, maybe from being on the receiving end of so many questions for so many years. Or maybe she's just more perceptive than most.

After a quick glance at me, she pushes on to the next question instead. "Scariest moment in your life."

The prepared response is easy, right there on the tip of my tongue. The second audition for *Starlight*. It wasn't just the casting director, but a whole room full of studio executives and producers. My mouth had felt like it was coated in moss, and I thought I might literally choke.

I've told the story so many times it barely feels real anymore. But it is.

So that would be an honest answer. To a degree. And it would be the "official" answer.

But I've already strayed from official. My press sheet says very little about my family and absolutely nothing about cow diarrhea, both deliberate choices for entirely different reasons, obviously.

And the dark interior of the car is lulling, creating a false sense of security and encouraging confidences that I am probably better off keeping to myself.

"When I woke up in the hospital with three broken ribs, a fractured wrist, and no memory of what happened." I keep my gaze fixed on the road ahead. We're on the freeway now, and the rhythmic flash of the white center lines is soothing.

That's not quite the whole truth, but it's as close as I'm willing to get, right now. Which is still closer than I've ever come with anyone else.

"Bar fight," Amanda says.

I blink. "Yeah, that's the official . . . how did you know?"

"I was out by then," she says easily, as if talking about her release from prison, which, I suppose in a way, she is. "Someone must have told me. One of the therapists, maybe. They read it online or saw it on TV." She glances over at me. "After the interview when I talked about the poster, everyone went out of their way to share the latest Chase Henry rumors. I'm a warehouse of gossip about you."

I wince. "Really?"

"Yep." She hesitates, sliding a speculative glance in my direction. "Did you really have a . . . I don't know what to call it when there are four people involved. A foursome? With some Cirque du Soleil performers?"

"No," I say with a groan. Did someone really say that?"

"What about losing one of your cars in a bet?" she asks.

"That is true," I admit. I still miss that Audi. It was the first vehicle I bought with my own money. And to lose it playing High-Low with Eric? Stupid.

"What about you buying all the presents for the charity trees at, like, six Starbucks?"

"Yeah." I shift uncomfortably. Elise suggested that I pick one location and buy all the gifts, but once I got started, I didn't want to stop. It felt so good to focus on someone else besides myself and the current fuck-up I was trying to make up for.

"Was any of it spin?" Amanda asks.

I frown. "What do you mean?"

"I mean, from what I remember, Brody Taylor was always quick to pound someone's face in and he had . . . issues with alcohol, too."

Interesting that she hadn't chosen to question me about that last part. Then again, mug shots made public tend to eliminate a lot of doubt.

"Not spin," I say. "Just art imitating life this time instead of the other way around, unfortunately."

That reminds me of something, though. I'm not sure how to bring it up without offending her, but it has to be said. "Listen, I should have mentioned this earlier, but this agreement, all of this, what we're doing, you can't tell anyone. If word gets out that I'm trying to manipulate the media, it would be bad." Speculation is one thing; a tell-all interview from Amanda would be something else entirely. She would be the innocent victim, and I, the exploitive asshole using her, which is kind of true. And it would destroy what remained of my career. Way worse than anything they might print from today's fiasco.

Just thinking about it makes my stomach hurt. Telling Amanda the truth—well, most of it—was a huge risk, one that feels riskier by the second.

She frowns at me, her expression serious. "Yes, because I feel the deep and abiding need to explain to a bunch of re-porters that I willingly went along because I missed my imaginary friend who happens to look a lot like you. That'll go over well."

"Fair point." We both have something to lose.

Amanda smiles to herself. She seems a little calmer, so something in this completely bizarre question-answer session is working for her.

"Okay," she says, settling back into her seat. "Next question. Most embarrassing—"

"Wait," I say, lifting one hand from the wheel to stop her words. "Why is it always your turn?"

"You want to ask me questions?" she asks, sounding surprised.

And exactly in that instant, I realize the inherent fallacy of that endeavor. "Oh. Uh . . ."

Amanda shrugs. "Anything you can think to ask me, I've already answered and probably on record. Most of it I can talk about, as long as it doesn't bother you to hear it." Her voice holds the emptiness of someone used to poking at an old scar, repeatedly.

I don't know what to say. "What's your favorite color?" I blurt finally.

She makes a face. "Really? That's what you want to know?"

"Yes?" It seems a relatively safe topic.

"Sometimes I think it's harder for people to listen. Like maybe I should just have a name tag that says, 'Amanda Grace, abducted and raped.'" She lifts her hands, blocking out the square space of the proposed label. "Gets the ugliness right out there, using the words no one wants to hear, so we don't have to dance around them anymore. I mean, it's all there anyway, underneath the surface of every conversation. Avoiding it, pretending it never happened, just makes everything else feel fake, forced."

Which is exactly what I was trying to do—pretend that part of her life never happened. I wince.

Amanda looks at me, a challenge in her gaze. "So come on," she says. "If you're going to do it, then ask something you really want to know."

Words run through my head, but none of them makes it to my mouth except the two that have been circling relentlessly since I read Elise's folder on Amanda. "Why me?" I'm the last person anyone should ever imagine in a life-or-death crisis. I can barely keep myself together, let alone help someone else. "The poster, I mean. Was it the only one there?"

Amanda turns her head to stare out the side window, her breath moving across the glass in a fog. "No. But that's the one that reminded me of home. And I think probably it had something to do with Brody and how real you made him seem."

She sighs, and the fog on the window reveals a heart that someone has clumsily drawn on the glass on a previous outing in this car. "Do you remember the episode with the bus after Skye's track meet?"

It takes me a second to make the leap. She's talking about *Starlight*. First season sometime, I think. "All the episodes tend to blend together after a while," I admit.

"The bus crashes on the way back from the track meet, and Brody saves Skye, as he always does," Amanda says.

Now I remember. We shot on a bus set that week, the vehicle cut in half for easier filming, and on location on an abandoned stretch of road in the middle of nowhere. My biggest memory of that episode is freezing and trying not to let it show. Calista as Skye had it much worse in track shorts and a T-shirt.

"But then they learn that if he changes things in the crash to save Skye, these other three kids will die," Amanda continues. "According to Brody, Skye needs to live to stop the apocalypse, and those other kids . . . they don't have a role in saving the world. Skye and Brody try everything to find a work-around, but there isn't one. She begs him to save the other kids and let her die because she doesn't believe her life is worth more than theirs. She doesn't believe Brody when he says she is important."

It was the mid-season finale, bringing even more doubt to Brody and Skye's future together. If he does what she wants, the world is doomed and he loses his chance at redemption. But he knows she'll never forgive him if he doesn't.

"Brody ignores her and does it anyway, of course," she says with a laugh, but her voice sounds soft, vulnerable. "He saves her. Because he believes she matters. Not just to the world but to him." She shifts in her seat. "I guess . . . everybody wants to be the one worth saving," she says with a wry twist of her mouth. "When you were there, talking to me, telling me I needed to keep fighting, I felt like it mattered, like I mattered. And I wasn't alone."

My throat is tight with emotion. "Amanda—"

My cell phone rings then, loud and shrilly, disrupting the quiet and making me jump, even though the meditation-chime setting is supposed to be soothing.

"Shit. Sorry." I fumble for it in my pocket to shut off the noise, but the screen is flashing Elise's picture, one she took from my bed one night and set for her contact on my phone. It's obvious what was going on immediately before the picture, from her rumpled hair to the bedsheet wrapped under her arms.

Amanda would have to be blind not to see it, and she most definitely is not blind.

I swipe the answer button. "I can't talk right now," I say curtly. "I'm driving back to the hotel." Then for good measure, I add, "And I fired you, remember?"

"Oh." It's more of an exhalation than a word from Elise, but that's it, enough to assure me she gets it, then a click as she hangs up. Shortest conversation I've ever had with her, but then again, Elise is nothing short of dedicated when it comes to one of her schemes.

I set the phone to silent and dump it in the cup holder by the gearshift. "Sorry about that."

"You don't need to apologize," Amanda says. But I can feel that something has shifted here in the darkness, creating a distance that wasn't present a few seconds ago. "That was your publicist? The one who took your car?"

I have the feeling she's asking more than that, but that ground is far too dangerous to tread at the moment. "Yeah, that's her."

"Ah. Okay."

"So I think it's your turn for a question," I prompt, trying to steer the conversation back on track. It feels, oddly, like we lost something in that interruption. We're back to being strangers in the dark.

Amanda shakes her head. "No, it's not important. We should talk about the plan."

"The plan?"

"How we're going to get them to take pictures," she says pointedly.

"Right, yes. Okay." I have to shift gears mentally, running through my schedule. "There will probably be a couple of photographers and reporters hanging around the hotel tomorrow, especially after what happened today. If you leave with me in the morning, when I go over for hair and makeup, that's probably a good start. Then we can—"

From behind me, I hear the very familiar opening guitar and banging piano chords of a song that they will probably play at my funeral. The *Starlight* theme.

I stiffen. "What the hell—"

"It's my phone," Amanda says with a grimace, shifting in her seat, squeezing past me, so close I can smell the light scent of peaches or nectarines in her hair, to reach into her bag on the backseat. "My sister's idea of a joke. She downloaded a bunch of songs and attached them to certain numbers."

"Liza?" I ask.

Amanda snorts. "No," she says, her voice muffled as she rummages. "Mia. *Starlight* is no joking matter to Liza."

Amanda returns to her seat, phone in hand. "It's Dr. Knaussen."

"You have your therapist programmed into your phone?"

She raises her eyebrows at me. "You don't?"

"Touché," I mutter.

"If I don't pick up, she's going to keep calling." Amanda stares at the screen as if consulting it for wisdom. "Maybe set my parents off in a panic."

"Okay, so answer." But clearly there's more to it than I'm aware of, especially given how reluctantly she lifts the phone to her ear.

"Hello?" she says.

"Amanda, it's Dr. Knaussen. Are you all right?" The woman's

voice is low and smooth but pitched to project confidence, like one of those radio-show-host doctors. I can hear her as clearly as if she were on speakerphone.

"Yeah, I'm fine," Amanda says, fidgeting with the button on her shirt cuff.

"I just got out of a session now to a panicked message that you left town. With Chase Henry, the actor?" Dr. Knaussen sounds alarmed.

Amanda grimaces. "It's not what it sounds like. He's in Wescott filming a movie, and he heard about the poster and everything." She hesitates. "He invited me to visit the set, and I thought it might help."

The silence on the other end of the phone speaks volumes.

"Amanda," she says slowly. "As we've discussed, Chase Henry was an important coping mechanism when you needed it, but you need to understand that Mr. Henry, the real person, has no capacity to help—"

"Yes, I know," Amanda says sharply with a quick glance at me. I stare straight ahead, not sure if she wants me hearing any of this. "It's not about that."

"I have to admit, I'm concerned," the doctor says, clearly choosing her words with care. "When we agreed to try a more aggressive approach to exposure therapy, we talked intensively about the possibility of setbacks and the need for small steps. I know you're eager for progress, but you could do more harm than good." The scolding tone is faint, barely detectable, but still there.

Amanda sinks deeper in her seat, her shoulders curving in protectively.

I tighten my hands on the wheel, struggling to keep my mouth shut.

"I understand," Amanda says in a weary voice. "But the small steps weren't working. It's been two years," she adds with a flare of anger. "I needed to do something different."

"Something different," Dr. Knaussen repeats. "Amanda, there

are other, far less rash options." She sighs. "We've talked about you trusting your choices. You need to be able to trust your decisions again to be able to function. I believe most of your anxiety comes from your fear that you somehow brought what happened to you on yourself, that you could have done something differently and prevented it."

I can't help it this time; I'm staring at Amanda. How could she possibly think that she was, in any way, responsible for being taken?

But Amanda says nothing, just continues studying an invisible pattern on her pants, her finger tracing aimless lines in the fabric, which I take to mean that she does, in some way, believe that.

"My fear is that you've made an impulsive decision to trust someone you don't know anything about."

Me. Amanda's trusting me, and she probably shouldn't. The good doctor is right about that.

"He's a stranger with a familiar face, and if that doesn't work out . . ." The doctor pauses with another sigh.

"But how am I supposed to trust my choices if I don't start making some?" Amanda demands, showing a bit of her earlier fire.

I could almost admire it, if I wasn't so busy feeling sick to my stomach.

There's a long pause where I can practically hear her therapist debating how hard to push. Maybe it's the cynic in me, but I'm betting there's a certain cache to being the shrink who finally "cured" Amanda Grace, even if that means sticking through some unexpected turns along the way. Just makes the book or journal article that much more interesting.

"All right," the doctor says eventually. You can almost hear her lifting her hands in the air in surrender. "I'm just concerned. It's about you making smart choices."

As if anyone knows what those are until it's way too late to change them.

"Okay," Amanda says. "I'll call you tomorrow."

She hangs up, and it's quiet in the car again.

"Is that true?" I venture, unable to stop myself. "Do you really blame yourself for—"

"I don't want to talk about it," Amanda says, folding her hands over her phone.

I close my mouth with an audible click. She's right. This is none of my damn business.

The rest of the journey—only about fifteen minutes, thankfully—is conducted in silence.

But that changes as soon as we pull into the Wescott Inn parking lot. Wescott is a tiny town, pretty much like Springfield in that respect, and most of the cast and crew are being put up in this, the nicest of the hotels in town. Which isn't really saying much. Max, along with Jenna and Adam, are reportedly in a much swankier B and B, but I'm not about to complain.

Police cars are blocking the main entrance, beneath the overhang, their red and blue flashing lights turning the white facade of the hotel a faint shade of purple.

Amanda tenses next to me. "Is something wrong?"

I frown. "It's probably nothing. Just a security issue. It happens sometimes, especially on location. It's harder for them to keep the crazies out." I wince at my word choice. I don't think Amanda's crazy, but she may take offense at the term.

Amanda just nods knowingly. "Stalkers."

It occurs to me then that even though her experience has been completely different than mine in some very big ways, we overlap in certain areas. "Yeah. Some are just fans who go a step too far, some are . . . something else. This one girl, Sera Drummond, actually broke into my condo and told the cops she was my girlfriend. Then she threatened to burn down my building, and we had to get a restraining order. It was seriously fucked up."

"I got letters. I had to have a protective detail for a while." Amanda makes a disgusted noise. "People are sick to capitalize on someone else's misery."

"Agreed," I say, navigating through the mostly empty parking lot. Then a thought dawns rather belatedly. "Is that . . . do they freak you out?" I ask Amanda, nodding at the police cars. "I can try to park around back, go in through a delivery entrance or something." So far, no one in town seems all that interested in us, so I haven't been reduced to sneaking in and out here. But I can figure it out.

She shakes her head. "No, I'm fine."

I'm not so sure about that, though. Even less so, when she climbs out of the car and looks around as if she's been dropped off on an alien planet instead of a town practically next door to the one where she grew up.

"We'll get inside, get you checked in, and everything's going to be great," I promise, even though I have absolutely no business making those kinds of promises. Especially with what I've done. What I'm doing.

Amanda takes a deep breath, squaring her shoulders, and nods.

We head toward the main entrance, in step with each other. I'm careful not to touch her, though it feels impolite not to guide her or at least let her walk ahead of me. Elise would laugh at that and point at my Texas upbringing again. Guess I never realized exactly how deeply ingrained it is in me.

It's only as we skirt the squad cars that I realize they're both occupied. The officers inside open their doors simultaneously and get out.

"Amanda Grace?" the closest one asks. Barks, more like. He's older, with graying hair, and built like a barrel.

She freezes, and I'm right there with her. What the hell is this?

I pivot to face them, putting Amanda behind me. "Officers. Can I help you?" I plaster on a smile. I can feel my hands tightening into fists already. One of the small problems I've had in my life is that I don't particularly respond well to authority, even when I'm in no position to resist it.

"We're responding to a request through Officer Beckstrom in

Springfield for a welfare check on you." They are theoretically talking to Amanda, but both of them, big beefy authoritarian types, are glaring holes through me. Clearly, they've seen my record. Great. I'm not proud of the stupid shit I've done, but I am trying to get past it, if people will let me. These guys don't seem inclined toward the whole "fresh start" idea, though.

"Your father, Miss Grace, is concerned about you," the older cop continues, watching me as though I might lunge at him for his keys and take off on a joyride or something.

Ah, so Amanda's dad isn't the "chase a car down the driveway" sort of dad. He's the "call the cops on the sleazy Hollywood type taking my daughter" kind instead.

Good to know. Wish I'd known it a little earlier.

7

Amanda

At first, I'm not sure I heard the officer correctly. My dad? My dad, who can't even really look at me, can barely talk to me, sent the police after me?

He doesn't want to deal with me himself, but I guess letting me "run off" would be an equally unacceptable outcome. Better to send someone else to handle it. To handle *me*.

A rush of fury and hurt floods through my veins, and I can feel my face burning with it, my eyes smarting with tears.

But I've got a more immediate problem. Chase is in front of me, and his body language screams trouble. His shoulders are tense, his back stiff, and I can't see the front of him, but I'd bet there's chest puffing going on.

Crap. He'd have to be stupid to challenge armed men who are just looking for an excuse to take him down, and yet that doesn't appear to be much of a deterrent at the moment. I seem to remember that resisting arrest might have been one of his various sins.

"Excuse me?" I step out from behind Chase. How did he do that anyway? Manage to put himself between them and me? I didn't even notice it happening until it was done. "I'm fine. You can see that I'm fine. Thank you for checking, though."

"Miss Grace, your father would feel more comfortable if you returned home," the closest officer, the older of the two, says, his gaze flicking to me briefly.

"I'm sure he would," I say. "But I'm going to stay here." The key is to remain calm, keep my voice even and unaffected. If I shout or look like I'm about to cry, they'll only press harder.

"I have Beckstrom's office and cell number programmed into my phone," I continue. Probably set to the *Cops* theme, if I know Mia. "If I run into trouble, she'll be my first call." I hold up my phone, as if to demonstrate.

This doesn't seem to do much to convince them. I can feel the tension rising, like a string binding all four of us tighter and tighter. Someone's going to snap and lash out, any second.

"I have a daughter not too much younger than you," the older cop says. "I wouldn't want her out here with a stranger." His voice goes dark on the last word, like it's a synonym for murderer. Or worse.

Then it clicks. He *knows* me, or thinks he does. He followed the Miracle Girl story, probably imagining the horrors as if they'd occurred to his own child. I can see it in his face. It's his worst nightmare, and like most of the police I've encountered, they see what happened to me as some kind of failure, personal or systemic. *It never should have happened.* I've lost count how many times I've heard that. I'm proof that there are gaps and inefficiencies that can destroy lives.

And he's determined to make up for it, even if in just this small way, by delivering me back to known safety. I get that, I do, but I'm a person, not a symbol.

"I understand," I say as patiently as I can. "But I'm twenty, and I'm here of my own free will."

"You sure?" the second officer chimes in, his gaze fixed on Chase, who bristles at the implication.

Enough. I'm so tired of everyone second-guessing me today. I get plenty of that in my own head.

"I think *I* would know, don't you?" I ask sharply. "I've got some experience in that area, as I'm sure you've heard."

The words hang in the air like the echo of a slap. And all three of them are staring at me.

Finally the older cop gives a curt nod. "Sorry to have disturbed you." His voice is stiff with formality. He's pissed now because I seem like an ungrateful snot.

Great. "Thank you for following up on the call," I say. "I appreciate it." Even if I don't need the help, somebody someday might, and I don't want the memory of my reaction to slow them in responding on future welfare checks. I don't want that on my conscience.

The older officer jerks his head at the younger one, and they retreat into their cars without another word.

I wait to make sure they're actually leaving, then I turn and head for the sliding doors into the hotel. There are five or six curious faces turned in my direction, watching through the glass. Other hotel guests who happen to have been in the lobby or those drawn by lights and the promise of drama.

But as soon as they see me coming, they turn away, pretending to be occupied by something else. Checking in, reading a free newspaper from one of the little metal stands, or, God, staring up at the ceiling. Really?

Chase is behind me, his steps slower. "You didn't need to do that," he says. "I could have handled it."

I turn and wait for him to catch up. "Really?" I ask. "I'm not sure this would have worked nearly as well if I had to visit you in jail."

He makes a face, that generous and wide mouth twisting with displeasure. "I'm working on it, okay?"

I'm distracted momentarily, flustered. Why would I be paying any attention to his mouth? "Do you have a problem with the police?" I ask evenly, determined to keep this conversation—and rehabilitation plan—on track.

"No," he says, stuffing his hands into his pockets as we move deeper into the lobby.

I look at him.

"Not anymore," he says. "They have a problem with me." He sighs. "I did some stupid shi . . . stuff when I was younger."

He's censoring his language in front of me? I can't decide if that's funny or kind of insulting, like he still sees me as a child. Lots of people do. Once you're in the victim role, it's hard for people to treat you as anything other than someone who needs to be protected.

But I'm only four years younger than Chase, and I don't have a whole lot of innocence left to protect, unfortunately.

"I had friends who maybe didn't have my best interests in mind," he continues. "Not that I'm trying to pin the blame on them," he says quickly, in a manner that suggests he's been accused of doing just that. "I did it. All of it. Willingly, eagerly, even." He hesitates. "It's just . . ."

"Easier to lose track of yourself when there are all these other voices shouting at you?" I offer. I know that feeling. I've been living with it for the last two years.

He glances at me sharply, as if seeing me for the first time. "Yeah, something like that," he says with a hint of surprise in his voice.

"Welcome back, *Mr. Dean.*" The front desk girl practically leans across the polished wooden counter to beam at him as we cross the lobby.

I raise an eyebrow at Chase.

"Fake name," he mumbles. "Not my idea."

Yeah, *that's* what I was reacting to. "James or Jimmy?" I ask instead.

It takes him a second. "The sausage guy?"

I nod.

His mouth—what is wrong with me?—quirks in a wicked smile. "Definitely the sausage guy."

I roll my eyes. Good grief. But a part of me is pleased that he didn't hesitate to play with the innuendo.

"Hey," he says to the front desk girl. "Thanks. This is . . ." He hesitates and lowers his voice, in deference to those who are lurking around the lobby. "This is Amanda Gr—"

"Oh, yes, sir, Mr. Dean." She—her brass-colored name tag says SHARA—smiles at him so hard it makes my cheeks ache in sympathy. "I know who she is. All the arrangements have been made, and I have the reservation information right here."

Pulled up, no doubt, the second she saw us through the windows. Or, rather, the second she saw Chase.

At least, that's what I think until she turns that same awe-struck smile on me. "Miss Grace, we'll be checking you in under the name Mrs. Dean to preserve your privacy, as requested, and you'll be in the room adjoining Mr. Dean's." A faint pink blush rises in her cheeks.

"What?" Chase and I say at the same time. I can feel a sudden heat crawling up my neck. What exactly does she think is going on here?

Shara looks startled. "I'm sorry. Do I have that wrong? Ms. Prescott left very explicit instructions before she checked out."

Next to me, Chase stiffens. "I bet," he mutters.

"Ms. Prescott?" I murmur.

"Publicist," he says.

Ah, Elise. The one he fired, who, from the looks of her photo on his phone, might have been more than just an employee. So, she was pissed, and this was her passive-aggressive parting gift. Nice.

I plaster a polite smile on my face. "I'm sure Shara can find another room in the hotel for me. I don't want to intrude on Mr. Dean's privacy."

Her confused gaze flicks between Chase and me. "I can check," she says to me with a nod. "I also have a note for you, Mr. Dean, from Ms. Prescott before she checked out." Shara holds out a folded slip of paper.

Chase takes it from her, his mouth curving down in distaste. He barely glances at the message inside before crumpling it and shoving it into his pocket. Then again, it doesn't take long to read "fuck you," which is likely the spirit of the message, if not the exact wording.

Shara types on her computer, each loud clack of the keys echoing through the quiet lobby. It feels like a Klaxon going off, drawing even more attention to us. We're the only ones at the desk, which helps, but I can still sense other people in the lobby. Footsteps across the floor behind us. The quiet whoosh of the automatic doors opening or closing. A cough from the club chairs arranged in front of the big stone fireplace. I don't know if they're people Chase knows or not.

Experience keeps me facing forward, away from prying eyes.

"I do have something on the first floor," Shara says after a moment. "It's not one of our luxury rooms. But it is handicapped accessible, so it's right near the door." She offers this last tidbit with a hopeful smile, as if that will make up for the lack of a mini-fridge or king-sized bed.

But all I hear is "right near the door"; in other words, kidnap adjacent. Easy access. Prime bad-guy territory. Just prop the door open and lurk nearby, waiting for your victim. Or break open the room window and drag her out into a van. Smash and grab.

My palms start to sweat, and I surreptitiously wipe them against my pants.

I force myself to maintain my smile, even though I can feel the muscles protesting. "Sure, that sounds great." I'm proud that my tone stays mostly level.

"I'll make the change right now," Shara says.

Chase frowns at me, studying my face, and something must have shown in my expression, despite my efforts.

"Wait," he says, stopping Shara as she begins to type again. "The original arrangements are fine." He hesitates. "If that's okay with you? There's a door between the rooms," he adds quietly. "You can keep it locked."

Shara looks away, pretending not to listen, and awkwardness spills out all over the lobby. My face is hot, and I'm not even sure why. It feels like there's a spotlight shining down on us, even though I can't see anyone other than Shara.

"It's a deadbolt, so the key card won't open—" Chase says.

"I'm familiar with the mechanics of a deadbolt," I say quickly and under my breath. I just want to get out of here. It feels like all my vulnerabilities and "issues" are on display.

Shara, thankfully, seems just as relieved to be moving on to the next stage of check-in. Key cards, two, for me. She pushes them in a little envelope across the counter to me without comment, her smile dimmed a little but still firmly in place.

"Thank you for choosing the Wescott Inn," she calls after us as we step away from the counter.

Chase leads the way, stalking toward the elevators without waiting for me.

I follow him. His head is down, his shoulders hunched, his hands jammed in his pockets, and I'm not sure if that's an unconscious defense against anyone who might be watching or if it's just his way of pushing off any potential conversation with me. He didn't seem angry a few seconds ago, when he offered to keep the adjoining room arrangements, but now I'm not so sure.

I catch up to him at the elevator doors and stay quiet, just in case. He jabs at the button for the elevator with enough force that it sounds like it hurts, and suddenly, I'm leaning toward the "angry" explanation.

Great.

I study the mirrored doors in front of us, my reflection next to Chase's. He is staring at the floor, pinching his lower lip between his thumb and forefinger, lost in thought or just avoiding me—I'm not sure which—which gives me plenty of opportunity.

It's like an image out of bizarro world, the two of us in one place. I know his face almost as well as my own, but this version, the real, non-Photoshopped version, is different, not just older, and I catch myself playing "find the difference."

The thin line of a scar above his left eyebrow. The spray of faint freckles across the bridge of his nose. The dark circles under his eyes that speak to stress and sleepless nights.

His T-shirt is rumpled. There's a tuft of dark blond hair sticking up a little at the crown of his head, which is, frankly, kind of adorable.

He is so . . . real. Which sounds completely ridiculous. Of course he's real. He always has been. Just because I didn't know him then didn't make him less of an actual person.

But it's a strange feeling, a duality of sorts, as if the guy who posed for the poster I know so well and this man next to me are two different people.

Despite the intimacy of the perfect Chase who lived in my head for years, talking to me and soothing me, this Chase, the one with the flaws and money problems, the one who knows about cows and mucking barns, feels so much more real, more approachable, even. He understands what it means to screw up, to be afraid and desperate.

Without even knowing why the first-floor room bothered me—I doubt my logic about the accessibility for criminals would leap to mind for most normal people—he intervened, at the expense of his own privacy. Something he probably doesn't get a lot of.

And then there's that bit of sticking-up hair that I just want to reach over and smooth into place . . .

My heart gives a funny little quiver, and a vaguely familiar warmth floods through my chest. It takes me a second to place the sensation. The last time I felt this way, I was staring at C. J. Weymouth in the trumpet section of band freshman year, with my best friend, Casey, whispering in my ear about how she heard that trumpet players were the best kissers. Strong lips and all.

No. *Oh, no. No, no, no.* I *cannot* be attracted to Chase Henry.

I spin to face away from him, though he's not even looking in my direction.

This crazy plan is already shaky enough; I don't need to take it out at the legs. And that's exactly what letting myself be attracted to him will do.

I don't need this. I can't have this.

Someday. That's what my mom always says with a distant smile whenever the topic of guys or relationships comes up. I mean, I have trouble leaving the house sometimes. Dating is a little out of the question.

Besides, who in their right mind would undertake the challenge of . . . well, me? I still flinch when well-meaning people pat me on the shoulder.

Not that any of that even remotely mattered. When the part of you that registers attraction is dead, or at least in a coma, for more than four years, it's kind of a nonissue.

Until now. Apparently.

I cast another glance over my shoulder at Chase, who's jabbing at the elevator button again, his jaw tight with frustration. I can see the muscles ticking beneath his skin, and the faint stubble on his cheek catches in the bright cast of the overhead light, making it glint like gold.

And I find myself imagining what that would feel like under my fingertips.

What is wrong with me? This is absolutely the worst time for that part of my brain or limbic system or hormones or whatever to wake up.

Tearing my gaze away from Chase, I force myself to focus on the floor, on the random shading patterns in the tile.

I'm not going to do this. It would look completely pathetic from the outside, maybe even to Chase himself. Like I'd transferred all my feelings generated by a poster to the real thing, regardless of the person beneath the face.

Besides, even if I was ready, Chase Henry would be the very *last* person to consider a viable candidate.

I saw that picture of Elise on his phone, looking warm, naked, and sated. And that was someone he worked with. It was clearly casual, coworkers with benefits. I doubt very much that he'd be interested in the kind of challenge I'd present.

A flash of bitterness zips through my veins before vanishing. There's no point in focusing on hating what happened to me, wishing it hadn't. Been there, done that. I'm here to move on. Or at least try to.

That's what I need to concentrate on. Nothing else.

"Amanda?"

Chase's voice startles me, and I turn to find him at the threshold of the now-open elevator, his arm across the door to keep it from closing.

"You coming?" he asks, his eyebrows raised in question or possibly concern.

"Uh-huh." I lift my chin and do my best to pretend that my face is not red as I hurry toward him.

He edges a step out of the way, still holding the door but making sure that I have plenty of room to pass without bumping into him.

And the recently awakened part of myself gives a tiny appreciative flutter. How did Elise give this up? Granted, Chase wants something from me, but I don't get a forced vibe from this. If anything, this thoughtfulness seems more like habit. A really nice habit, actually.

"She must have been really pissed at you." The words escape before I can stop them, and I clamp my lips together belatedly.

He pushes the button for five and looks over at me, his brows drawn together in a frown. "Who?"

"Elise." It's unavoidable now that I've blurted it out.

"Yeah, she . . . definitely has her own agenda," he says with distaste.

Silence falls as the doors close.

I shift my weight from foot to foot. The space feels too small with Chase on the other side of it. I'm too aware of him now, unfortunately, and that brings with it a whole slew of thoughts and questions I don't really want to contemplate.

Like, what does he look like naked?

Stop, stop, stop.

How long can it possibly take for an elevator to get to the top of a five-story building? Seriously.

"I'm sorry about not being able to take the other room," I say, more to distract myself than anything else. "It's just that the first floor kind of—"

The elevator dings, interrupting me, and the doors roll back.

"You have nothing to apologize for," Chase says shortly, holding an arm across one of the doors and gesturing for me to exit first.

But clearly, though, I do. Or someone does. Chase has practically shut down in response to something. He was positively chatty in the car, by comparison.

He passes me by and leads the way to our rooms. They're in the far corner of the floor, tucked at the end of a hall. His room is to the left of mine, according to the numbers.

I fumble in my fleece pockets for the key cards. Now that we're here, I'm not exactly sure what's going to happen. I mean, we talked about pictures tomorrow, and that's fine, but what about the rest of the time?

How exactly is being in proximity to him supposed to help? Suddenly my plan seems sort of stupid and not well thought out.

I tug my bag higher up on my shoulder, jab the key card into the lock, and manage to shove the door open, bracing it with my foot.

"Is this going to be okay?" Chase asks, tipping his head toward the room.

"Oh. Yeah, I'm sure it is," I say, confused. At first glance, it appears to be a normal, slightly upgraded hotel room. Basically like the ones my family used to stay in when we used to go on summer car trips to Gettysburg or wherever, only a little nicer. But that's true of the entire building.

The two beds are draped in pristine white comforters with room service menus propped against a multitude of pillows. The bathroom is dark and to the right, so I can't really see it, but I'm assuming it has all the required facilities.

The door to Chase's room is immediately to my left, on the other side of the closet.

The closet. Two sliding panels, both mirrored. Inside, there's a safe on one half of the floor, limiting the space. The carpeting looks even newer, cleaner, which is saying something, considering it looks great in the rest of the room.

In short, it's a perfect little hidey-hole. And I hate myself for noticing that.

"Good. I'll be right here later, if you need something." Chase gestures toward his room door in the hall. "But I need to go. I have to take care of something right now," he says, avoiding my gaze.

Uh-oh. I knew I shouldn't have agreed to this adjoining-room thing. He can't wait to get away. But all I say is, "Okay."

We stand there in silence for a long moment.

"Do you want me to check it?" he asks eventually.

"What?" I ask.

He hesitates, faint color rising in his face. "The room. Do you want me to check it to make sure it's, uh, secure?"

It's only then that I realize he's been waiting for me to go inside. And now he wants to know if I need him to look under the beds for monsters and rapists?

Oh God, how humiliating. Even if that would have made me

feel better—maybe—there's no way I can say yes now. "No, it's . . . I'm fine. Just . . . yeah." Clinging tighter to my bag, I cross the threshold into the room and turn to face him.

There, I'm in. Now what?

"Okay." He pauses. "If you're hungry, you should order room service, whatever you want. Charge it to the room."

"Um, thanks."

He nods and turns away without another word, striding off down the hall, the way we came.

I stand there for a second, staring into the space he used to occupy, fighting the urge to laugh at the ridiculousness and myself.

I was worried about being attracted to him, while his primary concern, evidently, was figuring out how far away he could get from me and how quickly.

A small snort of laughter escapes before I stop it. Well, this certainly makes things easier.

A teeny-tiny part of me is mourning the loss, though. Because even just *thinking* about him that way was a step forward, albeit one I wasn't expecting.

I step back from the door, letting it shut. As soon as the latch clicks into place, I throw the deadbolt and the U-shaped security-lock thing.

I look around the room, noticing for the first time the strong, impersonal smell of newish carpeting and cleaning supplies. It reminds me of the hospital a little, which sends a shiver through me.

Even though the room isn't that big, it feels empty and exposed somehow. I remember suddenly an article I read online a few months ago about a guy who installed secret cameras in hotel room heater / air-conditioning units to creep on the guests.

Key cards aren't that secure, you know. The evil voice pops up in the back of my head. *Someone might still be able to get in with an old one. And the security latches aren't that hard to beat.*

With an effort, I push those thoughts away and go about

turning on all the lights I can find and pulling the drapes tightly closed.

I have a small moment of indecision when trying to decide which bed, the one closer to the door or the window. Where is the greatest threat?

After deciding that anyone leaning a five-story ladder against the outside of a hotel is bound to be noticed, I settle on the bed farthest from the door.

I perch carefully on the edge of the bed with my bag on my lap, the fluffy white comforter rising up to surround me, and try to ignore the unfamiliar silence and the rapid beat of my heart, which is only getting faster.

8

Chase

GO WITH IT.
Find me later. Room 222.

The note is crumpled from where I stuffed it in my pocket, but Elise's message, in her smooth, curling cursive, is still legible.

It doesn't take but a few minutes to find her room on the second floor. The bar latch is flipped, keeping the door from locking. She's expecting me to show up here, as ordered, and that just pisses me off further.

I shove open the door to find her pacing at the foot of the double bed in the much smaller, non-luxury room, her phone pressed to her ear. Her laptop and tablet are both set up on the desk and glowing—she's working.

On what, though? That's the question. I have a bad feeling about this.

"What the hell, Elise?" I demand as the door bangs shut behind me.

She holds up her finger in the classic "wait" sign and gives me a patronizing wink.

"No, no, I totally agree," she says into the phone. "I think you should wait until tomorrow. There'll be more to work with then."

Why does that fill my stomach with dread?

"Uh-huh, uh-huh. Yep, exciting, I know! Tomorrow." She hangs up, puts the phone down on the desk, and turns to face me with a seductive smile. "Sweetie." She looks as sleek and pulled together as she did this morning, which feels like eons ago. Her skirt is one of those that hugs her curves and yet looks smooth and untouchable.

Usually, that only makes me want to touch her, to rumple her, even more. Right now, though, I'm too angry.

She makes a production of sitting on the edge of the bed and patting a spot next to her, each individual motion calculated for maximum allure.

I don't move. "What are you doing?" I ask darkly.

She makes an innocent face, her hand resting on her chest and playing with the buttons on her blouse, until one of them pops free "accidentally." "Who, me?"

I'm beyond allowing myself to be distracted. "The rooms?" I press. "Whatever you told that girl at the front desk?"

Her hand drops to her lap with a definitive slap, and she gives me an exasperated look, all hint of temptress vanishing. "Okay, before you get all *rah-led up*," she mocks my accent, "just listen for a minute."

I glare at her.

"No, seriously, I want you to think about this." She sits forward. "We knew that photos of you and Amanda would attract some attention."

I nod grudgingly.

"So, after you told me you got her to come here, all I could think was, imagine what kind of response we'd get if people thought you two were . . . together?" She smooths a nonexistent wrinkle out of the comforter.

"Together?" I stare at her, my brain refusing to compute what she's just said. Then I get it. The adjoining rooms. The way the front desk girl watched Amanda and me, her cheeks flushed with excitement, like she was in on a secret. "As in, *together*? You're fucking kidding me."

Elise stands up, following me as I take a step back and locking her hand on the front of my shirt. "No, think about it. It's so meta! Your poster saved her in that room and now, you save her in real life." She smiles up at me.

"What happened in that room was real life for Amanda," I point out. Very real. Too real.

"Right. Of course." Elise taps her finger lightly against my chest. "But you know I'm right. The media will eat it up, and all those teen girls who watched *Starlight* will remember why they fell in love with you in the first place."

More like, why they fell in love with my image or the character of a guardian angel. Not exactly the same thing, but for Elise's intents and purposes, it's one and the same.

"Elise," I say, my jaw tight. "You saw what happened at the store. Amanda . . . she's messed up." I feel vaguely guilty telling Elise this, as though everything that Amanda told me in the car is somehow protected by confessional status or something. But it's true, and Amanda would be the first to admit it.

"And yet she managed to make it here," Elise says wryly, her mouth quirked in amusement.

"You think she's faking?" I ask in disbelief. Maybe Elise was too far away when Amanda panicked at the store, but my seat was front and center. You can't fake that kind of terror. And there were plenty of us who tried for a living.

"No," Elise says, sliding up against me, back in temptation mode. "I just think this face is awfully persuasive." She cups my chin, running her thumb over my lower lip. "It doesn't have to be a big deal, Chase," she says softly, her breath touching my mouth. "She doesn't have to know. The rumors will take care of most of it. You just stand a little closer to her, maybe put your arm around her shoulders—"

I pull out of Elise's grasp. "She doesn't like being touched." I could still feel Amanda flinching away from me.

Elise waves her hand dismissively. "By creepy old guys against her will, yeah. But that's not you."

I rub my forehead. "Jesus, Elise, no." Pretending to be in a relationship for attention is bad enough, but to do that to Amanda after everything she's been through? That feels wrong. It takes away her choice. Maybe she doesn't want to be "romantically linked" with me or anyone else. I imagine that kind of thing might be an issue for her in real life, let alone adding a layer of fake.

Elise's expression shifts, hardening around the edges. "I thought we were in this together. I thought you had my back."

"I do," I snap. "But this is not what we agreed on. You're taking it too far and—"

"Even if it's working?" she asks.

"What?"

She stalks to the desk and snatches up her phone.

"Look," she says, unlocking the main screen and handing the phone over to me.

"I don't know what I'm—"

"The call log, Chase." She sounds impatient and bored, which is a bad combination when it comes to Elise.

I click to her recent calls and find a very familiar number at the top. George, her boss, my former publicist, has called twice in the last two hours.

"Some of the photos from today already hit gossip sites," she says, folding her arms across her chest. "It's generating buzz, negative for now because they got a shot of Amanda freaking out."

I wince.

"But that'll change," she says. "If we move on to phase two, which I already told George about."

Of course she had. I hand her the phone.

Elise takes it with a frustrated noise. "You know why George called? Because Rick called him, wanting to know if he was involved. They were curious."

Rick, my agent? It's been months since either of them asked *anything* about me. I'd ceased to exist for them.

"It's working, Chase," Elise says fiercely. "You just have to trust me. Don't quit now, don't turn it all into nothing, not when we're so close. Please?" She gives me a pleading gaze that might be just as calculated as her seductress routine earlier but feels far more real.

I sigh. She has a point. If we quit now, there was no purpose behind any of it, including any pain I might have caused Amanda just by showing up in her life. And, honestly, on a practical level, there's not *that* much difference between what Amanda and I have already discussed and Elise's new plan. We would just be deliberately cultivating the media's instinct to blow everything up into a bigger story than it actually is. Without Amanda's knowledge.

I can feel my resistance and initial outrage waning, and it makes me hate myself more than I already do.

"No one's going to get hurt," Elise says quickly, sensing my capitulation. "Not even Amanda. As soon as the rumors start, we'll issue denials to the press, and we'll even include her, if she wants."

Denials will only fuel the fire of speculation, which is exactly what Elise is counting on. And I'm not quite sure how "we" are going to do this when I "fired" my publicist, but . . . whatever.

"All right," I say.

A slow smile spreads across Elise's face. "Admit it—I'm a genius," she says, as she sways toward me.

"An evil genius," I say. But there's no fire behind the words, and she knows it.

She tosses her phone on the bed and hooks her fingers into the collar of my shirt. "Evil genius. I like that. Want to visit my lair?" She raises herself up on her tiptoes and presses her warm mouth against mine. Her tongue is very persuasive, and the taste of her lipstick, familiar from our past encounters, has me hard in an instant.

She tugs at my coat, pushing it off my shoulders, then steps back, pulling me with her to the bed.

But I can't shake the nagging feeling that's eating at me, making it hard to lose myself in the moment. It takes me a second to isolate the source: Amanda is upstairs by herself.

Why that should bother me, I'm not entirely certain. She said she'd be okay. But something tells me she says that a lot, while maybe not being sure that it's true. It's obvious she doesn't want to be a burden to her family or anyone else, including me.

Elise's hand slides smoothly to my fly while I continue to argue with myself.

If there was trouble, Amanda would have called. But my phone, which is in my pocket, has been silent, no texts or calls, this whole time.

I focus on trailing kisses down the side of Elise's neck, using just a hint of teeth, the way she likes it. The breathy noises she makes in response go straight to my head. It's the only time she ever sounds out of control, and I love it.

Normally. This time, though, I can't get my brain to fucking shut off.

How do you know everything's fine? Maybe Amanda would have called. Except you didn't give her your number, stupid.

Shit.

With a sigh, I admit defeat and pull away from Elise. "I have to go back upstairs."

Elise sits up, her mouth open in shock. "Are you serious?"

"Your idea," I remind her, pushing myself off the bed. "I don't feel right about leaving Amanda up there by herself."

"She's not an unattended infant, Chase," Elise says with a forced laugh.

"No, but she is my responsibility." I shrug my coat onto my shoulders and adjust my jeans. "Unless you want to change the plan?" That's the only compromise I'm willing to make. If we're doing this, I'm not going to let Amanda suffer through it.

"This is ridiculous." Elise straightens up, swinging her legs to the floor and then touching the corners of her mouth to correct her smudged lipstick.

Maybe, but I have to be able to sleep at night.

I start to head for the door.

"You're lucky I'm so understanding, Chase Henry," she calls after me in a teasing voice, but when I glance back, her smile is full of sharp edges.

The warning comes through loud and clear: *Don't cross me.*

Be careful who you get into bed with. That's what my grandpa used to tell my dad all the time when they were dealing with the local ranching political bullshit. It was one of his favorite sayings, right up there with "Good fences make good neighbors."

My grandfather meant it in terms of alliances and taking sides in land disputes, town council votes, and local ordinance changes.

I never thought he might have meant it literally as well, until this exact second.

But it's too late to do anything about it now, so I nod. "Agreed."

It's quiet upstairs on the fifth floor when I arrive via the stairs, too uneasy to wait for the slow elevators. I'm not sure what I was expecting. Half the Wescott Police Department pouring down the halls with guns drawn? Amanda's family pounding on her room door, demanding that she come home?

Unless all of that happened while I was gone.

I quicken my pace.

The doors to our rooms are shut and look exactly the same as when I left—no angry family members, no police, no noticeable scuff marks on the door from someone trying to break in.

Jesus, maybe Amanda's paranoia is catching.

The only difference is a room service tray at the foot of Amanda's door.

I let out a breath of relief. She's fine. She did exactly what I suggested and ordered some food. In other words, exactly what any normal person would do.

I'll check on her after I've had a shower and a second to myself to wrap my head around everything that's happened since I left the hotel this morning. At this moment, it's hard to believe that was only twelve hours ago. Hell, for that matter, I was in California less than a day ago. I'm exhausted, and I just got here. I haven't even memorized my lines yet.

But as I'm reaching in my back pocket for my room key, I get another look at Amanda's room service tray.

The metal cover is still on the plate, and the silverware is still wrapped in the black cloth napkin. A piece of plastic wrap across the top of her water glass kept the water from spilling out in transit, but there's a wide circle of condensation around the base.

With a frown, I kneel and touch the top of the cover. Warm, but not hot. I lift the lid and find a hamburger and french fries completely untouched.

The receipt is stuffed under the edge of the plate, and I'd bet just about anything—if I had anything left—that the black, hasty scrawl across it is not Amanda's, especially considering that her fake name is spelled wrong (*Miranda Deen*).

Neither, most likely, was it Amanda who left a—holy shit—twenty-five-dollar tip on a ten-dollar meal. I'm calling someone tomorrow to reverse that. If I can figure out who. There are times when I really miss having a personal assistant. Evan always just seemed to know that kind of stuff without having to talk to twenty people. He's a screenwriter now.

Without any other recourse, I stand and knock on Amanda's door. "Amanda? Is everything okay? It's me, Chase."

A quiet rustling noise, barely audible, comes through the door.

"Um . . . yeah, I'm fine. Thanks." She sounds distant.

I frown. Maybe she fell asleep waiting for the tray to come?

"There's food out here," I try again.

"I'm sorry about that," she says. "I tried to cancel it. I found some protein bars in my bag."

Who turns down a burger for protein bars? I lived on those for a few weeks during training sessions—no carbs allowed before shirtless scenes—and they got disgusting pretty fast.

Not to mention, I saw the time it took Amanda to pack: less than five minutes. If she remembered to chuck protein bars in there as well as her clothes and makeup and whatever other girl stuff, I'd be impressed.

"So, really, I'm all set." Her voice holds a determined cheerful note in it, but it's hollow, like she's trying not to cry.

It takes me a second to put the pieces together.

Room service delivers to the room, obviously. Amanda is not great with strangers. I'm betting she's even less great with strange guys showing up at her room, even when she's expecting them.

I lean my forehead against the small expanse of wall between our rooms, trying to absorb the coolness. My eyes are gritty with lack of sleep, and I really want that shower. "Did the room service guy scare you?"

Silence.

"It wasn't his fault," she says eventually.

Okay. I let out a slow breath. "Well, it's just me out here now. You want to open the door and I'll hand you the tray?" I ask. She needs to eat. It would be bad if she fainted tomorrow morning in front of the cameras. (Though, Elise would probably find a way to spin it into a pregnancy rumor, God help me.) Plus, Amanda's too skinny. The bones in her face are frighteningly prominent and not in the way of someone on the third week of a cleanse.

I realize then it's been quiet on the other side of the door for too long.

I knock again, feeling the start of panic. "Amanda, are you all right? You're not, like . . ." How do I ask this? I have no fucking clue. "You're not hurting yourself or anything, right?"

"No, I said I'm fine," she snaps, her voice louder and stronger than before. I pissed her off. Good. "Why does everyone make that assumption?"

"I don't know—maybe because you're not letting me in to see for myself," I snap right back at her.

There's another long silence, and shadows flicker in the gap beneath the door. She's moving in the room.

"I pushed the table to block the door," she says quietly. "When he was banging on the door."

I feel a flicker of temper rising. There was no need for him to bang on the door. So he *had* scared her. And then tipped himself 150 percent.

Asshole. I'm definitely going to make some calls tomorrow.

"I don't think I'm ready to pull it away yet," she says with a hint of defiance, as if she's expecting me to try to talk her into it.

But nope, I'm moving on to Plan B. "All right. Hang on a second." I bend down and scoop the tray from the floor, juggling it with one hand while I fumble for my room key. I manage to get my door unlocked and shove it open with my foot, all somehow without spilling anything.

My room feels like a foreign land with a few familiar objects scattered around. The "suite" is really more of a slightly-larger-than-standard hotel room, with a half-wall dividing a small sitting area—couch, TV, mini-fridge—from the bedroom. My tablet is charging on the coffee table and my suitcase is on the floor of the bedroom, the top flap hanging open. I was only here a few minutes before Elise called to tell me the car was picking us up.

Thinking of Elise prompts me to check my reflection in the mirror above the couch to make sure she hasn't smeared lipstick all over my mouth—that would be tough to explain—and then I pop the deadbolt on the adjoining room door and knock on the door to Amanda's room. She has to flip the deadbolt on her side to let me in. And I'm hoping convincing her to do that will be an easier task than talking my way in from the hall.

"It's me," I say. "I'm in here alone. The door to the hall is shut, and no one else has a key."

After a long pause, I hear the sounds of the deadbolt scraping back on her side and she cracks open the door to look up at me. Her hair is pulled into a sloppy ponytail now, with loose strands damp and curling around the edges of her face, as if she just splashed water on her cheeks. Her eyes are swollen and red, leaving no doubt as to her earlier tears.

"Except for a select number of groupies, but I assure you they're carefully screened," I add, to make her laugh. Though it wasn't exactly untrue in the past.

She gives me a wary smile, opening the door a little wider. "I can't tell if you're joking."

"Always," I say. I hold out the tray with a dramatic flourish. "Dinner is served."

She looks at the tray with both longing and reluctance.

"I wanted to open the door, you know," she says fiercely, but makes no move to take the food. "For room service, I mean."

It clicks then: she wants the burger, but she's holding off, some part of her punishing herself for not being able to do more.

My stomach, detecting the scent of freshly cooked meat nearby, is not so indecisive and gives an embarrassingly loud growl. "Well, it's here now, so eat up," I say firmly, pushing the tray toward her.

Amanda steps back, making space for me to enter her room.

I hesitate on the threshold.

"Come on." She waves me forward. "Sounds like you need to eat too."

"I can live without eating protein bars, thanks."

She smiles wryly. "Good thing. I don't actually have any."

I point at her with my free hand. "I *knew* it."

She shrugs, dismissing the accusation. "I'll share. You can have most of the fries, but half the burger is mine."

I move past her and stop just inside the room, which is pretty similar to the bedroom part of my suite, only with two double beds instead of one king. A leather chair on wheels sits abandoned in the corner, the accompanying round table wedged firmly against the door on the opposite side of the room.

It must have taken some serious effort to drag that table into place. Serious effort or serious panic.

It also presents a problem because now I have no idea what to do with the tray. Her bag is on top of the dresser, and the only other flat surfaces in the room are beds.

She takes the tray from me, puts it down on the edge of the farther bed, and sits without hesitation. After lifting the lid on the plate, she promptly divides the hamburger into two ragged but mostly equal halves.

After a moment, she glances up at me with an expectant expression, so I sit across from her, which puts the tray and plenty of space between us.

She peels back the bun on her half of the burger and lays out a tidy row of french fries in the layer of ketchup on the patty.

"What are you doing?" I ask, half intrigued and half revolted.

She raises her eyebrows. "Eating?"

"No, I mean with the fry . . . construction."

"I like the taste," she says with a shrug. "It all goes to the same place anyway."

I make an exaggerated face. "Yeah, if you can get it there."

She rolls her eyes, her mouth quirked in a small smile.

Taking my half of the burger, I make a point of eating a bite of it alone and then returning for a french fry.

Shaking her head, she puts the bun on her burger and digs in.

It's quiet for a few moments, and it's probably the most relaxed either of us has been all day.

But I have to ask: "Why did you lie?"

She goes still. "What?"

"Why not just tell me what happened with room service?"

Amanda puts her burger down and fidgets with the edge of the plastic wrap covering her water glass before answering. "I don't want this to be my whole life, you know?" She looks up at me. "The more people who have to coddle me, the more it feels like this is going to be forever. I'm going to be ninety and still messed up." She lets out a frustrated breath. "And I'm doing everything I can, even some off-the-wall stuff," she adds pointedly, gesturing to the room around us. "But it never feels like enough. And talking about it, telling people what's wrong, I've been doing that for literally years. It doesn't help. They're just words."

The angry desperation in her voice strikes a chord in me.

Sometimes the hardest thing to live with is knowing that you *can't* do anything. You can only push the wheels so far, make so many changes, but control is ultimately out of your hands.

At that point, really, all you can do is whatever you can to keep yourself from going crazy. I understand that, maybe too well.

I swallow a bite of hamburger and clear my throat. "You know how to throw a punch?"

She regards me steadily for a moment, her dark eyes seeming even darker against her pale skin. A redhead with brown eyes—it's a combination I haven't seen often.

Then she says, "Therapist number three," and returns to eating her strange burger concoction.

"What?"

"That was his suggestion. Self-defense classes," she says with a bit of a sneer.

"Well, yeah. What's wrong with that?" I ask.

She wipes her mouth with a corner of the napkin. "Nothing.

If you don't melt down every time a stranger touches you," she says.

I put down my half of the burger on the plate. "I'm not talking about judo or a masked guy full-on attacking you in a darkened hallway."

She shudders.

"I just mean a decent punch, without breaking your fingers." If she feels she's got a shot at defending herself in a bad situation, maybe that would help. Plus, hitting something—or someone, in my experience—usually helps vent a little steam.

"Sorry, they don't teach that in PE." She pauses. "Or, if they did, I was absent that year," she says dryly, the corner of her mouth turning up.

It's that smile that pushes me into a decision. She is trying so hard not to be a victim to all the fallout, but from the outside, it looks like one of those losing battles, an endless game of Whac-a-Mole. I *know* that feeling.

Yet she's still capable of finding humor in all of this. Okay, really dark humor, but still.

I wipe my hands on my jeans and get off the bed. "Come on. Stand up."

Amanda narrows her eyes at me.

"I won't grab you or come at you—promise." I hold my hand palm up, like I'm swearing to tell the truth, the whole truth, and nothing but the truth.

After a long second, she nods and puts down her burger/fry combo.

As she slides off the bed to stand, I shrug out of my jacket and toss it onto the other bed. Amanda tracks it with her gaze, a faint pink blush rising in her face and neck, which I don't understand. I'm still fully dressed.

"Face me," I instruct.

She does, and we're toe to toe, about two feet apart, an invisible line dividing us.

"Step back with your right leg," I say, doing the same myself. "Your other right," I add when she moves her left.

Glaring at me, she makes the change.

"Now angle your body at forty-five degrees, but keep facing me," I say.

She frowns.

"Ninety degrees would have you facing the wall, so half of that," I offer, trying to help.

"I understand basic math, thanks," she says. "I'm trying to figure out how to both turn away from you and face you at the same time."

I watch her struggle to mimic my position, not quite getting it.

"Can I help you?" I ask eventually.

After a split second of hesitation, she nods.

She sways slightly as I cross the invisible line into her space, but she doesn't step away. I stand behind her, careful to keep several inches of distance. The nectarine smell of her hair is much stronger, this close to her.

"Forty-five degrees, aim your toes and hips that way." I point to the corner diagonal to us.

She shifts in the right direction. But it's still not enough.

"Can I touch you?" I ask in the best brisk tone I have. It sounds crazy intimate to ask that and it's not at all what I mean, but I'm determined not to make her jump away from me again.

The pink in her face deepens, but she nods.

"Touching your waist," I say, then I wait until she nods before moving my hands toward her.

Her breath catches audibly when I make contact, but she doesn't flinch.

I keep my grasp light, guiding rather than grabbing her hips. Her skin is warm through the fabric, and I can feel the points of her bones beneath my fingers. She really is too thin.

She lets out a shaky breath, and some of the tension eases out of her body.

"Now your shoulders." I wait until she nods again, and then I settle my hands carefully on the rounded tops of her arms, angling her toward where I would be standing.

Then I cross back to my side of the line.

"This makes you a smaller target," I explain, waving a hand at her now-turned body. "It's harder for someone to land a direct hit because there's less surface area within reach. And by facing forward, you can keep both eyes on your opponent."

She cocks her head to the side in curiosity. "How do you know all of this?"

"They hired a trainer for that kickboxing scene in the second season of *Starlight*," I admit.

She stares at me blankly.

"The shirtless scene that launched a thousand GIFs?" I prompt with an internal wince at the term. I didn't name it that. But that's apparently what the scene is known as.

"I stopped watching after season one," Amanda says.

"Ouch." I clutch my chest in mock pain. "Well, at least you missed the zombies. Wish I could say the same."

"I like beginnings," she says with a shrug. "First books, first movies, first seasons. Everything's a possibility, you know? Once they start making choices and narrowing things down to a specific storyline, it's less fun."

I never thought about it that way, but yeah, I can see her point.

"In any case, they brought this guy, Jason, on set to teach me kickboxing, and I liked it so I kept going for a while." Until I got caught up in being an idiot instead. "I figured Brody was supposed to have been around for a hundred years, so he should probably be pretty good at boxing, if that was his thing."

"You take it seriously," she says with some surprise. "Knowing your character." She pauses. "Acting."

I set my jaw against the by-now-automatic surge of frustration. I know she doesn't mean it the way everybody else does, like it's so shocking that I want to be good at something. She doesn't know me, doesn't know how often I run into this particular attitude. To be fair, though, I can't blame her or anyone else. My behavior for a while pretty much guaranteed that people would think the worst of me: superficial, self-destructive, stupid.

Sometimes, though, it feels like no matter how far I've come from that version of me, it's never quite far enough.

But all I say to Amanda is, "Yeah, I do."

Then I gesture to her in a beckoning motion. "Okay, make a fist."

She balls up her hands and holds them up for presentation.

I circle her wrists with my hands, one in each, and I can feel her pulse thrumming against my fingers. "Always keep your thumb on the outside of your fist. Otherwise you'll end up with a broken thumb if you connect."

I make the adjustments, moving her fingers closer together, one fist at a time. "Now, when you hit, aim with these knuckles." I lightly touch the bones on the top of her fist. "You're going to extend your arm, but don't lock your elbow. Like this."

I pull carefully on her left wrist, as if she's driving a punch at me. Her sleeve rides up slightly with the movement, and that's when I feel the band of raised and rough skin beneath my fingertips. It's a scar about a half-inch wide in a perfect circle all the way around, right at the bones where her hand connects to her arm.

My gaze snaps to Amanda's in question before I can stop myself.

"The chain," she says matter-of-factly. But her blasé tone is betrayed by a nervous swallow. "He kept me chained to the wall."

My reaction is instinctive, visceral and stupid—I drop her hand like it's on fire and step back.

She stiffens, a mix of emotions flashing across her face before vanishing behind a smooth, blank mask. It's like watching the life drain out of someone, Amanda turning into a marble version of herself.

I feel like a complete asshole. My mouth works for a second before words come out. "Sorry. I'm sorry, Amanda. That was shitty. I just . . . I wasn't expecting that."

"It's okay," she says in a flat tone that suggests this is not the first time this has happened to her.

Except I'm pretty sure it wasn't just hurt that I saw on her face, but disappointment as well. Like she expected better from me.

That eats at me more than anything. I am not living up to the Chase Henry in her head. I'm not living up to anyone's version of me, including my own.

Amanda meets my gaze defiantly. "Bruises heal. But there's the scar on my wrist, formerly fractured cheekbones, some cracked ribs that healed on their own over the years, and a mouth full of broken teeth. He didn't want to do too much serious damage. I might have died before he was done with me."

It's like she's daring me to run. But she lived through it, so I'm determined to stand my ground in hearing about it. Anything less would make me the worst kind of coward, and I've played that role too often already.

"And then, of course, there's the truckload of psychological damage." She waves a hand in a vague gesture at the table braced against the door. "Obviously."

I don't know what to say, so I keep my mouth shut.

"A dentist donated his services to fix my teeth. Made them even better, straighter than they were originally," she says with a small smile, her gaze fixed on a distant spot somewhere over my shoulder. "A plastic surgeon offered a consultation on my wrist, too. But that's one thing I want to keep."

"Why?" The question pops out before I can stop it. Why

would anyone want a permanent souvenir of such a horrible time in their life?

Her eyes refocus on me, zeroing in until I feel like she can see through me. "Because it helps me when I wake up in the middle of a panic attack. It's proof that I got out. And because it reminds me I survived."

I take back anything I might have ever thought about her being messed up or weak.

She's a fucking warrior.

"So." Amanda puts her hands on her hips. "Are you going to teach me to hit or what?"

That's a challenge if I've ever heard one, and I'm up to it, yeah.

I clear my throat. "So, in boxing and kickboxing, you use combinations. Left, right, left, left, whatever. Basic punches are the hook and the cross. But for right now, let's just stick with the cross." I demonstrate a couple times, and she follows along.

"Feels weird to lead with the left," she says with a frown.

"It seems backwards, but it's actually making the best use of your dominant hand. You get more force behind a punch from your right hand because you have more momentum from the follow-through motion," I say.

I walk her through throwing a couple punches to make sure she's got the form close to right. Then I grab one of the pillows from the bed.

I take a breath. "Okay, I know this is the douchiest thing anyone is ever going to say, but please don't hit my face. I really need this job, and they'll kill me if I show up tomorrow with a black eye. Real bruises are harder than hell to cover up."

"I know," she says simply.

It doesn't take but a few tries before she's landing some solid hits into the pillow. Nothing that would put a serious dent in someone determined to hurt her, but enough to make him think twice. More important, Amanda looks like she's having a good time. Her forehead is furrowed with concentration, her cheeks are flushed with the effort, and she seems somehow more present in the moment, less haunted.

"Nice," I say, when she connects hard enough that it almost knocks the pillow from my hands.

Panting from the exertion, she bends at the waist to catch her breath.

"You okay?" I ask with a grin, lowering the pillow.

She nods without looking up. "Yeah," she says. "That was fun. Dinner and a boxing lesson. Not exactly what I had in mind when I asked to come with you."

I grin and toss the pillow onto her bed. "It's a full-service operation around here."

She straightens up, then, and smiles at me. "Thank you."

It's a broad, genuine expression that lights up her entire face, the smile that was broken but is now repaired, undimmed.

Amanda Grace is beautiful. The realization strikes with an uncomfortable amount of force. And she's looking at me like I deserve the gratitude she's beaming at me. But I don't. I so don't.

I duck my head, my hand flying up to rub at the back of my neck. It's a tell: Chase breaking through the role. My first acting coach did his best to hammer that home, to rid me of the habit, but he wasn't entirely successful.

"Sure, yeah. You're welcome," I mumble.

Her smile slips a little, and she tilts her head to the side in confusion.

I can feel the question coming, and I can't be here to try to answer it. I'm an actor, a professional liar. But I don't want to lie to her any more than I already am. She deserves better than that.

"I should go," I say. "Early day tomorrow."

"Okay," Amanda draws out the word, making it clear she's not buying my excuse.

But she doesn't say anything more as I grab my coat from the bed and bolt for the adjoining door.

Once safely on the other side, I close the door and lean against it, my shoulders sagging with the weight of the situation and my choices.

This "simple" plan is only getting more and more complicated, and, if I'm being completely honest, it's not all Elise's fault.

9

Amanda

I must have been high when I packed yesterday.

It's the only explanation for the array of disastrous clothing options on the bed in front of me this morning.

With my hair dripping down my back, I pull the hotel towel—too short and too thin—tighter against my body and search through my shirts, as if a more acceptable one might have been born from two lesser choices in the few minutes I left them alone.

Boatneck with red stripes and three-quarter-length sleeves, no. Pink with ribbons, *no*. The snug-fit purple V-neck with a flowered pattern, definitely not. Oversized flannel shirt that used to be my dad's, no. A faded long-sleeved T-shirt from Liza's college advertising a "3K Popcorn Festival Fun Run" from three years ago, no. White see-through blouse with built-in cami and short sleeves—even worse, puffed short sleeves. No, no, *no*.

I rub my hand over my face, my eyes gritty from lack of sleep. Last night was a bad one, and waking up this morning to discover this problem isn't helping.

I brought a mishmash of the new, bold items my mom picked out for me, anticipating better days, and my absolute worst "dressing for comfort" clothes. What the hell was wrong with me yesterday?

It had to be the adrenaline rush. With my heart thundering in my chest, five minutes to pack, and Chase Henry waiting downstairs, I felt mostly invincible, determined, and in motion, a step ahead of my fear, but cautious enough to include my feeling-vulnerable favorites.

And now, this morning, my fear has caught up with me, clobbering me in the process, and my packing extremes have left me with nothing to wear. Nothing I want to be photographed in, anyway.

I bite my lip. I don't want to blow this. I'm asking Chase for a lot, and these photos are the only thing he's getting.

And he's been so . . . considerate. Last night was actually fun.

Until I freaked him out and he took off for the safety of his room. I'm still not sure what I did. One minute we were laughing, relaxed in each other's presence, and the next he's backing away, trying to get to minimum safe distance.

With a sigh, I return my attention to my choices. My plaid flannel from yesterday is my best option. It isn't dirty exactly. But I ran home in it, in a sweaty panic—yuck—and there were pictures taken at the store, which means it'll be obvious I'm wearing the same thing two days in a row.

Someone will notice, and it'll be commented on, speculated about, then likely deemed a sign of dysfunction rather than limited wardrobe options. (The irony that I spent an inordinate amount of time in my closet yesterday and still managed to come away with this dilemma is not lost on me.)

But walking out with my head down and my shoulders

hunched, wearing my dad's ratty shirt that's long enough to be a dress, is not the image I want people to have of me or for me to have of myself, either.

I want to be stronger than that.

I pick the pink, the least offensive of my options. I used to love the color. Then I spent two years in a room where everything, including me, was decorated in an obnoxious shade of bubble gum, Jakes's version of "teen girl" decor.

I shudder involuntarily.

But this pink is so pale it barely deserves the name, which helps. And it's a solid color, which, I vaguely remember from my TV interview days, is better for film. Not sure if that's true for photographs, too, or not.

Unfortunately, this particular shirt, with matching pink ribbons threaded through the cuffs, also seems to scream "happy, untainted innocence." Hello, false advertising. And wishful thinking on my mom's part.

But without a better choice available, I add it to my pile of jeans, boyshorts, and bra to carry to the bathroom.

Next door, the distinct beep-grind of the lock releasing sounds, and I look toward the entrance to Chase's room, my heart pumping extra hard. The doors between our rooms aren't very thick. Noise travels.

He left about forty-five minutes ago, so early it was dark out. That's what woke me in the first place. Not that I was sleeping all that deeply, anyway.

The anxiety of spending the night in a strange place for the first time in years had combined with the unexpected feelings Chase had stirred up.

As I lay there in bed, my mind replayed the careful way he'd touched me, arranging my fingers just so, and the steady concentration in his expression. He really thought my learning to punch would help, and he wanted me to feel better.

But because my mind is a fucked-up maze with monsters

around every corner and no guiding thread out, the second I dozed off, Chase would turn into Jakes, transforming a gentle touch into an unwanted, greedy, and painful one.

That meant hours tossing and turning in sweaty sheets and misery, halfway between sleeping and awake.

So when I'd heard Chase's door open and close earlier this morning, my eyelids snapped up. We hadn't discussed a schedule or a meeting time.

I'd sat up sharply in bed and waited for the knock on my hall door, though it would have made more sense for him to knock on the door between our rooms.

But the knock never came.

He's back now, though. The hall door closes with a loud thud, and then I hear the small sounds of him moving around the room. Footsteps. Mini-fridge opening. The clatter of something hard landing on a table or counter.

I fidget with the edge of my towel. Early meeting? Breakfast? Gym? Girl? I have no idea. I'm a little uncomfortable with how much I don't like the last option.

Chase Henry doesn't owe me anything, especially not like that.

I grab my stack of clothes to go to the bathroom and get ready.

I'm passing the door to his room when a horrible idea hits. What if he saw those feelings in my expression and that's why he bolted?

The image of me beaming up at him, like a pathetic fifteen-year-old with a crush, completely oblivious to his discomfort, flashes front and center in my brain, and humiliation burns through me.

I'm struggling to remember exactly what I said and did and to what degree, when I hear close-up movement on the other side of the adjoining doors.

Like someone approaching, getting ready to knock.

I flee for the bathroom.

* * *

Twenty minutes later, I'm slightly calmer, soothed by routine. I'm dressed—in a shirt I hate—with my hair mostly dry and mascara and concealer applied, which is the extent of my makeup repertoire.

Swallowing hard, I make myself walk out of the bathroom. After wrestling the table back into its normal place, I collect my cell phone from the charger and my key card from my jacket and step reluctantly to the doors between our rooms.

Unless you're going to quit and go home, this is your only option.

I flip the lock on my side and pull the door open. Chase's door is already unlocked and cracked an inch or two.

My nerves returning, I knock as loudly as I can without pushing the door open.

"Yeah. Come in." Chase sounds muffled, distracted.

I push open his door to find a room a little larger than mine. To my right, a sofa and coffee table in front of a big flat-screen TV and mini-fridge in an entertainment center. To my left, a table and four chairs.

Straight ahead is a half-wall, dividing the living room from the sleeping area.

Chase is on the room phone in the bedroom section, the black receiver between his ear and his shoulder as he tugs an off-white shirt down over his chest.

Or tries to, anyway.

His hair is darker, damp from a shower, and sticking up in places, with water dripping down his neck.

He evidently didn't bother much with the towels, as inadequate as they are, because his skin is visibly damp, which is why the fabric is sticking to him, giving him trouble as he attempts to pull it into place.

And giving me plenty of time to look. The hair under his arms is darker than the blond on his head, and the skin there is lighter, but what catches my attention is the curve of muscle from his side to his stomach. I don't know what it's called, but I like it.

He doesn't have the ridiculous fake-looking bubbles of abs, the ones those guys in the Perfect Pushup infomercials are so proud of.

Instead, his stomach is flat with those yummy unknown muscles on the sides, calling attention to his belly button, which I'd never previously thought of as a sexy feature, and the top button of his jeans, which is, fortunately . . . or not, fastened and in place beneath his belt.

It's his job to look this good. I know that. And yet, I feel the effects like an actual physical blow, taking my breath from me in a not unpleasant sensation.

What is wrong with me?

"Hey," Chase says to me with a distant nod. "I'm on hold. I knocked on your door, but I think the hair dryer—"

I turn sideways, shifting my gaze from him to stare at the couch instead, my face warm in a whole new way. "You don't have a tattoo." The words come out in a horrifying squeak before I can stop them, and I wish for the dark spaces in the patterned carpet to open up and swallow me.

From the corner of my eye, I see Chase frown at me, confused. Then he looks down at himself. His expression clears, and a mischievous smile tugs at the corners of his mouth.

"I thought you said you didn't watch after season one," he says.

"I didn't," I say, managing a quick glance in his direction. His teasing look forces me to rally. "But I recognize the wallpaper photo from my sister's phone when I see it."

In that image, half of his stomach was covered in five thick black lines, like a giant hand swiped at him and missed, marking him from the lower left side of his rib cage across to the right side of his abdomen.

He laughs. "The devil's claw was fake. Part of Brody's backstory. I don't have any tattoos."

"Really?" I blurt.

"I don't want them to get in the way of getting a part. They can cover them with makeup, but it doesn't ever look right." He cocks his head to one side, his mouth quirking with amusement. "Why? You want to check?"

Oh God. I want to simultaneously melt into a puddle and run away. But I make myself stay still. "I'm good, thanks," I say, attempting to sound dry, unaffected. That's easier now that he's managed to get his shirt—a Henley with the top two buttons undone—down the rest of the way.

He smiles, a real, full one that crinkles the lines up by his eyes, not the broody half-smirk I'm used to from my head version of him, and I grin back at him, unable to resist the real Chase peeking out.

But then, like someone flipped a switch in him, his smile fades, and he drops his gaze from me. "I'll be ready in a couple minutes," he says, and it's last night all over again. Only this time, he's not physically retreating. Probably because he can't get any farther from me and still be in the room.

The pleasant warmth of the past few minutes drains away. What just happened? If it was the semi-flirting—that's what that was, right?—then that's on him because he started it.

But before I can say any of that, his head jerks up. "No, yeah, I'm here," he says into the phone, turning his back to me.

I'm not sure whether I should stay or go, but I figure if he didn't want me in here, he would have said when I knocked. Plus, I'm just pissed enough at him to stay, regardless.

"Uh-huh, yes. That's exactly it," Chase says, and if he was a bit chilly with me, he's downright arctic with whoever is on the other end of that phone.

Somebody's in trouble. I wonder if it's the publicist, though I don't know why she'd call the hotel phone when she has his cell.

"It *is* unfortunate," he says, biting off the words. "You know what else would be extremely unfortunate? If I had to bring this up during every interview between now and the premiere next year."

I can't hear the person on the other end of the phone, but I sense frantic backpedaling.

"Thank you," Chase says after a moment, sounding more frustrated than grateful. "I appreciate you taking care of it."

He hangs up the phone with a sharp clack, then lets out a loud breath, raking a hand through his damp hair, making it stick up in more spikes.

"You ready to go?" he asks, with barely a glance in my direction. He moves to the table near me, gathering up a rumpled stack of folded pages—script, maybe?—his room key card, and his cell phone, after pulling the earbuds from it.

He means: go outside, find the photographers, get our picture taken.

Strangers. Wide-open space. No place to hide. People staring. Right now.

Somehow I managed to put this moment out of my head in favor of worrying about what Chase was or was not thinking about me. But now my anxiety comes roaring back, drowning out my temper.

I shift from foot to foot in the doorway between our rooms. "Um, yeah?"

This was part of our deal, and I'm not about to renege. But my hotel room has, in the last twelve hours or so, become a relatively safe space. And now, we're leaving, breaking the bubble.

Suddenly, I feel ridiculous. The ribbons on this shirt make it too frilly, as if it were a costume or disguise. And as loose as it is, it's still more form-fitting than anything I've worn in years. I want to fold my arms across my chest to keep people from mentally stripping me.

"You know, maybe I should change," I say to Chase as he tucks his phone and key card in separate pockets, my voice coming out too high. "I have the plaid shirt I wore yesterday, which

I know isn't the perfect solution. But this shirt is pink and kind of tight."

Chase turns to stare at me.

I tug at the bottom of the hem, feeling a nervous sweat break out at my elbows and knees. "It's just short sleeves are out because the scar makes people panic. And bright colors draw too much attention."

I can hear the irrational panic in my words, but I can't stop them from tumbling out any more than I can stop the purely illogical conviction that if I just had the right shirt, I would be okay.

It's like people who are convinced that turning a light switch on and off seven times keeps them safe. I've been in enough therapy to recognize what's happening—my attempt to control what is uncontrollable.

But the worst part is that *knowing* it's ridiculous—*knowing* it doesn't matter what I wear (within reason), that it's just my brain pushing out a cocktail of neurochemicals to make me feel this way—doesn't change anything.

Damnit. "Never mind," I say, my face flushing and tears burning in my eyes. "It's stupid."

Chases hesitates. "You don't have to—"

"I know," I say sharply. "But I'm going to. It's just . . . I did a shitty job packing." Lame, but true. Actually, the truth would be that no matter what I'd brought, I'd feel this way. Because focusing on my clothing is just a dodge, a substitute, for what's really bothering me.

Consciously engage your rational mind, Dr. Knaussen would say. *What are the odds of your being taken or harmed in front of witnesses, including Chase Henry, a celebrity?*

Fairly small.

But my issue with that exercise is that the odds of me being taken in the first place were pretty small. Just because they're smaller now isn't all that reassuring.

"Okay." Chase nods slowly, watching me.

I squirm under his scrutiny. "Let's just go. I'm fine." I knew Chase would not be a magical solution, but I guess some part of me was hoping it would be easier with him here.

He frowns, and I brace myself for the polite, brittle brush-off: *Maybe it would be for the best if you went home.*

"Hang on," Chase says instead. He turns away from me and crosses the room in a couple of long strides to his closet.

The wooden hangers clatter, and then he's back in front of me with a white button-down.

"Here." He holds it out to me. "Fold up the cuffs, and do that thing with the ends that girls do." He mimes a bow at his waist with an awkward gesture that, in spite of everything, makes me choke out a laugh.

"You don't need it?" I ask, taking it from him. It's soft, well-worn cotton. Not a dress shirt, but probably something he wears over jeans.

He shrugs. "Not today, and there's laundry service here. I've already got a bag started." He jerks a thumb over his shoulder to a plastic drawstring bag on the floor, workout clothes—the edge of a T-shirt and the blue leg with white stripes of athletic shorts—hanging out.

I slide my arms in his shirt and then flip my hair out so it's not tucked underneath. His shirt smells good, but what I like most are the worn parts on the cuffs and edges, threads coming free, as if it's been washed, dried, and worn dozens and dozens of times. It has history.

The shirt is loose but not swimming on me, and I immediately feel better with it on. After folding up the cuffs, I button most of the buttons and tie the two sides in the front into a loose knot at my waist.

Chase nods. "Yeah, that." He steps back and gives me a professional look from head to toe. "Pink is covered, and it's definitely not tight." That hint of teasing in his voice from earlier makes a brief reappearance, and I nod like a pleased idiot.

"Give me your shirt from yesterday." He holds out his hand. I return to the pile of clothes on my bed to pull it free.

When I give him the shirt, he puts it in the laundry bag on top of his clothes, pulls the drawstring tight, and drops the bag on the table.

"It'll be ready for tomorrow, okay?" he asks.

I bob my head. "Thanks." I hate that I need to be coddled like this, but I'm grateful that he's treating it like something semi-normal instead of asking me twenty times if I'm okay.

Of course I'm not okay. Some part of my brain is convinced that picking the right shirt will keep me safe. And the reverse also: that picking the wrong shirt is somehow tempting fate to strike twice in the same place, like lightning. If that's not crazy, it's knocking distance.

But Chase just shrugs. "No problem. You want to go out this way?" He gestures toward his hall door.

"Yeah." As we pass his mirrored closet doors, I catch a glimpse of myself. He's right; the pink is reduced to a narrow V at my chest, and the white fabric is loose around my shoulders and blousing outward until it reaches my waist, where I've tied it off.

It is very clearly not *my* shirt.

But I like the way it looks. In my reflection, I don't see the innocent child my mother is trying desperately to revive in me, or the girl who's hiding beneath miles of flannel or old college T-shirts from a school she didn't even go to.

This person, the one in the mirror wearing *this* shirt, looks like someone who has a connection to another person. A connection that might be intimate or just friendly, but definitely personal. I might not have that yet, but it feels good to see myself as someone who could. It's like a peek into a hoped-for future.

I touch the collar gently, feeling the softened and curled nubs of the formerly pointed edges.

But I have to warn Chase, because the image in the mirror also screams something else.

"This might start rumors," I say, gesturing down at myself as he pulls open the hall door.

He stops so suddenly I almost collide with his back. Then he turns with a frown and looks at me, his gaze sweeping me up and down. After a moment, the muscles at his jaw tighten and jump, like he's grinding his teeth.

Uh-oh. My heart sinks for reasons I'm not sure I want to identify, and I take a quick step back.

Before I can say anything, his frown vanishes beneath a smooth, empty expression. "I don't care if you don't." His tone is carefully neutral, a little too much so.

I don't know what I expected him to say, but that doesn't stop the swell of disappointment in me at his response.

"No," I say. Because I don't care. Not in the way he means. But what I'm thinking is maybe that's not quite the same thing as not caring at all.

10

Chase

Amanda is quiet in her corner of the elevator, studying her clasped hands, peeking out from the cuffs of my shirt, or the tiles on the floor. I can't tell which.

I drag my gaze away, only to find myself staring at her reflection in the shiny gold-tinted doors before us.

I like that she's wearing my shirt. It looks good on her. And it sets off this greedy sense of *mine* in me.

It sounds caveman, but it's more like pride. *Look, this girl who is strong and fighting so hard—she trusts me.*

Watching the tension roll out of her shoulders when she pulled my shirt on made me feel stupidly like a hero.

But letting myself feel that, just like wanting her smile last night to be something I deserved, is dangerous. I'm navigating a fine line between truth and a convenient fiction, and my conscience is threatening to throw a rod.

Elise will love that Amanda's in my shirt, which means I probably should have taken it back once Amanda pointed out the implications, but I couldn't.

I wanted her to wear it. I wanted to help.

Even now, when I should be focused on locking in the scene and Smitty and preparing for the first day of shooting, which never runs smoothly, I can feel Amanda's nervousness rising with every floor we descend, and I want to fix it, though I don't know how.

I know better than to ask her if she's sure she wants to do this, because she's made that pretty clear. But that doesn't stop me from feeling the need to do something.

I clear my throat, and she looks up at me. "So, it should be pretty easy," I say, my mouth absurdly dry.

She nods, though I'm not sure if that's agreement or simply encouragement to continue.

"We'll have transport to location. A van." I had the identifying information in an email on my phone from the driver, a guy named Ron.

"There might be a couple of photographers waiting outside the hotel or when we get to set," I continue. "So we'll stop, let them get a few shots, and then move on. Five minutes, tops. Simple, no pressure. Okay?"

Amanda nods again, mute.

I desperately want to see a flash of the girl who stood in my doorway this morning, turning six shades of red, and still held it together enough to be smart with me.

Unfortunately, I suck at this kind of stuff in real life. "So it's my turn to ask questions, right?" I ask.

She frowns at me.

"The car, last night," I prompt. "You never told me what your favorite color is."

Her eyebrows lift in amusement. "And you know that's still the lamest possible question you could ask, right?" she asks.

I grin. Better. "I'll work on it," I say.

The doors open, revealing a lobby bustling with activity. A group of businesspeople in suits are gathered around the check-in desk, their rolling briefcases lined up around them with the pull handles extended, like an impromptu cage.

I step out, Amanda just behind me, and head for the hotel turnaround, where the van is supposed to be waiting.

"Mr. . . . uh, Dean? Mr. Dean?" A balding man in a dark blue suit coat behind the registration desk—the manager, presumably—calls out as soon as he catches sight of us.

The muscles in my neck tense, shooting pain down to my shoulders and up into my head, and I ignore him, heading toward the glass lobby doors.

"Don't you think you should—" Amanda begins.

"No," I say. "He just wants to apologize again."

Amanda looks up at me, waiting for an explanation.

I sigh. "The room service guy."

"Because he banged on the door?" Amanda asks. "That was my fault. I didn't—"

"No, because he signed a fake name to the receipt. The wrong one," I add when she opens her mouth to point out the obvious. "And he tipped himself anyway, thinking we wouldn't notice because we're probably throwing money around like crazy." I pause. "And yeah, because he scared you." Mostly because of that.

Amanda stays silent.

Slowing down, I say, "Look, I know it sounds like some kind of star temper tantrum or whatever, but people who don't see you as a real person, for whatever reason, are dangerous." Especially when they have relatively easy access to your room.

"Did they fire him?" she asks quietly, stopping next to me.

"Yes." Theoretically. I was assured that it *would* happen.

"Mr. Dean?" The manager sounds breathless now, and his hurried footsteps echo in pursuit of us. He's left the counter to chase us down.

I start walking again quickly. *Not now.* It shouldn't have

taken me pushing that hard to get the manager to take action, and I don't want to hear any more excuses.

"Good," Amanda says at my side, surprising me into glancing down at her.

She gives me a tight smile. "Makes me a bad person, right? Admitting that I wanted him to be gone?" She shrugs. "Guess I'm not the virtuous, selfless victim everyone makes me out to be." Her tone is light and breezy, but there's a thick layer of guilt underneath.

"Nope," I say. "Makes you human." I nudge her side gently with my elbow. "They can always hire him back next week."

She nods, relief playing across her face, and then, as we approach the tinted glass doors that will let us out, she loops her arm through mine, resting her hand on my bicep.

It's a friendly, maybe even playful, gesture, but the jolt of it runs through me.

Her hand is small and light on my arm, and I can't believe it's there.

The shock of her voluntarily touching me is quickly surpassed by that same warm burst of pride and the squeezing, conflicted feeling of having earned trust that I don't deserve.

But I don't get a chance to feel too guilty about it. Because as soon as the doors open and we step out, flashes explode around us, dozens of them. It's blinding, disorienting.

I throw my free arm up instinctively, though that will make most of the photos unsalable.

What the hell is this? Way more than the photographer or two Elise had mentioned. This is a fucking mob scene.

The air is full of shouting and the hiss-click of digital cameras.

"Amanda! Amanda, look this way!"

"Chase, give us a smile. Are the two of you together?"

"Chase, any truth to the rumor that you're quitting the business?"

"Amanda, baby, you're beautiful; just give us a smile. Show everybody how you're doing."

Amanda's hand tightens into a claw on my arm, and my heart is pounding like it wants to run away without me. I forgot this. How quickly exhilaration at the attention converts into panic, especially when you're not expecting a barrage of it.

Like when you feel like shit after your second attempt at a thirty-day dry-out and the cameras are there, waiting to capture you at your worst.

Like when your former costar is arrested on drug charges, and the paparazzi show up outside your gym to make sure you know about it.

Suddenly I want a drink. I can feel the burn of it down my throat and into my gut and the smooth confidence it would provide. It would make this situation so much easier, just like it did before. I'd have the right thing to say, a cocky smile to give, or I just wouldn't care if I didn't.

But that is not an option at the moment. Next to me, I feel Amanda shaking. A glance down shows her dark eyes glassy with panic, not unlike yesterday morning at the grocery store.

Shit. I loop my arm around Amanda's shoulders and turn her around with me toward the hotel. Her hand clutches hard at the back of my shirt, pulling the fabric tight.

Once we're far enough into the lobby again, the glass doors slide shut behind us, muffling the noise.

Amanda releases her grip on my shirt and slowly moves to the nearest pillar, pressing her back against the side facing away from the doors. Then she sinks to her knees.

"Are you okay?" I ask.

She nods, her head down. "Yes." But her breathing, artificially slow and steady, says differently. She inhales through her nose and exhales through her mouth, in a controlled manner. Her face is pale, and her hand is trembling when she pushes her hair back.

I fidget, wanting to help, but in this case, there's no one to punch. Or too many of them, depending on how you look at it.

"Are you sure?" I ask gruffly, my hand in a fist at my side.

"Just took me by surprise," Amanda says. "I wasn't expecting that many of them," she says, glancing up at me. "I kind of froze. Sorry." Her face tightens with regret.

"Nothing to be sorry for. I wasn't expecting that, either." Fucking Elise. She's behind this, I'm sure.

Footsteps approach from deeper in the lobby, and I pivot, moving to block Amanda, crouched low, from view.

But it's just the blue-coated manager. "I'm sorry, Mr. Dean," he says, his gaze darting to Amanda and then back to me quickly. "I was trying to catch you to warn you. They got here a few minutes ago, and our security—"

"It's fine," I say, fighting the urge to yell at him. They're not used to this kind of thing in middle-of-nowhere Wescott any more than they would be in Tillman, and he did try to warn me. "Can you just get us out another door?" I ask. "I can call Transportation and have them pick us up there."

"Of course." The manager nods so rapidly his double chin wobbles with the motion. "If you'll follow me—"

"No," Amanda says.

I turn to look at her. "What?"

"No." Amanda pushes to her feet, one hand pressed to the pillar to steady herself. "This is what . . ." Her eyes shift to me, and she gives me a significant look.

This is what we came for. That's what she's trying to say. And she's right, to some extent.

But I never thought we would be dealing with it at this level. And beyond that, following through with the plan suddenly doesn't seem as vital as it did yesterday.

I shake my head. "Amanda—"

"This is important," she finishes instead, her chin tipped up. "I'm not going to let those assholes tell their version of me, selling pictures of me running away. No." She folds her arms over her chest.

Amanda might be feeling bold, but I'm not. I'm responsible. For her, for the situation, and for whatever the combination of the two brings about, and the weight of that is making me a little panicky.

I blow out a loud breath in frustration and lift a hand to rub the back of my neck. "This is not what we talked about, and you don't have anything to prove," I say, all too aware of the manager waiting nearby.

But Amanda just laughs and gives me that look, the one that's older and wiser than twenty, the one that's a little bitter and a lot tired. "Yes, I do."

And you know it. The words hang unspoken in the air between us, but I hear them anyway.

Even if she's not proving it to the paparazzi and the world in general, she has something to prove to herself, which is the whole point of this exercise for her.

Damnit.

I hold my hands up in surrender. "All right." I look to the manager. "I guess we're leaving from here," I say reluctantly.

He nods. "Of course. We'll have stronger measures in place by the time you return." He holds a card out to me. "If you'll contact us to let us know when you'll be arriving . . ."

I take his card and shove it in my back pocket with my key card.

As he departs for the counter, a white van pulls into the turnaround, and the low murmur of the photographers outside grows louder.

My stomach churns with acid. "Ready?" Even though this is what Elise wanted to happen, even though it's what I need, I hate it. Way more than I was expecting.

Amanda nods and steps closer. Without a word, she ducks under my arm and slides her hand around my back and grips my shirt again, taking me by surprise.

"I don't want them to know I was scared," she says with a hint of defiance. "I'm sure they got shots of it before. I want them to think it was deliberate."

I don't deserve to be anywhere near this girl.

I rest my arm carefully across her shoulders, like before, although it feels different. I'm not sure where my hand should be. Closer to her neck? Or down by her shoulder? When I put my arm around her a few minutes ago, it was pure protective instinct, done without any thought other than getting her out of there.

Now, I'm aware of her warmth under two layers of shirt, the proximity of her skin to my fingertips when I rest my hand between her neck and shoulder. "Okay?"

"Yeah." She squirms closer, tucking her shoulder behind me, so our sides are pressed together, and a flare of awareness shoots through me. The memory of her this morning, hectic color rising in her cheeks when she caught me getting dressed, surfaces unexpectedly. And the urge pulses in me to see more of that. To see if I can *cause* more of that.

Shit. I should not be thinking like this. It's too fast. And she's Amanda Grace.

We move toward the doors, and they slide open. "Remember, they can't touch you," I say, and I feel Amanda nod. "Keep your eyes focused on the van and try to smile," I say through my own tight, forced smile. "We'll be out of this in under a minute."

The photo snapping and flashing starts immediately, even before we're outside. And so does the shouting.

It's just as blinding and overwhelming as before, maybe even more so because they feel they missed their opportunity the first time.

But it's not a surprise this time. Amanda, to her credit, holds it together, her eyes straight ahead and a grim smile plastered to her face.

When one guy lunges too close, she shies away, curving toward me, and I stick my hand up, blocking his lens.

"Move, asshole," I say in the most pleasant tone I can muster under the circumstances. Because shoving him is only going to get me in trouble with Max, and I've got enough of that coming already.

The photog glares at me and flips me the finger while continuing to shoot, but we're still moving and he's missed his chance at Amanda's face.

As we approach the van, a girl in the front passenger seat pushes her door open but then freezes in place, her expression uncertain. The walkie-talkie in her hand—seemingly forgotten—tells me she's a production assistant sent to collect me. Her hesitation says she's probably a local, a college student, maybe. Or one of Max's cousins. She's not used to this, for sure.

I catch her eye and jerk my chin at the van. She gets it after a second and pulls herself back in and shuts the door.

After picking up the pace for the last few steps, I lean forward without dropping my arm from Amanda and yank open the rear passenger door.

Amanda climbs in without hesitation, but her hand catches mine as it moves away from her shoulder and she tugs me in after her, not sitting down until I'm inside.

I'm not sure if she's continuing the act she started for the cameras or if she somehow knows I need the support. She might be right on the latter. It's been years since I've done this parade of bullshit sober and never with this much riding on it. Or at this level of deception.

I slam the door shut and drop into the seat next to Amanda. My mouth feels coated in sand, my tongue dried up and sticking to the roof of my mouth.

In the old days, I would have had a bottle stashed in my trailer. But this is not like the old days and can't be again for so many reasons.

The older guy behind the wheel, presumably Ron from my email, turns to look at us. "Everybody okay?"

"Yes," Amanda says, sounding surprised but calmer than earlier.

Despite the available space, her body is a solid line against mine, the two of us pressed together in the center of the bench. Her hand is still in mine, and she squeezes once in reassurance. For her or for me, I'm not sure.

She lets go after that, but it doesn't matter. Guilt is throbbing in me like the worst hangover headache ever.

And I really want a drink.

11

Amanda

Next to me, Chase drops his head, running his hands through his hair. His body is wire-taut with tension, like any sudden movement on his part or mine might cause him to snap into pieces.

I'm not sure if touching him will help or make things worse, so I stay still.

The driver, a guy with white hair and wearing a black *Coal City Nights* baseball hat, mutters to himself and finally manages to navigate out of the turnaround without running anyone over.

As soon as we turn out onto the road, the muscles in my stomach relax a little, but dread creeps in almost immediately. Now that we're away from the hotel, I have no idea what will happen next or even where we're going.

My heartbeat ratchets up, and I fight the urge to scoot deeper in the van.

"So, yeah, hi, I'm Emily," the girl in the passenger seat says uncertainly, twisting to face us.

She's about my age, maybe a little older. She's wearing an ID badge on a lanyard around her neck, and a black T-shirt with *Coal City Nights* in swirling cursive print. Her skin has the healthy glow of someone who goes outside, and her blond hair is pulled into a perky ponytail that brushes her shoulders.

Her gaze skates over me without recognition and dismisses me in favor of focusing on Chase.

She regards him with a mixture of awe and concern. "Are you okay, Mr. Henry?" The sugary-sweet deference in her tone makes me squirm.

"Chase." He lifts his head and gives her a smile, but it doesn't make his eyes crinkle and there's strain around the edges.

Doesn't matter, though. The desire to give her laser "back off" eyes is a steady drumbeat in my veins.

"Okay. Chase," Emily says with a big smile, her eyelashes fluttering.

My jaw clenches so tightly I hear my new, perfect teeth squeak in protest. Batting her eyelashes? Seriously, who does that outside of cartoons?

"I'm fine, thanks, Emily," Chase says with another tight smile.

Her face lights up, hearing her name. Should I even be here, interrupting this lovefest?

"Just thirsty," he adds, rubbing his eyes with a harsh laugh, though nothing about what he said was funny.

I frown.

Emily doesn't seem to notice. "I have water!" She turns and rummages at her feet and produces a small bottle damp with condensation, her face glowing with pride.

I realize suddenly this is probably what Liza would have been like around Chase yesterday, if I hadn't been in the middle of the mess.

And if Liza's version of flirting didn't include harsh back-handed compliments and critiquing a guy's grammar. I've seen her in action. It's ugly. The girl equivalent of pulling pigtails.

Out of the corner of my eye, I watch Chase take the water with a polite nod of thanks. He cracks it open and takes a sip, but his expression is more of mirthless amusement instead of relief.

Then it clicks.

He's a recovering alcoholic. I don't know much about the disease; my family has plenty of issues, but not that one. I'm guessing, though, that stress—like, say, oh, trying to jump-start your career, or running an unexpected gauntlet of paparazzi with a certified head case clinging to your arm—might make things worse for someone who's trying very hard to avoid temptation.

Emily beams at him and then produces a clipboard from somewhere.

"You'll have about twenty minutes to change in your trailer before you're supposed to be in Hair and Makeup," she says with an anxious glance at Chase.

He nods with no outward indication of irritation. I have no idea if that amount of time is actually an issue or if she's being ridiculously obsequious again.

While they're preoccupied, I dig my phone out of my pocket and do a search. One good thing about being stuck in the hospital or in the house for extended periods of time is that you learn pretty quickly how to make the internet cough up anything you need, on demand.

It doesn't take me long to find what I'm looking for.

While Emily is going over schedules, locations, and other stuff I should probably be paying attention to, I download the app and enter what I think is the zip code for Wescott, or close enough.

When I've narrowed the results, I nudge Chase with my elbow.

Instantly his attention shifts to me, and I feel the weight of it like it's a physical sensation. It's as if I'm the only person in the world who is of any interest to him.

My face grows warm under the intensity of his gaze, and for a second, I understand exactly what Emily's feeling when he smiles at her, even if it is forced.

Then I remember myself and shake it off, tilting my phone screen toward him.

He squints at it until I lift it a little higher: *MEETING FINDER: AA Meetings in Wescott, PA, General Area.*

Relief and gratitude mix with shame on his face, and he nods.

I click on the one listed at 6:30 p.m. in the basement of the courthouse.

"Still shooting then," Chase says to me quietly, watching over my shoulder.

Knew I should have been paying attention to Emily's schedule rambling.

I search again and find one that's later: 9:30 p.m. at St. Paul's Lutheran Church. I don't know how far it is from where we will be, but Wescott's not that big.

"Yeah," Chase says. "That could work." His smile is crooked and tired, but real, as far as I can gauge it.

I highlight the information to send it to him, only to realize that I have no way of doing that.

Before I can say anything, he takes my phone from me, types for a few seconds, and then hands it back.

It's open to Contacts, and I have a new one: Chase Mroczek. And a cell phone number with a 323 area code.

Liza would know for sure, but I'm guessing that's his real last name rather than another alias.

Something about the fact that he not only trusts me with his number but also lists himself by his real name makes me slushy with warmth.

I text him the information because he's watching me, and I feel the buzz of his phone in his pocket against my hip.

My breathing catches, and he's still watching me.

We are sitting *so* close, and . . . it's not bothering me. It's the opposite of bothering me.

Emily makes an obnoxious throat-clearing noise, snapping the delicate thread of the moment and startling us into looking at her.

"Sorry," she says but mostly to Chase. "I just really need to get through this." She waggles her clipboard in a gesture that manages to be both hurt and snippy.

"No, that's my fault," Chase says easily with a hand up in apology, as if vouching for his sincerity. "I'm sorry. Go ahead." He gives her an encouraging nod.

And it's like watching time-lapse photography: Emily blooms under his attention like a long-neglected African violet positioned under a sunlamp. Even though it's been, what, three minutes since he last talked to her?

Geez.

With a blush and more eyelash fluttering, Emily continues her clipboard recitation. Chase keeps his full attention on her, asking questions or clarifying details just frequently enough that she can't help but feel engaged. Engaging, even.

I lean back in the seat, watching their interaction. It's partially an act, I think. Not insincere, but he's working to make her feel comfortable.

He's good at what he does. Very good. Giving pieces of himself away to her.

To me.

It makes me wonder if he gets to keep anything for himself. It also makes me wonder how much of it is real.

It doesn't take us long to get to where they're shooting.

Three beefy security guards stand over sawhorses borrowed from the Wescott police and possibly Home Depot, based on the orange color. The barricade blocks the street, holding back a cluster of photographers, who snap pictures as our vehicle passes them.

Once we're dropped off on the other side of the barrier, Emily leads us to a row of trailers parked along a side street in a mostly deserted industrial area.

Empty—or mostly empty—warehouses with broken-out windows dominate the scenery, though there are small square houses with overgrown yards about a block away.

I shudder. It would be even creepier, but the whole area is buzzing with activity. People in the black *Coal City* crew shirts and hats are hustling with a purpose. Some of them have walkie-talkies and clipboards like Emily. Others are carrying random pieces of equipment: moving blankets, two plants in terra-cotta pots, a shiny metal screen, one of those fuzzy microphones on a long pole.

Unidentifiable black cords stretch between the trailers, X-taped to the ground, and somewhere nearby there's the loud, persistent hum of a generator.

Across an open field that might have once been a warehouse parking lot, I can see behind one of the other abandoned warehouses, which is where most of the activity is centered. There are tall lights on metal stands, what look like small railroad tracks on the ground, and a couple of big cameras. And that's just what I can pick out.

From the look of it, they're already filming something. Or maybe just testing equipment? I have no idea.

At this point, I'm utterly out of my element.

"Here we are!" Emily stops in front of the second trailer from the end. It has horizontal orange and brown decorative stripes along the side. Chase's name is on the door, written in black marker on a crooked strip of white tape.

The utter lack of glamour is shocking. Not just with the trailer but the whole setup. It doesn't look like a movie set as much as a moderately upscale trailer park. I wonder if Mia knows this is what it's like, if that would change her mind or her ambitions at all.

Probably not. Mia comes with glamour—and drama—included. Just add water and air.

Emily climbs the two metal steps, pulls the handle to swing the door open, and then hops down, making room for Chase to ascend.

"Remember, twenty minutes," she says to Chase in a stern voice, which she then ruins by giggling.

I hurry to follow him in before she can close the door on me. She's staring at me like she can't figure out what I'm doing here.

Honestly, I'm not sure either. I don't have any specific task. That was done as soon as we pulled away from the hotel and the photographers.

The door snaps shut after me, and I'm squinting in the dim light to see.

Chase steps in deeper and fumbles for the switch.

After a second, my eyes adjust and . . . wow.

"It's really, uh, peach in here," I say, reaching to touch the edge of a curtain. It's a hideous Southwestern pattern in the aforementioned washed-out peach with blue and green as accents. The whole trailer—couch cushions, walls, countertops—follows the motif. It's blindingly ugly.

Chase snorts. "Yeah."

"I didn't even know wood paneling came in this color," I say.

"I don't think it's wood," he says.

I'm not sure what I was expecting. Something with a heart-shaped Jacuzzi in the floor? Strobe lights overhead? A special cocaine drawer, the handle a custom-designed star in 24-karat gold?

But it's a standard RV, aside from the stunning decor choice, and smaller than the one my grandparents used to take to Arizona. The right side holds a small seating area with a bench sofa and a table that folds down. To the left, there's a tiny stove top and sink set in a kitchen area with narrow wooden doors that, if the layout is similar to my grandparents', lead to a pantry and a bathroom.

Through a doorway at the opposite end of the kitchen, I see a double bed covered in a spread that matches the Southwestern pattern, only with blue as the dominant color.

Unsurprisingly, that does not help.

It smells mildewy in here, with a faint hint of cleaning spray, as if someone opened the door, squirted some 409 in the air, and then ran away.

When Chase moves past me to the table, it stirs the air and the musty, moldy scent grows stronger. For a moment, I'm back in Jakes's basement. The smell of the thick black mold in the leaky shower and the barely functional toilet pervaded the dim and shadowy room, the boarded-up windows allowing nothing more than thin slivers of light.

I reach out and steady myself with a hand on the kitchen counter, curling my fingers around the sharp edge of the corner, grounding myself in reality.

I must make a noise, because Chase pauses in emptying his pockets onto the table and turns to face me, his phone and script pages still in hand. "All right?" he asks, his forehead furrowed with concern.

I nod, concentrating on my breathing until the moment fades. Which it always does, but it's hard to remember that when it's happening.

"What about you?" I manage.

He blinks and his gaze skitters away from mine. "It comes and goes," he says finally, putting his phone and pages down next to his hotel key card on the table with more care than necessary. "Eleven months sober. It's . . . I'm a work in progress, I guess."

"I know the feeling," I say.

He gives me a rueful grin. "Yeah."

After a quick look around, he locates the wardrobe bag hanging on the bedroom door.

He doesn't bother shutting the door to change, though. He's stripping off his shirt before my brain catches up with what's happening.

I turn quickly, but it's a split second too late for true self-preservation. I shut my eyes for good measure. But that turns the black curtain of my eyelids into an uninterrupted screen on which to play that moment of Chase undressing himself. Over and over again . . . in slow motion . . .

Kicking off his shoes, he reaches over his head, grasping the neck of his shirt and pulling it forward. Revealing those muscles in his stomach, the ones that so entranced me this morning. They shift and flex beneath his skin with the movement.

And watching him take clothes off is so, so much better than watching him put clothes on.

What are those muscles called? They should have monuments built to them. Statues in museums. Paintings by the masters.

But, mainly, to truly appreciate them, I'm beginning to think I might want to touch them.

Just the thought makes me shiver, though whether in excitement or fear I'm not sure. How quickly it might slide out of control, and that's if he didn't run away screaming at the idea first. With my history and hang-ups, I'm a tricky prospect, more than most guys would likely want to deal with.

With that cold slap of reality, I swallow hard and try to focus on something, anything else.

"It's safe, Amanda," Chase says after a moment, the amusement plain in his voice. Clearly, it doesn't bother him, getting dressed and undressed in front of strangers. Probably a job requirement.

But I think he and I might have different definitions of the word "safe" in this context, so I wait until I hear the zip of a zipper going up and the jangle of a belt buckle before I risk peeking over my shoulder.

He's dressed but . . .

I frown at him. "They buy the clothes used?" He's wearing a

grungy white sleeveless undershirt that, while tight and lovely on him, looks like someone stomped it into the dirt for a few hours first.

"Yeah, or they distress them." Chase shrugs into a dark blue hoodie, reaching back to pull the hood out. "Rub them with sandpaper or whatever else they've got to do the job."

"The sleeves are disgusting." One arm of the hoodie is marred with what looks like dried blood and white trails of snot. The other is covered in bleach spots and clumps of mud, and the cuff is torn and flapping loose.

"We're filming out of order," he says with a grin.

I know that happens, of course. I just never thought about the practicalities of it. The clothes would have to be dirty before the mess that dirties them. There has to be a massive spreadsheet somewhere for keeping track of all of this.

Liza would probably want to take it home for the evening and stroke it.

With a strange pang, I realize that's the second or third time I've thought of my sisters in the last ten minutes.

When I was "gone," I couldn't let myself miss them. Not and stay sane. But once I was back, it was even harder to appreciate having them again. My condition, for lack of a better term, dictated everything. Jamming us together, pushing us into each other's paths, and I became the stumbling block for everyone, tripping them up, dragging them down.

As Chase shoves his feet into battered construction boots, his face a mask of distant concentration, like he's preparing for the day ahead, I think about pulling my phone from my pocket and sending a text to Mia or Liza.

But doing that now will only generate a series of angry and concerned texts—or God forbid, calls—asking if I'm all right or if I've learned my lesson and am ready to come home now.

Uh, no.

Besides which, so far today, my phone has been suspiciously

quiet. That makes me think my family is up to something. Better not to trigger that, whatever it is.

A sudden banging on the trailer door behind me makes me jump and spin to face it, my hand clapped against my chest.

"Come in," Chase shouts, unfazed.

The door swings open, and Emily's head appears, then her upper body as she steps up and in. "I'm so sorry," she says breathlessly. "The schedule . . . something happened. They need you in Hair and Makeup right away." She bites her lip hard, as if she's delivering news of an unmitigated disaster and expects to get slapped down for it.

"It's okay," Chase says soothingly, and her shoulders relax. "I'm ready."

He reaches down and scoops up his clothes from the floor, making it blindingly obvious that he changed right there, with the door open.

My face goes hot.

For the first time, Emily's gaze flicks over me with true, albeit hostile, interest. I watch her catch on to the fact that I'm wearing a man's shirt. Chase's shirt, likely, given the situation.

A tiny crease appears between her eyebrows. Ooh, she's not happy.

"Is your friend staying here?" Emily asks in a cheery tone that still somehow manages to convey her idea of the "right" answer.

Chase glances at me in question as he drops his clothes over the back of a chair.

I don't love the idea of being out in the open and surrounded by strangers staring at me all day. But when compared to the possibility of being alone in this dim, musty-smelling space for hours . . .

"I'd rather tag along," I say. "If I can."

"Well . . ." Emily says slowly at the same time Chase says, "Sure."

That settles that. A tiny evil part of me feels a little triumphant at Emily's crestfallen expression.

Once Chase has his phone and key card back in his pockets and his pages in hand, a sulking Emily leads us out of his trailer, across the crumbling street, and to the former warehouse parking lot. She stops at a trailer much closer to the lights and the action.

HAIR/MAKEUP is labeled on the outside with tape, just like Chase's trailer, but the exterior looks newer.

"I'll be back to pick you up," Emily says with a sniff.

"Thanks, Emily," Chase says as he steps up and pops open the door, but even the mention of her name isn't enough to warm her up this time.

She spins on her heel and stalks off.

"Sorry," I murmur. "I think that's on me."

He shakes his head as he climbs into the trailer. "No. She just—"

Chase stops dead, his gaze fixed on someone or something I can't see.

"What's the . . ." I begin.

But instead of answering, he turns with the bleakest look I've ever seen. Then he says quietly, "I am so sorry, Amanda."

12

Chase

"Hey, Karen," I say, my voice cracking in a way it hasn't since I was fucking thirteen. I stuff my hands in my pockets because I don't know what else to do with them. "I didn't see your name on the crew list."

Karen looks up from her kit, brushes in hand, distaste written plainly across her face. I haven't seen her in a couple of years, but she looks the same. She's a few years older than me, short, wire-thin, every movement full of purpose and energy. Her black hair is divided into pigtails that should make her look like a little kid but somehow reinforce the idea that she's bad-ass, doesn't care what you think, and is not someone you want to be on the wrong side of.

Too late for me on that, I'm guessing.

"Max asked me to fill in for Keelie, so I'm pulling double duty, hair and makeup," Karen says after a moment, as if she contemplated ignoring me and only reluctantly decided against it.

Behind me, I hear Amanda coming up the stairs, and a cowardly part of me wants to send her back to my trailer before it's too late. Amanda likes me, I think. And I like that she likes me. Not many people do these days, and quite selfishly, I want to hang on to her regard. I don't want to see the disappointment and disgust slowly filling her expression as Karen details my every fuck-up and failure, as Karen will definitely feel compelled to do. She's not one for holding back.

But hiding the truth—or avoiding it—is how I got into this mess so deeply in the first place. I can't go back to that. So I keep my mouth shut.

"Her kid has the measles, if you can believe that." Karen's bright tattoos look like watercolors across her chest and down her arms, bared by her tank top. They move and shift with her muscles as she sets up her station with her tools and supplies. She's a walking work of art. Something and someone my mom would have appreciated.

I told Karen something like that once, blurted it out one extremely late night early in the first season. We were both new then, nervous novices on a set of experienced professionals. She laughed at me. Told me her family didn't think so. We were friends pretty much from then on. Until I messed it up.

The trailer door slams shut after Amanda, and she edges carefully around the side of me. There's not much room to maneuver in here. "Hi," she says to Karen.

Karen's eyes move from me to Amanda, and confusion dominates her expression. She's trying to place Amanda.

This has potential for complete disaster.

I clear my throat. "Amanda, this is Karen Vega. She was one of the makeup artists on *Starlight*. She's the one who did the tattoo, actually."

Amanda smiles at her. "You did a great job," she says with a self-deprecating laugh. "I thought it was real."

Karen gives a quick bob of her head in acknowledgment of the compliment. "Thanks."

"Karen, this is Amanda Grace. She's here visiting for a few days." I hear the distant, professional tone in my voice, as if that will cover and contain the situation, like one of those boxes the bomb squad uses when detonating strange packages at LAX.

It doesn't help, though.

Karen jolts, her eyes widening as she stares at Amanda, clearly comparing her against whatever image she has from the media.

Then she looks at me and gives a tiny shake of her head in disgust. She may not know what I'm up to, but she suspects something.

I stiffen, waiting for the tirade.

But she ignores me, looking away from me as if I don't exist. In a way that's worse than her yelling.

"Come on in, hon," she says to Amanda. "You can sit over there if you want." She points to an open swivel chair at the next station over.

There are only two stations in the trailer and not much space between. It's smaller than what I'm used to from my *Starlight* days. But so is everything on *Coal City Nights*, and I don't care. I'm just grateful to be here.

Hair and Makeup is your first stop on a working day, so the people there generally see you as you are. In my case, that was: frequently hungover, tired, and a little late. During the second season, at least. Toward the end of the third season, it was more like: still drunk, belligerent, and really late.

Being late to a set is a huge deal. It's disrespectful, a slap in the face to everyone else, not to mention pricey. Time is literally money because the equipment is rented, the clock is running, and everyone is being paid whether you're there or not.

But no one's going to take a chunk out of the star for being late, not at first anyway, so instead the crew catches shit for it. They're the ones pushed to move faster, to make up the difference and still produce quality.

I knew that, but I didn't care. Not then.

Yeah. I was a massive dick. There's no arguing or excusing it. Nothing to do but take responsibility. Which I'm ready to do, but that doesn't mean it's going to be easy.

It's always harder with someone who knew you before everything went to shit. They have, or had, expectations that you've managed to disappoint in every way possible.

Karen's mouth tightens as she looks me over from head to toe, taking me in with a professional eye and also a jaded personal one.

"You're on time. Early, even. That's a first," she says. "Are you actually sober or just doing a good imitation of it?"

I flinch, though she's dead right to be asking.

"I'm sober," I say to Karen, standing my ground. It's the only thing I can do. Besides apologize, which is also on my list. Making amends.

"Everyone else is already on set," Karen adds, and it sounds like an accusation, even though I've done nothing wrong. This time.

Amanda gives me a guarded look but says nothing as she sits in the designated chair. She knows something's wrong.

Karen lifts her hand in an impatient, what-are-you-waiting-for gesture at me.

I shrug out of Smitty's carefully and precisely dirtied hoodie, hanging it on a hook behind me, and sit in the chair at her station.

She wraps a cape around my neck before handing me the tube of industrial-strength moisturizer to apply myself. It's almost like sliding backward in time to the first days on *Starlight*.

"You don't look quite as much like a rough patch of road," Karen says, eyeing me critically, as she works a glob of product into my hair.

"I'm trying," I say, then wince. Because I know I've said that to her before. So many times over the years.

She grunts in response, which is more than enough to convey her skepticism. Her touch is cool, brisk, professional.

I swallow hard. "Listen, Karen," I say quietly. "I need to apologize—"

"So what are you doing mixed up with this circus?" she asks, raising her voice to direct the question to Amanda. She's obviously not interested in my apologies—something she's said to me more than once as well.

"Amanda's here to—"

Karen glares at me in the mirror, hard.

I shut my mouth.

Amanda, watching the interplay from three feet away, frowns. "I'm a *Starlight* fan," she says simply, after a pause.

Her gaze catches mine in the mirror in a small private moment, and a tiny smile plays at the corners of her mouth.

I want to laugh. Yeah, such a fan.

"You're a fan. Of his?" Karen asks. "Really." Her tone conveys both skepticism and severe disapproval at once.

"Yes," Amanda says, tipping her chin up in defiance. I know her well enough now to hear the pique in her voice. She doesn't like to be questioned. Too many people try to question her, to make her into their own vision of her.

"No accounting for taste, I suppose," Karen mutters.

"Hey," I say in warning. It's fine for her to take a chunk out of me; I deserve it. Amanda doesn't, even if her fandom is fake.

Karen lifts her shoulder in a half-shrug and redirects. "How long have you been visiting?"

"Just since yesterday," Amanda answers warily.

"What did you do last night?" Karen asks.

She's digging, trying to work out what's going on, what I'm up to. Fuck. Elise's scheme, and my going along with it, will only confirm that Karen's right to think the worst of me.

I'm feeling queasier than ever about what I've done.

But Amanda has it well in hand. "Ate dinner," she says with

an economy of words, a challenge to Karen's nosiness. "Went to bed."

Karen raises her eyebrows.

"Alone," Amanda adds dryly. Her face is a bit pink, but she's holding it together. Is it weird or wrong that I'm proud of her? I don't know, but I am.

Karen continues to pepper Amanda with questions as she works, applying the base layer of foundation before adding the details.

Amanda watches the bruise appear around my left eye. The cut over the bridge of my nose. The redness around my eyelids and at the base of my nostrils. All signs of an addict, a user, on a bad day in a hard life. Which could just as easily have been me in reality as Smitty in this version of the world.

"Wow," Amanda says to me. "You look terrible." But her eyes are bright with humor.

Before I can respond, Karen cuts in. "You think this is rough, you should have seen him when he was drunk and fell over a chair on set."

Humiliation burns up my neck and into my face, and I want to look away, hide from the judgment, but there's nothing I can say. It happened; I did it. I can't change the past.

Eric and I were out late the night before. And then the night before stretched into the morning of. It was the tail end of the third season of *Starlight*, and I could see the show unraveling week by week and taking my career with it.

Before that, I tried to stop it, tried to make things better, to point out where Brody was no longer being Brody, not just changing as a character, but becoming completely inconsistent. That was my job, right? To look out for Brody. To be the best Brody I could be. I'd been playing him for a couple years by that point, so I felt like I knew him, even cared about him like someone separate from me.

But unsurprisingly, my input was not welcome. I sort of knew that going in—actors are actors, not writers—but I felt like I had to try, even as a last-ditch effort.

Which then utterly failed.

And hey, when your life is spinning out of control and you feel helpless and useless, what better way to handle it than to get wasted and blot out all your worries?

The only problem with that method is that sobering up is inevitable, though not always timely, and the worries and fears come pouring back in with a vengeance and compounded by whatever stupid or shameful thing you've done in the meantime.

Like stumbling into work and falling over a chair in front of everyone.

"They had to write a fight scene into the next episode to cover it," Karen adds with that amused, bitter, angry edge, punishing me for my stupidity.

Amanda's gaze shoots to me. "Real bruises," she murmurs.

I focus on staring at my right shoulder in the mirror, avoiding Amanda's eyes.

"Or how about the time you all took Eric's dad's jet to Cabo and left Marcus behind to find his way back?" Karen asks. "Fun times, right, Chase?" The sneer in her voice is cutting, and it's hard not to try to defend myself even though there's nothing to defend. She's right.

"I apologized to Marcus," I say quietly. "And to Calista, too," I add before she can bring that up. Though no amount of apologizing will make up for what I did in that case.

Karen raises her eyebrows. "They let you in to Safe Haven to visit? Perks of preferred-customer status?"

"I wrote her," I say, fidgeting with a loose flap of faux leather on the chair arm.

That startles her into silence. She stares at me for a long moment as if trying to decide whether or not to believe me.

Then she shakes her head and moves to consult the script and her notes on the counter.

"You'll have your sleeves down in this scene, so we can hold off on the track marks for today." She pauses. "Unless you've already got your own." She looks pointedly down at my arms at my sides.

Amanda makes a sharp, surprised sound.

I close my eyes. "No."

A solid and commanding knock sounds at the door.

I open my eyes in time to see Karen step back from my chair, almost as if she's been expecting the interruption.

Max pops his head in. His dark curly hair is rumpled from where he's been running his hands through it—a classic frustrated-Max move. I watched him do it so often on the couple of *Starlight* episodes he directed, it's surprising he's not bald. And his glasses, those thick, J. J. Abrams–inspired frames, are slightly crooked on his face, the lenses cloudy with visible smudges.

Max is not having a good day. I can tell that before he even opens his mouth.

"I need to talk to you," he says abruptly, his gaze drilling into me. He doesn't seem to notice Karen or Amanda or he doesn't care.

If his lack of pleasantries and greeting didn't give it away, the bluntness of his tone tells me all I need to know. I'm in trouble. Whatever shit is raining down on Max's day, he's already narrowed the source down to me.

My fists clench, the muscles in my arms going tight and my heartbeat accelerating for a fight. A dozen arguments leap to mind, each one louder and angrier than the next.

I haven't done anything wrong.

I'm here, I'm ready to work. That's what you wanted, right?

You said you wanted to give me another chance. You call this a chance?

Fighting, with fists or words, is my automatic response to any kind of authority. A counselor during my second rehab attempt said once that anger is fear turned outward. That I was afraid of people leaving or taking away what meant the most to me so I sabotaged myself instead. Doing the damage myself provided the illusion I was still in control.

Even knowing that, it takes serious effort to keep my ass planted in the seat and my mouth shut.

If I start arguing with Max, I'm screwed. It won't change his mind about whatever it is. And even worse, he'll just see my reaction as proof that he's right to blame me, that I haven't changed at all, no matter what I say.

Besides, it's entirely possible he's right to blame me this time. The scheme Elise cooked up is already spiraling beyond control, and if someone from the hotel called Max . . .

I let out a breath and force my hands to relax.

"Sure," I say, and it sounds almost normal.

Before the word is completely out of my mouth, Max turns and leaves, letting the door slam behind him.

"I guess I'm supposed to meet him outside," I say to Amanda, trying a forced smile.

Her forehead furrowed, she nods with that watchful wariness.

My stomach is tight with dread. He might fire me. I might be getting fired.

The idea is a rock in the back of my throat, making it impossible to swallow.

I've never been fired. Not even from *Starlight*, when I certainly deserved to be.

But the truth is, if it's going to happen, now would be the time. Recasting would be a hassle, but we haven't shot anything yet. If Max is at all concerned about my ability to pull this off, he's probably already got someone in mind to replace me.

Panic flaps in my chest. What am I going to do if he fires me? There goes the audition for the Besson movie. And anything else that might come along. My tarnished reputation will be completely blackened. I'll be done, for good.

Suddenly, the familiar smells in here—the foundation, hair

spray, the various pungent removers and glues that linger in the air long after use—give me a nostalgic, homesick feeling. I felt the same way backstage just before the last performance of *Twelve Angry Men* my senior year in high school. Like I was losing something I wouldn't be able to get back—not just a door shutting but an escape tunnel to another life being blown up in front of me.

I want to be here. I want this life. I need it. This is what I'm meant to do.

It's the only thing I've ever done well or right. I need to be here, to be Smitty.

With determination burning in my veins, I get up and snag Smitty's hoodie. If I need one last chance to convince Max that I'm right for this role and that he's right to trust me, then I need every advantage I can summon, and looking the part can only help.

A glance in the mirror shows me Karen watching, her expression a mix of pity and hardened resolve.

I face Amanda.

"I'll be right back," I say in an attempt at reassurance, for both our sakes.

Then I silently curse myself for saying the one thing that, in a horror movie, at least, guarantees the exact opposite.

13

Amanda

The trailer door bangs shut after Chase, and I lean forward in my chair to track his movements through the window in the door.

He looked so grim, the lines of his face tight and screaming misery.

But the window is frosted glass, so all I see is two shadowy figures, one shorter and gesticulating wildly, the other standing stiff and unmoving.

I can't be sure, since no one used his name, but I'm betting the shorter shadow is Max, the director.

The dread on Chase's face told me that this guy Max, or whoever he is, is in a position to hurt him in some way.

". . . any idea of the trouble this has caused?" A strident voice comes through, slightly muffled.

The Chase-shaped shadow ducks his head and mumbles something I can't hear.

". . . call from the hotel . . . I had to pay for extra security, more barricades, not to mention the last-minute overtime . . . killing the budget, for Christ's sake!" The shorter figure pulls at his hair, making it stand out in a wilder halo.

Extra security. Crap. Is this because of the photographers? Is this because of me? The plan wasn't mine, but I went along with it, encouraged it, even, because I didn't want to feel bad about getting something without giving in return.

"This is not *Starlight*, okay? This isn't television. We can't afford to fuck around, Chase. I only have so much money. Nobody is paying—"

"You know he's using you, right?" Karen says.

I glance over to find her watching me in cool evaluation, taking my measure against some standard in her mind.

Irritation flashes through me. I'm not sure whether she's holding me up against what she knows about Amanda Grace, the Miracle Girl, media darling, innocent victim, or if she's comparing me to other girls she's met in Chase's company.

I suspect it's the former and despise the idea of the latter, but either way, she doesn't know me. I didn't ask for her opinion, and her unsolicited, condescending "let me give you some good advice, sweetie" attitude, one I encounter frequently these days, is pissing me off.

Ignoring her, I turn my attention back to the door and the conversation happening outside.

"—cleared a guest, but she never said it was *that* Amanda Grace." The man whom I suspect to be the director throws his hands in the air. "Jesus Christ, Chase, are you *trying* to mess this up?"

I wince.

"I'm not sure who's pulling his strings these days, so it's impossible to know exactly what he's up to. Maybe he's looking for a publicity boost by having you around," Karen says. "Or maybe he wants to make himself look better. Soothing his guilty conscience or trying to give the haters something else to talk about." I register her careless shrug out of the corner of my eye. "I don't know, but he's working an angle. You need to know that."

Annoyed, I turn in my chair to face her. She's not wrong, exactly, but the motives she's ascribing to Chase are the least generous interpretation.

"What makes you say that?" I ask finally. I'm not going to deny it because then she'll just waste time trying to convince me. But I am curious about *why* she'd say it.

"Because Chase doesn't do anything that doesn't benefit Chase," she says, gathering up her brushes and sponges and putting them away.

That doesn't match with my understanding of him at all. Maybe he was that way once, but now, in my experience, he's been considerate, maybe even overly so, of my feelings.

So he's a changed man, one who's learned from his mistakes. Or maybe she never had the right measure of him in the first place.

But something in Karen's air speaks of bitter experience.

Experience she's obviously determined to share with me.

With a last, reluctant glance toward the door and the conversation going on just outside, I swivel my chair toward hers.

"Okay," I say. "If that's true—"

She frowns. "Of course it's true."

"Then why does it matter so much to you?" Because there's a strong undercurrent of anger in the air in here. It tastes like betrayal, distrust, disappointment. Almost like . . . an ex-girlfriend?

No, that's not quite right. The vibe is different. But then again, my real-world experience with ex-girlfriends is limited to what I've seen on *The Vampire Diaries* and old episodes of *One Tree Hill*, so what do I know?

Karen hears my unvoiced thought and laughs. "I didn't sleep

with him. You don't get to write me off that easily." She shakes her head. "Crazy ex-girlfriends never get the benefit of the doubt of being right," she says with a wry twist of her mouth.

"I didn't say that's who you were," I point out.

Karen sighs. "It's more complicated than that." She flips her braided pigtails behind her shoulders, where they don't stay, and steps around her chair to sit down.

"You ever meet someone who's really got something different, someone who is wildly, unfairly talented, and yet it's still not enough?" she asks.

I shake my head.

She sighs. "Yeah, well, you have now."

"I don't—"

"His first day on *Starlight* was mine, too. He's from Texas; I'm from Alabama. Red-state refugees, you know? We bonded. We were both terrified and desperate to be there and stay there," she says with a small reminiscent smile that triggers an ugly burst of jealousy in me. Regardless of the current status of their non-relationship, they were once close, and some part of me envies that.

Karen pauses. "I don't know how much you know about television production, but it's a bitch. The hours are grueling, and the pace for a weekly show is brutal. And Chase worked harder than anyone. Even harder than me," she adds with an arched eyebrow, as if this were some impossible, herculean-type feat.

Who is this girl?

"You don't really have time for a life outside of work, so you better have one at work." She shrugs. "Your coworkers become your friends, your on-set family. And most of the time, that works out okay. It did for us, in the beginning. We had fun." That fond smile returns but with sadness. "I crashed on Chase's sofa for three weeks when my girlfriend bailed on me and the rent. He's . . . he was a good guy."

"I sense a 'but,'" I say.

She sits back, hesitant for the first time. "I don't know how much he's told you about his family."

I frown. That's a twist I wasn't expecting. "Not much," I admit cautiously. "I know he has a brother, Aidan. And he grew up on a ranch." *Thank you, question-and-answer game.*

Karen looks surprised. "He told you about that?"

I hate that she already seems to know the few details I have about Chase's personal life. I bet she knows his real last name for sure, without Googling it. "Yes," I say.

Karen fusses with her bangs, straightening a few stray strands until they fall in line with the others, all without looking in the mirror. "Look, I don't know them, never met them, don't want to, but something there . . ." She shakes her head. "I don't know. All I can say is that nothing he did was good enough."

I open my mouth to protest.

"I don't mean for me or the show; I mean for him. He was always pushing so hard. He was driven, but past the point of ambitious, to the point of self-destruction. He needed something he couldn't find. Nothing was ever good enough, and that just left this huge . . . hole in him."

She lifts her hands, revealing an ornate and beautiful diamond pattern on the insides of her arms. Her skin looks almost like jeweled fish scales, as if she's secretly a mermaid underneath. "I tried to help him, when the drinking and gambling and other stupid stuff started. But Eric was louder than me." Her mouth curls in distaste, as if just saying the name disgusts her. "You know how that is?"

I nod because I know what she means, though I'm not absolutely sure who Eric is. He's either the one who played Skye's overprotective brother or the goody-goody boyfriend. I can't ask without giving away my earlier lie of being a fan.

"Eric made Chase feel like he needed Eric's approval," Karen says. "Eric's dad is a producer. Rawley Stone. He's been around forever. You know the big TV show in the mid-2000s about runway models who were also international espionage experts?"

"*SpyWear*?" I vaguely remember it from reruns on the higher cable channels.

She nods. "That's Eric's dad. And he's had a bunch of others. Eric's never worried about a damn thing a day in his life." Disdain drips from her words. "I think Chase felt if he had Eric's stamp, that would be enough. He would belong. And that would fill . . . whatever it is." She waves a hand vaguely about her middle as if indicating the general location of the hole she mentioned.

She leans forward, then, her expression intense. "But I can tell you this: Eric Stone has *nothing* on Chase. Eric is coasting, one or two bad movies from being a lifelong has-been, famous for nothing but being Rawley's kid, but Chase is the real deal." Her mouth pinches in. "Or he was until he messed it up."

For the first time, I catch a glimpse of the fear and sadness beneath her hardened exterior. She seems smaller, more vulnerable. Like someone missing a friend.

"He's lost," she says, staring down at her hands. "He doesn't know how to be okay with himself, so he's always chasing some quick fix or a better way to hide. I've seen it happen to other people. I watched it happen to Chase in slow motion over five years." She looks up fiercely. "I don't care what he says, how sorry he is, how much better he says he is now. He's not done fucking up yet, but I'm done trying to help."

And just like that, the bitterness and anger are back.

"So why are you telling me this if you don't care anymore?" I ask. I can't figure out if she's trying to punish Chase, warn me off, or remind herself why they're no longer friends.

"I never said I don't care," she says, offended and maybe a little hurt. "I just don't believe him. I can't. And as for why: you."

"Me?" My hand flies up to my chest.

"He's taking advantage of you, whether you see it or not. Maybe just for company or comfort or something bigger—who knows? I don't want anyone else caught up in the fallout." She levels a knowing look at me. "You've had enough trouble in your life. You don't need this. Trust me."

In the momentary gap of our conversation, words filter in from outside.

". . . want me to give you another chance, but I don't have time for this, Chase. If this is the start of more trouble—"

"It's not. I promise." Chase's "I" sounds more like "Ah." His accent is stronger when he's upset, I think. "I'm sorry, Max. I didn't mean for it to—"

"You never mean for it to—that's the problem!"

When I glance out the window again, Chase's outline seems shrunken, like he's pulled into himself. My heart contracts hard in sympathy.

Maybe he deserves this treatment because of his past sins, maybe he doesn't. But he hasn't done a damn thing wrong in front of me, and I can see him trying, so hard. Why can't they? How are you ever supposed to start over if people won't give you a chance?

Suddenly, I'm angry on his behalf and mine. Are we always going to be trapped by our histories? Is Chase forever going to be the guy who had it all but messed it up? Am I always going to be the girl who got taken, the innocent who was tainted? Or, worse, the girl so damaged, so ruined by what happened to her that she can't have a real life after? Perpetually to be spoken of in solemn whispers.

Screw this.

I stand and head for the door.

Karen shakes her head, her mouth turned down. "Don't say I didn't warn you," she mutters.

"Thanks, I've got it covered," I say and shove open the trailer door and head down the stairs.

The door bangs shut behind me, and I stop.

In front of me, a few feet away, Chase and Max are still

arguing. Rather, Max is arguing. Chase is just standing there, shoulders stiff but his head ducked down, as if he wants to fight but knows better. Like a kid being shamed by the principal.

My anger flares immediately.

Chase has his back to me, but Max catches sight of me right away.

His mouth clamps shut, and his face flushes red, his gaze skating wildly from side to side as if he doesn't know where to look.

And then I know exactly what to do.

As Chase turns to see what's going on, I move toward him, keeping my pace brisk, businesslike. People like Max don't know how to handle someone like me; they don't know how to relate, so they pretend not to see me. But I can use that.

Chase frowns. "What's going on?" he asks, clearly not sure why I'm out here so suddenly.

I ignore him, focusing on Max, who can barely stand still now. He's practically vibrating with the need to leave.

"I just wanted to say thank you so much for letting me visit," I say, forcing a smile. "I can't wait to tell everyone about what a great experience it's been and will be over the next couple of days." I pause, waiting a beat for him to get it.

His forehead wrinkles in confusion.

Come on; you can do it. Put the pieces together. This can be very good or very bad for you.

"Um, yes, I . . . we . . . ," Max stutters. "Well, it's not something we had planned so I'm not sure—"

"*People* magazine has been asking what I've been up to," I continue. "I know they'll be so happy to hear about my visit to the set and the good work that you're all doing here."

Or not. It depends on you.

Max's gaze jerks toward me involuntarily in surprise, and I meet it without flinching.

Then, I watch as his expression shifts lightning fast from reluctance to naked avarice.

There it is. Now you're with me.

Max gives me a grudging nod of respect. "Of course," he says. "We're pleased to have you here for as long as you want to stay."

An awkward moment of silence passes among the three of us, before his attention returns to Chase. "Whenever you're ready," he says in a slightly less snarly tone.

Then he turns and stalks away.

Chase rubs the back of his neck, ruffling the deliberately mussed look Karen created. "You shouldn't have to do that," he says to me, the muscles in his jaw jumping. "You're already doing more than—"

"He was being a jerk." I fold my arms across my chest. "And nobody made me do anything. *I* decided."

"Huh," I hear a voice say behind me.

Startled, I turn to see Karen standing on the steps of her trailer, her expression one of surprise and faint admiration. "I guess you do."

It takes me a second to replay our previous conversation to the last thing I said.

I've got it covered.

She gives Chase a hard look, then nods at me before disappearing inside.

"If people are going to judge us by our pasts," I say to Chase, "then I'm at least going to control how it happens and make it work for us. We are not our mistakes, our tragedies. We're more than that. And *he*"—I wave a hand toward where Max stood—"should know that."

Plus, this way, Max might think twice before taking out my presence on Chase. I'm a potential asset now instead of a liability.

I expect Chase to argue further, but instead he's looking at me oddly, his head tipped to the side.

"Amanda," he says hesitantly. "Whatever Karen told you—"

I stiffen. "It's fine. It doesn't—"

"—I'm sure it's true," he finishes as if I hadn't spoken. "You don't have to come to my rescue. I deserve what I'm getting. And I'm willing to take whatever Max hands out to get a second chance. I *need* this chance," he says, his eyes boring into mine, pleading with me to understand.

Tears blur my vision. He really believes what he just told me. He'll let them say anything, do anything to him as long as he gets his "chance."

I blink them back and step closer to him. "The whole point of a second chance is that no one ever deserves it."

He rocks back like one of my punches from last night connected.

"Everyone messes up, Chase; the degree just varies," I say with a weariness that feels bone deep. "And the perspective."

No one thinks I made a mistake in the course of events that happened to me, but I did. Of course I did. I trusted someone I shouldn't have, wasn't as smart as I should have been, maybe didn't fight as hard as I could have in the moment because I didn't believe the world was that messed up. That doesn't mean it was my fault, but I have to live with all of those things, the choices I didn't make and the ones I did.

Chase opens his mouth and closes it without saying anything, emotion writ large on his face: regret, shame, despair, and determination. And I'm familiar with every damn one of them.

"I have to believe that we're all on our second or third or fourteenth chance, one way or another," I say. "And anybody who says otherwise and tries to make us feel bad about it"— I jerk my chin in the direction Max took—"is fucking lying to himself and everybody else."

Chase laughs, but it's a choked sound. "Thanks." He lifts his arm and, after making certain I see the gesture coming, wraps it around my shoulders, pulling me close. "Thank you for that."

My cheek rests against his chest lightly. His arm is warm and comforting across the back of my neck, and his fingers on the cap of my shoulder seep heat through my shirts. Beneath the faint scent of sulfur, like old eggs, that clings to his hoodie, I smell him, the shampoo and soap from the hotel . . . and his skin.

My heart is thumping in my chest like a rabbit on crack, but it's not fear I'm feeling. I want to curl closer to him, press full-on against him, and possibly stretch up to press my mouth against the side of his throat.

I can actually feel my toes tensing, as if they're preparing to lift me up for that last item, with or without my consent.

"Sure," I mumble and pull away.

He lets me go immediately. I rub my arms up and down, trying simultaneously to retain his warmth and also banish the goose bumps.

The shivers aren't unpleasant except in their newness and what I know they mean. Want. Lust. Everything I can't have right now.

Chase frowns and opens his mouth to say something.

But I beat him to it. "We should go, right?" I ask brightly.

Involuntarily, his head swivels in the direction of the cameras, the lights, and the activity. "Yeah."

"Good. Because you smell kind of horrible," I tease. It's an exaggeration but an effective change of topic. I wrinkle my nose. "Does this fight you're in take place in a pile of garbage?"

He raises his eyebrows and lifts a sleeve to sniff at it. He grimaces but tries to hide it. Then he grins at me. "We are committed to authenticity here," he says in mock solemnity.

"Awesome. Could you maybe be authentic more downwind of me?" I ask.

He laughs and stretches his arm toward me, looping it loosely around my neck as we start to walk. "You just don't understand dedication to the craft."

I make a face. "I'm not sure that's the same thing."

"I don't know—maybe you just need another whiff," he says in pretend thoughtfulness.

Another hug? Another ten seconds of closeness with him? *Yes.* I'm already turning toward his chest.

But then, with a teasing grin, he raises his other arm as if he's going to hold it in front of my nose, and disappointment flashes through me before I can clamp down on it.

Playing my part, I lift my hands quickly to cover my nose. "No, thank you!"

"Oh, well, your loss," he says with a shrug, releasing my shoulders and dropping his arms to his sides to stuff his hands in his pockets.

Yes—yes, it is. A surge of wistfulness overwhelms me momentarily, and I catch my breath.

A fearful impulse tells me to push the emotion away, box it up for safety and send it to the farthest reaches of my mind. At the same time, some part of me wants to hold it up to the light and examine it, to feel the wonder of *wanting* again.

I don't have much time to consider either option, though. Because once we're on the set, I learn a couple things very quickly.

The first is that, despite my initial worries, after a few curious glances, absolutely no one seems to care about my presence. They're too busy, all of them moving in a hundred different directions at once. The set is an anthill that's been stomped on and then lit on fire for good measure. Which is a relief because if I can't hide from so many strangers, being invisible to them is the next best thing.

Chase settles me in the chair with his name on it and heads to the relatively calm epicenter, an open space where a battered car, a cooler full of ice and beer, two ragged lawn chairs, and the other two actors are waiting beneath the lights and the watchful eyes of the cameras.

I watch as Chase and the others run through the scene, under Max's direction, trying different approaches with the same words. It's fascinating to see the shades of character emerge without knowing anything about the overall story. There's the push-pull of old friendship and envy between Chase and the other guy, and simmering resentment and bitterness between Chase and the girl.

But that's when I learn the second thing: Karen was right to warn me. Chase is extremely talented. So much so that he disappears into Smitty in front of my eyes. The Chase I knew, or thought I knew, is gone and in his place is a temperamental addict with shaking hands and a short temper. Even his gestures, the way he moves his body, are different. It's like watching a stranger with Chase's face.

It wedges a tiny crack in the little bit of confidence I've regained, letting in a chill. Because, in spite of my fierce defense of Chase only a short while ago, I have no choice but to recognize that someone this good at pretending to be another person might be impossible to ever really know. Or trust.

14

Chase

I forgot what it was like, having someone on your side.

I don't like how Amanda did it, sacrificing herself on the altar of more unwanted media attention, but that she was willing to means a lot. The warmth of that belief, deserved or not, stays with me, and I catch myself staring at her off and on while we rehearse.

She's taking in the sights around her, the hive of activity, the strange and new in what is so familiar to me. Her hair looks redder in the sunlight, and the pink shirt she hates, the one she wears under mine, adds color to her pale skin.

When I check on her, she asks questions—quietly at first, worried about making too much noise in case the cameras are already rolling—wanting to know the purpose of that piece of equipment that looks more like it belongs on a construction site or what that person with a harness does.

She's observant, smart, wry . . . and beautiful.

The moony tenor of my thoughts sets off an internal alarm. I know, better than others, the dangers of falling for your own fiction, believing the lies you had a hand in making.

I try to keep an eye on her, but once we're rolling, I lose myself in being Smitty. I forgot what that was like, too, how good it feels to be someone else.

Smitty is an unapologetic mess, and it's a relief to be an unflinching disaster of a human being. Because, as horrible as it sounds, it's exhausting trying to be a better version of myself. As Smitty, the bar is much, much lower. I can be a dick sometimes, but Smitty, as written by Max, has turned it into an art form.

When I remember to look up during a break, someone has given Amanda a script, and she's absorbed in reading.

Then, when I glance over later, the AD has pulled her over by one of the playback screens. Amanda's watching us, watching me, with an intent expression, her forehead creased with concentration.

She's interested in the story and in what we're doing. Other girls I dated, they only cared about the results—the cameras, the magazine spreads, the party invitations—not the work.

Not that I'm thinking about Amanda that way. The dating way. Being attracted to her is one thing, an uncontrollable, biological or chemical thing, but acting on it would be just like pressing the button to blow up my life.

I've done dumb things, but I'm smarter than that. And she deserves better.

Reminding myself of that whenever my gaze strays toward Amanda, I concentrate instead on doing the best work I can.

In the scene we're working on today, Smitty and Keller, best friends since kindergarten, are forced to realize that their shared future, long planned and loosely envisioned as owners of the Blue Palace Bar with a little dealing on the side for Smitty, is just a childish fantasy. Keller has an opportunity to get out of

Westville, to go to school and become the writer he's always dreamed of being.

But Smitty can't handle it. He doesn't have the opportunities that Keller does, and the Blue Palace was his bright future with his best friend. In one horrible moment, he's losing both.

The day passes in a long, strenuous blur with a tense director and a cast and crew new to working together.

So it's not until we break for dinner, when I'm settling on to a piece of curb next to Amanda with my paper plate in hand, that I realize she hasn't said much lately.

Actually—I frown, thinking about it—she hasn't said much since this morning, other than perfunctory answers to direct questions.

Momentary panic grips me.

"Is everything all right?" I ask, wondering if I've missed something. She was tense when she confronted Max, but after that, she seemed all right, or so I thought. But I was more than a little distracted.

"It's fine," she says, but she doesn't look up from where she's putting a layer of potato chips under the bread of her turkey sandwich.

"Are the blueberries going in, too?" I tease, tipping my head toward the only other food on her plate. "I just want to be prepared."

"No," she says with a distant, polite smile, like I'm a stranger approaching her at an airport. Nothing like this morning.

"Amanda, what's wrong?" I ask. Then a belated thought occurs. "Is this about Adam?" I glare in his direction, where he and the other cast and crew have gathered to eat, twenty or thirty feet away from us.

Adam DiLaurentis, the guy who's playing Keller, approached her this afternoon, blowing right past me to say awkward things like, "It's so great to see you up and around." Like she was stuck at home with a broken leg for a few years. And then he pressed her on eating dinner with him, away from me, so they "could get to know each other because you seem awesome."

She was staring him down into awkward silence by the time I intervened.

At the memory, my hands clench, bending my plastic fork until I make myself relax.

"No, no," Amanda says quickly. She pauses. "You know that was more about you than it was about me, right?"

I pause in the middle of stabbing a forkful of salad. "No."

She shrugs. "Adam is Keller. Even when he's not being Keller, you know what I mean?"

Sort of, yeah. Adam doesn't have the chops. That's what my acting coach would have said. Adam will always play this type of character. Friendly, guy-next-door, nothing that's too much of a stretch from who he is in reality. There are a lot of actors like that.

I'm not sure what that has to do with me, though.

But Amanda is done talking, picking up her turkey–potato chip sandwich to eat around the edges.

A secondary and self-centered fear kicks in on me.

She read the script, watched part of it play out today. Granted, it wasn't the finished version, but there should have been more than enough for her to form an opinion about the story. About Smitty. About me.

Oh, Jesus.

Have you ever watched someone do something they claim to be good at but they're so clearly not, you can barely stand to be near them? I've been in auditions like that, where I'm fighting the urge to cringe on someone else's behalf. And then there's that weird fear their incompetence and overconfidence are contagious, ready to leap through the air and land on you like germs blasted out into the room by a sneeze.

Don't be stupid. Amanda's not like that.

But now that the idea has taken root in my head, I can't get rid of it. "Did you enjoy what you saw today?" I ask.

She puts her sandwich down and pulls out the napkin tucked beneath her plate to wipe her mouth before answering. "It was great," she says, with a bland smile.

My heart plummets to my feet.

I drop my fork on my plate, appetite gone. "Shit, Amanda, if it's not . . . if I'm not . . ." I shake my head, trying to find the words. Acting is the only thing I've been good at. I thought I was locked in on Smitty, but it's hard to judge your own performance. Max hasn't been effusive with praise, but he never is.

Amanda looks up at me, alarmed. "No, Chase." She reaches a hand toward me in a placating gesture, but stops well before making contact. "No, that's not it."

"But there is something," I persist, my pulse thumping hard with dread. Laughter and conversation from the others drift over.

Lowering her hand, Amanda sighs, studying her sandwich. She looks tired, dark circles under her eyes. Her shirt, my shirt, is limp and rumpled.

"It's stupid, but Karen was right," she says finally. She balances her plate on her knees and folds her arms across her chest.

My breath catches in my throat. "Right about what?" I manage after a second. I never did hear exactly what Karen told her.

Amanda lifts her shoulder in a halfhearted shrug. "You're good. Really good," she says. "That's why Adam's trying to stir up trouble. You're better than he is, and everyone who sees this movie is going to recognize that." She hesitates. "Watching you today . . . it's like you disappeared."

I relax slightly. "Why does that sound so ominous?" I say, trying to joke.

"Because Smitty is kind of an asshole?" she shoots back.

I laugh. "You're not supposed to like him. He's basically the bad guy, the antagonist." For most of the story, anyway. Then he gets his redemptive moment, a chance to save Keller and give him a future without Smitty, or he can take them both down. That's why I fought for the role. Smitty does what I wish Eric would have done, what I *should* have done. Stepped up and cared more about someone else than myself. I can't change what I've done, but this part feels like a step in the right direction, like blocking a scene before you do it for real.

"Yeah, I get that," Amanda says.

I wait, but she doesn't say more, and an inexplicable tension hangs thick in the air.

With a grimace, I keep pushing. "I'm sorry, but I feel like I'm missing something here. If I've done something or . . ."

Amanda looks up at me, her face shadowed in the dim light. "It's one of those weird things that I . . ." She gives a rueful smile. "Forget it. I'm just being a freak."

"No, tell me. Please?" I need to fix whatever it is, if I can.

She bites her lip. "I still have trouble trusting people. Actually, it's more like trusting my judgment of people, you know?"

I nod. That's completely understandable given what . . .

It clicks in my head then.

She has trouble trusting her judgment of people, and she just watched me be someone else, someone awful, selfish, and violent, for ten hours. Even worse, she knows I have a history of being all those things, at times, in real life. Probably in great detail, thanks to Karen.

So she has no idea what to trust, *whether* to trust.

I set my plate on the crumbling asphalt and turn toward her. "Amanda . . ." I begin, but I don't know how to finish. She's right.

Amanda looks at me calmly, but her dark eyes shine with tears. "I know it's ridiculous. This is your job, and there's nothing wrong with being good at it. It's just . . . me."

My throat aches with unexpressed emotion. I want to pull her close, wrap my arm around her, as though that would magically transfer her pain and hurt to me. But giving in to that instinct would be the worst thing I could do.

If I were a good person, the person she thinks I am, I would tell her to run from me, far, far away. But I can't. Even worse, I don't want to.

"I promise you, I am not being anybody but myself with you," I say hoarsely. That much is true. I hesitate, then decide to give her the honesty she deserves in the only way I can. "Maybe a slightly better version." I clear my throat, feeling the heat rise in my face. "More like the person I want to be. But that's all."

Amanda stays silent for a long moment, watching me, and I fight the urge to fidget under her gaze. Then she puts her plate on the ground and edges toward me, the narrow space between us growing smaller.

When she rests her head against my shoulder, her body is a warm solid line against mine, and I can barely breathe for fear of scaring her away.

"Thank you," she says, looking up at me, holding my gaze.

Staring down at her, I find my attention drawn to her mouth. When she bites her lower lip, pulling it into her mouth and slowly releasing it, pinker and damp, I *feel* it in the electric zip of attraction firing through me.

The atmosphere shifts, moving from nervous tension to something softer, heavier.

Don't do this. Just smile, look away, and pick up your food. This is a bad idea.

But I hold still, like I've been frozen in place.

She tilts her head up slightly more toward mine; her mouth is just a few inches from mine. Her breath moves against my skin, and on instinct, I lean in to close the gap.

"Hey, Henry, are we doing this or what?" Adam calls.

I jerk back from Amanda even as she straightens up and shifts away from me, her cheeks flushing with color.

Regret curls through me, along with the intense desire to punch Adam. I glare at him and give a wave in acknowledgment, resisting the urge to flip him off.

"I should go." I gesture in Adam's direction. "He wants to run a few lines before we start up again."

"Oh, yeah." She nods rapidly. "Sure." She's very carefully not looking at me, focusing instead on her dinner that she's reclaimed.

As I scoop my plate off the ground and walk away, I tell myself this is for the best. Amanda deserves better. Better than me.
Teasing, flirting a little to make her blush, that's one thing. But
more would be wrong . . . for both of us.

And I *almost* believe it.

15

Amanda

"You sure you'll be all right here by yourself?" Chase asks, his arm holding the hotel's service elevator doors open for me to exit first.

"I'll be fine. It's an hour," I say, turning to face him once I'm in the hall. "Besides, I think they kind of frown on bringing random tagalongs to these meetings, don't they? It's sort of a members-only thing, right?"

His forehead furrows. "I don't have to go."

"I was kidding. You should go. You *need* to go," I say.

Chase bobs his head in agreement as we walk toward our rooms, but he doesn't look convinced.

Ever since dinner, ever since that almost-moment at dinner, he's been extra considerate. Warm, friendly, checking on me during every break through the final three hours of filming . . . all while keeping a distinct physical distance.

In the van on the way back here, he kept a very circumspect two feet between us on the bench seat. Emily could have fit in that space. She probably would have liked to.

I'm not sure what to make of it. I keep replaying that moment at dinner over and over in my head, trying to understand it from every angle.

I almost kissed Chase Henry. I know that for sure.

I'm a little less sure if he meant to kiss me.

Leaning my head against his shoulder felt completely natural and the right thing to do. And when he looked down at me, the moment snagged and held. My head moved toward his like it was on a track or a wire, drawn along on a path without conscious thought on my part. I just felt this . . . pull toward him. But was it just me? I don't know.

"Amanda?" Chase asks, interrupting my thoughts.

My face flushes hot. "Sorry?"

"I said, I'm going to grab a shower first before I head out so I'll be here for a few more minutes. But after that, I'll have my phone with me at the meeting if you need anything," he says.

I shake my head. "Chase. It's fine. I'm going to find some boring television to watch and hopefully fall asleep at some point. The History Channel is usually pretty good for that." I shrug. "If not, there's always infomercial bingo."

He gives me a strange look, a smile tugging at the corners of his mouth, as he takes his key card out of his back pocket. "What is infomercial bingo?"

"Based on the name of the infomercial, you pick ten words that you think the host is going to use within the first fifteen minutes. But the name of the product doesn't count," I add sternly.

"Seriously?" he asks, amused.

"I invented it in the hospital when I couldn't sleep," I say. "Sometimes I still have trouble."

Everyone assures me nightmares are completely normal. But the weird part is the worst ones, the ones where I wake up struggling to breathe, take place on the porch, not in the basement. I'm standing just outside the front door, seconds before I make that choice to move my foot forward and change my world forever. Only this time, I know what's going to happen. I try to run away or cry for help. But I can't move and no noise comes out. All I can feel is that same paralyzing pressure in my throat and chest, robbing me of my voice.

I can't scream, even when his fist tangles in my hair and he drags me toward the basement, and in that way, the dreams parallel what actually happened.

I clear my throat. "Trust me when I tell you there's nothing on between three and four in the morning, no matter what cable package you have."

"Yep, been there," Chase says as we reach our rooms. "When I was drinking and even now sometimes." He lifts a shoulder. "I never sleep well in hotels, especially the first few nights."

"Okay, then infomercial bingo might work for you too. If I'm still awake when you get back, I'll teach you the finer arts of the game." I hold my breath, waiting for him to get that polite, panicky look that I'd expect from someone who was almost accidentally kissed the last time we were alone-ish together.

But he just smiles. "Sounds like a plan."

When he meets my gaze, the moment holds a beat too long, and I feel that same pull again. Like I might be able to step closer and wrap my arms around him.

"Chase—" I begin.

The *Starlight* theme song plays, tinny and violently loud in the hallway, making both of us jump.

I wince. "Sorry, I need to change that." I pull my phone out of my pocket and consult the screen, though I already know who it is. I send it to voicemail for the moment.

"Your therapist," Chase says.

"Yeah. She made 'special arrangements' to speak to me after hours tonight," I say, digging out my key card.

"That'll probably be her chapter heading," he mutters. "'Special Arrangements.'"

I stop, surprised.

He makes an apologetic face. "Sorry, I didn't mean to—"

"No, no," I say. "You've got it all wrong. This?" I wave my key card, indicating the space between us. "Easily sequel material for the Miracle Girl story."

He gapes at me.

"I mean," I shrug, "if she's going to get mileage out of me, it should be *at least* a two-book deal," I say with mock affront. "I think that's the going rate for Miracle Girl–related stories these days."

He throws his head back and laughs, and the sound of it warms me.

But it doesn't change reality, which is Dr. Knaussen waiting. So I slide the key card into the lock and push my door open.

"Do you want me to come in?" Chase asks.

I look at him, startled.

"I mean, to check the room before I leave," he adds quickly.

Oh. I glance into the room, confirming that everything is as I left it, with the exception of the bed now being made. "No, I think I'm good but . . . thank you."

"Right." But he doesn't move, just stands there watching me with that same intensity I remember from the moment at dinner.

Before I can stop myself, I step toward him, testing him, testing me.

Something that might be desire flickers in his gaze, along with wariness, as I approach, but I keep my hands—and my mouth—to myself.

He lets me enter his personal space, so close I can feel the heat of his body, the brush of his legs against mine. It makes me feel shaky, but not in a bad way.

I lean forward, and his breath catches in his throat. Never

would I have thought that to be a sexy sound, but it's such an involuntary desire response, I shiver with a wave of *want*.

But then I chicken out at the last second, and instead of lifting my chin toward his, I turn my head to the side to rest it against his chest. Which is a smaller victory, but a victory all the same.

"I'm glad you're here," I say. "I'm glad *I'm* here."

"Me, too," he says softly, and I feel the words vibrate in his chest, next to the too-rapid thumping of his heart.

But then he steps back abruptly and uncertainty rises to swamp me. Am I reading him wrong? Getting this, whatever it is, wrong?

"I should go," he says, turning toward his door.

I open my mouth to say . . . something. I don't know what. But my phone starts to ring again then, and my time is up. I have to answer.

When I shut the door to my room, though, I lean against it, taking an extra second or two to gather myself.

Then I answer my phone. "Hi, Dr. Knaussen."

"Amanda? I was worried there might have been a miscommunication," she says with that faint hint of reproof.

"No, sorry; I just couldn't answer quickly enough." Eh, sort of true.

I'm lying to my therapist. This has to be a new low and probably a sign that it's time to move on to number eight.

"That's fine," she says. "I'm just glad we didn't miss one another."

I frown. She sounds almost excited. Which doesn't make any sense. Maybe it's my imagination.

"How are you?" she asks, with even more of that cooing sympathy I've come to expect from her.

"I'm fine." I clutch the phone tighter against my ear, hating the defensive tone in my voice.

"Mmm-hmm."

I know this tactic, a bid to make me fill the silence, and I keep my mouth shut.

"And how is Mr. Henry? Are you finding him to be as you expected?" she continues in a carefully neutral tone.

Oh, come on. Is she really expecting me to swing at that?

"Yes, he's fine, too," I say. He would have to threaten to eat soup out of my rib cage before I'd admit to trouble now. Shouldn't she, as the trained professional, know that?

"I understand that there were some photos taken today," she says.

I tense. I was so focused on the right people in Chase's life seeing them that I forgot that people I knew would see them as well.

I pace at the foot of the bed. How widespread are those images for her to have seen them? Were they on the news or one of those entertainment shows again? I wince, imagining my family subjected once more to endless Miracle Girl coverage and speculation. My dad disconnected our cable at one point as well as our home phone. Are there reporters camped in front of our yard again?

Pausing by the dresser, I run my finger along a scrape in the finish. "The photos weren't a big deal. It was fine." I'm using the word "fine" a lot, and accordingly, I brace myself for a gentle chiding. "Fine," according to Dr. Knaussen, is an empty word. It's the one we use when we can't bring ourselves to say something positive but we know that "okay" often encourages questions we don't want to answer.

Whatever. "Fine" is a perfectly descriptive word in my book. I'm not good, not great—I would never say that. But I'm not falling apart at the moment, either. So how else would you describe that other than fine?

Fortunately, Dr. Knaussen's pursuing a different scent at the moment. "If you don't mind me saying, I've seen the pictures and you didn't seem fine. You seemed frightened." I hear her clicking her pen open and closed, open and closed.

I sigh and decide to give a little. She actually has helped more than any of her predecessors. "Yeah, it was scary," I admit. "It's been a couple years since I've been around cameras like that, and there were more than I expected. More than we expected," I corrected, remember the shock on Chase's face. "But we handled it."

There's a long silence on the other end, then: "I'm interested to hear you describing you and Mr. Henry as a 'we.'"

It's the deliberate casualness in her tone that tips me off. *This* is what she was after.

I exhale loudly. "Yes, 'we.' We're . . ." What are we? I have no idea. That moment at dinner and the echo of it in the hallway a few minutes ago didn't *feel* like something that happened between random strangers. But I'm not 100 percent sure I trust my instincts on this matter. Chase certainly moved away from me fast enough.

". . . friends," I finish lamely. I make a face at myself in the mirror over the dresser. After months of suggesting, unsuccessfully, that I expand my "comfort zone and social circle," she's going to have a field day with me labeling a guy I've known for barely twenty-four hours as a "friend." Especially when that guy is Chase Henry, the face of my pretend savior.

But I know I like him. And I think he likes me. What other word for that is there? "Happy allies"? "Pleasant acquaintances" doesn't seem to quite cover it. And neither of those terms even takes into account my other feelings for him—toward him?—which I am *not* going to bring up right now.

I close my eyes and wait for Dr. Knaussen's response.

She takes a deep breath.

Here we go.

"Amanda, at this point, I'd like to let you know that your parents are here with me, and after today, they have some additional concerns they'd like to share with you on this matter," Dr. Knaussen says.

My eyes snap open. *That's* why she was okay with rescheduling. That also explains the overly solicitous tone and hidden excitement in her voice. Family "conversations" are her groove. She's convinced I can't be completely healed without everyone on board. She's met with my mom and Mia, and Liza, even. My dad was the lone holdout. Apparently not anymore.

I hear some quiet murmuring in the background. Then my mom says, "Amanda?" Her voice sounds small, worried.

My free hand immediately flies to the scar on my wrist, tracing the line with my index finger. "I'm here," I say.

"Amanda, we're worried about you. I know you're an adult, and your decisions are your own," she says with a care that suggests she fears I might hang up at any second. "But those photos today—"

"You don't know what it looks like," my dad bursts in.

I jolt. It's one thing for my dad to be in the room but to jump in on the conversation? I picture him standing over Dr. Knaussen's desk, glowering. "Am I on speakerphone?" I demand.

"He's taking advantage," my dad continues as if I haven't spoken. "He sees that you're not well enough to make smart decisions about your—"

"Mark, shhh," my mom says. "We just don't want you getting hurt again. We saw the photos. You were wearing his shirt, and he was touching you—"

"It's not the same thing," I snap. "Not even close. It's okay when he touches me." Actually, if I'm being honest, it's more than okay. I *like* it.

That revelation stops me in my tracks for a moment. Somehow, somewhere, I crossed the line from tolerating to *enjoying* being touched. Granted, it's a phenomenon limited strictly to Chase Henry at the moment, but still.

My mouth is open in shock. I've managed to surprise myself.

How? When? Walking out to the van this morning, when he made me feel safe in spite of the cameras? When we were pressed

196 / STACEY KADE

together in that seat on the way to the set? Clearly, it was probably before I nearly kissed him at dinner.

I scramble to remember the exact moment it happened, this huge, monumental step for me, but I can't pin it down. It apparently wasn't a big Hollywood moment with trumpets blaring, but a smaller, more subtle transition.

"Amanda? Are you there?" My mother's voice breaks into my thoughts and I remember I'm supposed to be paying attention.

"Yes, sorry," I say quickly.

"I said, we're just concerned to see such a dramatic change in you so suddenly. You've been so resistant to anyone . . . and I understand that victims . . . of what happened to you sometimes—"

An old frustration rapidly overtakes my newfound astonishment. "Rape, Mom," I say. "Rape survivors."

"Everyone has your best interests in mind, Amanda," Liza says, barging into the conversation. "There's no need to be harsh."

My head jerks up. She's there, too?

"Who else is listening?" I demand. "Mia?"

"Don't drag me into this," Mia protests. "It wasn't my idea."

"You've got to be kidding me," I mutter, rubbing my forehead where a headache is developing.

"I think what Mom was trying to say is that studies show that sexual assault survivors may react in a variety of ways, including celibacy or promiscuity, sometimes vacillating between periods of each," Liza pronounces. "And you seem to be moving to—"

My patience evaporates. "Liza, I'm not sleeping with Chase Henry, but if I was, it would be my choice and nobody's business but mine. I don't need a study to tell me that."

The other end of the phone explodes with voices, all of them talking at once.

"Amanda!" my mom says, her voice choked. "You can't!"

"Don't take that tone with your sister. She's just trying to—"

"—understand your anger, but it's misdirected—"

"—go home now?" Mia asks, fury clear beneath her plaintive tone.

"Okay, everyone," Dr. Knaussen tries to interject. "Let's calm down and circle together. We're here for Amanda and—"

"—setting a good example for Mia—"

"Actors are notoriously unreliable, and Chase Henry has a reputation for—"

"—don't pretend this is about me. Like I even exist except when Amanda's—"

"—taking stupid risks, endangering yourself further. You should just come home!"

I listen to them talking over one another, and tears well in my eyes. I love them, and I'm certain they love me or they wouldn't try this hard.

But I can't do this. Not now.

"I have to go," I say loudly into the phone.

"Amanda, wait," my mom pleads.

"I don't think running away from this conversation is going to help," Liza says, oh so reasonably.

At that, my hand squeezes so tight around the phone that my knuckles ache.

"I'll check in tomorrow," I say, working to keep my voice calm.

Then, before the rest of them, including Dr. Knaussen, can chime in, I hang up and turn my phone to do not disturb.

16

Chase

Once I'm in my room, I shut the hall door behind me firmly.

My heartbeat is still thrumming hard, and I feel a ghost impression of the heat between us at every point of contact: Amanda's breasts brushing against my ribs every time one of us breathed, her legs bumping mine.

It was the least amount of body contact I've ever had in a hug, no hands involved anywhere, but it was also somehow the most intimate. I wanted to wrap my arms around her and pull her tight against me. I had to step back from her just to get myself under control.

A glance ahead of me reveals that Housekeeping closed the adjoining door to Amanda's room, and I'm both relieved and disappointed.

I would have shut it anyway to give her privacy for her conversation, but removing my action from the equation also removes temptation. Temptation to eavesdrop, temptation to stick my head in and see if she'll look at me like that again, temptation to ask her something dumb just to see her smile.

"Come on, Mroczek." I rub my forehead, feeling the greasy remnants of the makeup I missed removing. "Get in the shower, get cleaned up, and get your head back in the game."

I move toward the table to empty out my pockets.

"Aww, what's the matter? Things not going so well with Little Miss Tragedy USA?" a familiar female voice calls out coyly.

I freeze.

There's a rustle of fabric, and then Elise emerges from the bedroom half of the suite, leaning against the half-wall, her legs bare beneath one of my shirts. It's held together by a single button in the middle, revealing the curves of her breasts at the top and the juncture of her thighs at the bottom. She's not wearing anything underneath it.

"Jesus, Elise," I hiss, trying to look only at her face. "What are you doing here?"

"You did such a good job today, baby," she says with a sly smile. "You deserve a reward." She wiggles her index finger at me in a come-hither gesture. "You should have seen the pictures. Giving her your shirt was a stroke of genius."

I glance over my shoulder toward the door to Amanda's room. It's shut, but the lock is not engaged. I think I can hear the faint murmur of her on the phone. "Get dressed."

Her hand drops, and her expression goes icy. "Excuse me?"

Careful. Elise holds the keys to my future and possibly my destruction if I don't play this right.

"The doors are thin," I say. "You're the one who's all about selling the story." I tip my head in Amanda's direction, hating myself. "What do you think she'll say if she finds my 'fired' publicist in here half naked?"

Elise flips her hair over her shoulder, narrowing her eyes at me. "I wasn't aware that, after twenty-four hours, the two of you had the type of relationship where she might walk in unannounced."

Trap. There was no way to respond to that without landing in more trouble, for doing what she told me to too well or not well enough.

"Then again, maybe I shouldn't be so surprised," she says with that calm but dangerous tone I recognize from previous fights, "since you were so enamored today you didn't even have time to respond to my texts."

"I was a little busy working," I snap, which is both true and not. I drop my key card, script pages, and phone on the table. "Thanks, by the way, for the ambush this morning."

"I had to. Your reaction looked more natural that way," she says, folding her arms across her chest. "If you'd read my texts today, you'd know that. You couldn't slip away for thirty seconds to answer me?"

Yes, I could have. But it felt wrong, shady, especially with Amanda right there.

"Then I wouldn't have to risk a personal visit." Elise toys with the one engaged button. "Though why you wouldn't want this, I'm not sure."

Elise, the seducer, is back, but the hard look in her eyes tells me that the pissed-off version is lurking beneath the surface, ready to lash out at the slightest provocation.

I'm caught. If she starts yelling, Amanda will hear it even if she's on the phone. She won't know who it is or why, but she'll know there is an angry woman in my room. And there just aren't that many reasons—beyond pissed-off girlfriend—for that to be the case.

That would be the end of Amanda smiling at me like I deserve her respect, the end of her looking at me like she trusts me.

I should want that—wanting otherwise is a dangerous game—but I don't.

"I'm sorry," I say. "It was just a long day." I hope the door on

Amanda's side is shut, too. Or that she's preoccupied talking to her therapist.

I'm the shittiest human being alive.

Elise's expression softens slightly, her lips puffing out in sympathy. "I know, it's a lot on you, Chase, dealing with her damage and drama." She waves a hand in the direction of Amanda's room with an eye roll.

"It's not . . ." I catch myself. "It's fine."

"And it's working." The excited gleam is back in her eyes. "Did you check your email?"

"No."

She nods toward my phone on the table. "Do it."

I reluctantly follow her direction. It takes me only a second to see what she's talking about. At the top of my inbox, I have an e-mail from Rick, my agent. Complimenting me on the buzz around *Coal City* and suggesting that we touch base early next week.

Holy shit.

"Then there's this." As I put my phone down, Elise reaches for hers, charging on the half-wall behind her. "You have to see."

She flips through open links on her phone, showing me the photos of Amanda and me in prominent locations on all the various entertainment/celebrity news sites. The pictures look exactly like what Elise wanted: I appear flustered and protective with my arm around Amanda, who, despite her best efforts, has a deer-in-headlights look. Neither of us is smiling, and the tension is palpable. But the effect of being surrounded by the crowd is that we very much appear together, facing off against a common enemy.

Several shots focus on her hand clutching the back of my shirt.

The headlines are, as expected, awful. "True Love from Trauma." "Pity Party for Two?" "Amanda's 'Angel' in Real Life."

I make a face.

"And then . . ." Elise pulls up a video clip from *Access Hollywood*.

It's basically a short rundown of everything covered in the articles. First, the photos from this morning, while the host explains that *Coal City Nights* is filming in Pennsylvania near Amanda's home. Then a review of Amanda's story and her connection to me, or, rather, my poster.

But when the screen returns to focus on the host, my picture is in the upper left corner with the graphic *From Poster to Poser?* stamped over it. Which I don't understand until the last few seconds of the clip.

"But the suddenness of this 'relationship' "—the overly loud host pauses to make air quotes—"and Chase Henry's troubled reputation with the media, has some questioning whether it's all a publicity stunt orchestrated by Henry's team." His voice deepens to help demonstrate the seriousness of this charge.

"Oh," his female coanchor says, placing a hand over her chest in showy empathy, "that would be terrible."

Elise clicks away as the screen fades to black.

"That guy has never liked me," I say, my mouth tight. "He's still pissed I mixed him up with that other guy, the one on *ET* or whatever." Never mind that he's actually right.

"It doesn't matter," Elise says, curling her arms around me, her phone still in her hand. "Speculation fuels the fire. We just want to make sure it's burning our way." She rises to her tiptoes and plants a kiss near my mouth.

I tense up, and it takes effort not to break out of her grasp. "How do we do that?" I ask, hoping the redirection will distract her. I feel more trapped than turned on.

But she makes an offended noise. "Seriously, Chase? Now?" She inches closer, with that sharp smile. "I'm trying to seduce you."

And you should enjoy it is the unspoken message. And a week ago, hell, two days ago, I would have been all over it. And her. She's driven and ambitious, which means she's not offended or wounded when I'm the same way. And she doesn't want a damn thing from me, relationship-wise, so I don't have to worry about messing up or letting her down.

It's a mutually beneficial non-relationship, and continuing it is probably the smartest, safest choice I could make right now.

Besides, I have no *real* reason not to. As my grandpa used to say, *If wishes were damn horses, then everybody would have them . . . or something like that.*

But Elise's hands, crawling toward my fly, feel graspy and greedy and not in the good way. Her breath is warm and sticky against my neck, and I don't want this. Not now. Not anymore.

"I know . . . it's just I'm late for a meeting." I tilt my head away from her questing mouth.

She pulls back, a frown creasing her smooth forehead. "A meeting. With who?" She sounds suspicious.

"Not that kind of meeting," I say. "It's AA." Elise is well aware of my adventures with alcoholism and what I'm doing to fight back.

"Oh." Her nose crinkles with distaste. "Really? You've been here a day."

I stay silent. She doesn't understand—she never has.

"Just get it under control," she says, pointing a finger at me.

As if it were that simple. But Elise prides herself on having few weaknesses, and addiction of any type (other than to work) is something she classifies as a character flaw rather than a disease or genetic predisposition.

"I mean it, Chase. If you get wasted and smash up a car again—"

I flinch.

"—all of this will be for nothing."

"I know."

Elise stands there for a moment, studying me with a frown, and I can practically see her weighing her options, debating whether she should push me into it because she wants to know she still can or if she should get the hell out of the way and let me deal with my mess so it doesn't become her mess.

She throws up her hands. "Fine." She disappears into the bedroom, and I keep my back turned.

When she emerges a minute later, she's dressed again, though she's wearing my shirt over her tailored pants.

"Phone?" she asks, her hand out.

With reluctance, I hand mine over.

"The plan is simple," she says, almost absently as she clicks away on my screen. "I've created a few social media accounts. You're verified and all set up. The usual suspects, Twitter, Instagram, even Facebook." She makes a disgusted face before continuing. "Anything formal is going to raise questions. It needs to be real and from you. A few tweets or pictures of you and Amanda behind the scenes. Posts about spending a quiet night in. The two of you watching movies or swimming in the pool." She looks up at me. "Shirtless would be best."

"So I'm just supposed to start snapping photos of her and posting them? That wasn't part of my deal with her." Not to mention she'd hate it. And it would change how she is around me, guaranteed. She might start to see me like the paparazzi, someone who wants a piece of her. I don't want that.

Elise waves away my concern. "Please—I saw her today. She'll do anything you ask. And if you're so worried about her precious privacy, be smart. She doesn't have to be in the photo. Just have two drinks on the table. Or 'accidentally' show her sweater on the arm of your couch when you're posting about not getting much sleep." She flicks her fingers in a careless gesture. "You know how it goes."

I shouldn't be surprised. I really shouldn't. But the fact that she's talking about intentionally starting false rumors about the sex life of a rape survivor without a second thought or concern makes me stare at her in astonishment.

"I loaded a few examples of what I'm talking about in drafts on each one of the apps, okay?" Elise holds my phone out to me, but I don't take it. It feels as though she's turned it into a spy device, a traitor in the room that will report on me. On us.

That's dumb—there is no "us," and the phone won't do anything without me. But maybe I'm not so inclined to trust myself.

Elise cocks her head to one side, her expression evaluating. "You do realize that this girl is falling for your image, the version of you that has been very carefully orchestrated by *me*. She doesn't know the real you." Her eyes narrow at me. "She hasn't seen you bottom out, over and over again. She hasn't bailed you out of jail, picked you up from the hospital, or come to get you when your car got repo'd."

"I know that," I say sharply. Too well. Though most of those things are in my past. Or at least I want them to be.

But Elise doesn't seem convinced. She points my phone at me. "We've had fun and we're good together. But don't be stupid. If you get in my way, I will burn down your world and still get what I want. Are we clear?"

"Yeah," I say through gritted teeth.

"Good." She grabs my hand and slaps my phone into it. Then she stalks toward the door. "Start tonight," she calls over her shoulder without concern for who hears her.

Damnit.

17

Amanda

The light under the unlatched door to Chase's room is a solid reassuring line of yellow.

I shift restlessly in my bed, the sheets twisting around my legs. His lights came on about forty-five minutes ago, when he got back from his meeting.

I hope he didn't hear much of my phone conversation before he left.

I roll my eyes. If one could call *that* a "conversation."

It took me the better part of an hour to calm down after talking to my family. It had been a long day and would be again tomorrow. Better to forget everything about that call, get some sleep, and face the day with a clearer state of mind. Or so I told myself.

But I'm still lying awake, all too aware of the glow of Chase's light under the door, beckoning me, and I can't figure out whether it's a lighthouse signaling danger or a beacon leading me to safety.

I shut my eyes. It's Monday night. In two days, I'll be heading home again. And that's interpreting Chase's offer of a visit for a few days as generously as possible. If he counts Sunday, I could be going home as soon as tomorrow, maybe Wednesday morning.

And I'm not sure what will happen once I'm back there, if the progress I've made will hold steady.

If it does, that would be amazing, exactly the push I was hoping for from this experience. But that's not what's keeping me awake.

For the first time since I've been home, I want something. I want *someone*. I want to be able to want again. To feel that flutter of desire and to not be afraid.

Because I like it when he touches me. *I like it when he touches me.*

My eyes snap open, and I shake my head on my pillow, repeating the words in my head, hearing the awe they contain.

The lack of fear is a minor miracle by itself. But it's more than that: he makes me feel safe enough to take a chance.

I'm sure that Dr. Knaussen would say that I'm conflating the paper version of Chase with the real thing. But I don't think so. When Chase, the real one, looks at me, it's like he sees more than just what happened to me.

He doesn't treat me like Amanda Grace, the Miracle Girl, victim, survivor, girl who should be swathed in plastic bubble wrap or a straitjacket. He's careful, yeah, but I'm a person to him, not a label.

Not to mention, unless I'm really mistaken about the events of this evening, both the almost-kiss and that lingering moment in the hallway, he might even be attracted to me.

Another minor miracle, as far as I'm concerned. Someone

who isn't interested in me as an odd form of celebrity, a freak show, or a challenge. Someone not so disturbed or disgusted by the violence in my past as to be repelled by me.

The question is, what am I going to do about it?

Maybe at some point I'll feel this same way about someone else besides Chase Henry. I hope so. But what if I miss *this* chance to take back this part of myself, to feel this way about another person, and I don't have another opportunity?

You definitely won't have another opportunity to feel this way about Chase, a small voice in my head says.

That idea—and the anticipatory loss I feel from it—is the one that pushes me to action.

My heart is pounding so hard that it makes my breath come out unevenly, but I sit up and throw back the sheets.

I pause on the edge of my bed, half-expecting the light in Chase's room to go out or for some calamity to ensue, like a fire alarm going off. Either being a sign from the universe that I need to abandon this plan of action *right now*.

But everything remains quiet and still. And his light stays on. It seems the universe is willing to give me the rope I need to trip myself up.

I stand up. My body feels weak and shaky, but a crazy frisson of excitement runs through me as I make my way over to Chase's door.

I don't know what I'm going to say, if I'll even be able to get the words out. And then, if I do, I have no idea how he'll respond. What I'm thinking isn't exactly a normal request.

Standing in front of the door, I feel my breath puff out and bounce against the surface, dampening my nose in the process.

What if I can't go through with it? What if I make it all the way through the talking and he actually turns out to be okay with it, then I freak out?

Before I can talk myself out of it, I lift my hand and rap gently against the faux-wood door.

Chase pulls the door open almost instantaneously. He must have been nearby.

But he's tall and so close suddenly, so real, I take a step back.

"Is everything okay?" he asks, his phone in his hand. He's dressed in athletic shorts and a T-shirt with the sleeves ripped out. And he's wearing glasses, narrow dark brown frames that make him look like an incredibly hot professor. The appearance of physical and intellectual prowess in combination makes my knees a little wobbly.

I swallow hard. "Oh, yeah, sorry. I didn't mean to make you . . ." I hesitate. "Glasses?"

"I wear contacts," he says. "But they bug me at night. Especially in hotels. The air is too dry."

"Oh."

His mouth quirks in a half-smile. "Is that what you wanted to—"

"I can't sleep."

Chase raises his eyebrows.

I didn't realize how suggestive that sounded until I said it aloud. It's not all that far from what I want to talk about, but I'm not there yet.

"Infomercial bingo," I blurt, my cheeks burning. "But it's not a big deal, if you're busy." I nod at the phone in his hand.

He blinks down at his phone, seeming to have forgotten he held it. "No, no, it's nothing. Come on in." He steps back to give me space to enter.

I move into the room. His script pages are on the coffee table. I've probably interrupted him preparing for tomorrow. The cowardly part of me declares that I should go, leave him to his work.

But when I turn to say that, his gaze jumps guiltily from my legs up to my face.

He's checking me out.

I'm not wearing anything particularly provocative, just sleep

shorts and a long-sleeved shirt to cover my scar. But he's looking. Not with greed, hate, or punishment in his eyes, the way
Jakes did. Nor is he staring at me like I'm a freak or inspecting
me for damage. He's looking at me the way a guy does when
he's attracted to a girl. A normal girl.

It takes serious effort not to grin giddily at the realization.

"Are you sure everything's—" Chase begins, not quite meeting my gaze.

"Yeah . . . no." I take a deep breath, summoning courage, and
sit on the far side of the couch. "I wanted to talk to you about
something, but it's kind of personal . . . embarrassing."

Sliding his phone on the coffee table, he drops onto the other
end of the couch. "Is it about what happened in the hallway?"
he asks, rubbing the back of his neck.

"Yeah, actually. Kind of," I say, surprised.

"Listen, I'm really sorry. I didn't mean to . . ." He shifts on the
sofa, like he's trying to give me more room even though there's
practically a whole cushion between us. "I didn't mean to make
you uncomfortable," he finishes, color rising in his face as he
leans forward to rest his elbows on his knees.

I frown. I have no idea what he's talking about. I was the one
to initiate contact and—

"It's kind of an involuntary reaction for guys in certain situations, but I should have—"

I clamp my hand over my mouth to stop the astonished
laugh bubbling up inside me. *Oh. That's* what he's talking
about.

At the time I was so preoccupied with my own feelings, I
hadn't been paying attention to what was happening with him.
I should have been. That would have answered my question
about whether he was attracted to me or not. But to be fair,
my experience with the early stages of that kind of thing was
limited to Chris Matheson, my date at the freshman dance
and my first kiss. He ground his hips against mine for a dance
or two and I might have felt . . . something. But that was it.

There was no lead-up with Jakes, nor was that anything I *wanted* to dwell on.

Chase scowls at me. "What?"

I shake my head, not taking my hand off my mouth. I don't trust myself not to laugh, and I don't want him to think I'm laughing at him instead of my own inexperience.

"That's not it?" he demands.

I lower my hand, but I can't stop smiling. "Well, not exactly. It's related, sort of. In a good way."

"Okay," he says. "Can you try to—"

Deep breath. Just say it. "I like you," I say, turning on the sofa to face him more fully.

"Oh." He straightens up in surprise. "I . . . like you, too. What is this about?"

I bite my lip and pull my legs up onto the cushion next to me. "I don't really know how to bring this up," I say. "It's not something that people usually talk about because it just happens. But I don't have that—" I cut myself off, with a jerk of my head.

"It's all right," he says, the traces of frustration and embarrassment gone, replaced by a compassion that makes my chest hurt. He reaches out like he might touch my knee, but stops.

I track the movement of his hand. "I'm not afraid when you touch me." The words escape in a whisper, but saying them to him changes me, frees me.

I'm close enough to see the heat flicker in his eyes, behind the cool academic frames. "Good," he says, his voice rougher than it was a moment ago.

"Actually," I say, "more than that, I like it."

He draws in a sharp breath, and his gaze is tight on me. The strength of his response gives me the courage to continue. "I'm going home in a couple of days," I say. "And I . . . I don't want to lose out. I want this part of me back, the chance to feel this way about someone else." I hesitate, needing that extra second to go for broke. "I want to feel this way about you."

"What are you asking me, Amanda?" he asks. The sound of

my name from his mouth in that taut voice makes me shiver in a good way. "Because my imagination is kind of running away with me."

I scoot closer to him on the sofa cushion, and he watches with an intensity that makes heat flood through my body.

"I . . . If you're . . . willing to let me, I want to try something," I say, my throat tight with desire and nerves.

His head moves in a single jerky motion, a rough nod.

Before I lose my courage, I lift up on my knees and, bracing one hand on the back of the couch, brush my mouth over his.

His lips are warm and soft, and that golden stubble that I first noticed yesterday is as rough as I imagined, but it feels good.

His breath flutters against me, and I can feel how still he's holding himself, letting me explore. Then he touches my cheek, his thumb moving lightly across my skin and guiding me closer.

And when he opens his mouth beneath mine, I'm lost.

18

Chase

Her lips move against mine, tentatively at first.

I tilt my head toward hers, extending the contact, in a mostly chaste kiss. Her scent surrounds me, reminding me of sunny days with the smell of the orange trees in the yard of the house next to my former condo building.

When I dare to sweep my tongue over her lower lip, just where she bit that lip earlier, she makes a soft noise of assent, somewhere between a sigh and moan that goes straight to my dick.

I clutch the cushion beneath me with one hand to keep from pulling her onto my lap. She wants to try and I want to show her, that it feels good, that someone touching you can be the best thing in the world instead of the worst. I want to be that guy.

But you're not the good guy she thinks you are, remember?

My conscience, long ignored and handicapped by alcohol and ambition, roars back in force.

I could be, though. When her tongue tangles with mine briefly and she clutches my shirt front, inching herself closer to my lap, I think maybe I can ignore the voice in my brain telling me to stop.

You'll fuck this up. She's fragile, and she deserves better. If she knew what you were up to, she wouldn't be here, asking this.

This time, I can't blow it off. There's too much at stake. And I meant what I said to Amanda: I like her. I don't want to hurt her.

"Amanda . . ." I pull back reluctantly.

She blinks at me, dazed for a moment. Then she withdraws to her side of the couch with a guarded expression. "You don't want to." Embarrassment colors her cheeks.

"I do. Believe me. It's just . . . I'm not sure it's a good idea." I shift uneasily because parts of me are very convinced this is the best idea ever.

Amanda swallows audibly. "I don't want anything from you," she says with a quick but uncertain smile that splinters my heart. "If that's what you're worried about. I mean, I do, but not like that. Seriously. No strings attached. I'm just talking about for as long as I'm here—"

"I know," I say before I can cave. Because I want to. I really want to. And then because I'm a coward, I take the easy way out. "I'm just afraid it's kind of fast," I say, studying the blank screen of the television to avoid looking at her. "You're still trying to figure out what you want, what works for you. I don't want you to regret anything." That last part, at least, is true.

Out of the corner of my eye, I see her lurch back.

When I dare to glance at her, her expression is cold, remote. "You can say no to me for any reason you want," she says. "Because you're not interested or attracted to me."

We both know that's not an issue.

"Because you don't want the hassle or you think it's creepy or messed up or gross." Her eyes are shiny with tears, but she blinks rapidly, refusing to let them fall. "Or that I am those things because of what happened."

My jaw drops. "Amanda, no," I say. "That's not—"

"But you don't get to say no *for* me," she says, pushing off the couch to stand up, fire in her gaze. "Do you understand that, Chase? I'm my own person. I have enough people telling me what I can't do, what I should and shouldn't want, whether it's too fast or long overdue. Pick any reason you want, but not that one. It's mine." She steps around the coffee table, moving rapidly for the door.

"Wait." I sit forward and reach a hand out to stop her, though I'm not sure what I can say.

But she skirts me without so much as a glance in my direction and stalks to her room, closing the door softly after her.

It would have been better if she slammed it. Anger I could deal with. But that? That was straight-up hurt and disappointment. In me.

I flop back and bang my head against the sofa. Fuck. Could that have gone any worse?

My phone gives a sharp buzz, shivering against the wood of the coffee table.

The gray bubble is easy to read from where I sit.

Elise Prescott: Waiting . . .

I can hear her impatience in the spaces between the periods. Because I haven't posted anything yet.

It's only the knowledge that I can't afford to be without a phone that keeps me from throwing it against the wall as hard as I can.

Before Amanda knocked, I was looking through the apps Elise added to my phone and the "drafts" she talked about. Elise didn't miss a trick. She actually staged photos. There was one of my running shoes on the floor, one kicked over next to the other, like I'd just taken them off, which means she went through my closet. The accompanying text: *Nuthin like a good run rite?*

Complete with deliberate misspellings. Does she seriously

think that was something I would think? Or that I would spell it that way, even if I did? I didn't go to college like she did—lots of people don't—but that wasn't the same thing as being or sounding like an idiot. People hold that shit against you.

The next one was worse. It looked like a misfire at first, focused mostly on the movie selection page on the hotel television in my living room. The text was her suggested, *Quiet nite in is da best.*

But then at the edge of the photo, on the corner of the sofa, like it's been shed casually, is Amanda's plaid shirt, the one I sent through the laundry.

The shirt is hanging in my closet. I can see the edge of it from here, still in the clear plastic protective bag from the service. Which means Elise borrowed it, set the scene, and returned it.

She really has no boundaries, no lines she won't cross. I guess I knew that before—it's one of the reasons I wanted to work with her, besides the fact that no one else would take me on—but this is the first time I've been on the receiving end of that pushiness.

And I don't like it.

However, it does seem to be working.

I drop my glasses on the coffee table and scrub my hands across my face in frustration, hating myself, Elise, Rick, everyone who will read these posts and decide I'm worthy of interest again, regardless of any possible talent.

Damnit. I don't want to do this. I want my career back, I want to do what I love, but I don't know if I want to become the person that requires me to be.

Not if it means more of this sneaky, underhanded bullshit. There's already been enough of that.

I look up and catch a blurry glimpse of my reflection in the television screen in the entertainment center—the first time I've been "on" television in a long while. My features are blurred, dark holes where my eyes should be. Haunted, empty, a shell of a person.

I don't want to be that guy. The one who, like Elise, has no boundaries, who will literally do anything. I've been there and it's not a good place to visit, let alone to live. Half of my issues with alcohol were drowning loneliness and insecurity, but the other part of it was my attempt to choke out the shame from some pretty shady decisions.

But the only way out of that—or past it—is to stop making decisions that make me feel like shit. Or at least stop making them intentionally.

That means I owe Amanda a better explanation, or at least a more honest one.

The thought of facing her, though, tightens my gut. I'm good at fighting, but I suck at confrontation when it comes to feelings. And words. And words about feelings.

Far easier to throw a punch or pretend to be someone else (and read someone else's words) than it is to open my mouth and tell an unpleasant truth.

Putting my glasses back on, I push myself up from the couch, listening for signs of movement next door.

There's nothing. Which probably isn't good. But neither is she throwing things around and yelling.

That doesn't really seem like Amanda anyway.

Then it hits me: she could be packing. Folding all her clothes and jamming them in her bag, gathering her shampoo and stuff from the bathroom. She could be leaving right now.

I wouldn't blame her, not after that showing.

The thought of opening the door to find her gone makes me feel panicky, like my last chance has slipped away. I like who I am better when she's around. So, I don't want her to go, not just like this, but in general.

I open my door and knock on hers, which is closed. No surprise there, I guess. I find myself hoping it's not locked, as that would be a true sign of how much I fucked up the last few minutes.

But there's no scrape of the deadbolt when she pulls open the door a second later.

Hey," I say with relief. The lights are on in her room, but she's still in her pajamas, not dressed and ready to walk out.

She doesn't move, doesn't say anything, just stands there in the doorway, not quite meeting my eyes.

"I thought maybe you were leaving," I blurt into the silence.

Her eyebrows shoot up. "Are you asking me to?"

"No!" I say immediately, louder than I meant to, and she jumps a little.

I shake my head, frustrated at myself. "No," I say in a calmer voice. With my hands on my hips, like I've been running some exhausting marathon, I force myself to take a deep breath. "Can I come in?"

She steps back and holds her hand out in a limp gesture of welcome.

I step into the room and turn to face her. "I want to start this conversation over."

"I'm not sure there's a point." Her tone is not cruel or cutting, just matter-of-fact.

I can feel the urge to be defensive rising in me, demanding that I throw something back in her face, something that will make it her fault instead of mine. But I clamp down on that urge, my hands clenched in fists. It's not her fault. She didn't do anything wrong. I did.

Accept responsibility for your mistakes promptly. That was kind of one of the big ones in recovery.

"I'm sorry," I say. "That's where I should have started. I'm sorry."

When I dare to look up at her, she's watching me with a cautious expression, her arms folded across her chest. "Okay."

I sit on the edge of the bed closest to the door. "I was wrong to make my answer about you instead of me. That was bullshit."

She nods slowly and moves to sit next to me, leaving several feet of bed between us. "Thanks." Her toes poke into the carpet.

"I'm not . . ." I struggle to find the right words. "I'm not good at this kind of thing, at talking about stuff."

The edges of her mouth curve up reluctantly. "I've noticed."

"Right?" I say in relief. "So, just, uh, bear with me, okay?" I slide my hand across the comforter and space between us, palm up. And after a second of hesitation, she rests her hand on mine.

I slip my fingers between hers and squeeze gently. "I want to say yes; I *really* want to say yes."

She blushes, ducking her head, her hair sliding forward to hide her face.

"But I'm not the guy you think I am. I've made mistakes, some of which you know. Others you don't," I say evenly.

"Calista," Amanda says.

I jolt. "Did Karen—"

"No," she admits. "I could just tell there was something when you guys were talking about it earlier."

I hesitate. I don't ever talk about this with anyone, but if it makes her understand what I'm trying to save her from, then maybe it's worth forcing the words out now.

"Eric, Calista, and I spent a lot of time together when the show was filming," I say slowly. "But Calista was even younger than me. She was the only one playing her character's age. Her mom was her manager, kept her separate from the rest of us. Bad influences." I shrug. "She was right about that."

Amanda says nothing, but she's listening intently.

"We kept in contact after the show ended. By the time a year or so had gone by, some of us were having trouble finding more work. Eric suggested a reunion party of sorts." I can picture him now, grinning at me on the other side of the pool table at his house. Weirdly enough, as angry as I still am, I also miss him.

"Calista was eighteen by then, and she'd fired her mom," I say.

"Awkward," Amanda says with a wince.

"Yeah. She was trying to figure out who she was outside of Skye, outside of who her mom wanted her to be." I understood that better than anybody, probably.

I take a deep breath. "Anyway, Calista came out with me that night, the night of the reunion party. She'd been on the scene more and more, but Eric's parties were . . . on the excessive side." Which was part of what made them so awesome. Nothing says you've made it more than having a friend who threw house-destroying parties on a regular basis. Or so I thought at the time.

"I don't actually know what happened that night. We got crazy wasted. The memories aren't . . ." I shake my head. "I was blackout drunk," I say flatly. "And I drove. Trying to get to another party, apparently."

Amanda sucks in a sharp breath.

"Crashed Eric's car. I woke up in the hospital with broken bones and a complete blank space where the night should be. Eric's dad covered it up, paid people off, to keep it from coming back on Eric. Eric was mostly fine, cuts and bruises. He was wearing his seat belt when we hit the guardrail, I guess. But Calista's arm was shattered. She had to have a bunch of surgeries. And the pain was bad." I swallow hard. "Bad enough that she got hooked on the pain meds. To the point of buying illegal shit to supplement."

"Chase." Amanda tightens her hand on mine.

"She's in rehab now, and her life will never be the same. Because of me." I tighten my jaw, trying to adjust to hearing the words aloud. It never gets any easier, though. "I'm sober now, but I'm still making mistakes, no matter how hard I try." I look to Amanda. "So, I meant what I said: I like you. I really don't want to see you get hurt when I fuck up. Because I will. I am. A fuck-up. Okay?"

She's quiet for a long moment. "Are you planning on making a mistake, planning to hurt me?"

"No, of course not!" I say. "But that doesn't always mean it won't—"

"Then what makes you different from anyone else?" She shifts on the bed, turning to face me.

"I don't—"

She holds her free hand up. "Just listen."

I shut my mouth.

"Let's say I leave here and find someone else who makes me feel the same way you do," she says. Her voice is careful, but I hear her doubt. "I like him, and he makes me want things I didn't think would ever be possible for me."

"Okay," I grit out. I hate this hypothetical guy already. He's probably taller than I am. Yes, it's ridiculous. But that doesn't stop the throbbing pulse of jealousy that's taken up residence in my chest next to my heart.

"What happens when that guy goes to the media and sells all the details of our relationship, the good and the bad?" She lifts her shoulder. "Actually, probably more the bad than the good since that plays better. I mean, let's face it—'Amanda Grace is so messed up!' is going to mean a bigger paycheck than 'Amanda's doing great!' "

I can feel the muscles in my jaw jumping.

"Or," she continues, "maybe this guy just realizes he can't deal with my hang-ups and he bails."

Now my hands are clenched in fists.

"Chase." With a faint smile, Amanda lifts our linked hands, showing me her fingers are turning pink from my grip. "Didn't actually happen yet."

I loosen up immediately. "Sorry."

"It doesn't even have to be anything that big or out of the ordinary. Maybe he just falls out of love with me or finds someone he likes better. Happens all the time." She tilts her head, trying to catch my eye. "My point is that you can protect me from you, if you're so determined to do that, but you can't protect me from being hurt. No one can."

This is not what I want to hear. If I stay away from her, it seems like there should be some universal agreement that she'll be fine. Otherwise, it takes the legs out of my argument.

"But I don't want to be the one to—"

Amanda shrugs. "So don't." She takes a breath. "You've made mistakes, and you're living with them. I understand. We're all doing that, to a certain extent. But please don't treat me like I'm some kind of . . . damaged relic from the *Titanic*. I'm not something to be preserved in a glass case somewhere, as a living reminder of a disaster. I'm a person. I want to live. If I can't do that, then maybe I'm better off hiding in my closet." She laughs bitterly.

The mention of the closet catches my attention, and I look up. "What is that about? The closet thing. I heard you talking about it."

Her gaze drops to the floor. "I do okay most days now. But on bad days, in really bad moments," she says carefully, "sometimes I have to work hard not to retreat to the closet." An ugly red floods her face at the admission.

And in spite of that, she's here, and she's trying. I want to stare at her in awe, but that will, I know, only make her self-conscious.

I clear my throat and bump her arm with mine. "You're the bravest person I know."

Her hand still in mine, she shifts closer to me, resting her head against my shoulder. "Doesn't mean I'm not scared. I hate it; I wish I wasn't. But I am."

"Still the bravest person I know," I say, my voice thick with emotion. I press my mouth to the top of her head, her warm soft hair.

Her throat works audibly. "Thanks," she says after a moment. "And you're not a fuck-up," she adds.

I give a tired laugh. "Wait till you know me better."

"No," she says, her voice gaining ferocity. "By definition, a fuck-up doesn't care, somebody who's given up. That's not you."

She pulls away from my shoulder, sitting up straight. "I think you're just scared." ·

I look at her sharply. "Maybe," I allow after a moment. "But if so, it's with good reason." The litany of my failures is burned into my brain from frequent repetition, and it's not short.

"Being scared isn't a bad thing," she says, reaching a hand toward my face. Her dark eyes are intense, but her fingertips are light against the corner of my mouth, the lines I've noticed cropping up by the sides of my eyes, and the edge of my eyebrow—the one with the scar. All my flaws.

"Means you're just like the rest of us." Her mouth quirks in a smile. "But you have to decide if you're going to let it stop you. Other people may give you chances, but that doesn't matter if you won't let yourself take them."

My eyes are burning in spite of myself. No one has been this forgiving, probably because I've never deserved it.

Amanda starts to pull her hand away, but I catch it and press an open-mouthed kiss against her palm. And then, watching to gauge her reaction, I move down to her wrist, against the line of the scar there. Kissing it, not to make it better, but so she knows she doesn't have to hide it from me.

She sucks in a breath, and I have the distinct pleasure of watching her eyes change, the pupils expand to deep pools.

"You have to tell me. You have to talk to me. If it's going too fast or a direction you don't like," I whisper to her.

"Yes." She nods quickly, a tremor running through her, but I'm shaking as hard as she is.

I let go of her hands to frame her face, which is small and fine-boned beneath my fingertips. Her breath moves against my skin before I lean in and brush my mouth against hers, my fingers tangling in her hair.

Her lips part, a soft sound escaping.

That's an invitation I can't ignore. I lick the soft line of her lower lip, just on the inside of her mouth.

She moans, and I feel the vibration as much as hear the noise. I deepen the kiss, sweeping my tongue over hers, and she clutches at my arms, her hands warm against my bare skin.

I freeze for a second, not sure.

"It's okay," she says against my mouth, panting. "I just wanted to touch."

God. "Yeah, okay," I say, in a strangled voice.

Her hands skim over my biceps. "That's . . . yeah." Her touch has rendered me basically incoherent, and she knows it, by the mischievous look in her eye when she smiles at me.

Then she presses her mouth to mine again, her tongue sliding hesitantly between my lips, and I'm the one groaning now.

Pulling my hands from her hair, I move them to her hips and tug her closer, until she's half in my lap, and then she throws her leg over both of mine.

Her heat is radiating against my hip, and it's hard not to rock against her. To pull her fully on top of me until we're lined up and rubbing against each other. Those tiny boxer sleep shorts she's wearing wouldn't be much between us and neither are my shorts.

It's instinct and that desire to feel her moving against me that has me shifting, turning toward her and pulling us up higher on the bed.

The motion settles me between her legs and brings her breasts against my chest. She wraps her arms around my neck, pulling me tighter.

I press my hands against the bed to support my weight, but when I start to lower my arms to bring us both to the mattress, she stiffens suddenly and pushes her hands against my chest. "No. Wait."

Breathless, I pull back.

She pushes herself upright and away from me, shoving her hair back, which is messy from my hands in it.

"Too much, too fast," I say. "I'm sor—"

"Don't," she says quickly, her breathing still uneven. "Don't apologize. Please." Her eyes beg me not to make a big deal out of it. "You didn't do anything wrong. It's just me." She gives a rueful eye roll. "It's like there's a level in my head, you know, with the bubble?"

I know what she's talking about; my grandfather had one in his wood workshop in the barn.

"Only in my head, the center is green, and the bubble tipped from the green to red. I'm not sure I can do . . . that. You on top of me." She flinches.

"Maybe that's enough for tonight," I say, backing toward the edge of the bed.

"Maybe," Amanda admits reluctantly. But she won't look at me, her gaze focused at some undefined point on the dresser instead. "I was just hoping . . ."

Her sadness and disappointment pull at me. "Hey," I say gently. I move to kneel on the floor in front of the dresser, so she'll look at me. "This kind of stuff is going to take time, figuring out what you like. What's okay for you."

She opens her mouth to object.

"Not just for you, either," I add. "Everyone." I hesitate, not sure how much she wants to hear, but oh, what the hell.

"I've been with a few girls, women," I begin.

"A few?" Amanda smirks.

I hold my hands up. "I'm not trying to brag here, just make a point," I say. "None of them have been exactly the same, the things they liked, the things they didn't. It's just more complicated for you is all."

She nods, still looking too solemn and down on herself.

"But I could brag, if I wanted," I say, more to get her reaction than anything.

Amanda scowls at me.

I hold her gaze steadily. "I promise you, before we're done, you're going to know exactly what you love, exactly what you want. And you'll be asking me for it."

Her mouth opens slightly, and heat flickers in her gaze again, pushing back the fear and discouragement.

Mission accomplished.

"Okay?" I ask, standing up.

"Yeah," she says, watching me move with a hunger that sends pride streaking through me.

"I'll see you in the morning," I say, turning toward the door. I'm already looking forward to it, to more time with her. My head is full of Amanda—her courage, how she smiles at me, the calm, reasoned way she talks, and that soft noise she made when I kissed her and how I might get her to do that again. All of that should probably scare the hell out of me, but it doesn't.

"Chase?"

I glance back at her.

"Thanks," she says with a shy smile.

And then, I remember all that I've done to use her and her name. All that I'm still doing, technically, and guilt slams into me hard.

"Don't. I'm not a saint, and this isn't an act of charity." It comes out sounding harsher than I mean it to, so I try to smile. "I like you, remember?"

She plays with the edge of the comforter, and I expect her to object but she just nods.

Once I'm back in my room, I discover my phone has vibrated halfway across the coffee table, thanks to the texts from Elise that fill the screen. At a glance, each one is angrier and pushier than the last.

But her plan is already working, as she has so frequently pointed out. And with the email from Rick in my inbox, I know she's right.

It doesn't have to go any further. Who cares if people think Amanda and I are made up? It's probably better, given what just happened, if they do.

And if Elise gets pissed, what can she really do? She'll find a way to take it out on me, I'm sure. But she won't go public with what we did because that would only hurt her career. Make her look bad, too. Worse, maybe, even than me. I was just the pretty face following her orders, or that's how it'll seem anyway. Because that's always what people think of me, and she knows it.

I tap my phone against my palm, thinking of Amanda and that smile. The kind of guy she thinks I am. The person I want to be. After a second of hesitation, I click on the latest text from Elise and without reading it, I type, *No, I'm done. We're done.*

Then I delete all the apps and Elise's ridiculous drafts before I can second-guess myself, and I put in a call to the front desk to have new room keys sent up.

For a moment, it's like I'm free-falling with the ground rushing up at me. But the weight on my shoulders is gone.

19

Amanda

"Amanda?" Chase's voice intrudes, softer than normal.

I hear him, but I can't see him. I'm in the middle of a crowd, and I'm lost or I've lost someone. I'm not sure which. And it doesn't seem to matter against the rising tide of panic in my gut. People are shoving against me, their elbows in my sides, their shoulders pressed in my face, until I feel like I can't breathe.

I rise up on my tiptoes, looking for him. But all the faces around me keep blurring together, making it impossible to tell who's who. Choking back terror, I turn . . .

"Amanda?" Chase asks again. "You awake?"

I open my mouth to call his name, but before I can speak, there's the lurch and spin of a new reality settling into place.

Suddenly I'm awake in the dark, lying down, staring up at the ceiling. My body aches with the heaviness of sleep, both the recent exit from it and the lack of enough.

"Amanda?"

It's a familiar scenario. Chase waking me up after one of Jakes's visits, wanting to talk, trying to convince me to fight, to keep hoping.

But no, something is different. The pillow behind me smells strongly of a pleasant detergent, and . . . Jakes is dead. I'm not in the basement. Not anymore. Never again.

Struggling to orient myself, I blink a few times and my hand automatically moves to my wrist, confirming the presence of the scar, before I recognize that I'm in a hotel. In a big double bed, lying on crisp white sheets.

You're okay. The confirmation rushes relief over me in a wave.

The Chase Henry talking to me is real, the one staying next door, not residing in my head. The same one who made a stunning and still unbelievable promise to me last night, a promise that kept me awake for hours from equal parts anticipation and anxiety.

He's in the doorway to his room, backlit into shadow.

"Chase?" I ask, my voice croaky.

"I'm sorry; I knocked. A few times," he says, hovering behind the door.

I sit up and fumble to turn on the bedside lamp. Only the faintest hint of gray light emerges from beneath the curtains. "What's wrong? What time is it? I . . ." I squint at him. "What are you wearing?"

He grins at me from beneath a baseball hat and aviators. "Standard celebrity disguise."

I grab the glass I filled with water before bed and take a swallow. My throat is dry from the nightmare or dream, whatever it was.

"I don't think you're disguising much," I point out. If anything, he's calling attention to the fact that he's trying to hide, and besides which, that jawline is kind of unmistakable. Strong, a little stubbly at the moment, and kind of delicious, like maybe you want to bite it a little. Not hard, just a nibble . . .

Or maybe that's just me.

Chase shrugs, taking off his sunglasses and hooking them in the collar of his gray T-shirt. "Doesn't matter. It's mostly a precaution. We're going out the kitchen exit anyway." He's filled with an excited energy I've never seen from him before. Though I would never have described him as slow, exactly—weighed down, maybe—there's a spark to him this morning, a new urgency that I don't . . .

Crap. "Did I oversleep?" I shove my hair out of my face and throw back the covers, scrambling out of bed and barely noticing his appreciative look in my haste.

"Go to the set without me," I say, searching for my jeans. They have to be around here somewhere. "You can't be late." I finally locate my jeans on the back of the rolling leather chair and grab them.

"No, no." Chase holds his hands up in a placating gesture. "It's still early. Do you have anything to cover your hair?"

"My fleece has a hood," I say, confused. "What is this about?" I'm never my best in the mornings, but that is especially true after two successive nights with little sleep.

"It's a surprise," he says, rocking back on his heels with a very self-satisfied grin.

I stop, with one leg in my jeans. "You do realize why that might not be reassuring to someone like me."

He frowns. "It's a good surprise," he offers.

"Uh-huh," I say, unconvinced. "Good" is a matter of opinion.

"Do you like bagels?" he asks.

"What?" I blink at him, not sure if this conversation is really this all over the place or if it's just me. "Yeah, I guess."

"Good. Come on." He waves me forward. "I have food."

I fold my arms over my chest. "No," I say flatly. I'm a ridiculous figure, I'm sure, with bedhead, sleep lines on my face, and, knowing my luck, that white crusty stuff from toothpaste dried on my lips. So attractive, he'll be revoking any and all promises made in my direction. "Not until you tell me what's going on."

Chase pauses. "You trust me with your body but not in general." It's not a critical statement, but a statement nonetheless. Like he's still trying to figure me out.

My face burns like it's on fire, and I'm not sure whether it's the idea of trusting him with my body, which sends another surge of heat through me, or being caught in the loophole I was kind of hoping he wouldn't notice.

"It's outside, no one knows we're going, we'll have it entirely to ourselves," he adds, his eyes softening.

From anyone else that might have sounded like a threat of the no-one-can-hear-you-scream variety, but it's the reassurance I need. Fewer people means fewer variables to try to predict, fewer surprises of the negative variety. Plus, I want to trust him, which makes it easier.

"Okay," I say slowly. "Do I have time to actually get dressed? As in, not wearing my pajamas under my clothes?"

He nods. "Yeah, we have a few minutes before the cab gets here. Can't take the car or the photographers will follow us."

"But why?" I can't be more coherent than that.

Fortunately, he seems to understand what I'm asking. "I'm working this whole week. If we want any time together, we have to be creative with timing."

"You know you don't have to . . ." I pause, flustered. He said he liked me last night, but this is different. I don't want him pretending to feel more than he does.

"I mean, the courting"—I roll my eyes at myself and the old-fashioned word that popped out of my mouth—"that part is not what I was asking for last night." I squirm inwardly at the mention of the previous evening. My bravery at the time now feels like brazen stupidity.

Chase cocks his head to the side, his eyebrows rising. "So maybe you should ask for more."

"I don't—"

"Amanda, it'll be fun. And I want to have fun with you, if that's okay," he says patiently.

I open my mouth.

He holds up his hands in surrender. "If you need a reason to justify it, then think about it this way: spending time together helps us get more comfortable with each other." He gives me a heated look that suggests he would like to be very, very comfortable with me. I can almost feel his hands on my skin again, and it sends an instant bolt of lust through me.

With that, he leaves my room, closing the door after him.

I kick my one leg out of my jeans and stand there for a second, just trying to collect myself.

Then, scrubbing my hands over my face, I head to the bathroom.

Five minutes later, after I'm dressed and my teeth are brushed, I stick my head in his room and find he's busy packing up food from a room service tray on his dining table.

When he sees me, he holds out a plastic-wrapped bagel, a tiny cup of cream cheese, and a plastic knife. "To go," he says.

I step deeper into the room and take them, stuffing the sealed cream cheese and knife in the pocket of my fleece and holding on to the bagel, for lack of anywhere else to put it. It's too big for my other pocket.

"You know this is alarming," I say in a grumpy voice, picking at the edge of the plastic wrap. I think the bagel is a blueberry one. He was paying attention at dinner last night.

When he doesn't respond, I look up to see him stopped in the process of stuffing napkins in his coat pocket, wearing a stricken expression.

"I mean," I say quickly, "you're entirely too peppy for oh-God-thirty in the morning."

He relaxes. "Morning person," he says with an unapologetic smile. "Rancher DNA, I guess."

I grunt in response.

He wraps my free hand around a paper to-go cup of coffee.

"Do you need cream or sugar? Or ketchup?" He waggles the packet at me. "I wanted to be prepared."

I glare at him. "I wish I knew *what* you're prepared for."

"You," he says simply, and warmth spreads through my chest. "But beyond that, you'll have to see."

He grabs his cup of coffee and then scoops up his key card and phone, putting them both in the pocket of his jeans.

"Ready?" he asks, putting his sunglasses on and gesturing for me to lead the way to the hall door.

"I don't know, am I?" I ask pointedly. I'm not scared, exactly, but I can feel that nervous ball of tension in my stomach, the one that always forms when I'm not sure what's going to happen.

He pauses. "Is this really okay, Amanda?"

I swallow the impulse to answer automatically and make myself really think about it. Right now, it's just the sensation of mild anxiety. The potential for panic is there—it's always there—but it's actually manageable right now. "Yeah," I say, a little surprised.

Chase grins at me. "Good." Then he reaches around me and pulls open the door with his free hand, which is good because I don't have one to spare. "Are you always this grumpy in the morning?" he teases.

I stick my tongue out at him. "Only when someone wakes me from a dead sleep to be annoyingly vague," I say.

"Noted."

Out in the hall, it's a little brighter, the window at the far end letting in the dull gray pre-dawn light.

But there's a strange smoky smell, covering the scent of new carpet and cleaning supplies that I've come to expect over the last day and a half.

I wrinkle my nose. It's not cigarettes, which is good, because that smell sends me over the edge sometimes, but it's definitely something charred. And it's close. I turn, looking for the source.

As Chase exits behind me, pulling the door closed, I find what I'm looking for.

A blackened square of something rests on the carpeting in front of his door, between Chase and me. I must have narrowly avoided stepping on it when I walked out.

I point at it. "What is that? Did room service really screw up your toast?"

He frowns, nudging it with the edge of his boot to flip it over, then kneeling down for a closer look. "No," he says flatly. "It's a picture. What's left of one, anyway."

When I bend down to see for myself, I pick out my own features first, then his, though there's not much left of either. It has to be from yesterday.

That is seriously creepy. I shiver. "Someone wanted you to see this?"

He sighs and stands. "Yeah. Elise is big on symbols. I burned her, she . . ." He lifts his shoulders. "You get the idea."

"Elise. The publicist you fired?" I ask.

"Yeah." He steps over the burned picture and leads the way down the hall toward the service elevators.

I follow, taking an extra step to stay at his side. "She's still hanging around?" I ask. "That's kind of stalker-y, isn't it?"

"You'd think," he says grimly.

I wait for him to expand on that, but he's silent as we take the elevator down. It's hard to read his expression behind his sunglasses, but his enthusiastic spark seems to have dimmed slightly.

Oookay, definitely something strange there, but considering the end of their relationship likely consisted of a personal element as well, maybe it's not that weird.

I mean, probably not any weirder than burning pictures of them together or driving by his house at night or any of the other slightly crazy ex behaviors you hear about on *Jerry Springer*, right? As usual, my experience is limited to what I've witnessed thirdhand.

And if Chase isn't worried, or at least not talking about calling the police, then it must not be that big of a deal.

Besides which, it's not really my business. He's *not* my boyfriend.

The reminder of that grates unexpectedly, surprising me. I don't want that from him. I just explained that to him, and I meant it, too.

But . . .

It's too early to be thinking about this stuff. I push thoughts of Chase, his ex, and her weirdo behavior out of mind and concentrate on keeping my worry about where we're going and why in check.

True to Chase's word, a cab is waiting for us at the back entrance of the hotel.

The ball of tension in my stomach grows bigger, reaching out tentacles into my arms and legs and dragging them into slow motion as we exit the hotel into the parking lot, where the taxi waits.

"Come on," Chase says. He opens the back door of the cab, but seeing my hesitation, slides in first.

I follow him, and the driver bobs his head at me in greeting as I close the door. He looks normal. No hint of sociopathy in his wrinkled face. Not that that is so easy to see, as I know too well.

Chase's leg brushes against mine as we turn out of the parking lot onto the street, and I find I'm distracted, at least temporarily, by the feel of him against me, and as ridiculous as it sounds, the way his legs look in his faded jeans.

He's toned beneath the velvety-looking fabric. No skinny chicken legs for him. Does he lift weights? Go running? Definitely something because I saw workout clothes yesterday.

The noticeable cut of his thigh muscle beneath the denim sends a greedy surge of desire through me. I kind of want to run my hand over it.

Chase takes my coffee and tips his head toward the wrapped bagel I'm still clutching tightly in my now sweaty hand.

"You should eat," he says. "We won't have time once we're there."

"Wherever there is," I say, in one last attempt to elicit details. But he just nods.

Gah.

I do my best in the moving vehicle, juggling the open bagel, the cream cheese, and the plastic knife.

But the blueberry bagel sticks in my throat, despite my clumsy slathering of topping, and I'm struggling to swallow.

Chase takes the plastic knife from me and gives me back my coffee.

But as I take a sip, I watch him, momentarily stumped by the messy utensil and the lack of a place to discard it. A small flaw in his otherwise perfectly thought-out plan.

He looks around for a second, as if searching for a handy receptacle that he somehow previously missed. Then he shrugs and sticks the knife in his mouth to clean the cream cheese from both sides before sticking the knife in his pocket.

I choke on a laugh.

"I am resourceful, if nothing else," he says with a grin as he wipes the corner of his mouth.

After about ten minutes, the cab slows on a nondescript patch of road. I lean away from Chase to look outside for something, anything, as a clue to our final destination. In the patch of woods to my right, a brown peak pokes out sharply above the rapidly changing colors of the tree line.

A mountain? But it's painted brown, like an oversized science-project volcano made of papier-mâché.

The cab makes a turn onto a gravel drive toward the "mountain." A metal gate, the kind found at parks and cemeteries, stretches across the drive, but half of it has been left open. There's an eerie, abandoned air to the area.

I sit up, tense, on the edge of the seat.

The cab bounces over potholes and crunches over fallen leaves until the driveway expands into a parking area. And beyond that, a familiar setup: an open area spotted with small patches of fake green grass that looks almost black in the pale early morning.

It's a miniature golf course.

But dark shadowy figures and shapes crouch over the Astro-turf squares, turning it into a nightmarish landscape.

Um, hell no.

I look to Chase for explanation as the cab pulls to a stop, but he just shrugs with a smile.

Then the course lights snap on, along with brightly colored bulbs strung on lines around the perimeter of the course, and the space is transformed from creepy abandoned playground to a festival-like atmosphere.

The course appears to be a mix of fairy tale and nursery rhyme characters and settings. The mountain I saw from the road is decked out as the mine from *Snow White,* with pick-axes drawn on the side of the mountain, each bearing a Dwarf's name.

A giant red boot dominates the center of the course. The Old Woman Who Lived in a Shoe, maybe?

It's tattered around the edges—a chunk of the boot has broken off to reveal the white concrete beneath, and the mountain appears to be streaked from sun discoloration or a bad paint job—but the effect is charming. Like a tiny forgotten town tucked away as a secret but only for those who deserve to find it. Something out of a fairy tale itself.

Tucking his sunglasses into the neck of his shirt, Chase slides out of the cab, and I climb out after him. My fear is receding under the weight of curiosity.

"It's closed for the season, so none of the water features are on," Chase says. "But we have it to ourselves." He frowns at my fleece jacket. "You're not too cold, right?"

"No, I'm fine," I say, looking around me in amazement. Now that I'm out of the cab, I can see a bridge over an empty basin painted blue that's likely meant to represent a river. A shiny green troll—it looks more like a Martian—crouches beneath the bridge with a greedy expression. A dark line divides his head from his body, probably where the water would normally hit.

Beyond that are a small gingerbread house with old-fashioned Christmas tree lights playing the role of candies to lure Hansel and Gretel and a "tower" that's only a little taller than me with a tattered rope braid of "hair" hanging from a window at the top.

A kid, probably only a few years younger than me, wanders over from somewhere with a huge yawn to stand by the first hole, two metal putters in hand. He nods at us in acknowledgment but, other than that, looks utterly bored and half asleep.

"How did you do this?" I ask Chase, unable to keep the delight off my face.

He shrugs. "Max is from Wescott. They're excited to be the location for a movie and involved in any way with the production. Emily made a few calls."

"Emily the production assistant who showed us around yesterday," I say. The one who wanted so badly for me to leave that I think she would have carried me out, piggyback style, if required.

He grins at me. "She called late last night to ask if I needed anything. So I told her what I wanted."

I couldn't help it; I laughed. "I bet this is not what she was thinking." But once he asked, it would have been tough for her to find a gracious way out without admitting why she truly called.

"Probably not," Chase agrees with a wicked smile. "But she did it."

And would hate me so much more for it. Oh, well.

"This is okay?" he asks turning toward me, hesitation in his voice. "I wanted to do something away from the movie, something outside."

Because you haven't had much of that lately, is the unspoken thought.

And he's right.

It strikes me, then, that his excitement this morning was to share this with me. All because . . . I let him?

Who messed him up so badly that a little kindness and forgiveness went so far in his currency?

"Yeah," I say softly, moving to thread my arm through his. "It's awesome. Thank you."

"Good." His pleased smile is something to behold; it makes me want to do crazy things to see it again.

Chase leads the way to the kid and collects our clubs and balls, along with the scorecard and requisite tiny pencil, which he stuffs in his coat pocket.

"We've got half an hour to get in nine holes," he says, offering me a club and my choice of either a green or blue ball. I take the green one. "Think you can keep up?" he asks with a challenge in his voice.

Ha. Guess he is right that we could certainly know each other better.

"I don't know," I say, doing my best to inject doubt into my tone. "I'll do my best."

20

Chase

"You're a fucking ringer," I say in disbelief, as Amanda's ball clunks off the giant's heel, spins into the green-painted metal pipe presumably meant to represent a bean stalk, and then bounces neatly into the hole.

We're on the sixth hole, and she's under par. Well under it. My score is almost double hers.

Amanda laughs and steps onto the concrete curb bordering the putting green. "Nope, just lots of practice."

"How is that?" I ask, glancing at her and then back down to line up my shot. They give you three holes in the little plastic mat at the entrance to serve as tees. Why? Doesn't that make it unnecessarily complicated? Real golf is nothing like this.

She shrugs, walking on the curb as if it's a balance beam. "My dad is one of four brothers. But he has three daughters and five nieces. I don't think he knew what to do with us. So he took us miniature golfing and bowling—"

I swing and my shot ricochets between the giant's feet and then rolls back out at me. "Damnit," I mutter.

"I can also play poker, change a flat tire, and fix a leaky shower head." She hops off the curb and makes her way past the giant and the bean stalk toward me.

I raise my eyebrows.

"Not my favorite things to do," she admits. "But I felt bad for my dad. He was always outnumbered. And Liza approached everything like her entire future depended on getting it right on the first try. You should have seen her trying to line up the plumber's tape." She rolls her eyes. "Super-stressful for all involved. Mia was, still is, in her own little world." Her mouth curves into a wry smile, and she tucks a loose strand of hair behind her ear. "That left me."

Her smile fades slowly. "Until I was . . . gone. Now he doesn't seem to know what to do with me." She gives a forced laugh, rolling her club between her palms.

"I'm sorry," I say, fully feeling the inadequacy of those words but having nothing else to offer.

She lifts a shoulder in a stiff shrug. "It's okay."

Except it clearly isn't.

Amanda leans her putter against the score stand and then moves in front of me. "All right, so here's the deal: you're swinging from your arms."

I stare at her. "Yeah, that's kind of how it works."

"No, you need to use your shoulders. Stiffen at the elbow, like you don't have any joints from the shoulder down." Her hands are light on me as she makes adjustments.

The sky behind the fake mountain is orange with the impending sunrise, and the light sets the red in her hair on fire. She's beautiful. And her forehead is wrinkled with concentration, which is fucking adorable.

I work on maintaining the new stance she's given me. "Why do you think that is?" I ask, taking a couple of practice swings when she steps back. It feels weird not to bend my arms. But I can't do much worse this way than I've done on my own. "Your dad, I mean."

"I don't know," she says, reclaiming her club and resting it over her shoulder, like a baseball bat. "It wasn't like that at first. Everyone was so excited I was alive." Her mouth pinches in. "But it didn't even feel real to me. You know, when you've imagined something so many times—" She cuts herself off.

I look up from where I'm attempting to line up my shot again. "No, I get it." I spent my first couple years in L.A. imagining a triumphant return home to Tillman after my Emmy win or my big payday as a lead in a box-office hit.

Yeah, well. Everyone defines success differently, and as it turns out, no one else in Hollywood agreed with my definition.

By the time I realized I had peaked—surprisingly, there is no "this is as good as it gets" banner strung ceremoniously across your doorway, just people making promises about even better things in the future that never come to fruition—my life was declining so fast and so furiously that there was no way I could go home for anything resembling a victory lap.

"I think he's angry with me," Amanda says quietly. "For not being smarter, faster, fighting harder."

I step out of position, toward her, the denial immediately leaping to my tongue. But I hold it back. She won't believe me. Because she blames herself, she assumes everyone else does, too.

Instead, I make myself return to the tee area. "No," I say. "I bet he blames himself."

She makes a skeptical noise.

"Think about it. His job was to protect you, keep you safe, and that didn't happen." I shrug. "If it was me, I'd feel like I failed my kid." And kept failing her by not being able to deal with it and face her. "He probably feels guilty for messing up your life."

"Yeah? He has a hell of a way of showing it," she says, but her tone is thoughtful. She watches my ball slowly putter its way past the giant's feet without trouble. "Good job." She steps toward me, her hand out for a high five.

But I ignore it and lean in to kiss her.

Her lips are cool, but her mouth is warm and vaguely coffee flavored. With my free hand, I tug on the front of her fleece, pulling her closer. Her fingers are cold against my skin when she rests her hand at the back of my neck. When her tongue slides boldly into my mouth, I can't stop a groan from escaping.

I catch her lower lip gently between my teeth, and she makes that soft gasping sound that goes straight to my head. I want to hear that noise when I'm inside her.

Moving from the corner of her mouth, along her jawline, I leave open-mouthed kisses, and her hand clutches tighter at me. "We could get out of here," I murmur against her skin, soft and scented with the hotel soap.

Amanda laughs, a bit unsteadily, and pushes me away. "We're in the middle of something here." But her eyes are bright, her cheeks flushed with the cold and want.

"We could definitely be in the middle of something else," I offer.

"No way—you're not getting off that easily," she says, tipping her club handle toward me.

I smirk. "Really?"

She blushes. "I mean the golf game. The one you're currently losing," she says pointedly. "Besides, this was your idea."

"You know I occasionally have terrible ideas, right?" I ask.

She sticks her tongue out at me.

I heave an exaggerated sigh. "Fine."

"What about your parents?" she asks as we make our way around the giant, which is pretty much just a pair of legs and the lower part of a torso, to the back half of the hole so I can finish.

The question catches me off guard, which is stupid because

I should have been expecting it. It's a logical progression from talking about her family.

"Not much time for mini-golfing," I say. My ball has stopped about three feet from the hole, but there's a weird outcropping of "beans," stones painted green, that might get in the way.

"Elbows," she reminds me, resuming her perch on the curb.

For a second, I think she's going to let me get away without answering. But then as I straighten my arms, she says, "So you trust me with your body but not in general."

I glance at her sharply and yes, she's teasing, but there's a level of seriousness in her expression as well. Her personal life is, by circumstance, far more exposed than mine. Which means I have her at a disadvantage.

"I don't know," I say. "I haven't talked to my mom since I was eight." I look up from the Astroturf to Amanda. "She left. She's an artist in Sedona, last I heard. Silversmith, I think, or something like that. She makes jewelry and metal sculptures and stuff."

Amanda frowns at me. "But you said your brother—"

"He's my half-brother. My dad remarried when I was ten. Layla. She's cool." She tried. I had to give her that. But I was miserable and my dad was determined to ignore it, which only made the environment at home that much worse. Heavy with poison, resentment, and unspoken words.

I knock the ball toward the hole with a clumsy move that's more bump than swing. But it goes in, giving me the best score I've gotten all game.

I retrieve the balls from the hole.

"What about your dad?" she asks, stepping forward to take the pencil and scorecard from my pocket and writing down my new number.

My jaw tightens. "Do we have to talk about him?"

She looks up, startled.

"What I did . . . it's not something I'm proud of," I say, trying to explain, but the words come out sounding clenched.

Her expression softens. "No," she says. "We don't have to." She tucks the pencil and card into her jacket pocket.

But now that the topic is hanging out there, I can feel it pressing down on me.

As we follow the sidewalk to the tower, the one with the weird rope dangling from it—*Oh. Rapunzel. I get it.*—I feel the words gathering at the back of my throat, pushing forward.

"La Estrella, that's our ranch, has been in my family for a long time," I say. "My great-great-grandfather came from Poland. Learned English, moved to Texas from New York, and bought land on the cheap. Or won it in a poker game, depending on who you talk to." I shrug, my mouth curving up at the memory of my grandfather detailing exactly how that supposedly happened—it involved a hot blonde and an extra ace of hearts, according to him. The story got more and more outrageous every time he told it.

Amanda stops at the tee, listening to me, her club forgotten in her hand.

I shift uncomfortably. Having her attention on me while I'm talking about this is harder than I'd thought.

Handing Amanda her ball, I nod for her to go ahead. "Don't stop. We're burning daylight now."

She hesitates.

"Please?" I ask.

With a look of sudden comprehension, she takes the ball and lines it up on the tee. "Keep going," she says.

"It's what the Mroczeks do. We ranch. Every generation," I say. "'We're raising the food that feeds America.'" Hearing my dad's words—the ones he recited over and over again, then shouted at me—come out of my mouth gives a weird sense of déjà vu.

"So what happened?" she asks, her club connecting with the ball, the soft hollow sound loud in the silence.

"I left," I say flatly. "The night I graduated from high school. Took what little money I had and went to crash on the couch of a friend of a friend in L.A."

"But what—"

"I left even though they needed me, my dad, my grandpa. Aidan was just a little kid. The drought was killing us, and we couldn't afford the help we needed. They were talking about selling off land, which was technically more my problem than theirs, because I was 'the future.' But I didn't care."

She glances back at me, and I smile tightly. "I told you, I'm a selfish asshole. I did what I wanted—fuck everyone else. If the ranch failed . . ." I shake my head. "I had to get out of there. I couldn't breathe." I search for the words to explain. "La Estrella . . . it's not just the family business, it's your whole life. No extracurriculars, no late nights out because you have to be up early the next morning. Football might have been okay because, hell, it's Texas, but forget acting in plays or musicals, the rehearsals, the performances."

You expect someone else to pick up your slack because you want to sing and dance around in a pair of tights? You can do that here.

That's what my dad said when I told him I got the lead in *Our Town* my junior year. Never mind that acting was the only time I ever felt like I was in the right place, the only time I ever felt like I had found a home. His disdain for anything in the arts was corrosive.

"You were, what, eighteen?" Amanda asks, pulling me out of the memory. Her sympathetic frown eases something tight inside me.

"Yeah, but that doesn't matter," I say, waggling my finger at her as I move to set up my shot. " 'Every Mroczek son knows his responsibility from the time he's able to walk to the barn.' " That's another Dad-ism, and this one almost makes me gag. I can hear myself saying it to another kid. Maybe even to Aidan, and I just can't do it, couldn't do it.

"You didn't ask to be born into that life, that responsibility, though," Amanda says.

I'm struck by what a difference it must be, raised by someone for whom work is a job, maybe one you're passionate about, but not a family heritage.

"I tried that argument, believe me," I say. "It didn't work. Then I told him I thought I would die if I had to stay there, which apparently was what my mom said when she left." I grimace. "That didn't help." I steady the club and start to swing.

"Elbows," she says quietly.

I stop mid-swing and make the correction. "And the fact that I wanted to move to Hollywood and be an actor . . . now that really pissed him off."

"Because of your mom? Because she's an artist?" Amanda asks.

"Maybe. He never said. Duty, responsibility, loyalty—those are the only things worth anything, according to him. That and hard work, not playing around with make-believe and relying on your looks to get by."

"Ouch," she murmurs.

"Yeah." I hit the ball harder than I should have, and it thunks into the side of the tower instead of the tunnel through it, then slowly rolls down the pity ramp to the lower part of the green, to join Amanda's.

"Plus, as he liked to point out every time we fought about it, it wasn't like I was going to be doing Shakespeare or *Schindler's List*," I say, bitter and tired, even after all these years. And who knows, maybe he had a point back then and now. What did I have to show for the last few years but a series of fuck-ups? A good start followed by a mess, mostly of my own making.

Amanda winces. "You look like your mom?" she asks, looping her arm through mine as we walk down.

I hesitate, surprised by the question. "Yeah. I guess. People used to say that."

She nods thoughtfully, her cheek rubbing against my sleeve.

"You know, the stupid thing is, I could see my dad hated it, the choices he made," I say, squeezing the club in my hand so hard I can feel the tattered rubber grip digging into my palm. "He hated being on the ranch, hated that my mom left because she didn't want to be a rancher's wife. But he wouldn't do anything about it, and he wouldn't let me do anything about it either."

"What about your grandpa?" she asks, striking with unerring accuracy to the broken heart of the matter.

I clear my throat, trying to dislodge the growing lump. "He was the only one who supported me. When I was in high school, he told my dad to let me act, to be in the plays." I smile, remembering him arriving at the auditorium in his sagging bolo tie, program in hand, and bragging on me to anyone sitting near him.

My smile fades, though, as I recall the rest. "To get it out of my system, he told me later." The betrayal stings as harshly now as it did then. "I didn't find out about that part until we were all fighting that last night. Then he, uh, died. A few years ago, I guess. Layla sent me his obituary. It was right when everything was going to shit. I was . . . not good." I swallow hard. "Aidan was listed as his only grandson."

Amanda makes a sympathetic noise, pulling my arm tighter against her.

I'm not sure if the decision to leave me out was my grandfather's decision or my dad's. Either way, it was a kick when I was already on the ground.

"I didn't go back for the funeral. I didn't see him after that last night. He was just so fucking disappointed in me." The words come out in a mirthless bark of laughter.

It's hard to think of that moment, of him staring across the battered kitchen table at me. His face wrinkled and weathered from all his years in the sun, distaste and disdain embedded in his expression. I let him down.

I stare into the distance, focusing on the broken-down mountain so the stinging in my eyes doesn't turn into tears. "I was scared of being trapped, of giving in and getting stuck because that was almost easier than trying. So I stayed away. And now it's too late. I'll never know if he forgave me or if he even sort of understood why. I don't even know if they still have La Estrella." Generations of work gone because of my selfishness.

"Hey." Amanda lets go of my arm to stand in front of me on the green, rising on her tiptoes to force me into making eye contact. "Sometimes you have to do what's right for you, even if no one else agrees."

I meet her gaze and she nods, giving me a significant look. She understands. Of course she does. She's here with me, against her family's wishes and her therapist's recommendations.

"You weren't trying to hurt them," she says softly.

I reach out and touch her cheek, my thumb rough against the smoothness of her skin. "Does it matter?"

"Yes," she says simply. "Just because someone loves you doesn't mean they own you. That's something different." Her expression darkens, with pain and remembrance. And I want to take it away.

Instinctively, I move forward, my hand sliding into her hair, and she tilts her face toward mine, her arms slipping inside my open coat to hold on to me. Her breath is warm against my skin and—

"Um, excuse me?" a voice asks hesitantly.

Amanda jolts back from me, taking a quick half-step away, like she might run with the slightest prompting.

"What?" I ask over my shoulder, more curtly than I intended.

"I'm sorry, Mr. Henry," the kid who gave us our clubs says. "But you asked me to let you know when your cab was here." He points to the parking lot, and sure enough, when I lean around the tower, I can see the splash of taxi yellow.

"I did," I acknowledge gruffly. "Thanks."

He nods, his head bobbing like it's on a spring, and leaves at a quick clip. I scared him. I swallow a sigh. Bad enough that being the owner's grandson means you're dragged out here literally at the crack of dawn, worse when the guy behind it is an asshole. I make a mental note to tip him extra, from what little I've got, anyway.

"Guess our time's up," I say to Amanda. And I can feel it: the spell of togetherness in this isolated place in the half-dark before sunrise is broken now.

She nods. "For the moment."

"Did you have fun?" I ask, and then make a face. She spent half the time listening to me whine about my family. "Never mind."

"I did," she says quickly as we head back toward the first hole and the parking lot. "It's not every day I get to school someone *so* badly." She grins.

"No, no." I shake my head. "We didn't finish. I could have made a comeback."

She snorts. "No, you couldn't have."

At the tiny "clubhouse," made to look like an ice-covered castle, I'm in the process of handing the kid—Luke, if I remember right—our clubs, balls, and an extra ten, when cameras start flashing from the parking lot.

"Amanda! Chase!"

"Look up!"

"Over here!"

"Is this a date?"

Squinting, I glance over to find a phalanx of photographers surrounding our cab and at the entrance to the course. Behind them in the parking lot, their hastily abandoned SUVs are still running, doors thrown open.

It looks like most of the vultures circling the hotel entrance have flown here instead. But this time, it's not just paparazzi. Reporters have joined in. I see familiar entertainment-show logos on the side of video cameras.

Son of a bitch. How did they all know? Someone, somewhere is talking.

Automatically, I step back, blocking Amanda from their view. "I'm sorry. I'm not sure how they found us."

Amanda touches my arm, and I glance back at her. "It's fine," she says.

"No—" I begin.

"It's what I'm here for," she says pointedly, a smile lurking beneath the tension in her expression. "Remember?"

She's right, except suddenly that idea sends a weird pang through me. That's not all we are, all this, is it? Maybe once, but not anymore, right? The Amanda Grace I picked up at her house on Sunday is not the same Amanda I know and like now. That Amanda was a name, a symbol, a media magnet and a chance at career salvation.

This girl, the one tucking her arm around my waist in the face of flashing cameras, the one who's grumpy in the morning, who eats french fries on her burger, who listens without judgment to the worst things I've done, she is someone else entirely. A real person who happens to share the same name.

I don't want to let go of *this* girl, this Amanda, for the previous incarnation, no matter what the benefits might be.

The realization staggers me, literally.

"You okay?" Amanda asks with a frown as I recover my balance with an extra step.

"Yeah," I manage. *Get over yourself, Mroczek.* Now is not the time for any kind of philosophical revelation, not with dozens of cameras present and lots of work to be done this week.

But even that doesn't stop me from wanting to stand between her and the cameras, wanting to find a way to protect her from something I know she hates.

Amanda takes a deep breath to steady herself. "Let's do this," she says, giving me a nod.

We move swiftly, my arm around her shoulders, pulling her close, so that the crowding assholes don't get too pushy.

Once we're in the cab, it's a parade back to the hotel with our vehicle in the lead. The driver drops us at the front entrance, because, at this point, there's no reason to try to hide.

A few of the paparazzi and reporters have raced ahead to beat us back.

They're shouting again as we get out of the cab.

"Chase, were you out all night together?"

"Is this all just a play for more publicity, Henry?"

"Amanda, is Chase Henry your boyfriend? How do your parents feel about that?"

Amanda winces reflexively, and I take her hand. After a while, it all blends into a dull roar of noises and voices; the words lose their meaning.

But just as we're at the sliding doors into the hotel, one question breaks through the chaos.

"What do you say about the rumors of security issues?" a female voice rings out shrilly. "The threats against the two of you? Are you scared?"

Amanda stiffens, and even I, far more experienced with this kind of tactic, stumble, catching my foot on the edge of the threshold as I automatically look toward the questioner, who is lost in a sea of faces.

"Chase?" Amanda asks through clenched teeth, bringing me back to myself.

I face forward. "No, come on," I say in a low voice. "It's just to get our attention."

I hope. God. It never occurred to me that the craziness that surrounded my former life might potentially intersect with the nutjobs that Amanda has had to deal with. Threats might be the least of our concerns. People are so weird sometimes. They forget that the tiny dancing characters on their screen are real people.

We make it through the sliding glass doors and into the lobby. Unlike yesterday, where most people didn't seem to notice or care, it feels like everyone's staring at us now. But that's probably because of the madhouse outside rather than anyone recognizing us.

Amanda's hand is tight in mine, her fingers pressed hard against the bones beneath my skin.

"It's just them making stuff up," I say, keeping us moving toward the elevators and the eventual shelter of our rooms.

Amanda nods, her face pale and her dark eyes wide.

"It's okay," I promise. A promise I probably have no business making. Damnit, this is when having the resources of being an actual celebrity—rather than one who has fallen from the top rung to that of a *Mental Floss* trivia item—would come in handy.

"I know," she says, but she doesn't sound convinced.

"I'll talk to the manager here and our security on location. But I'm sure it's just bullshit. I haven't heard anything about it," I say. Except who would tell me now that Elise isn't speaking to me?

Elise. Fuck.

This has her written all over it. She did warn me that she had a backup plan, one I wouldn't like. And she has the contacts to do it: plant a few unsubstantiated stories with the right people and off it goes. It keeps the Chase/Amanda story going, which benefits her, and it doesn't destroy her rep. Just makes our lives more difficult. Amanda's, in particular. She lived with violence for so long, I can't imagine what the potential threat of its return is doing to her.

A shudder runs through her, one I feel through our joined hands.

I've got to talk to Elise, get her to call this off. Amanda is too—

Amanda stops dead in the middle of the lobby, her breath catching in her throat.

I move to stand in front of her, so she'll see me, see the truth in what I'm saying. "They create rumors to get reaction photos from us, to keep people clicking through to their websites—that's all this is."

But she's not listening, her alarmed gaze zeroing in on something over my shoulder.

Confused, I turn to see what's caught her attention.

"Oh, crap."

21

Amanda

I drop Chase's hand and make a beeline for the overstuffed chairs in front of the lobby's stone fireplace.

"What are you doing here?" I demand.

Mia looks up from the open snack-sized bag of chips in her lap. "Finally." She stretches her arms over her head and then flips her bright red hair over the back of the chair. "I've been here, like, half the night," she says through an exaggerated yawn.

I spin away from her, my gaze bouncing past the cautiously approaching Chase, to search the lobby for the rest of my family. My mother racing toward me, Liza's folded-arms avoidance, my dad hovering in the distance like a storm cloud on an already overcast day.

But . . .

"They're not here," Mia says. "Just me." She points a chip at

Chase, who's keeping a few feet back, his hands stuffed in his pockets. "You're welcome for that, b-t-dubs." She pops the chip in her mouth.

I glance at him, and Chase, eyes wide with surprise, holds up his hands in an "I'm innocent" gesture.

As she crunches away, Mia wrinkles her nose and tilts her head toward the ceiling in consideration. "'BTW'? I feel like maybe 'b-t-dubs' has become one of those, like, cliché things to—"

"Mia!" I say through gritted teeth. "What are you doing here?" *By yourself, in a lobby surrounded by strangers, in an unfamiliar town?*

It's hard to explain, but when she was at home, theoretically under the watchful eyes of my parents, I could relax a little. I couldn't control anything that happened there, so I couldn't make a mistake or miss something that might come to harm her.

But with Mia here, suddenly everything's a threat that requires vigilant attention on my part. Otherwise, if I mess up, she might be hurt or taken. Because that's how the universe works, or something.

It's ridiculous, I know, but that's the way it feels. And maybe it's not so ridiculous if there are actual threats against us.

The pinch of worry in my stomach grips harder.

Mia heaves a sigh, as if my question is such an imposition, or perhaps I'm an idiot to be asking it.

"What do you think I'm doing here?" she says flatly, squishing the chip bag into a crinkly ball.

It doesn't take me long to connect the pieces: the disastrous phone call last night, my parents' fears about Chase, their knowledge of my compulsive need to protect Mia.

"Did they send you here?" I ask in disbelief. Surely even my parents wouldn't go that far. My younger sister as babysitter and bait? It made a terrible kind of sense: her very presence—and my worries for her safety—would keep me preoccupied and therefore less involved with Chase.

Mia gives me a look that is much wearier and older than it should be. I can see the dark circles under her eyes, the downward turn of her mouth, the tangles in her normally smooth hair, the wrinkles in her sweater, and the baggy knees in her leggings.

"Only one way to find out, isn't there," she says, examining the edge of her thumbnail, where the cuticle has given way to blood.

By calling them, she means. Which, if I do, just gives them another opportunity to work on me, to make me feel bad, to tell me not just that I should come home, but that I should bring Mia with me.

Suddenly it seems very possible that my parents orchestrated this. I feel sick.

"Amanda?" Chase asks hesitantly.

I turn.

"I'm sorry," he says with regret in his voice, "but I'm going to be late if I don't . . ." He gestures toward the elevator.

"Oh, yeah, no, you should go." I nod so rapidly I feel like my head might pop off and roll across the floor. I hate that he's witnessing this, yet more of my family's dysfunction, from the front row, in full Technicolor and surround sound.

Trying to ignore the humiliation burrowing its way beneath my skin, I take a breath and strive for calm. "I'll catch up with you upstairs," I say to Chase.

I have the distinct feeling that if I go along with this bid to control my actions, by letting Mia into my room, it'll be that much harder for me to send her home or deny my parents' wishes to bring her there.

But Chase doesn't move, his gaze shifting from me to Mia and then back in obvious discomfort.

"I, uh, just brought the one key card," he says quietly.

Before I can say anything, I catch movement from the corner of my eye. Mia bolts upright in her chair, her face the dictionary definition of stunned, the balled-up chip bag rolling out of her limp grasp.

"Holy shit, you guys are really sleeping together?" she asks at full Mia-volume, which is like ten times that of a normal human being. It actually echoes in the high-ceilinged space.

Chase winces.

The rest of the lobby falls silent. Anyone who wasn't watching us before is watching us now. I hear the distinct hiss-click of cell phone cameras taking photos.

Damnit, Mia. I snag her arm and pull. "Up, now. Let's go," I say through my teeth. My face is hot enough to start a forest fire in rainy season.

Mia grabs her purse from the floor as she stumbles to her feet under my force. "What? What's wrong?" she asks as the three of us hastily make our way toward the elevator. "You know that's what everyone's talking about anyway." Then she, in typical brazen Mia fashion, waves at the people who are staring. "It's why Mom and Dad are losing their shit."

Thankfully the elevator doors open right away when Chase pushes the call button, and we have the car to ourselves.

"Not that I have a problem with it," Mia says, yanking her arm free from me once we're inside. "It's good; you're finally moving on. You deserve a little fun." She pats my shoulder in the manner of someone comforting a wounded puppy.

If it were possible to make the elevator plummet to the basement and kill us all, I might have taken that option. Unfortunately, I don't have that kind of power. And we're on the first floor.

"Shut up, Mia, please," I mutter.

Chase leans closer, his jacket brushing against my shoulder, and I have a vivid memory of sliding my arms beneath it to wrap around his warm body. Well, that's probably history.

But then he murmurs, "At least somebody in your family doesn't hate me." Amusement curls the edges of his words.

I look up at him sharply. "Not funny."

But Mia laughs. "True!" she says to him. Then she tilts her

head, eyeing him with a considering look. "But I'm not the only one. Liza still has a raging crush on you."

"Mia!" I snap.

"What? It's not like it's not completely obvious," she says with an offended huff.

Then she turns that calculating gaze on me. "And seems like Liza might not be the only one," she says in a singsong voice, pointing at me with both fingers in succession, like she's jabbing buttons on a vending machine.

I want to die, even though it's nothing Chase doesn't know already. It's just how she's saying it. Mia is an expert at manipulating volume and dramatic gestures for maximum attention and effect.

Chase, though, doesn't apparently feel the same way.

He gives a smothered laugh, and I glare at him. "Don't encourage her, please."

Mia ignores me. "That means you've got three-fifths of the Grace clan on your side," she says to Chase with a shrug. "Not bad. We're a tough crowd. Especially this one." She elbows me. "She's got trust issues," she says in a loud stage whisper.

I shut my eyes, praying for the doors to just please open.

When they do, Mia is blissfully quiet for a few moments, preoccupied by taking in her surroundings.

"No penthouse?" she asks, wrinkling her nose.

I cringe. Saying her name in a scolding voice hasn't had any effect so far, and I'm betting that's not about to change, so I don't waste the breath.

"Not this time," Chase says, seemingly undisturbed as he leads the way to our rooms.

"Huh," she says with that calculating look I've learned to dread.

"Mia—" I begin.

"So, is your agent here?" she asks Chase, ignoring me.

"Stop," I hiss at her. "It's not a talk show. You can't just pelt people with questions that are none of your business."

"More like a job interview than a talk show, I think," Chase says to me dryly. "And no, he's not," he says in answer to Mia. "He and I haven't exactly been on great terms lately." His mouth tightens.

Mia makes a speculative noise.

"But you can do better than him, anyway," Chase says, startling me.

That's what she's after? Wait, never mind. Of course that's what she wants—an agent, connections to the Hollywood life she feels is inevitably in her future.

Mia raises her eyebrows, surprised. "Really?"

Chase grins at her. "He didn't even get me the penthouse this time."

She nods thoughtfully, then gives him a finger-gun gesture. "Good point."

He opens the door to his room and steps in to hold it for us.

Mia starts forward, but I push past her to go first and drag her along behind me, straight to my room.

Left unattended for half a second, she'd probably be rummaging through Chase's suitcase, asking him about his underwear or commenting on his brand of toothpaste.

Once I get her into my room—"Oh, you're not sharing with him? I'm disappointed in you, Amma."—I glance back at Chase, who is shrugging out of his jacket.

"I'm sorry about everything," I say, with a wince. That word seems to encapsulate not only Mia's surprise arrival but also every word out of her mouth since.

Chase shakes his head. "It's fine. I'm just going to hit the shower quick." He starts to turn away, his hands pulling at the collar of his T-shirt.

I hesitate then follow, taking an extra step to touch his arm. "Thank you for this morning. It was perfect." Somehow I feel more self-conscious now. It's like Mia's arrival has reminded me of who I was before, and every action now feels new and absurd.

A slow smile spreads across Chase's face, one of genuine plea-sure, and a spark of that energy returns. "Yeah?" He stuffs his hands in his pockets, rocking back on his heels. He's pleased at having pleased me.

"Yeah." I grin back at him like an idiot, feeling the perpetual tightness in my chest ease in the glow.

He tilts his chin up in mock consideration. "Even though it was, what did you call it, oh-God-thirty?"

"You brought caffeine and put up with my grumpiness until it kicked in. You pass," I say. "Also, you brought bagels. Bagels make everything better. Even ridiculously early mornings."

"Good to know," he says. "I'll keep it in mind for future ref-erence." His gaze is warm on me and I think he's maybe imagin-ing other early mornings, and suddenly, I really, really want one of those. Even though I know it'll probably never happen, just the thought of waking up beside him makes me want to hug him because it tells me that this is working—the crazy plan that everyone was against is actually making a difference.

"I won't be able to answer my phone, but I'm going to leave the cast and crew directory here." Chase points to a sheaf of bent and slightly crumpled pages on the coffee table, propped up on the tissue box. "Call Emily if you want a ride to set later."

"Oh, she'll love that," I mutter.

"Probably," he agrees with no lack of cheer. "But I hope you'll do it anyway." He offers me an uncertain smile. "I'd rather have you there."

It dawns on me then that this is the first time we've been apart since leaving my house on Sunday, other than sleeping, and even then it's just been a door and twenty feet of empty space separating us.

And I don't like it, this impending separation. Not because I'm afraid of being alone or being away from him, but just because . . . I like it better when he's around. So much of my life for the last two years has been spent trying to adjust my behav-ior to other people's expectations or concerns, trying to keep up a happy, stable front or prove that I'm okay. It's exhausting. But the last two days have shown me that Chase isn't like that. He doesn't require that of me.

With him, I can just be myself. And because of that, I like *me* better when he's around.

The realization stops me short. What does that even mean? Worse yet, what does it mean after all of this is over? There's no question that this is—that *we* are—temporary, only happening while we're here. No strings—that's what I said.

But I just nod. It doesn't matter. This, right now, is enough. It has to be. I won't think about anything else. It wouldn't be fair to either one of us.

Chase leans in and, with a gentleness that makes my eyes sting, he tucks my hair behind my ear, touching my cheek with his thumb. Then he kisses me, light and soft, his mouth warm and lingering until I'm clutching hard at his shoulders.

Then he steps back, taking a deep breath just like the one I'm struggling to catch. "I'll see you later, okay?"

"Yes," I say, like the promise I want it to be.

He exhales with another of those bright, real smiles.

As I start to turn for my room, he says quietly, "It's none of my business, Amanda, but I think she"—he tips his head toward my door and Mia waiting beyond—"is maybe having a hard time."

My mouth turns down. "Yeah, I know." Guilt pulls at me like weights wrapped around my ankles.

"Not your fault," he reminds me.

Technically, that's true, but if I'm the proximate cause, doesn't that basically amount to the same thing? I'm afraid it does.

"I'll see you soon," I say instead, and close the door after me.

In my room, I find Mia lounging upside down on my bed, channel surfing, her long red hair just inches from brushing the floor, and her ankles crossed on one of my pillows.

I don't know what to say to her. Uneasiness flares in my gut. The wrong thing might send her running in the wrong direction.

She grins at me. "You like him."

I sigh. "Not up for discussion," I say. "And get your shoes off my bed, please." She's lucky I'm not a germ freak like Liza. Liza would be stripping the bed already.

"Guess you don't like him that much if this is still where you're sleeping," she says. "Poor Chase." She pulls an exaggerated sad face, which, upside down as she is, is extra comical.

But I hold firm. That is, and always has been, the only tack to take with Mia if you want any kind of a serious conversation.

With an exasperated sigh, she rights herself into a sitting position, swiveling to put her feet on the floor. "Oh, come on. He's obviously into you. I'm just having some fun."

Now that it's just the two of us—her audience cut in half and limited to someone used to her tactics—she's calmer. An eight on a scale of ten instead of twenty.

"What's really going on, Mia?" I ask, folding my arms across my chest. "Why are you here?"

Her expression grows wary, her lower lip jutting out mutinously. "You know. Mom and Dad—"

"Oh, please, like they would have dropped you off and missed the chance to yell at me some more."

The way she avoids my eyes tells me that my belated deduction is on target.

"That's true. Everything is definitely still all about you," she says under her breath, kicking her boots against the short carpeting.

Her words strike with the accuracy of a whip, and I wince. "Meez, I'm sorry—"

"I thought it would be better, you know? With you . . . here." The word "gone" hangs in the air between us, a mid-thought correction. "But it wasn't." Her frown shows lines on either side of her mouth that have no business forming on someone her age. She shouldn't be under that kind of stress. And yet I know she is.

"What happened?" I ask.

Mia looks up at me sharply. "You mean after Dad freaked out because you sent the cops away?"

"I'm here because I want to be," I say evenly. "And I'm an adult—"

"Or how about when your picture, looking half terrified and ready to faint, shows up on every local news station, *Access Hollywood* and *Entertainment Tonight*, and all those other shows?" She cocks her head at me. "Mom *loved* that."

The image of my mother watching TV, her hand clamped to her mouth to keep from crying, immediately springs to mind. "I'm fine. I'm doing what I need to do, what's right for me," I say, feeling like the lowest form of life on the planet. Who is this selfish? Me—that's who.

"I know that, Amanda!" Mia shouts. "But someone needs to convince them. Get it? They can't see anyone else or anything else except saving you, even if you don't need it." She flops back on my bed with a sullen expression and stares at the ceiling.

Dread fills me. "They don't know you're here, do they?" I ask, sitting on the other bed.

"They were talking about it last night, what to do," she says without looking at me.

"After the phone call," I say, more a statement than question.

She nods, rolling her eyes.

"Liza said that if you wouldn't come home, they should bring me here. Because maybe that would convince you." Her tone is angry and bitter, but worse than that, I can hear the wobble of impending tears in her voice. And unlike most Mia-weeping situations, where she's a one-woman opera of despair, she appears to be trying hard *not* to cry. Which only makes me feel worse.

Convince me? More like emotionally blackmail me into doing what they want. I might be willing to take risks with myself but not with her and they know that. And how shitty for

Mia to hear her family—our family—talking about her that way, like she's a chess piece to be moved to achieve another objective.

My emotional meter swings wildly between rage and guilt, the one burning through me with the fire of a thousand suns, the other threatening to pull me down until I can't breathe beneath its weight.

"So I just brought myself to save them the trouble," she says with a bright, false smile at the ceiling.

"If Liza thinks it's such a great idea, then why didn't she come herself?" I snap.

Mia pops her head up, bracing herself on her elbows, and gives me an incredulous look. "You're kidding, right?"

I wave my hand in dismissal. "Law school, classes, incredibly difficult, yeah, yeah." I've heard it plenty already from Liza herself, who seems to need everyone else to acknowledge the difficulty before she can unclench even a little.

Mia snorts. "No, because then she'd have to talk to you."

I stop, my mouth hanging open. This is the first time anyone has ever acknowledged the tension aloud. I knew it wasn't my imagination, but the way Mia is talking, it's something the rest of my family has discussed.

"I thought you would have figured it out by now," Mia says, flicking her fingers against the bedspread, removing crumbs that she was responsible for putting there in the first place.

"Someone would have to talk to me," I point out. "And since Dad and Liza avoid me, and Mom is pretending everything is awesome, that leaves you."

She seems momentarily nonplussed. "Oh, right." Then she shakes her head. "Okay, well . . . it's just a few years ago, Liza was being Liza . . ." She hesitates. "You know how she is, all logic and next steps. Emotion chip deactivated or whatever."

I nod.

"And I guess she was doing some research." Mia pokes at the comforter again instead of looking at me. "And she found out that you can't declare someone dead for, like, a bunch of years, I guess."

Suddenly I have a terrible feeling I know where this is going.

"So, that summer, right before you were found, Liza was pushing for a memorial service for you. For 'closure.'" Mia lifts her hands to make air quotes, but her shoulders are sagging, as if bent under the burden of holding and then sharing this knowledge. "She was leaning hard on Mom and Dad to make it happen. Then the police called, saying they found you."

The words hit harder than I expected. When I was in the basement, I knew that my family probably thought I was dead. I was gone for so long. But all anyone ever said when I came back was how they'd never given up hope.

Hearing now that that might not have truly been the case makes me feel like I clawed my way to freedom only to find everyone completely uninterested in my return.

Which is obviously not true. But it's a flash-burn of betrayal that's hard to ignore.

"It's not her fault," Mia says with obvious reluctance. "Mom and Dad were messed up, like really messed up. I think she was trying to help in her Liza way."

She's right. Liza would break the situation down rationally. The best solution would be for me to come home. If that couldn't happen, then the next best would be to move on as neatly and cleanly as possible, which would require some kind of resolution or closure. And a memorial service would be the only kind of resolution or closure that could be controlled.

It just sucks as the one who was intended to be memorialized while I was still alive.

"When you came home, Liza pretended she never even brought it up, and Mom and Dad told me not to say anything to you because of your 'mental state.'" Mia makes a face.

So, instead, my older sister either ignores me or speaks to me without quite meeting my gaze. Liza might lean toward logic, but she's not a freaking robot. In her mind, she wrote me off as dead and then she turned out to be wrong. That must really be messing with her mind. Liza doesn't handle being wrong very well at all, even on little stuff. And this time, it's probably not just being wrong, but the guilt of it, too.

No wonder we're so messed up.

I sigh and drop my head in my hands, attempting to alleviate the tension growing in my neck muscles and the gnawing feeling of hurt in my chest.

Then I straighten up and focus on Mia. "Okay, putting that aside for now"—because what else was I supposed to do with that information right now?—"coming here without telling Mom and Dad is cruel, Mia. They've already had one missing kid; they're going to be—"

"They'd have to notice I was gone first, Amma," she says wearily.

She holds up her phone. No texts, no screen full of missed calls.

My shoulders sag. I don't know how to fix this. I don't know if there is a fix for it. But I hate seeing her hurt. "What can I do to help?" I ask.

She scoots forward to the edge of the bed. "Let me stay here with you until you come home."

I gape at her.

"It's just another day or two, right?"

The reminder sends a pang through me.

"You make me crazy, but at least you notice me. At least I exist to you," she says bitterly.

"Mia . . ." I begin, shaking my head.

"I won't get in the way," she says, and my heart breaks, remembering her as a little kid following Liza and me around.

"It's not that," I say.

She scowls. "You just don't want me crashing your little lovefest." She flings her hand toward Chase's room. "But I told you, I don't care. Go for it."

Hmmm. Should I be questioning the wisdom of decisions that my wild-as-hell younger sister endorses? Possibly.

"No," I say. "Listen to me. First, hanging out here isn't going to fix anything at home. You'll have to go back eventually. We both will. I'm hoping to have a better grip on some of the stuff that's bothering me by the time I leave. What's your plan?"

She doesn't answer, studying her nails instead.

"Second, things are complicated here. There's a lot of attention on us and some of it's not good. I don't want you caught up in that."

She narrows her eyes at me. "Are you in trouble?"

"No." I pause. "Not yet. Maybe. I don't know. There might have been some threats. Chase is checking into it. But there are always threats, remember?"

"Yeah, but—"

"My choice, not yours," I say firmly, leaving no room for argument. Liza's the lawyer, but Mia's persistence is almost as wearing. "And I don't want you here in the middle of that. Plus, you've got school."

Mia snorts. "Please. Who cares?"

"*You* might, if you miss enough that you're sitting next to me this summer at the kitchen table, doing homework for Mom." A day or two wouldn't do that, but I'm guessing, with Sammy's influence, she might have been "liberating" herself rather frequently.

"Gross." She wrinkles her nose.

"Exactly." I hesitate, then add, "But you can stay here for today. And if they'll let you in, I'll take you with me to the set." Hopefully Chase won't mind.

She straightens up as if she's been electrified. "Are you serious?"

"Yes, but you have to promise you'll be quiet and stay right next to me. This is a big deal, and Chase can't afford trouble from us."

She throws her hand up, palm out. "I swear."

"And then you have to go home *and* go to school tomorrow."

Mia heaves a sigh. "Fine." She stands up, practically vibrating with excitement. "Can we go now?" Then she holds up her hands. "Wait. I need to shower and change my clothes." She has the air of someone who expects to be swept off in a private jet to a studio somewhere.

"You can borrow something from me," I offer.

She rolls her eyes. "I'm trying to make a good impression, Amma, not convince them to give me their spare change."

I raise my middle finger at her, and she laughs.

She heads for the bathroom, pausing halfway to look back at me. "You're going to call them, aren't you?"

Mom and Dad, she means.

"Yeah. I have to let them know you're here." I'm tempted to text, but since a little information might only alarm them further—I really don't want another visit from the well-intentioned Wescott police—it's probably better to bite the bullet.

But I'm going to do my best to control the conversation.

As if reading my thoughts, Mia shakes her head and continues toward the bathroom. "Good luck with that," she says over her shoulder.

"Thanks." I chuck a pillow after her, missing her by several feet.

She laughs as she disappears into the bathroom. "Wow, you suck."

"Hey, Meez?"

"Yeah?" She sticks her head out the door.

"No matter what, when I get home, it's going to be different. I'll talk to Mom. It's going to be better."

Mia nods, her gaze not quite meeting mine.

"You believe me?" I persist.

She hesitates. "I think you're going to try, and that's better than it was."

Not exactly the rousing vote of confidence I was hoping for, but probably what the situation deserves. I wish I could give her more guarantees. I wish we could all have them. But that's apparently not how life works. Stupid life.

I wait until I hear the shower running—and Mia singing something from a musical—before I pick up my phone.

Ignoring all the texts, voicemails, and missed calls, I pull up my phone book and tap the number for my parents' house.

It rings once before someone picks up.

"Amanda?" It's Liza, not bothering with a greeting.

"Yeah, it's me," I say.

"I'll get Mom," she says.

"Wait." The word pops out before I know what I'm going to say next, so there's a weird, awkward silence for a long second. "Mia told me," I blurt.

Her sudden intake of breath tells me she knows exactly what I'm talking about.

"Liza, it's . . ." Not okay, exactly, but what? "Understandable," I finish lamely. "You don't have to avoid me because—"

"Mom's here," she says, and there's a murmur of conversation and the rustle of someone's hand over the receiver.

Then my mom says, "Amanda, thank God." Relief screams between her words.

"Mom, I'm exactly where I've been for the last two days," I say, striving for patience. I'm a horrible person, feeling frustration with her after everything they went through while I was gone. But it's making me crazy. I haven't done anything off the wall. Well, okay, taking off with Chase, I suppose. But since then, I've done exactly what I said I would. I've been in contact, staying where I said I would be. Okay, last night I hung up on everyone. But that was all.

"I understand why you might feel like we were attacking you," my mom says. "But I think you just need to look at it from—"

"That's not why I'm calling," I say quickly, wanting to avoid the rehash.

"Oh."

"Mia's here. I thought you should know," I say.

"What?" My mom gives a strained laugh, like I've finally lost my grip on the few marbles still in my possession. "Amanda, honey, are you okay?"

"Yes, I'm fine," I say through gritted teeth. "And Mia is here."

"No, she's probably at school by now. She spent the night at a friend's. Sophia. No, Sarah."

"Sammy?" I offer.

"Yes, that's it," she says, leaping onto the name with confidence. "Sammy Lareau."

"Mom, Sammy is a guy. And he's my age." I rub the heel of my hand in my eyes.

A strangled noise emerges from the other end of the phone. "There must be more than one Sammy," she says. "She's been spending the night over there since the beginning of the year and—"

"Mom, no, trust me," I say. Which in a sentence sums up the exact problem. It's not that she doesn't, but she's so busy protecting me from myself and everyone else that she doesn't see or hear me. And how can I blame her for that?

"I don't . . . Mia is there? Can I speak with her?" She's still not sure I know what I'm talking about. Then again, my version of reality hasn't always been so unassailable.

"She's in the shower right now. She heard you guys talking last night about bringing her here. She just decided to take matters into her own hands." And probably severely pissed off Liza, who would need their shared car for classes this afternoon.

"Damnit," my mom says quietly, startling me. It's rare to hear my mother lose her temper or, for that matter, swear.

"I told her she can stay for the day, but she has to be back in time for school tomorrow."

"And you'll come with her?" my mom asks, hope lifting her voice.

My temper explodes, sending a rush of adrenaline through me.

"I just told you that your youngest daughter is not where you thought she was and probably hasn't been lots of times in the past, and you're asking about me?" I demand. "No wonder Mia's so angry with you guys. She thinks you don't care, that she doesn't exist to you. I'm beginning to think she's right."

"Amanda, we are doing the best we can with all of this," she says tightly. "And I don't think you have the right to judge us."

"So sorry to have inconvenienced you by surviving," I mutter, the words out before I can stop them.

She sucks in a breath. "You take that back, right now. The day we learned you were still alive was the best day in my life, followed only by the days you girls were born. But you don't know," she says, her voice shaking. "You have no idea what it was like to see you . . . after. You were so broken. It was like that man"—the hatred in her tone vibrates over the connection—"had taken our little girl and left us with this wounded, damaged creature that shook whenever anyone came close."

I shut my eyes, able to imagine it all too vividly. Sometimes it feels like those first days out of the basement just happened, like the wound on my arm is still healing and my teeth are still sharp, jagged peaks or blank spaces in my mouth.

"And you didn't deserve it; you were such a good girl—" Her voice breaks on a half-repressed sob.

I wince, hearing her refer to me in the past tense. But to some extent, that's accurate. The daughter they lost, the Amanda I was, no longer exists. "Mom, I'm sorry, I—"

"Are we making mistakes? I'm sure," she says. "But we're trying. We are doing everything we can to make you healthy and whole again."

Frustration wells in me again. "Yes, but that's not your job. I'm not fifteen anymore. Or even eighteen. I'm twenty, and I have to find my own way."

"If this is about him, Chase Henry, because of what he's saying to you—"

"No, it's not about him," I say. "It's about me. I'm doing this because I want to, because I need to. And I need you to let me, okay?"

"But it's a risk that you—".

"I like him. I . . . want him," I say in a voice barely above a whisper, squirming with discomfort but determined all the same. The confession tears something loose in me, a last restraint breaking free. "And I'm glad."

This is not something we talk about at home. But my mother knows what I mean. She's the one who sat with me through all the invasive tests and exams, who cried with relief with me when the doctors confirmed that I would heal, I would have children if I wanted them, and I was not—for the last and final time, thank you, merciful God—pregnant.

But none of those results spoke to my ability—or lack thereof—to form an emotional and romantic attachment to another human being. There wasn't an exam for that, nothing except living, waiting, and seeing.

"I know who he is and who he's not," I add, because I know she's wondering if my poor deluded brain has cooked up a fantasy about Chase Henry, the poster version, come to life.

"Oh, Amanda," my mom says in a soft voice with a pained sigh, "I want this for you, you know I do, but with him, this *man*?" She emphasizes the word, as if wanting to make the four years between Chase and me an uncrossable chasm, rather than a leap from one stone to the next. "You don't really know him. He's handsome, yes, but—"

"He's more than that," I say sharply. Even in the short time I've been around Chase, I've seen how others treat him like he's nothing more than the symmetry in his face, bone structure that looks good on camera. The worst part is, I'm pretty sure some part of him believes them. I think that's why he's so pleased when he *does* something right, versus just staying quiet and looking pretty.

Someone, somewhere along the way, convinced him that he

wasn't good enough, wasn't worth consideration just being who he is. And that sucks. Because he is.

"And as for knowing him well enough, yeah, you're probably right," I say with a shrug. "But I'm not sure it's possible for me to trust the way you mean, so completely, no matter how well I know someone. I don't think that's part of who I am anymore."

She makes a small, distressed sound.

It hurts me to hear it even as it makes the blood rush to my head in fury. "Mom, you can't unbreak me. I wish you could," I say, my jaw tight with frustration. "But you can't; the damage is done." When I look down, a dark circle appears on my jeans and then another. I lift my hand to my face, surprised to find I'm crying.

"So now I have to figure out how to navigate the new me, cracks and all." I wipe my cheeks with the back of my sleeve. "And if it blows up in my face, then it does. That's not the important part. What I'm trying to get you to see is that I *want* to try. That's the point." After so many years of hiding, I want something—who cares who or what it is. It should be recognizable as progress, even if she doesn't agree.

She's quiet for a long moment, to the point that I pull the phone from my ear to make sure the call hasn't ended.

"All right, Amanda," she says distantly. "You have to do what you think is best for you."

Even if it's a huge, messy mistake is what she's very carefully not saying. I hear it just the same.

"Just, please, be careful. I don't think I can see you hurting like that again." She sounds so wounded, so bereft, it's all I can do to keep from taking back everything I've just said, everything I've fought for.

"I will, I promise," I make myself say, my voice croaky with tears and effort.

"I'll talk with Mia when she gets home tomorrow. Thank you for letting us know she's safe," my mom says with that chilly formality usually reserved for strangers.

The polite distance growing between us in this call makes my heart hurt, but maybe it's necessary. Maybe that's what's needed to break the connection to the past, the one place we can never return to, no matter how hard everyone tries. None of us is the same and we never will be. Maybe it's time we acknowledge that, no matter how much it pains us.

"I love you, Mom," I say.

"Loveyoutoo." But she rushes the words together and hangs up before I can say good-bye, the click of disconnection sounding as resolute and permanent in my ear as any door slamming.

I lower my hand, phone clenched in my fingers, to my lap and sit still for a moment, feeling the surrealism of this instant. Mia is warbling in the shower, welcoming everyone to the cabaret, and out in the hallway, I hear the wobble and clatter of a loaded-down cart, either room service or housekeeping.

So here I am. In a hotel, next door to Chase Henry's room, not the Chase in my head but the real one, who's my friend . . . and maybe more, if I can take it that far. And I think I just got my mom to *listen* to me for the first time in over two years.

I'm all in. And all on my own. It's a strangely isolating and liberating feeling. Before, I had multiple people watching and weighing my every move, helping me see the pitfalls and dangers and steering my steps.

Now it's just me. And I forgot how completely terrifying that could be.

22

Chase

The van feels emptier without Amanda. It is, obviously. It's just me, Emily, and Ron, our driver from yesterday.

But I guess what I mean is that for someone who has a small "presence," as the theater people say, meaning she's quiet and doesn't require being the center of attention, I *feel* her absence so much more than I expected to.

I've been away from her for, what, twenty minutes? But I miss that word or two murmured in my ear. The warmth of her leaning against me, and the trust that symbolizes. The calm suggestion that seems to make everything better, whether it's finding the local AA meeting or correcting my mini-golf stance. The glare when I've overstepped my bounds by being too protective of her or when I've laughed at something I shouldn't, like pretty much anything her sister Mia says.

I wouldn't have thought twice about anything like that in the past. Actually, I probably would have run screaming at the first hint of sentimentality. There were girls who tried, in a whole variety of ways. Pretending not to care so I'd pay more attention, flirting with Eric or pretty much anyone else in the bar to try for a jealous reaction, or caring so much that I'd never have cause for complaint, like they could wear me down into feeling something I didn't.

I sound like a privileged asshole, but the truth is, it never felt like anything that was happening to me, the real me. Was it flattering? Hell, yes. Did I take them up on it? No question. It felt good to be wanted. At least, at first.

But once I got sober, or made a real effort toward it for the first time, I saw the situation more clearly. Would they have been so interested (or fake disinterested) in me if we'd found ourselves in Bart's Tavern in Tillman with sticky beer-soaked floors and peanut shells everywhere instead of some NoHo club with thumping bass and an elevated VIP platform? Not that I planned to be in a bar again anytime soon, either way.

But the answer was no: they wanted Chase Henry, and the real me was always either too much or not enough.

But this is different. Amanda is different. For whatever reason she looks at me and somehow sees me—messed up, struggling, recovering me—as worthy. And that just makes me want to prove her right.

"—didn't you think?" Emily asks, breaking into my thoughts. She's twisted around to face me, leaning into my space with earnestness. "It was so corny. All those falling-down fairy tale characters. Like I'm pretty sure they only had six Dwarves." She laughs.

It takes me a second to figure out what she's talking about. The miniature golf course from this morning. She obviously thought it fell short and is looking at me eagerly for agreement.

But I'm going to disappoint her. "I thought it was great. *We* thought it was great," I amend carefully. I don't want to hurt her feelings, but . . . no. "Thank you again for setting it up."

Her face falls. "Oh." Then she tries to rally, giving me a smile that's strained around the edges. "You're welcome, of course. Happy to help," she says. "I mean, it's my job." She swivels quickly in her seat to face forward.

"It's not your job," I say, trying to smooth things over without raising her hopes. "It was a favor, and I really do appreciate it."

Her shoulder rises and falls in a non-response response. "Sure."

Ron catches my gaze in the mirror and shakes his head with a smile and an old-man snort, which Emily doesn't notice as she's clicking madly away at her phone. Pretending she's responding to a text, if I had to guess.

Ron gets it. He understands. It's like she's knocking on a door, but I'm already gone.

The realization hits with a force that straightens me in my seat. The way I'm thinking about Amanda is . . . intense. Way more than it should be for someone I just met, and someone who will be going home tomorrow.

Tomorrow, holy shit. I can't decide which is more unsettling: the thought of finishing out the week here with Amanda sixty miles away—distant but not out of reach—or the pang that idea sends through me.

My hands are shaking and sweaty suddenly. I rub my palms against my jeans.

I don't want her to go.

But I'm not sure I'm ready for anything else, either. I mean, she's made it clear what she does and does not want from me, and it's nothing beyond these few days. And why would it be? We haven't even slept together, for God's sake. And we might not. Not that that's everything, but it's something.

And hell, I'm eleven months sober, which is my longest stretch ever. I'm on the path to not screwing up, to finally getting my life and my career back together, and one of the long-held tenets of recovery is that you should avoid getting involved with someone, like the kind of involved that messes with your emotions, for at least a year. If it ends badly, you might find yourself retreating to damaging but comforting habits in a weak moment. Which would pretty much destroy everything I've worked so hard to rebuild.

But when it comes to keeping my emotions out of anything to do with Amanda, it might be too late to hit the brakes.

"Chase, are you okay?" Emily asks, interrupting my thoughts.

I glance up to find her studying me with a puzzled frown. I must look as fucking confused as I feel.

I resist the urge to snarl at her. "Yeah, why?" I ask as calmly as I can instead.

"Um, we're here?" Emily gestures toward the window. And she's right: the van has stopped at the security barricade. I can see my trailer in the distance.

"Oh, right, sorry." I force a smile. "Just focused on the scene today." A convenient excuse, but it would be better if that were actually the case. Yet another reason I need to lock this down and regain my focus.

Emily climbs out and waits outside my door to escort me.

Ron gives me a salute and a nod as I slide out of the van.

Despite my worries about coordinating everything this morning and my lapse of attention for however long in the van, I'm still early enough for Emily to lead me to my trailer first.

Her sudden stop and gasp are my first indications that something's wrong.

I tense, glancing around, expecting . . . I'm not sure what. But I don't see any obvious threat. At first.

"Oh my God." Her hand covering her mouth, Emily races the final feet to my trailer steps and then stops to stare, which helps narrow down the cause for her reaction.

From a distance, it looks like a bunch of random scratches, but the closer I get, the pattern becomes more distinct.

On the door to my trailer, someone has scraped the word "no" over and over again in varying sizes. And then, in the dead center of the door, AMANDA is spelled out in uneven letters with a thick scratch through it. The gouge is deep enough that the metal is dented.

Elise. It has to be. She's following up on her threats rumor, making her own evidence.

I feel a flash of irritation that she's taken it this far and then a greater surge of relief that Amanda isn't here to see it.

"I have to call Security," Emily says, fumbling for the walkie-talkie on her belt. "Don't go in."

"It's not necessary," I say quickly. The last thing I need is for Security to decide the police should be involved. I step around Emily and tug at the door, confirming it's still locked. "I don't think anyone made it inside."

But Emily frowns at me and continues her call over the walkie-talkie for Leon, who is apparently the security co-ordinator.

It doesn't take long for Leon to appear. A bulky, balding guy in a black golf shirt and black pants, he radiates ex-cop in his eyes and the way he holds himself.

He takes a few pictures of the door and checks around the outside of the trailer, bending to look beneath. Then he gets the key from Emily, who's hovering nearby, and confirms that the inside seems undisturbed.

"Anybody got something against you?" he asks, eyeing me in a way that makes me feel guiltier than I already am.

I rub the back of my neck. "Where do you want to start? Alphabetical or by date?"

He chuckles, but I was being serious. I've been through this before. Sera, my stalker, started this way, with weird little unrelated incidents that built to her breaking into my condo.

"We had some other minor vandalism on set last night, a break-in and a small fire in one of the other trailers," he says.

I frown. Why the hell would Elise do that? Other than to cause general unease, which, if that's her goal, I guess she's succeeding.

"Could be someone pissed off some locals," Leon continues. "Maybe somebody picked a fight in a bar?"

He looks at me, and humiliation flares in me. My reputation precedes me again.

"No," I say flatly.

"Or it might just be some bored kids or lookie-loos, hoping to score some attention with all the extra press in town," Leon says.

Also my fault because they're here for Amanda and me. Max is going to kill me.

"We're increasing nightly rounds, and we'll be on the look-out," he says. "Nothing to worry about for now."

I hesitate. "You haven't heard anything about specific threats, right?" I promised Amanda I would ask, and if it turns out not to be Elise, we need to know.

"You hear something?" he asks with a frown.

"Just something one of the reporters said this morning," I say. "I . . . my friend . . ." God, I was so awkward at this. "Amanda Grace is here with me and—"

Leon nods. "I'm aware of her history. But I don't know of anything pertaining to her." He pauses. "Unless there's something you want to tell me."

"No," I say quickly, probably too quickly, given the way his eyes narrow.

But he just nods again. "Let me know if you hear anything else."

I wait until Leon leaves and Emily hurries away on one of her other duties before I step into my trailer and dig out my phone.

"Chase." Elise answers on the first ring, the gloating self-satisfaction thick in her voice. And if I had any doubt before, I have my answer now.

"What the fuck is wrong with you?" I demand in a low voice.

"Getting some interesting messages lately?" she asks innocently.

"If you want to call spreading rumors about threats, carving up my trailer door—"

"I think that might be a slight exaggeration. A few words here and there in the right ears, some scratches in an already battered surface—"

"Starting fires on set, and leaving burned-up pictures outside my hotel room?" It occurs to me, then, that with her ringside seat for the whole Sera-the-stalker business, Elise has the perfect blueprint for creating a believable "dangerous" situation.

Her pause is perfect. A beat, just enough to give me cause to think that I might have surprised her. "What? I don't know what you're talking about." She gives a dismissive sniff.

She almost sounds believable. Goddamnit.

"Stop or I'm going to call the cops," I say.

She laughs. "And tell them what, sweetie?"

"My former publicist and ex has gone psycho," I snap.

"The media will love that, especially when they work out *when* I became your former publicist and your ex," she says pointedly.

I flinch. She's right. They'll love it the way that sharks love discovering a wounded seal in the water overhead, an unexpected bounty from above.

My relationship with Elise is well documented if someone wants to dig into it. If there's even a hint that Amanda and I got together (for real or for show) before Elise and I were done, I'm screwed. I'll be the asshole who played Amanda Grace, the Miracle Girl, forever.

Amanda. I close my eyes. I can all too easily imagine her at the moment of finding out, the color draining from her face, the fear and betrayal sparking hatred where there's only warmth and trust now. Just picturing it opens a vast and sucking hole of loss in my chest.

"And if I'm called in for questioning, you know what I'm going to say," Elise continues, her voice hard.

The reminder of my own complicity in this mess just pisses me off further. "I was never on board with this," I say through clenched teeth. "I didn't even know about it!"

"I told you there was a Plan B. It was your choice not to co-operate," Elise says. "And really, maybe that was the smarter move. 'Young love standing strong in the face of possible danger.'" She gives a theatrical flair to the words. "That will sell even better."

"You are a bitch," I snarl.

"An evil bitch," she corrects. "And I know—you've said so before. Though usually in a slightly more complimentary tone." She makes a tsking noise at me.

I'm tired suddenly. Elise will always find a way to win. My only shot is to convince her that she's already crossed the finish line. "It's enough," I say. "Just stop. I don't care if you're punishing me, but Amanda doesn't deserve it, okay?"

As soon as that last sentence is out of my mouth, I know it's a mistake.

Elise sighs impatiently. "Amanda, Amanda. You'd think this girl was a saint instead of someone who knows how to spin her media."

"Elise—" I say through gritted teeth.

"No one is going to get hurt, Chase. It's all surface, no substance. Just enough to keep the public craving another hit." A horn blares loudly in the background, and Elise makes a disgusted noise.

"Where are you?" I ask.

"You do not want to know," she says dryly. "I don't even want to know." She clucks at me. "The things I do for you."

Panic rises in me. "Don't. Don't do anything else. I mean it, Elise."

But I'm talking to dead air. I pull my phone away from my ear to check, and yeah, the screen is flashing, "Call ended."

Shit.

I'm still standing there, trying to figure if there's a point to

284 / STACEY KADE

calling back, when a firm knock sounds at my trailer door. Amanda.

I'm caught by a wave of relief and fear, all twisted together, and the strength of it takes my breath.

I waste a second wishing I could tell her everything. This has gotten so messed up. But that would mean losing her, and I'm not ready for that, even if I'm confused about everything else.

Then I push open the door, my heart beating faster with eagerness in spite of myself.

But it's not Amanda.

"Oh. Hey," I say, pulling back.

Karen raises her eyebrows. "Nice to see you, too."

I wince. "Sorry, I was expecting . . ."

She cocks her head, listening with amused interest. The barbell piercing in her eyebrow gleams in the early morning light.

I shut my mouth. "Never mind," I mutter.

Karen ascends the steps and pushes past me, her makeup case, which looks more like a tackle box, banging into my leg as she goes.

"Wow, your light sucks in here." She yanks back the curtains, raising a cyclone of dust. Then she turns and gives me a skeptical up-and-down look. "And you're not dressed."

I scrub my hands over my face. Somehow this day, which started off so well, keeps spinning out of my control. "What are you doing here?" I ask.

"Some asshole broke into Hair and Makeup and trashed the place. Even tried to start a fire, I guess." Karen holds up her case. "Good thing I take most of my shit back to the room with me."

So that was the other vandalism Leon was talking about. I don't understand why Elise would do that. Or why she would tell someone else to do that. There's no way Elise does her own dirty work when it involves shimmying through broken windows or whatever and playing with matches.

And targeting the hair and makeup trailer, or even more specifically, Karen, makes no sense. Yeah, we used to be friends, but the general public wouldn't know that, so there'd be no rea-son anyone would connect the incident to me or Amanda.

"Chase?" Karen snaps her fingers in front of my face in that familiar, annoying way I know from our years of early morn-ings.

"Yeah, okay. I'll just . . ." I grab the wardrobe bag of Smitty-wear off the bathroom door and head into the bedroom to change.

"I probably shouldn't be asking this, but are you okay? You seem off," she calls to me over the rattle of tubes and jars as she sets up.

"I'm fine. Just a long morning." I shuck my shirt and pull on Smitty's dirty sleeveless undershirt.

"Drinking already?" she asks.

As I pull on the jeans with distinctly crusty patches—Amanda's right; these clothes are disgusting—I stick my head out the bedroom doorway. "No," I say.

"Recovering from drinking last night?" she continues blandly.

"I told you, no." Leaving the hoodie on the bed, because today is a track mark day, I make my way to the kitchen area, where Karen's case is open on the counter.

She nudges me toward the bench seat at the tiny table.

"Heard you went to a meeting last night," she says, hand-ing me the moisturizer. She's watching me curiously, and I don't like being a spectacle for her entertainment. Like the tightrope walker whose footing isn't quite sure, and the spec-tators are caught between hoping he'll make it and wanting a good show.

I glare at her. "It's supposed to be anonymous for a reason."

"Please." She snorts. "In a town this size with a movie in pro-duction?"

When I'm done with the moisturizer, she tips my head up, casting a professional gaze over my face and the work to be done there.

"So where's your girl?" she asks, amusement thick in her

286 / STACEY KADE

voice, as she picks up two tubes and mixes the colors together. "Scare her off already?"

"No. Not yet, I don't think." I hesitate, but the words circling in my head are brimming up, wanting to spill out. Even though we're not currently on the best terms—or, frankly, any terms at all—Karen and I used to talk. A lot. There's something confessional about being in the makeup chair, or bench, in this case.

"Amanda's sister came to town unexpectedly," I tell Karen. "So they're still at the hotel."

"Uh-huh." She busies herself plugging in her airbrush system. It sounds and looks very much like a paint sprayer.

"So I'm not sure if she's coming to set today. She may have to make sure her sister gets back home."

"And you don't like that," Karen says, taking my chin in her hand to angle my face.

I jerk back to glare at her.

"Stay still." She makes the adjustment again, and I stay put this time.

"It doesn't matter if I like it or not," I say. "She's supposed to go home tomorrow anyway." The airbrush gun thing whirs quietly in Karen's hand, spraying a light layer of base makeup over my face, covering every flaw with artificial perfection.

I expect her to "uh-huh" at me again.

But instead, the gun stops and she steps back, eyeing me with a mix of pity and repressed amusement. "Wow, you've got it bad."

"What?"

She shakes her head. "In all the years I've known you, I've never heard you stressing about where a girl is and when or if she'll be around again. Unless she was a studio exec or producer or something." She gives me a tight smile. "I wasn't aware you knew women weren't completely interchangeable."

I make a face. "Thanks."

"No point in lying to you about something you already know," she points out, tilting my chin the other way.

"Yes, I think you were pretty clear about that yesterday in front of Amanda," I mutter.

"Didn't make her run, did it?" Karen finishes with my face, then sits across the table from me, patting the surface. "Give me your arm."

I stretch my arm across the table, turning my wrist up to reveal the inside of my forearm. But more of those words are welling up. "I like her," I mumble.

"I can see that," she says, laughter bubbling in her voice.

I shoot her a dark look. "Stop."

She holds up her hand, brush between her fingers. "I'm sorry, I didn't mean to. It's just . . . not you."

"That's kind of the idea," I say. "I'm not the same. Or I'm trying not to be." The problem is, I'm still working out what that looks like, who I want to be.

Karen processes this silently.

"Is it a good idea?" she asks after a long moment, her dark head bent over my arm, scrupulously creating fake evidence of a serious drug addiction. Any humor in her tone is long gone.

"No, probably not." I consider it. "Definitely not. We don't make sense. At all. I'm still getting my life back together, two steps short of being a total mess. She needs someone calm, stable, patient."

"And you want to rip his lungs out, whoever he is," she says.

"Yes." The word escapes in a reluctant hiss.

"Like I said, got it bad," she says.

"That's helpful, Kare."

She opens her mouth and closes it again. "I don't know what to say to you. I mean, I used to. But we're not friends anymore. I don't know you, and I don't know if I want to help you."

Her words bring on a weariness and regret that feel permanently etched on my soul. I drop my gaze to the table. "I'm so sor—"

"Don't. Stop."

I look up, and she points a finger at me. "Don't apologize.

Not yet." She hesitates. "I want to believe you. This time. But I wanted to believe you before, too."

I stiffen.

"I'm not saying this time is like the others," she says quickly. "It's already different. I'm just not sure I'm ready to be friends and forgive."

"Okay," I say, but the word is bitter ash, tasting of all my previous failures. Karen was my one real friend from before.

"But if I was," she says, turning her attention back to her work, "I'd tell you that I think the changes in you are good ones. The fact that you're asking yourself the right questions and answering honestly is a big step in the right direction."

"Yeah," I say, forcing the word out. I know where this is headed.

But then she surprises me. "And I would also say that maybe some things don't have to make sense to everyone else, just to the two of you." She glances up at me, sadness moving fleetingly through her gaze, and I wonder if she's thinking about her ex, Steph.

"Here's the thing, though, Chase." She points her brush at me. "You're smarter than you give yourself credit for, but you will fuck this up if you don't believe you deserve it."

I try to smirk. "I don't think that was ever a problem in the past." But her words hit with a splash of cold water.

She throws me an exasperated look. "There's a difference between entitled asshole and having a genuine sense of self-worth, dumbass."

"I feel my self-worth improving already," I say.

But she ignores me. "I mean it, Chase. You're your own worst enemy. It's up to you to figure out if you can find a way around that. That goes for everything: acting, Amanda, all of it."

The idea of it being up to me alone, of it all riding on me making the right choices, sends a bolt of sheer terror through me.

I find myself swallowing hard and wishing for a drink to

smooth the rough edges and bolster my confidence. "I don't know if I can," I say finally.

"Then there's your answer, I guess," Karen says completely unsympathetically as she stands. "But whatever you do, you better make up your mind without hurting that girl any further."

I wince. She's right. "But—"

"No," she says sharply. "We're done here. That's all the non-friend friendliness I have in me today, Henry."

With that, she packs up her case and leaves, the trailer door banging shut after her.

23

Amanda

I should have known. On the ride over to the set, I stressed to Mia repeatedly that we had to stay out of the way and be quiet. That drawing attention to ourselves could cause problems for Chase.

But as always, I needn't have bothered. Everyone freaking loves Mia. No matter how hideously dramatic she can be, she's also extremely charismatic when she wants to be, one of those people who draws others into their circle, even when they don't particularly want to be drawn.

Right now, I'm watching her nodding and listening intently to the assistant director, who's explaining something to her, pointing at the playback screen, while the lighting people make adjustments.

And this is after she's already chatted with Karen during a

round of touch-ups for the actors, interrogated a gaffer, and even spoken once to Max.

I would have thought this crowd to be less susceptible, given their regular encounters with actors and other shining stars.

But evidently not.

Even today, when tension is running high because someone apparently vandalized the set last night, everyone seems to welcome the distraction or the opportunity to explain their work to an enthusiastically interested party.

Only Chase seems remote and possibly unhappy. He's stayed away from his chair, my chair, all day. And it feels deliberate. Or maybe that's just me. After that conversation with my mom, I'm highly aware of the chance I'm taking, that I want to take, and I'm squirming with that feeling of added vulnerability.

Now, a few minutes before the last take of the day, I find myself staring at him, watching for a hint of what he's thinking.

They're shooting today in a bedroom set constructed inside one of the big open spaces of the empty warehouse building. Apparently, it's a replica of a real room in a house here in town where the cast and crew will be filming. But something about the angles required that they have a version with only three walls for this scene. And since the homeowners weren't especially thrilled at the idea of renovation on that level, there's now a full-on girl's bedroom, decorated with college pennants, posters, magazine cut-outs, and a pink feather boa draped over the mirror, springing out of nowhere in the middle of this sea of dirty concrete. It's creepy as hell, honestly. Like the deluxe edition of Jakes's basement bedroom.

Chase is in Smitty mode. It's a subtle difference, but I can see it in the way he moves, the quicker, jerkier motions. He's consulting with Jenna, the girl who plays Iris. His dark blond head is bent over the pages, right next to hers, a few shades lighter than his. They're absorbed in whatever they're discussing, and it causes a weird pinching sensation in my chest. It's not jealousy, exactly. I don't think he's interested in her—I'm not getting that vibe at all—but it's more just that she has his complete and undivided attention. And quite selfishly, I want it for myself.

For this scene, they, as Smitty and Iris, have been arguing for the last few hours, like red-faced shouting at each other, in a variety of takes, while they debate about Keller's future.

It doesn't look easy or fun. And maybe that's all it is—Chase concentrating on being Smitty.

Either way, I kind of hate myself for the itch of worry that has settled beneath my skin.

"Hey."

I look up to see Keller himself, Adam, hovering a very safe distance of five or six feet away.

Adam as Keller is all puppy-dog eyes, rumpled hair, and wrinkled button-downs. He very much has the look of the good-guy-next-door, with a potential for greatness, but who also might end up working as a pizza delivery guy.

"Hi," I say cautiously.

Adam hasn't said much to me after yesterday's awkwardness. I don't think he meant any harm, but the intensity with which he sought me out was odd.

"Long day, huh?" He jerks his chin toward the lights and cameras.

"Not for me," I say pointedly. I'm not sure what's happening here, but I can feel him warming up toward something bigger than general pleasantries.

"So you and Henry, huh?" He scuffs his feet against the gritty concrete floor.

I stare at him. "Seriously?"

He starts to speak, but I'm not done yet. "Since I don't think you're here because you actually care about my well-being, I'm guessing this is more about Chase. So let me help. Recovering alcoholic, workaholic, and selfish bastard are already taken. Mostly by him telling on himself."

Adam's regarding me with open-mouthed astonishment.

"But a well-meaning speech about him possibly being an income tax avoider or dog-napper, if you have a shred of proof or a wisp of gossip about either, are both still available," I say.

Adam laughs, a little too loudly, and Chase's head jerks up and in our direction.

"Did it work? Is he looking over here?" Adam mumbles to me.

I look at Adam in shock.

"What, I can't do something to help?" he asks, taking my stunned silence as an invitation to plop himself on the ground at my feet, but still maintaining a safe distance, which I both appreciate and find annoying.

I narrow my eyes at him, but he just gives me a big innocent smile. That feeling that he's up to trouble only increases. "Considering we don't know each other at all? No, you can't."

"Such a distrustful view of the world," he says in a teasing tone. "What would ever make you think so badly of . . ." He flushes red, apparently remembering who he's talking to. "Never mind," he mutters.

That makes me like him slightly better, which still isn't saying a whole lot. "What do you want?" I ask.

"Honestly?"

"I doubt it, but you can try."

"Funny." Adam sighs. "All right, I can see you're a cards-on-the-table type of person."

"More like low tolerance for happy bullshit," I say, "but continue."

He laughs again, and this time it sounds genuine. Chase is now staring at us, even as Jenna talks to him.

"I'm going to take back some of the stuff I thought about you," he says, sounding insultingly impressed and surprised. "You're not what I expected." He jerks his chin in my direction. "I like you."

If Mia were over here, she'd probably be able to rattle off his

IMDb entry with awe. But I have no idea who he is, so Adam's stamp of approval means less than he'd probably like.

"What do you want?" I repeat, emphasizing each word.

He eyes me with consideration and then seems to come to a decision. "Petty ambition, frankly."

I raise my eyebrows.

"I'm bored, and he's trying so hard to avoid looking over here, I thought it would be fun to get under his skin." He grins at me. "You know, the amazing Chase Henry, the great washup trying to make a comeback—"

"Hey," I say sharply, glaring at him.

He holds his hands up in a protest of innocence. "I'm just repeating what others are saying."

Chase stalks toward us, closing the distance in a few long strides. Then he's looming over Adam. Adam would be taller if he were standing, but Chase is broader, more threatening by a long shot, especially with the frown on his face and the sleeves of his hoodie pushed up, revealing tensed forearms.

"Is everything okay here?" he asks me.

Unaware of Chase's presence until then, Adam jumps, unease and surprise skating across his expression.

I feel a greedy bit of pleasure at that reaction. For all Adam's smarmy confidence and smack talk about Chase, he's not 100 percent sure that Chase won't kick his ass. And I find I'm kind of okay with Adam's uncertainty on this issue.

"Yeah, everything's fine," I say with a smile. "Adam decided he wanted to chat. But if you want to—"

"I better get back," Chase says, jerking a thumb toward Jenna. He turns and walks away before I even have a chance to nod.

Hurt throbs in my chest. Is this because of Mia? Because she arrived unexpectedly? Because I brought her to the set? Or did I do something I'm not aware of?

When he left the hotel this morning, everything was fine, as far as I knew.

God, get over it, Amanda. He's not your boyfriend. You're friends in a mutually beneficial situation. That's all.

A mutually beneficial situation that involves taking me on the most romantic 5:30 a.m. date ever?

"Well, that worked better than I thought," Adam says as soon as Chase is out of hearing distance. "You might try not looking quite so crushed, though, when he walks away."

"Are you seriously trying to engineer some kind of jealousy freakout?" I ask in disbelief. Good luck with that, today especially.

"Oh, come on; he's not the only one allowed to play the system?" He gives me that boyish, aren't-I-such-a-scamp smile that probably tugs at the heartstrings (and ovaries) of every other female in swooning distance.

I stiffen. "I have no idea what you're talking about."

Adam snorts. "Right. Last week, Chase Henry was a name that sounded only sort of familiar to everybody but the most die-hard *Starlight* fans, but this week he's trending as part of the top-three hashtags on . . . well, everywhere." He's working hard to hide it, but I can hear the envy in his voice.

And I still don't know what he means.

Adam pauses and cocks his head to the side. "You haven't seen it."

"Social media and I don't get along," I say. I had a Facebook page and Twitter account, both of which were co-opted for the search (#findAmandaGrace). I've never bothered to reclaim them or start new ones. I have a hard enough time dealing with the real world, where most people try to respond to me with some sensitivity. On the internet, deliberate, anonymous cruelty is a sport. It only took accidentally reading a few comments after an interview—ones that suggested I should consider being abducted a compliment to my hotness—to convince me to stay away.

Adam pulls his phone from his pocket, taps into it, and then lifts it up to show me.

I lean forward in Chase's chair to see. And sure enough, the first three items on the Trending list are #AmandaGrace, #ChaseHenry, and . . .

"Hashtag AMASE?" I ask, wrinkling my nose.

"It's your 'couple name,' a mash-up of your—"

"I know what it is," I say. I'm just stunned to learn of its existence. "I was only in a basement for two years, not the last century."

Adam flinches, but my words don't dissuade him from continuing. "I think they're saying it like Amaze," he says with a casual shrug that seems a little forced. "But you can always ask Chase."

Now, there it is. This is what his windup has been leading to. I can feel it, like I can feel tension emanating from him, despite his relaxed position on the floor. And yet, I have to ask, the words burbling up like vomit, "Why would Chase know or care?"

Adam blinks at me, all innocence again. "Because he's the one who started it."

With another tap, he has a profile up for Chase Henry on his phone's tiny screen. The small photo in the header is definitely Chase, but taken from the side. He's wearing sunglasses, the same ones from this morning. His head is tilted back in laughter, his face lit by what appears to be either late afternoon or early morning sun. It is a surprisingly intimate picture. He seems relaxed, happy in the presence of whoever is taking the photo.

"Verified" is stamped across the upper left, taking away the possibility of an imitator trying to convince the world otherwise.

The most recent posts are mostly benign—talking about going for a run or staying in for a quiet night with lots of misspelled words. Each contains the #amase tag, though.

And the first one, just a day ago, is nothing but #amase, #amase, #amase, #amase, #amase, #amase. Just the hashtag repeated over and over again, to start the trending process.

That causes something in me to shift, metal tearing into soft vulnerable flesh. My heart pushed into an oversized meat grinder. Chase was on his phone last night when I came to talk to him. But he put it aside, telling me it was nothing.

It shouldn't hurt. It really shouldn't. It's just part of the process, no different than boosting his profile with the pictures of us. But we never talked about this, and somehow that makes it feel more exploitative, instead of the partnership I thought we had.

"I mean, I think it's awesome how much you're willing to help him. But I'm just wondering what you're getting out of it, especially when you're just sitting over here by yourself." Again, his studied mix of casual concern and indifference hits the wrong note in me.

I eye him carefully. "It is awfully considerate of you to be so concerned with my feelings, Adam."

He gives an aw-shucks shrug. He doesn't know me well enough to hear the sarcasm underneath. Too bad for him.

"So, what's in it for you?" I ask.

His mouth works silently in surprise. Then he shakes his head. "I'm just thinking about you and that it's not fair—"

"Not fair to me or to you?" I persist. I might have been naive and trusting enough once to miss the selfish motives at play here, but I am not that stupid anymore.

Anger flashes across his face, then vanishes beneath precisely cultivated amusement with a touch of condescension. "You think I'm making it up? Oh, honey." He reaches out as though he would pat my knee, but stops himself.

I shift away anyway. "No, I don't." Sadly, that is the truth: the posts exist under Chase's verified name and that's an uncomfortable reality that I'll have to absorb somehow. But that's not what I'm after right now.

His forehead creases with confusion. "Then why are you giving me—"

"I know why he's doing what he's doing. Why are you?"

But I've given him too much time to rally. He just looks at me with distaste. "Sad that you can't even recognize the good from the bad anymore."

His words strike home, an extra slap on an already sore spot, and I draw back, pulling in a sharp breath.

As Adam pushes himself up and walks away, Chase's gaze finds mine, his eyebrows raising in question.

Okay? he mouths.

I don't know how to answer that right now. My head is full of questions, and the sensation that I'm missing something, if I could just pull back enough to see it.

I nod, though, because this isn't the time or place for that conversation, even if I were ready. And I'm not.

But Chase frowns, not convinced by whatever he sees on my face.

Fortunately, Max calls for places and the resumption of filming before Chase can make his way over to me.

As Mia hurries back to my side, breathless with excitement, I'm struck with a sick feeling, wondering how these pieces I've been handed fit together and exactly *how* I'm being played. Because at this point, it's not really a question of "if" anymore.

24

Chase

The knock at the adjoining door makes me jump, even though I've been half-expecting it, hoping for it. The dull rumble of voices from the television, mixed with the higher pitches of Amanda and Mia talking, stopped a while ago.

Not that I was eavesdropping, exactly. Just trying to pick my moment to go over and talk with Amanda, without a lot of luck.

After I finished on set for the day, well after ten o'clock, with Karen's words of caution circling in my head, we all went back to the hotel: me, Amanda, Mia, Emily, and Ron. And the silence was awkward and huge, punctuated only by Mia's various proclamations and observations from what she learned on set.

Amanda nodded politely or made the occasional comment in response to her sister, but she was a different person from this morning. I didn't know what Adam said, but whatever it was, it caused a distant, troubled look in her eyes that the intervening time had not erased.

I should have followed my instincts and punched him, no matter how much trouble it would have caused.

Amanda spent the rest of the time on set with her head bent over her phone, and the few times she looked in my direction, her expression was vague, like she was seeing through me.

I didn't know if it was in reaction to whatever Adam said or if it was because I was keeping my distance for the moment. Karen was right: I needed to think it through and make a decision without hurting Amanda.

But the problem is, even now, I'm not any clearer on what I want, except that I'm not ready for her to leave tomorrow. Maybe that's enough of a place to start. Either way, with Amanda at my door, my time's up.

I chuck my pages for tomorrow on the table and get up to open the door.

"Hey," Amanda says with a tentative smile.

But my voice is lodged in my throat, as I stare at her. She's wearing my shirt, and nothing else. The top three buttons are open, showing that she's not wearing a shirt underneath this time, and her long bare legs poke out beneath the hem.

I know it shouldn't matter; I should keep my focus on what I need to say. But I'm only human. A human with an instant hard-on, apparently.

"Oh." She makes a face, her cheeks flooding with color. "Sorry. Mia ransacked the clothes I brought. I know I need to get it back to you." As she brushes her hands down the front of the shirt, I can now see that she is wearing those same boxer sleep shorts from last night, the hem barely peeking out from beneath my shirt.

That doesn't help much, though, because the mental image of her in the shirt alone, false as it is, is burned into my brain.

I clear my throat, trying to recover my voice. "No," I man-

age. "It's fine. Don't worry about it. Keep it as long as you want."
Forever.

But the tiny wrinkle of concern in her forehead suggests that my words are not entirely convincing. That, or she thinks I'm having some kind of breakdown, which is, sadly, not far from the truth.

"Okay," she says, the drawn-out sound another indicator of her doubt. "But that's not why I'm . . . I wanted to talk to you," she says. She squeezes her phone between her palms, interlocking her fingers around it.

"Okay," I say warily, dread accumulating in the pit of my stomach.

I step back to let her into the room.

"So, Adam is kind of a douche," she says, moving past me and settling on the couch, folding into a cross-legged position on the farther cushion.

That is not what I was expecting. The tightness in my gut eases a little.

I close the door and join her on the sofa. "What are you talking about?"

"He went out of his way to talk to me again today. And I think I figured out why. Well, at least his tiny-brain reasoning, but there's more to it." She hesitates. "Sorry, I'm not even sure if this is something you want to hear about . . ."

"No, tell me; I want to know."

"So, he came over to talk to me today mainly, I think, because he thought it might make you, uh, jealous." She shifts uncomfortably, her gaze darting from me to the table and back again as if she's not sure enough about that possibility to state it as unimpeachable fact.

"He's right," I say flatly. Faker asshole that he is, he is evidently good at picking up genuine emotion when he's in the same room with it.

Her mouth opens in a surprised O.

"Sorry," I say. "I have no reason to make that claim—I get that. It's just . . . I was." Admitting it actually makes me feel temporarily worse, more exposed.

But then Amanda smiles at me, that bright, perfectly perfect smile that speaks to all that she's been through. "I'm not unhappy to hear that," she says softly.

Then she shakes her head and holds up her hand, as if we're getting distracted. And we were. "But that's not all. I think he's pissed you're getting more attention than he is, and he wanted to see if he could do something to disrupt it. To disrupt . . . us." Her words quicken now with distaste and anger. "He showed me where we, you and I together, are trending on all these sites. Hashtag Amase." Her mouth twists in distaste. "It's our names put together."

Suddenly I have a very bad feeling where this is going. I deleted the account and all of Elise's stupid posts last night. But that just deleted the app off my phone. It didn't get rid of the accounts entirely. Like, say on the phone or tablet of the person who created them.

"Amanda, I . . ." The words crowd in my throat—*I'm sorry, Elise, I said no*—but all jammed together like that, none of them emerges.

"Then he showed me the Chase Henry account where it supposedly all started from. The hashtag Amase thing."

She clicks on her phone and shows me a screen: the verified Chase Henry account on Twitter.

Even though I'm expecting it, the sight of it makes me freeze.

Seeing Elise's words in black and white—her stupid text-speak, the stuff about running and the quiet night in, plus a post she did not show me with nothing but #amase in it—makes my vision cloud temporarily with rage. She did not, at least, post the photos she took in my room.

But this is bad enough. Amanda will see it as an intrusion, a violation. And she's right.

A crushing weight settles on my chest, and I slump back against the couch. This is it. It's over, right here and now. Fuck.

Swallowing hard over the lump in my throat, I close my eyes. "Amanda, I know you have no reason to believe me, but I didn't write or post any of that stuff. And I tried to—"

"I know you didn't," she says quietly.

The words are so different from what I'm expecting that it takes me a second to process them. My eyes snap open, and I blink, playing back what I thought I heard.

"You . . . what?" I ask, sitting forward.

"They don't even sound like you," she points out. "And the hashtag?" She rolls her eyes. "Please. Not even with a gun to your head, I don't think."

I'm staring at her, my mouth open in amazement.

"What?" she asks with a frown. "I do pay attention."

She knows me. Enough to recognize something that's not me. The real me.

"Anyway, someone is pretending to be you." Amanda hesitates. "Your ex, maybe? I don't know. But there's a way to report it," she says with that calmness and certainty that is a balm to the craziness we're currently embroiled in. "Mia showed me. It takes a few days, though, and—"

Relief washes over me in a great wave. I know what I want now. "Stay with me?" I blurt out.

She goes still. "What?"

"I wanted to talk to you about this before. I'm sorry if I seemed off today," I say, the words spilling out quickly. "I just wasn't sure if . . . I'm here until Saturday and I was hoping you might—"

"Yes," she says.

"Really?"

Her mouth curves in a smile. "Yeah."

She knows me. And she's staying.

With the rush of adrenaline from her answer fueling me,

I lean over and kiss her, drawing her bottom lip into my mouth. She responds eagerly, moving toward me on her knees to close the gap between us.

Her tongue teases mine, moving in and out, mimicking the motion I want elsewhere. I pull back, laying open-mouthed caresses down her throat. She smells so damn good. Her skin is smooth and heated beneath my tongue, and I feel her swallow reflexively.

With my nose pressed against the point where her neck meets her shoulder, I give in to temptation and nip at her collarbone, and she makes that noise, that involuntary exhale, something between a sigh and a gasp. It makes my head buzz and my blood hot.

She rises up on her knees, her hands clutching my shirt as she meets my mouth again. I rest my free hand on her bare leg, rubbing my open palm up and down against the silky flesh, and her hips move in an instinctive thrusting motion that stops my breath. It's hard to think.

Sliding my hand up the outside of her leg, beneath her shorts, I grip her hip, drawing circles with my thumb on the skin exposed above the line of her panties.

Her breath is coming in shuddering pants between kisses, and I can feel the heat of her against me. Every instinct I have is telling me to lean against her, guide her onto her back. But that's a no-go.

Something has to happen, though. Or I need to start the cooling-off process. My dick is pressed so hard against the button fly of my jeans, there might be permanent marks.

"Amanda," I try.

"Yessss," she says against my lip. I'm going to lose my mind.

"You can't, uh . . . me on top of you is bad, right?" I'm struggling to get words out in the right order.

She tenses slightly, and that helps me collect my thoughts a little.

"It's okay," I whisper against the skin at her chest. "I just want to try something different. But if it's too much or it's not good, you just need to say." And I will hobble as fast as I can for the coldest shower known to man.

She blinks at me, her eyes made darker by heat and want. Her lips are reddened from kissing, and the sight sends a primal thrill through me.

Then she nods.

"Come closer," I say hoarsely.

She's already pressed against me at the chest, but her lower body is angled slightly away. At my direction, she inches forward on her knees until they're pressed against my leg.

I slide my hand down her hip to behind her knee. "Trust me?"

She nods again, a swift, decisive confirmation.

I tug gently until she lifts her knee and then I swing her toward me until she's straddling my thighs.

She's not even sitting on me but just the sight of her above me is so fucking hot. I want her naked and riding me, her hair loose against my skin.

"Okay?" I manage.

"Yes." The word barely escapes from her mouth before she's leaning over me, her tongue plunging in my mouth, tangling with mine. After a second, she changes the angle, lowering herself to rest her weight on my legs, lightly though, as if she's still not sure.

I resist the urge to tug her into me. I want to grind against her, feel her damp heat even with our clothes in the way.

Instead, I stroke her back, feeling the warmth of her skin beneath her shirt, *my* shirt. And when the fabric rucks up beneath my palm, my fingers slip across bare skin at her waist.

Her breath catches, escaping in the smallest of moans.

"Okay?" I ask again.

Her response is to inch her way forward into my lap, but we're not pressed together yet, and I think I'm going to die if I can't push against her, feel her rubbing on me.

But I'm determined to keep myself in check.

306 / STACEY KADE

Then her mouth moves along my jaw. "I like the way you taste," she breathes against me. Right before her teeth tease my skin.

Instinct kicks in, and my hands tighten on her waist, pulling her into me as my hips thrust up.

"Chase!" She exhales my name in a sharp breath, and I'm already fumbling to lift her away.

But then she rolls forward into me instead, and I feel like crying, it feels so damn good. Even with the stupid button fly. I lift my hips to push back against her—I want inside so bad—and she rocks with me, leaving kisses across my forehead and down my temples.

I fumble for the buttons of her shirt, pressing my mouth against every inch of exposed skin.

Her bra is a pale purple with a shiny silky edge that begs to be touched. Her nipples are already budding beneath it, and the sight of them makes my mouth open in anticipation.

But when I cup her breast, running my thumb over the growing hardness of her nipple, she stiffens.

It's subtle, not a jerk away from me, but a sudden tension that wasn't there before.

I retreat immediately. "Not good?"

Her gaze darts away from mine. "No."

"Too much or just not that?" I ask. Communication is the only way I'm not going to screw this up.

"Just not that." She folds her arms across her chest.

"Hey," I say and wait until she looks at me. "It's okay." I hold her gaze so she knows I mean it. "I just want to understand what makes you feel good and what doesn't. Talk to me?"

I shift a little beneath her, trying to give us some breathing—and thinking—room.

She hesitates, biting her lip for a moment, then releasing it in a slow slide. "Your mouth is okay," she says, a gorgeous blush spreading across the pale skin of her chest and up into her neck. "I liked you kissing me there. But hands grabbing, I can't . . ."

"Okay, no, that's all I need to know." I rest my hand at the back of her neck, caressing the tight muscles there until she relaxes.

When she bends her head to bring her mouth to mine, I keep my hands solidly on her legs, making no move toward her chest or any move at all, for that matter.

After a minute or so, the stiffness leaches from her body and she's warm and soft in my arms again, leaning into me.

"Will you take your bra off for me?" I ask, the words thick in my throat. "My hands won't go anywhere near, I promise." Then a thought occurs belatedly. "Unless that's not—"

"No, that's . . . I can."

I watch with greedy eyes as she reaches behind herself, unfastening the clip.

The material slackens, the cups gape away from her body, but they're still hiding her. She hesitates, shy for just a second, before pulling it down.

Her tits are as perfect as I imagined, pale-skinned handfuls with pink nipples that are begging to be tasted. They're shaking slightly with her heartbeat and accelerated breathing.

"You are beautiful," I say, my voice a grating mess.

She smiles at that but ducks her head down as she works the strap off one arm and then the other, leaving her shirt in place, which is only hotter.

When she looks up, I lock my gaze with hers, to be sure I'm not missing a change in her expression, then I lean forward and extend my tongue to lick one hardened nipple.

She moans.

Her hands run through my hair, and then she's pressing me tighter against her breast.

I take as much of her breast into my mouth as I can, sucking her until she's whispering nothing but my name and "yes," over and over again.

I release one nipple, leaving it reddened and wet from my mouth, which is the hottest thing I've ever seen, and move to the other.

She grinds hard against me, then pauses, tilting her head over mine to whisper in my ear, "Can you take off your shirt?"

I release her breast with one final pull, and she whimpers, riding me harder.

But I lean away, yanking at my collar.

Being skin to skin is an irresistible siren song of an idea.

She backs off a little, her eyes wide as she takes in my chest and shoulders. And watching her watch me, her shirt gaping open to reveal her breasts, her mouth a soft pink O, makes my cock twitch eagerly in my jeans.

Her hands slide over my pecs and down, lingering near my hips and abdomen. "What are these muscles called?" she asks, trailing a teasing finger over the area in question.

"Um, obliques, I think," I manage, fighting the temptation to put her hand on my hard-on.

"I like them." She gives me a saucy grin.

"Yeah?" My head is spinning. Somehow I've lost control over this situation, leaving her in charge, and that's more than fine.

Before I can blink, she's bent down to press her mouth against the muscles she "likes," laying her tongue against them like a benediction, and my eyes are rolling back in my head.

I grab her arms and haul her up, thrusting my tongue into the damp cavern of her mouth. Her breasts are wet peaks against my chest, and the friction feels so good. We're moving in a steady rhythm now, her breath coming faster.

But I'm not sure if I can hold out, not like this.

I kiss her hard one more time, sucking her tongue into my mouth before leaning back.

"Can we . . . I need to move, do something else or this is going to be over too soon," I say in a strained voice. I haven't so much as touched her clit or slid my fingers inside her, and I want to make her feel good, if she'll let me. "Same rules as before."

With a smile reeking of female pride, she leans forward and bites my lower lip, growing bolder by the second. "What do you have in mind?"

"Stand," I say.

She slides off me, and I shift on the couch, lying on my side and stretching my legs out until my feet press against the arm-rest on the opposite side.

Hesitation flashes across her face.

"You're on the outside, no weight on top of you, and you can pull away at any time," I point out calmly. But I'm not going to talk her into it. If she doesn't want to, we'll find another way.

But after a moment, she edges to the couch, kneeling next to me first, then stretching out beside me. "Hi," she whispers, resting her palm against my chest, before leaning in to kiss my skin above her fingers.

I'm such a fucking goner. I just hope I don't embarrass myself.

25

Amanda

I'm not sure about this. But lying next to Chase voluntarily isn't nearly the same as being pressed down against my will, which is what triggers panic in me.

And right now, the level in my head has the bubble firmly in the green-go zone. So, okay.

I miss moving with him, though. It felt like it was building to something. But it wasn't scary, at all, to my surprise. Just exciting, with a level of safety preserved. Like heat lightning in the distance.

But this, this has the potential to bring that lightning much closer, which makes my heart trip in my chest with both anticipation and nerves.

Seemingly sensing that, he caresses my cheek and leans in to kiss me softly, no tongue, just lips and gentleness.

I lift my hands to the back of his neck to press him closer, to deepen the kiss. But he holds off.

His hand drifts to my hip and then lower, his fingers alighting for a brief second at the hot spot of sensation between my legs. Just that fractional touch makes me wiggle toward him.

"I want to touch you here, my hand against your skin," he says, watching my reaction carefully. He's been so attentive, I feel almost guilty, doing all the taking and virtually no giving. Not that it seems to bother him. "I want to make you feel good."

The idea of his hand between my legs sends a bolt of want through me, followed immediately by uncertainty. I honestly don't know. Will it be ... clinical, uncomfortable? That's been my only experience with that action.

I decide to follow the lust, and besides, nothing he's done so far has felt even remotely distant or cold, or like a violation. And if I don't like it, I trust him to stop.

I trust him. The sentiment is solid, throbbing in my chest like my heartbeat, no shadow of doubt or hesitation.

I clear my throat. "Yes."

He exhales shakily and kisses me, his tongue delving into my mouth until I'm clutching at him, arching awkwardly against him.

"Put your knee up on my hip," he whispers in my ear, his mouth grazing my cheek in an open-mouthed caress.

I do, and for a split second, the feeling of being vulnerable chases away the heat and desire.

But then his fingers graze my leg, stroking the hollow where my thigh meets my body, and that feeling of vulnerability disappears under the chant of *more, more, more* in my head.

He braces himself on one elbow, and I feel him pull aside the layers of material between us, and the slightly cooler air touches my overheated flesh.

The first touch, just the backs of his fingers, pressing lightly, sends a jolt through me, and I'm pushing into him, the reaction automatic and instinctive.

He groans softly. "You are so wet."

I might have been embarrassed by the frank statement of my condition, but my heart is throbbing in my chest, like an over-inflated balloon about to pop.

Then he turns his wrist, and his fingers skate over the damp and aching flesh. His fingertip presses lightly against the tight bud of sensation at the top of me while the rest of his fingers slip through the wetness, parting me, holding me open to his touch.

I squirm against the sensation. It's not the same as rubbing against him—this is more focused and in that way more torturous but good.

"So soft," he whispers. "You're so soft and wet, and I . . ." His words cut off in a groan, as he drops his head, his jaw muscles clenching visibly beneath his skin.

His touch remains gentle but persistent, though, and soon I'm writhing against him, wanting something more. Instinct tells me to close my legs over his hand so I can keep that pressure there, just so.

But then he lifts his head to kiss me, his hand between my legs stilling, much to my frustration.

I move my hips toward him. "Don't stop," I plead. My whole being is encompassed in this moment, in his touch.

That's when I realize one of his fingers is resting at my entrance, pressing lightly but not quite penetrating.

He hasn't stopped; he's asking a question.

But then he goes further. "What do you want, Amanda?"

I blink up at him. His cheeks are flushed, his eyes are dark with want. Chase Henry Mroczek is watching me like I hold the answer to everything he wants, to the whole universe.

He told me that I would know what I wanted and that I would ask him for it. And he was right.

The idea of saying the words out loud sends a brief flash of self-consciousness through me, but the embarrassment is a feather compared to the weight of want in me right now.

"I want you inside," I say, holding his gaze steadily, despite the creeping heat in my face. "I want you to put your finger inside me."

His nostrils flare as he bends forward, his mouth hot and open on mine. Then he gives a shuddering breath that I feel against my cheek, as his finger slides in.

Reflexively I tense up, expecting pain or at least the sense of being invaded.

He stops immediately. "Amanda?"

"Just getting used to it," I say quickly.

Which is true. It doesn't hurt. It just feels different. There's no painful or invading sensation; his finger is just a warm, persistent but not unpleasant presence inside me. It sends a shiver through me. He is in me. Part of him is inside me. And I *like* it.

He holds his hand steady against me, not thrusting or pushing, his warm palm cupping between my legs.

Then he ducks his head and nudges the edge of my shirt aside with his chin and cheek to trail his kisses along the top of my breast.

The rasp of his stubble against my skin makes me ache. Then his hot wet tongue laps against my nipple before he closes his mouth over it and sucks.

Instinctively, I push my hips toward him, sinking his finger deeper inside me. I gasp.

He stops, lifting his head from my breast with an audible pop.

"Yes, I mean, it's good," I babble.

He returns his mouth to my breast, his blond head bobbing before me, and the sight of him like this, combined with the sensations, only sends a flood of warmth through me.

And it doesn't take long before I'm pushing up against him, riding his hand while he remains still.

It's what I need and yet somehow not enough.

A whimper escapes me against my will. "I need more," I beg before he can ask. Because I think I'll die if he stops now. There's a constant roar of need in my head. That sense of something building has returned, but with it, more frustration. It's like reaching for the top of a shelf and being just a few inches too short.

His tongue swirls over my nipple as I feel the pressure of a second finger pushing inside me, next to the first. It's tight but it feels so good, more filling. Not as much as I want, but better.

His hand rocks against me now, his fingers moving in me and it's . . . so . . . yes.

I tighten my knee on his hip, tucking my foot behind his leg, trying to pull him closer.

Wet sounds, the audible proof of how excited I am as he moves his fingers in me, break into my awareness.

I turn toward him and bury my face against the arm he's using to support himself, embarrassed. "God."

He gives a strangled laugh. "That's good; it's so good." His voice is rough, unsteady. "It means you're close, that you're feeling it."

He shifts, changing the angle of his hand and curling those fingers inside me, and a helpless moan escapes me.

He bends his head toward me, his breathless voice closer to my ear. "And hearing that, feeling how wet you are for me, makes me so fucking hard. Because it means when you're ready, I would be able to slide in and get so deep and make us both feel amazing."

My eyes flutter open, and his gaze, so familiar to me now, is pinned to my face, but those dark blue eyes are but a sliver of color. The pupils have swallowed the irises whole. His cheeks are flushed with color.

As I watch, his mouth opens slightly, those perfect teeth sinking into his bottom lip, strain written across his features.

Looking down, I see the cords of muscle in his forearm tensing and relaxing as he works in me.

And suddenly I can imagine what it would feel like, moving with him inside me, connecting in the most intimate way possible.

Before I can say, *I want,* or even whisper, *Yes,* a sudden chill spreads over my skin, raising goose bumps, and then that building, reaching feeling hits a peak, catching me off guard. And it all falls, falls, falls down and I'm shivering and shuddering, helpless against the waves.

"That's it," he whispers in my ear, what sounds like pride, not for himself but in me. "You've got it; just keep moving."

My hips push against him automatically, and the clutching feeling slowly fades away, leaving behind a growing sensation of contentment and warmth. I feel boneless and relaxed in a way I haven't in, I don't know, maybe ever.

"Okay?" he asks as I sag into him.

I lean back to peer up at him, a ridiculous smile spreading across my face. I couldn't stop it even if I wanted to. "Yes." The word is slurred with pleasure.

He laughs, a deep rumbling in his chest that I feel, and leans down to plant a quick kiss on my mouth. "Yeah, it's pretty good."

He pulls his hand away from me, and satisfied though I am, a complaining noise escapes my mouth. Less for the specific action than the loss of connection.

"Greedy you," Chase teases, kissing my forehead.

"Yes." He's kidding but I realize he's right: I am being greedy. Just not in the way he means.

Glancing down our bodies, I see the front of his faded jeans straining, pulled tight against his erection, which looks so large as to be possibly painful to him and definitely intimidating to me.

But at the sight of him like that, a craving unfurls in me and spreads, like an itch in my blood. I want to touch him. I want to see him come undone, see his face slack with pleasure. I want to see all that control he worked so hard to maintain for me unravel spectacularly.

But to do that . . .

I bite my lip, and contemplate what that would mean.

Grinding against him, against it, isn't the same. That, I could do. Have done. But somehow the idea of touching him, of undoing his pants, feels like too much, like skating too close to the edge.

A tiny trickle of dread wends its way through my post-orgasm bliss, and I hate it, the fear eating acid-like at my contentment.

Fuck fear. I'm so sick of it. It's just a body part, a penis. So what? My first experiences with one were traumatic and horrible, yes. But that doesn't mean that *every* encounter will be the same. Chase has already proven that in general in a dozen ways since I met him.

Why would this be any different?

And he won't do anything I don't want him to. If he was that kind, he would have done it already. A closed zipper—or button fly, in this case—is no deterrent.

"Hey," Chase says, nudging me gently. I look up to see him frowning, sensing the change in my mood. "Where'd you go? Is everything—"

"What about you?" I ask, heart pounding so hard it's making me tremble.

His brows draw together in confusion. "What?"

"This." Tentatively, I reach out and run my hand over the hardened bulge behind his fly.

He sucks a breath in a hiss through his teeth, and his hips jerk forward into my hand, his face a fierce mask of want.

A heady rush of heat and power surges through me until I'm almost dizzy from it. I made him react that way, I made him *want*, but I'm in control. I could almost laugh from the relief and giddiness.

He tilts away from my hand. "It's fine. I'll handle it later." He gives a shaky laugh. Those crinkles at the edges of his eyes make my chest throb with emotion, sending a wave of powerful affection through me, so much so that it feels as if the undertow will pull me under to drown, and I'll go happily.

I push up and kiss the lines I can reach, on the right side of his face. The next words pop out before I can stop them, before I can change my mind. "Can I watch? I mean, if that's okay with you," I add hastily. It seems like a good compromise to me—I might not be ready yet to take on my reluctance directly, but watching him touch himself might help with the intimidation factor, not to mention then he won't be so miserable.

It all sounds very practical to me, but it evidently sounds like more to Chase.

His breathing stops abruptly, only to emerge in a harsh exhale against my throat. "Now?" He sounds hoarse, and that power-high returns.

"Yes," I say. After that reaction? Oh, hell, yes.

"You don't have to—" he begins, and I sit up because I want him to see me and hear that I mean it.

"I know that," I say calmly. "I want to."

He swallows hard, and I hear the click of his dry throat. Then he gives a jerky nod. His cheeks are flushed and he's biting his lip. I'm not sure if that's uncertainty or restraint. Either way, it is possibly the sexiest thing I've ever seen.

"Are you sure?" he asks as I settle next to him, stretching out on my side and propping myself up on one elbow. But he's already tugging carefully at the top button on his jeans, knowing my answer even as I nod.

Dark gray boxer briefs emerge from behind his fly as he yanks the rest of the buttons free. The shape of him is much clearer without his jeans in the way. Longer than my hand and thicker than I expected, too. That makes the tremor of uncertainty in me increase a little.

Before I have a chance to potentially panic, though, he lifts up and shoves his jeans and boxers down his body in one smooth motion, revealing everything the fabric was hiding.

The hair there is not quite the brighter gold he has elsewhere, and it's trimmed close to his body. His penis stands slightly away from his abdomen, the skin darker with the flush of blood. The rounded tip is wet, and I'm fascinated by the sight.

I touch lightly with one fingertip, unable to resist, and his penis twitches toward me, like I'm home and it wants nothing more than to come inside.

He moans at my touch. "It's not . . . I won't last . . . if we were together, it would be much better than this," he tries, his words coming out garbled, half finished.

"I'm not worried," I say, then I follow an impulse and lean forward for a quick second to swipe my tongue across his chest before retreating.

He groans and locks his hand around himself at the base.

"Keep looking at me like that, and I won't have to do anything at all," he says in a thick voice.

I raise my eyebrows. "Really?"

He pulls up and down in a motion I recognize, though it's rougher than anything he did to me.

"When you came to the door, I thought you were wearing my shirt without anything under it. I almost lost it," he says.

Interesting. The revelation sends flutters through me, centering between my legs.

"Is that what you want to see?" I ask, feeling daring after his confession and the heated expression on his face.

Without waiting for his answer, I lift my hips and shimmy out of my sleep shorts and underwear. His shirt covers me anyway, and it's actually a relief to peel the damp material away from my still-aching-in-a-good-way flesh.

His eyes go wide and then squeeze shut. "You're going to kill me," he mumbles.

I can't stop myself from grinning.

When his fist is on the downward motion, my boldness resurfaces and I reach forward to close my fingers lightly over the head of him.

He arches hard toward my hand with a groan.

"Can you tell me what to do?" I ask in a whisper; my insides are quivering with nerves and excitement.

"You're asking me to talk when your hand is on my cock?" he responds in a strangled voice, removing his hand from himself.

Instinctively, I move my hand down to take its place.

"Keep doing that." His hand closes over mine, guiding on speed and pressure until I've got it. The heat of him is intense and when I squeeze a little tighter around him, he grits his teeth and pushes harder through the circle of my fingers.

"Seems like it should hurt," I murmur.

"It doesn't, not like that. But it would be better with lubrication." He gives me a direct look that lights something on fire in me. He means me, all the wet I couldn't control. He wants that on him.

I shiver in delight at the graphicness of the image he's put in my mind.

He rocks his head back against the couch, his lip pinched between his teeth. When he releases it, he licks his lips and opens his eyes to meet my gaze. "Can you open your shirt? So I can see?"

The words alone send a primitive surge of heat in a lightning bolt between my legs.

Instead of answering him, I maneuver the arm that's supporting my weight to tug at the material of my shirt until the cool air licks my skin.

My hand is working on him, but he's staring at me. "You are so beautiful. Everywhere, inside and out." He leans forward and kisses me, his mouth demanding and hot.

I give him everything he asks for in that kiss, everything I can.

When he pulls back, his hand closes over mine again, tugging harder at himself than I would have dared. Impossibly, he seems to grow harder and his breath is coming faster and faster.

"Amanda," he says, my name more a suggestion of sound than an actual word.

Then his whole body shudders and he gasps, his eyes wide but unseeing for a moment. Warm fluid splashes against my arm, startling me, but I ignore it for the moment, caught by the sight of him.

He looks so vulnerable and alone, this man who came to get me, the one who stands between me and anyone or anything that scares me. I want to pull him against me and hold him, giving him shelter and strength.

After a moment, he blinks, shivering, and his chest heaves as he struggles to catch his breath. "Holy shit. I don't think it's been like that since I first learned to . . ." He stops himself and laughs with an edge of hysteria, and I remember the overpowering sensation of well-being that I felt, that he made me feel.

His face seems softer now, younger, more relaxed. "Thank you."

I shake my head. "No, thank you for letting me . . ." I hesitate. "I was afraid . . . I wasn't sure if I could."

He reaches over me and pulls a handful of tissues from the box on the coffee table to wipe my arm.

As he cleans me up and then himself, I lean into him, kissing his forehead, his temple, the crinkles by his eyes, until he looks up at me.

I capture his soft and willing mouth with mine, trying to convey the sweetness that is building in my chest, threatening to bubble over in some unknown manner. Tears, words? I don't know.

He touches my chin with his thumb. "Stay with me?" he asks.

My confusion must have shown in my face. "I am."

"I mean tonight, in here." He reaches down and tugs his jeans and boxers back into place, leaving the fly open.

Involuntarily, I look over my shoulder in the direction of the king-sized bed. "I don't know. Mia's here . . ." Though who am I kidding? She practically shoved me through the door into

Chase's room earlier. I take a moment to lift up a prayer that she's asleep by now and hasn't been listening with her ear pressed to the door. That would be embarrassing on a level I don't want to contemplate.

"We're right next door, if she needs something," Chase says. "And I promise, I'll keep to my half of the bed. Nothing else is going to happen tonight. I just want you here with me."

When I turn my head to face him, the honesty, vulnerability, in his expression breaks something in me, and words come flooding to my tongue, dangerous ones.

Suddenly, I'm all too aware of what this sweet, tight feeling in my chest is.

Love. I'm in love with him.

All my fears of penises suddenly seem small in comparison.

I can't love him. That's crazy. This is over in a few days. He's going back to California; I'm going home to finish my high school classwork and figure out if I can have something resembling a normal life. Maybe even apply to college, now that I feel like I have a shot at succeeding in a new environment.

But knowing those facts does not diminish the feeling in my chest. Not even a little bit.

Which is utterly terrifying in its own right. I don't need a broken heart on top of everything else. I have enough to fix.

But when I open my mouth to explain all of that, the only thing that comes out is, "Yes."

26

Chase

I'm true to my word, and I keep to my side of the bed.

But when Amanda comes back after waking Mia and seeing her safely on her way home, at, like, four thirty in the morning or some crazy-early hour even for me, Amanda climbs in on my side, sliding beneath the covers with a shiver.

"Everything all right?" I ask in a sleep-fogged voice.

"Yeah. She's supposed to text me when she gets home," Amanda says, but even half awake, I can hear worry in her voice. She scoots herself backward into me, fitting herself snugly between my chest and my legs, her butt pressed against my dick, which is only too happy with that arrangement.

"She'll be okay," I say. I back off, putting a few inches of space between us. It's not enough, not when she's warm, almost naked, and well within my reach. But I want us to start right. We don't have to hurry.

So I work very hard on counting backward from one hundred by threes, and concentrate on matching my breath to Amanda's. She relaxes against me, her muscles going slack, and that trust, I realize, means more to me than the rest.

"Do you hear something?" Amanda asks in a sleepy voice, startling me into awareness a few minutes later. At least, I think it's just a few minutes.

I squint at her, her dark red hair spread over the pillow in front of me. Light is breaking through the curtains behind us, creating a blinding white line on the wall.

No, I didn't hear anything, I don't even hear anything now. Because somehow, I've lost the distance I put between us and she's pressed right up against me, and the rush of blood in my ears is drowning out everything else.

I can't stop myself from pushing up against her, and she makes a soft sound of approval, her hips rocking back into me.

But then she stops, her hand on my arm.

"Listen," she says.

I do. It's a faint and tinny sound of bells ringing.

"The alarm next door." I kiss her neck, at the warm juncture with her shoulder, and she shivers. "Probably Housekeeping bumped it and it's going off."

Which I would like to be, too. All my good intentions are rapidly dissolving with the feel of her warmth pressed against me, with only the thin layers of her shorts and my boxers between us.

Pushing myself up on my elbow, I run my free hand down her leg, from hip to knee.

When my hand rounds the back of her knee, barely touching just the inside of her thigh, she shifts her left leg forward, giving me access.

I let out a sharp breath. I should stop. Doing anything more right now is going to leave us both frustrated and wanting what we can't have at this precise moment, not when I'm supposed to be up for work soon. But my body and mind are on opposite sides of this debate.

324 / STACEY KADE

Amanda's legs move restlessly. "Chase," she whispers. "Please."

Debate over.

I slide my hand between her thighs and up, her skin growing warmer from the heat where her legs have been pressed together.

When I pause at the top of her leg and slide my hand beneath her shorts, she makes inarticulate sounds of encouragement. I stroke a finger lightly against the soft folds between her legs, and she makes a pleading noise, arching toward me.

But I maintain that teasing touch on her, up and down, the torment only heightening the moment.

Then to my surprise, she reaches down and presses her fingers against mine, holding it in place against her clit as she moves.

It sends an electrifying surge of lust through me.

I set my teeth gently in the skin at her shoulder, and she throws her head back.

Her breath is already coming faster when I lift my mouth, pressing a quick kiss against her skin.

"Keep going," I tell her, sliding my finger down to where she's already wet and warm and entering her.

She moans in response and moves faster, bumping against her hand and riding my finger.

I slide a second into her, gritting my teeth as my hard-on throbs with the need to be in that smooth, soft heat instead.

But it's just a matter of seconds before her muscles clamp down hard and a ripple of spasms sends a shudder through her whole body.

Yeah. I grin. That would be Amanda: 2, Chase: 1, and I'm feeling pretty good about those statistics.

But then, in a breath of silence between Amanda's gasps and my own thundering heartbeat, I hear the ringing again. Though distorted by distance, the bells sound familiar, more than they did a few minutes ago when I was still half asleep. I'm more than alert now.

With a sudden growing sense of dread, I pull carefully away from Amanda, even as she protests. And then my brain puts the final piece in place, and cold panic sweeps in.

"It's the alarm. On my phone," I say.

Suddenly the light beaming through the crack in the curtains seems way too bright. How late is it?

I lurch upward, reaching for the pillows next to me and sweeping them toward the foot of the bed. The bells get louder.

I feel blindly for my phone across the flat, smooth sheet. It was here when I went to bed, but I moved over when Amanda joined me and the pillows got shifted.

Her cheeks still flushed, Amanda crawls over the top of me, shoves her hair out of her face, and then reaches into the crack between the headboard and the mattress. "Here." She hands my phone to me. "Happens to me all the time at home," she says by way of explanation.

One quick look at the screen tells me I'm in trouble. "Fuck, the van's going to be here in five minutes, and Emily's called three times."

"What do you need?" Amanda asks with that calm possession I so appreciate in a moment like this.

A drink. But I take a deep breath, in and out, forcing myself to think. "No, it's fine; I can do it," I say, more to myself than to her. "I showered last night. I just need to get dressed and get out the door." Maybe Amanda's unruffled demeanor is contagious because I'm far calmer than I would have been before in these circumstances.

But then again, it's not nearly as bad as it has been in the past. I'm not hungover, unprepared, or in the wrong state. Yeah, that happened.

"I can do it," I say again to myself, as much in surprise as confirmation. So I'm not going to fuck this up. Not today, anyway.

She grins at me. "Yeah, you can."

I shove back the covers and stride toward the bathroom, only to take three steps back and lean over to kiss her. How is my life this much better so suddenly?

"Are you coming with me?" I ask with a smile as I pull away. "Because we're probably at the four-minute mark now."

Her eyes go wide and she scrambles off the bed, running for her room, a gorgeous blur of hair, pale skin, and white shirt.

She's dressed and waiting for me by the time I'm out of the bathroom.

"You okay for clothes this morning?" I ask as we head into the hall and hurry toward the elevator.

"No time to freak out about it," she says with a shrug. "I wanted to brush my teeth more."

I laugh. "I respect the choice."

"And I've got my jacket on." She tugs at the front of her fleece. "So no one can even tell if I'm wearing short sleeves anyway."

"But you are," I say as we reach the elevator and I push the button.

"Yeah. I am," she says with a tiny pleased-with-herself shrug.

"Is it weird if I say I'm proud of you since I had nothing to do with it?" I ask.

"No, I'll take it." She smiles up at me and rises on her tiptoes to kiss my mouth and then chin.

The five floors go by quickly that way, Amanda picking random places on my face to kiss—including the lines by my eyes, the ones much discussed by various professionals, which she says she likes—and the doors open on the lobby as Emily calls my phone again.

"How do you feel about making a small spectacle of ourselves?" I ask, stuffing my phone in my jeans pocket. I don't want Emily reporting back that I'm not answering my phone, but neither do I want to call her and offer an excuse for why I'm not already outside and in the van.

"Only a small one? We're scaling back?" Amanda asks, her eyes bright with humor.

"You know, just for today," I say with feigned indifference. "Change it up a little."

"Uh-huh. What do you have in mind?"

"Running." I take her hand and tug her after me, and she's laughing giddily as we dart across the shiny floor, flying past other guests and gawkers, heading for the front doors.

And for the first time in years, my heart feels light, weightless, even. In spite of everything Amanda and I have to figure out, the work still ahead of me and truths I have yet to confess, in this moment, I think I'm actually happy.

27

Amanda

"Oh, shit." Chase comes to an abrupt halt, a step ahead of me, and I stop next to him, staring.

Beyond the hotel's glass doors, the crowd is double what it was yesterday. Hotel security has corralled them behind wooden barricades to keep the entrance clear. But now, mixed in with the photographers and reporters are full camera crews and what appears to be just random people. Mostly women and girls, some of them younger than I am. They're bundled up in jackets and scarves, their faces pink with excitement and cold. Some of them are holding thermoses and others . . .

I frown. "Are those—"

"Signs. Yeah," Chase says, his jaw tight.

Now that I'm looking, I see dozens of homemade poster board placards with messages, decorated in puffy paint and glitter.

Most of them are for Chase exclusively, including a few marriage proposals and offers for childbearing. Does that ever actually work? And would you really want somebody who chooses you for matrimony or to be the mother of his children based on your masterful glue pen skills?

Others, to my surprise, bear the hashtag AMASE. Other variations include things like: WE LOVE YOU, AMANDA & CHASE; FAIRY TALES DO COME TRUE! <3; TRUE LOVE IS 4-EVER, AG+CH; LOVE FROM ABOVE. On this last, our names are surrounded by what I think is a depiction of angel wings. A connection to Chase's guardian angel character on *Starlight*, maybe? Is this the *Starlight* fan contingent?

"Whoa," I murmur. It's sweet and more than a little intimidating. I don't think Chase and I are even sure what we're doing, and suddenly, strangers seem to have a vested interest in the outcome of something we're still trying to figure out.

But a few of the signs bring tears to my eyes. They're the simpler ones: AMANDA GRACE LIVES; GOD BLESS AMANDA; MIRACLES DO HAPPEN.

Wescott is only an hour from my house. Some of these people might well be the ones who spent their free time searching empty houses, drainage ditches, and stretches of uninterrupted forest trying to find me. Other people hung flyers, worked in a volunteer center, or called tip lines.

I clear my throat. "Did someone organize all of this?" I ask, leaning closer to Chase.

"It's possible," he says, "but usually, someone tells you ahead of time if it's a planned spontaneous thing." He gives me an ironic smile, raising the eyebrow that has the scar.

"Oh."

Beyond the crowd, the roof of the white van that takes us back and forth to the set is barely visible. Emily is standing on her seat, looking over the top of everyone, her cell phone pressed to her ear.

A second later, Chase's phone rings in his pocket again. He grimaces.

The blue-coated manager from the other day approaches hesitantly. "Mr. Henry, the service entrance is available to you again, if you'd like to contact your people and have them pick you up there instead."

Chase looks to me.

"No, it'll be fine." I'm not 100 percent sure of that, but I feel more confident than I did the other day. Either way, I'm going to try.

Chase takes my hand, gives it a reassuring squeeze, and we head for the doors. As soon as the outer set opens, the crowd noise explodes and they lift and wave their signs into the air.

His fingers tighten on mine, but his smile is smooth, professional. If you didn't know him, couldn't feel the grip of his hand, you'd think he was thrilled.

But I can see the difference, the slight variation between public Chase and the private version. I like mine better.

He waves at the gathered people, but we move quickly for the van as voices shout at us.

"Chase, over here!"

"Chase, Amanda, do you have plans for what happens after filming?"

"Chase, I love you!"

"Amanda, is this all a publicity stunt?"

"Amanda, how do you feel about Chase saving you again?"

I fight to keep my expression neutral, but really? Where is that coming from? Of course that's probably how it looks: poor traumatized girl suddenly pulled into the spotlight and falling in love, a modern version of Cinderella with celebrity standing in for royalty. But still, it makes me uncomfortable. Chase's poster in that basement and the connection it had to my home and family gave me strength to fight, to escape, definitely. But now?

The whole point of coming here for me was to try to regain that courage I once had.

Because if all I've done is hand that responsibility over to

Chase, then I haven't made any progress toward trusting myself. And I don't think that's the case at all.

"Can you sign this for me?" someone close to my elbow asks, her voice quiet compared to the shouting. Then, there's a magazine being shoved in front of me, and I have to stop or knock it down.

It's a copy of the *People* magazine with me on the cover.

I look up, startled, and the asker, a woman probably my mom's age, smiles at me, perfectly pleasant, holding out a marker.

I freeze.

Confusion crosses her face, and she starts to frown.

Chase steps in, taking the Sharpie from her and handing it to me. I scrawl something that might have been my name or just a bunch of loops that vaguely resemble letters.

"Thank you," the woman says, beaming at me, as Chase tugs on my elbow and leads me to the van door.

"She's going to sell that on eBay the second she gets home," he says in my ear with a grin. "Probably with one of those crocheted toilet roll dolls that's supposed to look like you."

I nod, but I'm shaking, my heart rattling in my chest. I'm not even sure why. She was nice enough. It's just the idea of being singled out, which, duh, is what the entire crowd is doing to us. But I guess I always thought of it as more for Chase, not anything to do with me.

It occurs to me right then as I climb into the van that if this is something Chase and I want to do, to try to be in a real relationship, then this kind of reaction—crowds, signs, insulting questions, people asking *me* for autographs—will probably happen again. A lot. Eventually it would die down, but until then, we would be the focus of a lot of attention.

Before I was thinking of this only as a temporary obstacle, something to survive until it was done and I could go home. I want a normal life, have ever since I got back. But now, I'm not sure if that's possible, not if I also want Chase.

"What happened? Why weren't you answering your phone?" Emily asks Chase as soon as the door shuts behind us.

"I'm sorry," he says. "This morning didn't go the way I expected." But he smiles at me, and his thumb rubs over the back of my hand, easing something tight in me.

We can figure this out; we just need a chance. I know it. I feel it.

But Emily isn't so easily soothed. "Were you drinking?" she demands, as the driver pulls out. "They warned me about that."

Chase tenses, but I'm faster to anger.

"Hey," I say sharply, even though it's none of my business. But it's none of hers, either. "He's your job, but he's a person, too."

Color floods her face as she glares at me.

"It's fine," Chase says to me. "No. I'm not drinking." He doesn't even seem all that offended. But I'm seething on the inside that she dared to ask. She's not the director, his agent, or his mother. It's not right.

But then he'll always be owned, partly by other people, by their expectations and public perception.

I was aware of these things before, but somehow now, it feels more personal, like the loss of something or someone I barely had a chance to know.

As soon as we're on location, Emily rushes us toward the makeup trailer—no time for a stop at Chase's this morning.

"Are you all right?" he asks me as she hurries ahead of us, talking into her walkie.

I smile. "Yeah, just a little overwhelmed." In truth, I'm longing for the moment when we get to go back to our rooms, not because of the "naked stuff," as Mia would say (well, not only because of that), but because that just feels more real.

Chase slides his arm around my waist and stops us both right there in the middle of the line of trailers, with people bustling all around us, and turns to face me.

He hooks his fingers in the open pockets of my fleece to tug me close. "Tomorrow we're moving to shooting nights," he says, his expression serious. "How do you feel about breakfast out?

I did some research, and there's a pancake place near here that boasts twenty-seven different syrups. It's supposedly free if you try all of them at once." He grins at me. "A challenge."

In spite of myself, I laugh. "That sounds disgusting." But I love that he found time, at some point, to look into random places that might be interesting. It makes me feel like no matter where we are or what's going on, he'll always find a way to show more of the world to me than I would have let myself experience otherwise.

"What, no blueberry-banana–cotton candy–pecan combo for you?" he asks with mock confusion.

I wrinkle my nose. "Some things are good in combination; some are not. It's a fine art, knowing the difference."

"Such a limited palate," he says, tsking at me. "I bet you still like maple from the plastic bottle."

I raise my eyebrows. "And you have, what, a special syrup collection, vintages gathered from all over the world?"

"Maybe." He flashes me a smile that warms me down to my toes. "Want to see it sometime?"

I roll my eyes at him, but I can't help laughing.

He lifts his hand to touch my cheek then, his smile turning into something more serious as he regards me with a strange expression. "Thank you for defending me. It was . . ." He drops his gaze to somewhere near my feet. "No one's done that for me in a long time. I haven't deserved it in longer than that."

When he looks up at me again, his eyes are shining with an emotion that makes my chest tight. This is someone unused to being loved, the true kind of love where you want the best for the other person instead of what's easiest for you.

"She was out of line," I point out, uncomfortable with praise for something that was automatic when it came to him.

"And you cared," he argues.

I frown at him. "Well, yeah."

"Chase," Emily calls, her voice huffy.

But he ignores her, leaning his forehead against mine before dropping down to brush my mouth softly with his. "Thank you."

"Aww, adorable. Late but adorable."

I look up to see Karen standing in the open door of the makeup trailer. She folds her arms across her chest, the mermaid scales on her forearm rippling with the movement, but she looks more amused than angry.

Emily is at the base of the stairs, shaking her head at us. She, on the other hand, looks angry.

As Chase climbs into the trailer, Karen steps back to make room and punches him lightly on the arm as he passes.

"What?" he asks, but the grin on his face says he knows exactly what's going on.

"So I guess you're listening to me this time," she says to him, flipping one of her braids behind her shoulder. "That's a pleasant change."

"Told you—new version."

I have no idea what they're talking about, but he looks happy and even she seems slightly less grumpy, which I'm beginning to think, for Karen, is the equivalent of someone else laughing hysterically. The two of them are an odd pair as friends, but they make sense in that way, too, because they're opposites. If this is the first step in repairing that friendship—one that obviously meant enough to both of them that he felt horribly guilty and she was seriously pissed—then good.

As Chase sits in Karen's chair, I take my place in the extra one on the opposite side of the still-open doorway. Despite the fresh cool air from outside, the trailer reeks of chemical cleaner and acrid smoke. The walls are covered in dark smudges and attempts at fresh paint.

"Yeah, sorry," Karen says, catching my expression in the mirror as she starts her work on Chase. "It's getting better, but they were pretty thorough. Thanks a lot, assholes."

Oh. The vandalism. "That happened here?" I ask.

"Unfortunately," Karen says. Then she frowns at Chase. "What is going on with your hair?"

I smother a laugh, but apparently not well enough as he gives me a sharp look.

"I didn't have time to shower this morning," he says.

Karen just sighs and pulls out a spray bottle and starts squirting him with it. And Chase looks about as happy as a soaked cat about that.

"Something came for you," she says as she works. I think she's talking to Chase until she jerks her head at me. "I put it on the other counter."

I glance to my right to find a large gold box I hadn't noticed before, pushed against the mirror. It's one of those pre-wrapped jobs, where the lid just lifts off. My name, in fancy calligraphy-like letters, is written on a matching tag.

I look at Chase questioningly.

"Not me," he says with a frown.

A faint quiver of trepidation ripples through me. I've had enough experience with unannounced packages and letters—the FBI was, for a short time, monitoring our mail—not to reach for it without more information.

"Where did it come from?" I ask Karen.

"One of the runners brought it over an hour ago, maybe," she says with an odd look at me.

"You saw her drop it off?" Chase asks, his gaze meeting mine in the mirror. He's not sure about this, either. He told me yesterday that Security said there was nothing verifiable about the threats the reporter mentioned. But this confirmation that I'm not being paranoid sends a warm rush of relief through me.

"Yes. What's wrong with you?" Karen asks him, frowning.

He shakes his head. "Nothing." Then he says to me, "If a runner, a PA like Emily, brought it, then it's from someone on set. They wouldn't bring you anything just left outside."

As soon as he says that, it clicks. *Adam.*

I roll my eyes. Probably phase two of whatever stupid jealousy/ revenge scheme he's working on to cause trouble for Chase.

I scoot it closer and lift the lid cautiously, just in case, and find . . .

Nothing but mounds of gorgeous, individual red rose petals, reaching almost to the top of the box.

My shoulders relax, and the tightness in my stomach vanishes.

Plucking out a petal, I hold it up to show Chase. "Adam," I say by way of explanation. To fill a box this size, it must have taken dozens of flowers. An expensive and showy gesture, exactly something he would do to piss off Chase.

Karen snorts.

"Such a dick," Chase grumbles.

"He's just trying to provoke you." I stick my hand in deeper, seeking the note that will no doubt contain either overwrought— and likely stolen—poetry with rose metaphors or some kind of suggestive proposal, whichever he thinks will bug Chase more.

"He wants you to break. It's like a little kid poking at . . ." I stop, the words dying in my throat. My fingers, now an inch below the velvety surface, touch cool metal. But it's not the substance beneath my fingertips that makes me go still as much as the all-too-familiar shape.

My heart seizes. Acting instinctively against the terror barreling through me, I yank my hand away. But my wrist catches the edge of the box, and it tips in slow motion toward me.

Hundreds of dark red petals spill over the edge of the counter and float to the floor, like a slow-motion rendering of blood droplets falling.

And then the chain, metal links bright and blindingly shiny in the overhead lights, clatters out, tipping over the counter and piling onto the floor with a rapid chink-chink-chinking sound that I still hear in my nightmares.

28

Chase

Behind me, Karen gasps. "Oh my God."

Amanda is frozen for a moment, her hand in midair, the chain and petals in a heap at her feet, then she scrambles out of the chair. She presses her back against the trailer wall, as far away as she can get from the chain, but her eyes are showing edges of white from terror and her chest is heaving like she's run for miles.

I throw myself out of my chair, putting my body between her and the "gift" on the floor, like that will help, as if it's a snake that might strike.

But Amanda doesn't see me; her gaze is fixed on the chain and the rose petals, which, now that I'm looking at them from over here, resemble blood. And I'm sure that was intentional.

Goddamnit.

Amanda slides down the wall, curling into a tight protective ball but staying balanced on the balls of her feet. As if she might have to run.

My heart feels shredded, like someone is actually stripping away pieces of it, at the sight of her this way. She's so scared she's trembling; so pale and gray that she looks ghostlike. Was this what she was like right after she got back? No wonder her family is so fiercely protective and angry at the idea of her leaving with me.

I'm ready to tear someone apart for this.

But Amanda has to be my first focus.

"Amanda?" I kneel down cautiously in front of her, my hands out in an I-mean-no-harm posture. Touching her right now would be a bad idea, no matter how comforting I mean it to be.

"I'm fine. It's fine," she says, but she's rocking herself. Her right hand is locked around her left wrist, her fingers tracing the scar.

I'm caught between the sting of tears in my eyes and the incontrovertible and unstoppable rage welling up in me. Someone is going to pay.

"Shit," Karen whispers from somewhere over my shoulder. "Amanda, I'm so sorry; I didn't know."

She didn't, but I should have. My back stiffens. This is Elise. It has to be. Which means it's my fault. "Motherfucker, I'm going to kill her," I say.

"Kill who?" Karen asks, moving closer. "Adam? Chase, I don't think he—"

"Emily," I shout over my shoulder.

"Chase," Karen says.

"Emily!" I bellow.

She appears in the doorway with a disgruntled look. When she sees the flower petals, the chain, and Amanda, her eyes widen. "What—"

"Get Leon on your walkie. Get him over here," I say. This has gone too far. He needs to know everything. No matter what.

Emily hesitates. "I'm not sure if he—"

"Fucking get him now," I snarl at her. Once Leon tracks Elise down, I'm sure she'll tell him everything and Amanda will never forgive me. But I can't let this go. This has to stop. Now.

Emily blanches but nods rapidly and backs away, her walkie already raised to her mouth.

"Chase," Karen says again, her voice holding an odd and trembling note.

I glance over my shoulder to see her holding a slip of paper, the edges charred faintly, like a decorative effect.

"I found it on the floor. It must have been inside," she says. Then she turns it around so I can see the printed words on the other side.

GO BACK WHERE YOU BELONG, BITCH.

I reach up and punch the wall as hard as I can. The cheap plastic surface gives easily under my fist, denting from the impact but raising surface shards that slice into my skin.

"Chase!" Karen shouts.

But the pain feels good; it reminds me I'm not helpless.

"Dumbass, you're making it worse," Karen hisses at me as I shake out my hand, blood on my knuckles. She jerks her head toward Amanda, who is cowering to the side, away from me, away from the noise.

Fuck.

Automatically, I reach for her but stop before I touch. "I'm sorry, I'm sorry. I won't do it again. I'm sorry," I repeat, babbling in my panic.

"Let's maybe just get this cleaned up," Karen says, stepping around us, heading for the broom in the far corner.

"Don't," Amanda says tonelessly.

"No," I snap. "You don't have to look at—"

"They'll want to see it all as is. For evidence." She sounds so hollow that it makes me want to hold her or carry her away or both.

"Then how about if we go outside while we wait?" Karen offers, returning to her station. "Chase is going to need ice for his stupid hand anyway." She glares at me and hands me a wad of tissues from the box on the counter. "Dumbass."

It was once her favorite word for me; it is again, apparently.

And she's right. I stand and press the tissues against the cuts, sucking in a breath at the pain. Bruised knuckles, for sure; that's going to fuck up continuity. Max is going to kill me.

Amanda shakes her head. "No, I'm okay." She takes a deep breath and straightens her shoulders. But when she stands, she folds her arms over her middle, as if she's preparing for or recovering from a blow.

"It's not even the right kind of chain," she says after a moment.

I go still.

"The links in mine were much heavier," she continues. "I could have maybe eventually broken through these." She kicks the toe of her shoe in the direction of the chain.

"Amanda . . ." I don't even know how to finish that sentence.

"But mine, he knew better than to take that chance."

But she's not crying. Her eyes are dry and dull, and she gives a mirthless smile. "You know, the doctors told me that the muscles on that side were more developed, just from dragging the extra weight."

"Jesus Christ," I say in a croaking voice.

"Knock, knock." Leon's voice comes from behind me as he climbs the steps into the trailer.

I whirl around on him, fury and panic finally finding a suitable outlet. "What the fuck is this?" I demand, jerking my hand toward the mess on the floor. "How did this happen? Elise shouldn't have had credentials to be on set." When I'd "fired" her on Sunday, she told me she turned them in, all to sell the story in case someone "from Amanda's camp" checked.

Leon frowns at me, his bald scalp wrinkling with the expression. "Who is Elise?"

Raking my uninjured hand through my hair, to Karen's

audible cluck of dismay, I step to the side so I can see him and Amanda. "Elise Prescott, my fucking crazy ex."

"And former publicist," Amanda adds with a hiccuping laugh that holds an edge of hysteria.

Leon's frown deepens. "You think she did this?"

"Who else?" I shake my head. "She's probably the one who scratched up my trailer door, too."

"Someone damaged your door?" Amanda asks.

"Scratched some bullshit words into it, yeah." Warning me away from Amanda, which fits with this whole narrative Elise has going now.

"You didn't tell me," Amanda says with a frown.

I hesitate. "I didn't think it was anything serious." *Yeah, but more like you didn't want to tell her the whole truth. That you thought it was just Elise taking her stupid plan up a notch.*

Emily pops her head back in the trailer, her face tight with worry. "Chase, they're going to need you in, like, ten minutes."

"We'll check into the publicist," Leon says. "But I want you to look at something first." He pulls a manila folder I hadn't even noticed from under his arm.

"I've got some contacts with the local PD here, and they gave me these. Images from a security camera one of the warehouse owners still has active, trying to keep kids from trashing the place or turning it into a damn rave."

He flips the folder open, revealing a stack of photo printouts, camera stills, and turns it toward me. "Do you know her?"

The black-and-white image is slightly blurred, the subject caught in motion, but it's clear enough for me to recognize her. I will never, ever forget that face. It's narrow, her chin pointed, giving her a furtive, shady appearance. Her hair is thick and frizzed, sticking out of a dark, possibly black baseball cap.

The blood drains from my head, and I feel dizzy. "She's here?" I manage.

Karen pivots to look on Leon's other side and freezes. "Is that who I think it is?" Karen asks, her voice low.

"Yes," I say. Unbelievable. I should have known. The kind of media attention Amanda and I've been catching the last few days would be irresistible to her. Though she sure as hell didn't seem to care as much when I was hitting the pages for drinking and getting arrested.

"Son of a bitch." Karen sounds stunned, and I'm right there with her.

Amanda inches closer to me to look, and I want to put my arm around her, pull her close, as much for me as her, but she still has that bruised, don't-touch air about her. "That's not Elise," she says.

"No," I say flatly. "That's Sera Drummond. The girl who went fucking apeshit and tried to burn down my condo building when my assistant called the police on her. She was stalking me back in the *Starlight* days."

"She broke into his place and told anyone who asked she was his girlfriend and moving in," Karen says to Leon. "And studio security caught her hiding under his car on the lot once, waiting for him. I was there for that one."

Leon's overgrown eyebrows shoot up. "You have a restraining order against her?"

"Yes. No. I don't know. I did. It's probably expired by now. Fuck." I run my hands through my hair again before I think to stop myself. "Are restraining orders even valid outside the state?" I ask. "The one I had was in California." Jesus, did she drive all the way out here? Follow me? How did she get here so fast?

My mouth is so dry right now. It's killing me.

Amanda touches my arm gently, her fingers ghosting over my shoulder before retreating.

I turn toward her. "I'm sorry," I say, feeling helplessness and frustration rise up in me. "I used to have a whole team to handle this stuff. And now I'm on my own with no fucking clue what I'm doing." And now—I look at Amanda, her dark eyes watching me so seriously—I have so much more to protect.

"This is my fault," I choke out. "I should never have—"

"It's okay," she says, with a strained smile. "We'll figure it out."

We shouldn't have to. *She* shouldn't have to.

"Chase," Emily says in a pleading tone from the door.

"You." Karen spins toward her. "Tell Max there's a delay in Makeup, and it'll be a few minutes."

My heart falls. "Karen, no. You shouldn't have to cover—"

"You." She points at me. "Shut up and sit." She steps back to stand behind her chair, swiveling it in my direction. "I can work and you can talk."

I glance at Amanda, and she seems okay. Well, not okay, still too pale and shaken looking, but better than she was. She nods at me, jerking her head toward Karen, so I take my seat again.

"Thanks," I say reluctantly to Karen. I hate everything about this. Somehow even trying my best, I'm still managing to screw everything up.

"Shut up, I said," Karen says easily.

"I'll check on the RO, see if it's still in force," Leon says to me. He closes the folder and returns it under his arm. "In the meantime, you want to talk to me about this?" He points at the chain and flower petals on the floor.

"A PA brought the box . . ." Karen trails off, looking uncertain for the first time.

"Which one?" Leon asks. "Which PA?"

"I don't know. Not the one that brings Chase around," Karen says.

"Any chance it could have been her?" Leon points to his folder.

Karen stops, clutching one of her brushes so tightly in her hand that her knuckles are white. "It could have been," she says slowly. "I was working on Jenna, so I wasn't paying much attention. It was definitely a girl, a woman. She had a *Coal City* crew jacket on. I think. It was black, I know that. She might have had an ID tag on. I thought I saw it . . ."

"Anything else going on?" Leon asks. "Usually we see a pattern of escalation but—"

"The burned photo," Amanda says.

And that's when I fucking lose my mind. She's right. Burned stuff—that's Sera's thing.

"It was outside Chase's room yesterday morning when we left," Amanda says, looking to me for confirmation. "Early."

I nod, my neck muscles creaking with tension. Which means Sera has been in our hotel and also somehow knows which rooms are ours. It would only take one lax member of House-keeping and she could be in our room waiting for us. Or worse, waiting for Amanda.

I can see Leon making the same connection, his expression troubled. "Don't suppose you kept it?" he asks.

"No. We left it in the hall, and I think it was gone when we came back." Amanda looks to me for confirmation again, but I'm too far gone because I'm realizing that Sera might have been in the hall, watching us the whole damn time.

"I'll talk to the hotel. See if they caught anything on camera." He glances at me. "We'll get you new rooms or at the very least new keys in case she's managed to bribe someone on staff. You might have to forgo room service or cleaning until we can get this woman's location pinned down. Don't let anyone you don't know personally into your room, no matter what they say."

It's a solid first step, but it's not enough. I can't take the chance. The realization of what I have to do curdles in my gut, but it's inescapable. If I want to keep Amanda safe, I only have one option.

"Leon," I ask, my tone gritty and harsh. "Can you take Amanda back to the hotel?"

He shrugs. "Sure."

"I'm standing right here," Amanda says, frowning at me in the mirror.

"I know, and it's not safe here. Clearly." I shove my hand in the direction of the chain and flower petals.

Amanda raises her eyebrows. "So you're sending me to stay in the hotel alone."

I steel myself against her reaction and the sense of loss already building in me. "No," I say. "I'm sending you to gather up your stuff so you can go home. I'll find someone to take you. Or I'll hire a car. Something."

Her mouth falls open in shock.

Karen sighs and mutters something unintelligible. I'm pretty sure one of the words might be "dumbass."

I ignore her, focusing on Amanda. "It's the only way I know for sure that you'll be safe," I say, pleading with her to understand. "You don't know what it was like before. She would pop up everywhere. It was creepy as hell. She wanted to be with me. I have no idea what she might do to you." Just the thought of it makes me want to pull Amanda into a corner and block the rest of the world with my body.

"No," Amanda says.

I pause, flummoxed for a second. "No, what?"

"No, I'm not leaving." She sets her jaw stubbornly. Color has returned to her face, but in the form of a flush in her cheeks.

"It's not up to you," I say, getting louder and my accent breaking through, much to my chagrin. "I can't keep you safe here."

Which is apparently the exactly wrong thing to say.

Amanda's eyes flash anger. "That's not your job," she says, stepping closer to me.

"You don't know what she could do, Amanda. She's unstable. Jesus, she might have a gun. It happens," I argue.

"And I could die tomorrow because a bus runs me over or because some nutjob kidnaps me off the street and I'm not as lucky the second time."

Her words are a cold knife to my insides. "That's not funny, Amanda."

"I didn't mean it to be," she says evenly. As Karen swivels the chair to finish her work, Amanda steps around to maintain eye contact with me. "I know this is simple for you, but it's not for me."

I squeeze my hands into fists, the injured one sending dull pangs up to my elbow. "I don't want you getting hurt," I say through gritted teeth. "How is that complicated?"

"Because it's about more than that," she says, maintaining that infuriating calm. "I spent two years under the control of someone else. I lived literally at the whim of another person." She gestures at the chain. "He decided if I lived or died, if I suffered."

And everyone in hearing distance collectively sucks in a breath.

"That's not . . . I don't . . ." I struggle to find words, to put them in any kind of sentence that can follow that.

"Then I spent two more years hiding, being afraid, letting my fear control me," Amanda continues. "I'm here trying to change that." She levels a steady look at me. "You know that."

"This is someone trying to hurt you; you're supposed to be afraid!" I shout.

"This is someone trying to control me," she corrects. "And I can't let them." She hesitates. "I can't let you."

I jerk back in the chair as if Amanda just took a physical swipe at me, and Karen makes a frustrated noise, coming after me with a makeup sponge. "I'm the bad guy because I want to keep you safe?" I ask. "Are you saying I'm like . . ." I can't even finish that sentence.

"Of course not!" Tears fill her eyes, and she wipes them with the edge of her fleece sleeve. "Never," she says fiercely. "But what you're asking me to do . . . I can't. I'm sorry."

"Amanda, you aren't listening—"

She throws her arms up in frustration. "You want to protect me, I get it, but how am I supposed to learn to trust myself, to feel safe with my decisions, if someone else is always making them for me? Whether it's you, my parents, or my freaking anxiety?" She laughs bitterly. "Someone else is always in charge."

Karen pulls the cape from around my neck, signaling that she's finished.

I stand up, facing off with Amanda. "Okay, then tell me this: How am I supposed to live with myself if something happens to you on my watch?" I demand.

Her eyelids flutter down. "I'm not on your watch."

"Yes, you are," I say, frustrated. "That's what loving someone means." The words are out of my mouth before I realize I'm going to say them. It's something I haven't even acknowledged to myself, let alone shared with Amanda. But I know in this moment it's true, as clearly as I know my own name. And I don't care who hears it.

Amanda's mouth falls open slightly in surprise.

"I meant it," I say to her. "And I'm not taking it back," I add.

"Chase?" Emily is back at the door, hopping from foot to foot like a kid who waited too long to find a bathroom.

"Go," Karen says to me with a softer expression than I've seen from her in a while. "I'll finish in here while she answers whatever questions Leon has."

The big man looks up from taking pictures of the petals and chain with his phone, unfazed by the drama unfolding around him, and just nods.

"I'll bring her over when I come to set," Karen says.

"I don't need a babysitter." Amanda gives Karen a hostile look, which means she has more balls than I do.

I wait for the explosion.

But Karen just shrugs. "Then don't call it that," she says. "Think of me more like an anti-stalker solution. Because I will cut a bitch if she thinks she's coming near any of us again. Especially my trailer."

We all stare at her.

"What? She ruined my favorite set of brushes." Karen snaps the cape I was wearing in the air with ruthless efficiency and then hangs it on a hook on the wall.

A snort of laughter escapes from Amanda, and she clamps a

hand over her mouth to stop it. And, to my surprise, Karen winks at her.

"You guys are crazy," I say in disbelief. I have no idea how this conversation derailed so badly and so quickly. I blame Karen. I glare at her, which only makes her shake her head at me mockingly.

"We're not done talking," I warn Amanda as I head for the door and Emily impatiently waiting for me.

"I am," Amanda says.

And with Emily practically pulling me down the stairs and Max and the others waiting on me, there's nothing more I can say or do.

29

Amanda

"You know they're not really hurting him," Karen whispers in my ear as the actor playing Carl, the arresting officer, slams Chase against the trunk of the police car. There's a pad on the car, beneath the camera's line of sight, to protect Chase, and another on the ground. But it doesn't seem like enough.

"Well, not much," she says as Max calls, "Cut!" and yells for the medic to look at Chase's hand again.

Evidently, Max wasn't too upset about the injury—something I hadn't thought of until Karen mentioned it on our way over. Or at least, Max wasn't upset enough not to use it in the scene. Now Chase's bruised knuckles appear to be the result of being shoved to the ground before he can catch himself.

It's Smitty's big redemption scene. He's not fighting back. Instead, he's taking the fall for Keller, who got caught in a drug

350 / STACEY KADE

buy—the kind of fun Smitty has spent the entire movie/day trying to talk Keller into—so Keller can leave town, go to college, and have a future. It hurts to see the pain on Smitty/Chase's face when he realizes that he's losing his dream of the future and the only true friend he has left, even as he's doing the right thing.

"I know," I say to Karen. But it doesn't feel that way. I feel like they're busy beating up the outside of him while I took my shots at his feelings earlier today, making him the total damaged package.

"You did what you needed to do for you. He'll figure it out. He's just scared." She shrugs, one arm wrapped over her waist in the rapidly cooling evening air. I can see my breath now. They've been at this scene a dozen different ways, and we're about to lose the light, apparently. So the tension is running high, a silent, thick cloud choking out any of the conversations and laughter I've witnessed on previous days.

"It's partially our fault," Karen says conversationally as everybody resets, including the gloved medic, wiping Chase's blood off the spotless white paint of the squad car.

"What?" I ask, distracted as I watch Chase shake out his hand, stretching his fingers like they hurt. I hope they're not broken. He hit that wall so hard.

"His friends, his agent, his manager . . . his former manager. His assistant, Evan. All of us," Karen says. "He's messed up so many times before, his head is full of voices, including mine, shouting at him that he's going to fail, that he's going to fuck up. So he's not going to leave you alone about going home. He doesn't want to make another mistake."

"But I'm the one arguing to take the risk," I point out.

"I know. I'm just telling you, no matter what you say, you're swimming upstream against all of that."

Great.

"So you're in love with him, huh?" she says without looking at me.

I open my mouth and close it without speaking. I'm not ready to talk about that yet.

Karen snorts. "Please—I've been watching you watching him for hours. You flinch every time he hits the ground."

"It looks like it hurts," I argue.

She ignores my weak attempt at rationalizing. "Just be careful with him, okay? There aren't many people in his life."

I wait for her to finish that sentence. There aren't many people in his life looking out for him, people who care about him, who love him?

But she doesn't. *There aren't many people in his life.* The words hang in the air, making me unbearably sad. That this guy who took the time to teach me to punch, to make me feel good, to research pancake places with a bizarre number of syrups doesn't have anyone else to share that with. It seems like a loss for the world.

My throat swells with a lump, and I want to cry for him.

"His family cut him off when he came out here instead of staying in Texas to help at the ranch. Most of the ass kissers fell off when he couldn't get steady visible work. The rest of us got fed up with his bullshit when he was drinking." Her mouth tightens. "I stand by that decision, but that doesn't mean it was easy to watch him hit the bottom all by himself."

My heart sends up a sharp pang. "Yes, I love him," I say quietly, even as I realize it should be something I say to Chase.

"Good," she says, whether for the sentiment or that I voiced it aloud, I'm not sure. "Life is too short to hold yourself back." A sad expression flickers on her face before vanishing into the smooth, hard look she wears so well. I don't know what caused it, other than a broken heart in her past—Karen holding herself back or someone else holding back from Karen. It doesn't matter in the end. It's true either way.

Life is too short to hold yourself back. From love, from

happiness, from the fear of falling when you could have the joy of jumping.

And I, of all people, should know that.

Chase doesn't say much in the van on the way home. He has a cold pack bound to his sore hand with an ACE bandage, but as soon as I slide in next to him, he lifts his arm so I can curl up next to him.

I hesitate for a second, just long enough for the wounded expression to flash across his face. He looks away from me to stare out the side window and starts to lower his arm.

Catching him in mid-motion, I duck beneath his arm, moving so quickly that my shoulder connects with the side of his body harder than I meant.

But he doesn't protest, beyond the surprised grunt.

He wraps his arm around my shoulders, pulling me closer, as the van starts off. All I can think of is what Karen said earlier: that he's trying to save himself by saving me, trying to not be the failure everyone has told him he is, in one way or another.

I'm bracing myself for round two of our earlier argument. I can practically feel him gearing up to talk to me again, but he's evidently waiting for his moment, which is not now.

Emily makes quiet, idle chitchat with the driver, who murmurs replies that I can't quite hear.

It's dim and warm in here, a cozy cocoon of safety.

I snuggle into Chase, moving past his open jacket to rest my head on his chest, feeling the heat of his skin beneath the soft cotton of his T-shirt, the steady rise and fall of his breathing, and the more distant thump-thump of his heart.

I could stay like this forever.

But the van arrives at the hotel in what seems like seconds, dropping us off at the service entrance in the rear of the building without any discussion.

The night manager, a woman this time in a blue suit coat, is waiting at the kitchen to hand us new keys to our existing rooms, per arrangements made with Leon.

I remain glued to Chase's side through this, my arm wrapped around his waist, inside his jacket. I want to soak up every moment of him, of this temporary peace between us and the idea of what we *could* be. Before he tries again to send me home for my own good and shatters the moment.

Upstairs, we nod hello to the security guard, one of Leon's contacts, stationed a few feet away from our door. I didn't like the idea of a stranger being so close when Leon first suggested it to me in the makeup trailer, but now, I find the presence of someone who is definitively on our side, paid to be there, reassuring.

Chase uses one of the new keys to access my room and bolts the door behind us. Then he searches my room and his, including the closets and the tubs, and bolts his door before letting go of me in his living room area.

He stands near the dining table and pulls at the ACE bandage around his hand, unwinding it so he can remove the cold pack.

Dread spirals from my heart down to my stomach. I recognize this tactic for what it is: he's stalling, working out the words he feels he needs to say.

"Amanda," he begins.

I knew it.

Panic sprints through me. "I'm going to shower," I say, turning toward my room. I can't have this argument right now. I won't.

"We need to talk," he says.

"No, I'm going to shower."

He sighs, his face a mask of grim determination, but I move past him, heading for the door to my room, where I pause, a belated thought occurring to me.

"If you're thinking you're going to pack up my stuff for me in some kind of heavy-handed tactic to try to force me to leave, then you'd better be prepared to share whatever clothes you have left in your room." In the doorway, I fold my arms over my chest. I'm taking a stand.

He frowns at me, but doesn't deny the possibility.

"In fact, gimme." I wave my fingers at him in a summoning gesture.

He stares at me like I've taken sudden trauma to the head. "Give you what? My shirt?"

"Yes."

"Why?" he asks, even as he's shrugging out of his jacket. God, I love this man.

"I have an incomplete collection." Because I want it. Because no matter what happens, I need another piece of him to carry away from this place.

He gives me an exasperated look but pulls his T-shirt over his head.

"This doesn't change anything," he reminds me, as he tosses me his shirt.

I catch it easily, but I'm momentarily distracted. He is just as beautiful as he was when I first saw him without his shirt that first morning. But he's not preening now, tempting me to look at the work he's put into his appearance.

Instead, he rubs a hand self-consciously over his chest and down to his stomach, where the edge of his black boxer briefs peeks out over the top of his jeans. And that only makes me love him more. This is the real Chase, and I want him. For as long as he'll let me have him.

"It does," I say. "I want to have a shower because I didn't get one this morning. Then I want to go to bed, with you."

Chase opens his mouth to object.

"In the morning, I want to wake up with you." My voice breaks a little, but I push on. "I want to go have pancakes with orange–goji berry–caramel syrup."

In spite of himself, Chase makes a disgusted face.

"Ha!" I point at him. "Yes, see? Told you. It doesn't work for everything. Good individually, not so good together."

He rolls his eyes.

"But I want all of that," I say, trying not to plead. "There will

be plenty of time to fight tomorrow morning, after that. Right?"
I'm working hard to play to the rational since I know that's
what he'll respond to, but it's also true. How long will it take
for him to tear us apart in his need to protect me, in his need to
be a better person than he was before? A few minutes to crush
something so delicate, so carefully but fragilely constructed.

Chase hesitates.

Screw it. Pleading works sometimes, too.

I swallow hard and meet his eyes unflinchingly. "I just want
tonight. Please?"

He drops his gaze, but not before I see the flash of guilt and
uncertainty. He stuffs his hands in his pockets, dragging his
jeans lower. "Amanda, I don't know—"

"I do," I say with as much firmness as I can manage. And that
is huge for me, a victory I want to celebrate *with* him. Then,
before he can respond or I break down in tears, I turn and walk
away.

With his shirt in hand, I hurry to my bathroom, shut the door,
lock it. I'm not worried about the crazy stalker person. Well, not
as much with Leon's guy in the hallway and Chase right next
door.

I'm more worried that Chase is going to follow and try to
talk to me. Even through the door, those words can't be un-
heard. And if we have this conversation tonight, I'm afraid I
might give in and agree to leave. Then I'll never forgive him or
myself for it. And yet, if I keep fighting him on this, he might
begin to resent me for being stubborn, for putting myself at risk,
for making him take the chance of what he sees as failure.

Reaching for the tub faucet, I crank it full blast, drowning out
everything but the white-noise roar of water pouring into the
basin.

Then, and only then, when I know Chase won't hear, when
I can barely hear myself, I sit on the edge of the tub and let
myself cry. Great racking sobs that I held in earlier when I
opened that stupid box; when Chase told Leon to take me

home; when I watched Chase hit the ground, over and over; when I listened to the beat of his heart in the van and wished I could stop time to live in that moment.

For the first time in forever, I know what I want. And instead of it being a negative—an absence of pain, fear, or anxiety—it's something positive. Love, belonging, acceptance.

But I'm going to lose all of that before I even really have it. Frustration and despair swell in me in equal parts. Because what am I supposed to do? What can I do?

Why does it have to be so complicated? Haven't I earned something simple? I survived, damnit. I'm Miracle Girl, a title I never wanted, never felt like I deserved. But I'd take it right now if it meant I could have this without all the pitfalls, trip wires, and nooses.

I wipe my face and try to catch my breath. Chase's shirt is in my lap. Against my better judgment, I lift it to my face, feeling the softness of the cotton that covered the rise and fall of his chest, and smell the scent of him.

My heart twists in my chest. But with that pain—one that is also somehow pleasure because of what it means—comes a small burst of clarity.

Maybe it's always complicated. Nothing I've seen from people who aren't even as messed up as I am suggests that love is easy.

Maybe what matters is what you do when it isn't, when it looks too hopeless, too difficult.

That idea gives me the kernel of fortitude to get up, wipe my face, and *do* something instead of bemoaning my fate.

I know what I want. So I'm going after it.

In the shower, I take my time, though I know Chase is building an argument against me every second I'm away.

When I'm done, I towel-dry my hair, not wanting to bother with blow-drying it. My pulse is thrumming, but not with fear.

I pull Chase's shirt over my head, and it stops at my upper thighs, barely covering everything. Perfect.

This time, when I walk to the doorway between our rooms,

I'm shaking with anticipation, determination, and desire in a heady mix.

Chase is at the half-wall between the bedroom and the living room area, heading toward the bathroom. He's wearing just another pair of dark boxer briefs. The sharp cut of his leg muscles is plain when he's in motion like this. His hair is damp, too, and he's holding a bunched-up towel.

He stills when he sees me.

"Hi," I say.

He clears his throat and chucks the towel toward the dining table chair, where it catches. "Hey."

I turn and shut the door, locking out my room. I'm not going back there tonight. I'm not retreating. I'm moving forward.

I face him.

His throat works audibly. "Amanda, you don't—"

I raise my eyebrows. "If you tell me that I don't have to do this, I'm going to scream loud enough that Leon's guy calls the cops. I am my own person, Chase, and I make decisions for myself, including this one."

He makes a frustrated noise. "Even if you're going to ignore everything that's going on—"

"Yes," I say.

"—I don't want to be a dare to you, some boundary you're pushing against just to prove something to yourself," he says, the hurt in his voice achingly obvious.

I stop, stunned breathless. "Do you think that's what this is?"

Studying the ground, he lifts his shoulder once, mute.

"It's not," I say, stepping up next to him. I press my lips against his bare shoulder. "Remember I told you I wasn't going to run anymore, that I'm not hiding?"

Chase makes a soft noise of assent, his chest moving rapidly against mine as I trail kisses across his collarbone, tasting him. His skin is slightly damp from the shower and a little slick from the fresh soap.

When I reach his throat, I stop and look up at him. "I figured

out that's not enough. So now I'm going to chase what I want."
I wait until he looks down. "You," I say. "I love you, and I want
to be with you."

He draws in a sharp breath.

Before I lose my nerve and with a blush that is probably visible to somebody on the moon, I take his hand and tug him
toward the bed.

I'm half-expecting him to argue or pull back, but instead,
I feel him move with me, following without resistance.

His silent acquiescence to—and respect for—my choice and
my desires heats my blood faster than anything else.

When he steps past me, I watch as he pulls back the covers in
a smooth arc on one side and then slides beneath them, waiting
for me, with an intense, watchful gaze.

He's giving me the lead.

I love him so much in that moment that it feels like my heart,
inadequate for this level of emotion, might just burst.

When I kneel on the edge of the ironed-smooth sheets, he
rolls up on his elbow, watching me, his attention so taut I feel it
like a caress on my skin. Along my neck, between my thighs. I'm
fairly sure his shirt is transparent with the bedside lamp on
behind me, which means he can see everything, all of me. And
just that thought makes my pulse throb at the center of me.
I want his hands on me.

An idea occurs to me then, probably much too late, but I'm
hoping he'll have the right answer.

"Condoms?" I ask.

Heat flickers in his gaze. "In the bathroom, my shaving bag."

I pull my knee off the bed and take the few steps to the
bathroom in a hurry, the warmth between my legs already a
distracting ache crying out for attention.

His shaving bag is organized to a level I've never seen, everything in its place. And sure enough, I find three condoms tucked
neatly in a side pocket.

"All of them?" he asks when I hold them up on my return.

I set them down on the nightstand within easy reach. "I'm not getting back out once I'm in." Then feeling daring, I add, "And you're not, either."

He makes a sound that's half moan, half laugh.

I kneel on the edge of the bed and turn off the light, but there's enough moonlight shining through the gap in the curtains that, once my eyes adjust, I can see him on his side, his arm curled beneath his head on one of the pillows.

He holds his arm out to me. "Come here," he says in a husky voice that makes me want to press myself against him until we're falling together.

"Wait," I say. I shimmy out of his shirt, pulling it over my head and catching my breath as the fabric in motion teases my already sensitive nipples.

He makes a strangled noise. "You are so beautiful, like a statue or something." Then he gives an embarrassed laugh. "Sorry, I'm not the best with words."

But I know exactly what he means. The moonlight through the window has turned him into a silver and black outline, and the shape of him strikes a chord deep within me, the desire to possess, to take some part of that beauty into myself and hold it forever. And knowing him, knowing that he's kind and protective and fierce, only makes that desire stronger.

I lean over him, pushing at his shoulder gently until he lies back on the pillows. He goes willingly, his hand still tucked beneath his head.

The triangle of his elevated arm reveals the paler, intimate skin beneath his arm, the darker hair a shadow. It feels like something private, vulnerable. I want to make it mine.

I lean down and press my mouth against that soft skin, breathing in deep the scent of him.

He shivers, the goose bumps rising against my lips.

I look up at him. "Cold?"

"No," he whispers.

Pressing my hands against the mattress for support, I kiss a line across his chest, opening my mouth to scrape my teeth against the curve of his pectoral muscle.

He gasps. And I smile against his skin; the rush of power is heady. To make him feel the way he makes me feel, to *cause* him to want, to be in control. I am invincible in this moment.

Then that muscle shifts beneath my mouth, his arm moving. I feel his hand slip between my knees and up. One long finger strokes me once, teasing, before plunging inside.

My hips automatically arch toward him, throwing the top half of me back.

Chase stops abruptly, catching my wrist.

"Hold up."

"What's wrong?" I ask, my voice throaty, barely recognizable to my own ears.

He shifts toward the center of the bed, tugging at me to follow.

"I was afraid you were going to fall off the edge," he says with a soft laugh.

Love for him rises in me in a wave that feels so thick it might fill my lungs and block the air, and I welcome it.

Bending down, I let my mouth wander over his chest to the center dip, a small hollow that is perfect for licking, and to the heartbeat throbbing on the left side.

His hand returns between my legs, touching the top of my thigh, the hollow to the side, just an inch above where my skin is throbbing for him, everywhere but where I need him to touch. I squirm against his fingers, moving my hips, trying to manipulate his position, but he resists.

Making a frustrated noise, I slide down to press my tongue against his abdomen. His erection is right there, just peeking out of the top of his boxer briefs.

It looks impossibly uncomfortable and incredibly hard.

I ghost a breath across that part of him, and his hand between my legs ceases its torment and slides over the center of me.

My eyes snap shut. *Yes. Want.*

I open my eyes and stroke my hand down him, and his breath catches even as he pushes into the pressure, demanding more.

When I slip my fingers into his waistband, touching him tentatively, the skin so hot and tight, he groans.

Then his hand leaves me and he pushes his boxers down, giving me free rein.

Moved by instinct, I duck my head and trace his hardness with my tongue, curling over the top.

He moans, his hips thrusting up toward my mouth. As it seems like I'm doing something very right, I keep going, licking down the length of him. Then when I reach the top again, I close my mouth over him carefully.

His hand fumbles, shaking, between my legs, and then he presses his fingers inside me.

I suck in a breath over his skin and he groans, pushing himself deeper into my mouth.

Now we're moving together, my mouth on him, his hand in me.

I'm sideways to him, my breasts brushing over his stomach and his hip, but that doesn't seem to matter. Rocking myself against the friction of his hand, I can feel the return of that spreading warmth in my lower half.

And I know what it means, but I want more. I want all of him.

With one last suck against his skin, I release him from my mouth and straighten up.

His hand falls away from me when I tap gently at his wrist. Then I swing my leg over to his hips to straddle him, my heart racing with anticipation.

The heat of his body rises up in a wave, and I lower myself carefully against him, not pressing down, not yet, but making contact.

It's a strange feeling. I'm in control, his hands rest lightly on my legs, nothing more, but it's the feeling of being exposed, of opening myself up, that sends a faint tremor of uncertainty through me for the first time.

Chase lifts up, propping himself on his elbows, which brings his stomach against me, and I feel the muscles contract with the motion. "Kiss me," he says.

I lean forward and press my mouth to his. His kiss is lazy, unhurried, as he bites my lower lip gently and then slides his tongue over it to soothe.

The tension in me eases, and I can feel the slow, easy languor returning. My position over him doesn't seem quite as overwhelming or the tiny bit frightening that it did only moments ago.

He presses his mouth against the tops of my breasts, his tongue caressing every inch of skin he can reach. His chin, rough with the beginning of stubble, scrapes over my nipples.

A whimper escapes me, and acting on instinct, I lift myself up, bringing my breast to his mouth.

His tongue flicks out against my nipple before his mouth captures it, sucking it in deep.

I buck my hips against him, but the angle is all wrong. I'm too high.

His hands move to my thighs. "Open your legs just a little more," he whispers, sliding his palm between the side of his body and the inside of my leg. "You're safe; I promise."

I relent, following his gentle pressure to ease my knees away from his body, and to relax my weight onto him.

This brings the sensitive wet part of me in direct contact with the heat and solidity of him, still damp from my mouth. It feels shockingly good.

His head falls back, exposing his throat.

It feels natural and easy then to slide up him to press a kiss against his Adam's apple and then down again.

The angle presses him against the sensitive nub at the heart of me, and suddenly we're moving smoothly together in slick rhythm that feels effortless.

He grips my hips, dragging me over him with more pressure.

The tip of him presses into me barely, and I wiggle in frustration, trying to find a way to take him in deeper.

"You okay?" he asks tightly.

"Yes, don't stop!" I push against his shoulder.

But he gives a shaky laugh and lowers himself against the pillows. "Too close to the edge."

Dazed with lust, I reflexively look to the side of the bed in confusion. We're miles away from it.

"Not that edge," he says breathlessly. Then he reaches for the condoms on the nightstand.

"Lift up for me?" he asks, tearing one open.

Pushing up to my knees again, I watch, partly curious, partly uncertain as he grips himself and rolls the condom in place.

He looks away to discard the wrapper on the nightstand, but he must see something in my expression when he returns his attention to me.

"Come here," he says, and I lean up, bracing my hand on either side of his head to kiss him. I'm still holding myself above him, and he patiently returns to petting me softly, rubbing his knuckle against me until I'm pushing hard to take his finger inside me.

"Easy, just go slow. Give yourself time," he says in my ear. "We can always stop."

But I don't want to. This is my night, the one I asked for. And damnit, I'm not letting anyone, including me, take it away.

I slowly sink down against him again.

As I rub against him, the smooth glide returns, albeit with a little more friction.

I tip my hips toward him and then he is pressing into me, stretching me in a not-unpleasant way as he enters.

Chase swallows hard. "There you go—that's it." He arches up toward me, pushing in deeper, and it feels so good I instinctively press down against him.

When I lift up again, the moisture from my body has coated him and makes the slide down on him that much easier.

He groans.

"Am I hurting you?" I ask, hesitant about how much pressure is too much, and all my weight is pressing on him.

"Not even a little," he says with flash of a smile. He pushes himself up on his elbows then, changing the angle and making me gasp at the feel of him inside me.

Experimentally, I push down and feel the thickness of him slide deep into me. Instead of feeling violated or invaded, it just makes me feel . . . full.

"Look," he says hoarsely, lying flat on his back.

I push myself up to sit directly on him and glance down to see where he ends and I begin. He's buried inside me; we are as close as two human beings can be. And I'm not hurting, feeling scared, dirty, or used.

"Oh." I clamp a hand over my mouth. "It's amazing." Tears of gratitude, relief, and love flood my eyes.

Chase laughs and reaches up to touch my cheek, where one of the tears has rolled free. "Yeah, you are," he says softly, and I'm crying for real this time and smiling, too.

His hands settle on my hips as he thrusts up in me, helping me push down against him in counterpoint.

Then he moves his hand to press his thumb against me so that every move gives that extra brush of friction.

He moans. "Yes, that's it. You're letting me in so deep. Just a little faster."

Hearing him talk to me, guide me, flips a switch in me that I didn't know existed and I move against him harder, straining once again for that very top shelf.

And before I realize it, I'm falling, that cascading dizzy sensation spiraling through me.

"Amanda . . ."

But I can't speak; I fumble for his hand and squeeze it.

Chase moves harder against me, then, seeking his release, and I try to keep up with him but my limbs are slow and loose with pleasure.

He shudders beneath me, his body racked with spasms, and I love it.

I love him. And I'm not letting go.

30

Chase

The bright sunlight slicing into the room wakes me up with a jolt.

Late. I'm late.

I lurch up in a panic. But Amanda, curled against me, raises a hand, patting vaguely in my direction until she finds my shoulder.

"Thursday. Night shoot tonight," she mumbles against her pillow.

And I relax, sagging into the mattress. That's right. She's right.

But then what is the lingering unformed sense of dread hovering over me? Then I remember. Sera. The chain. Amanda refusing to go home. Everything I haven't told her.

Glancing over at Amanda again, I find that sometime in the night she got up and put my shirt on again. Her dark red hair is all over my pillow again, and I love the sight of it.

I should let her go. I should wake her up, tell her everything, even if it means pushing her away. Especially if it means pushing her away. She'll be safer at home, away from me.

But the thought of that makes my chest ache. I don't want it to end; I don't want us to end. Not yet. I'll do what's best for her, but I just want a few more minutes, a couple more hours.

Looping my arm around Amanda's waist, I pull her tighter against me, kissing the back of her neck.

She grumbles vaguely but wiggles against me, pressing her back to my chest, and her ass against my very awake cock.

"Sorry," I say into her soft skin, which still smells of soap. "Definitely a morning person."

I expect her to pull away or make a complaining noise. We didn't get much sleep last night, and it's early still.

Instead she pushes back against me with a soft moan.

I slide my hand down her leg, remembering yesterday morning and how quickly she came. She might not be a morning person, but parts of her seem to like it well enough.

At my gentle nudge against the back of her knee, she slides her leg forward eagerly to let me touch between her thighs.

"Are you sore?" I ask, gently nipping at her ear as I run my fingers lightly over her lips.

"A little, maybe," she says between gasps. "But different. More swollen feeling than hurt, if that makes sense."

Yes, yes, it does.

"Tell me if it's too much," I say as I slide a finger into her. But she's wet and slick for me already. Definitely a morning person.

"Chase, yes. Chase," she says, riding my hand with a fervor and desperation I haven't heard before.

I love hearing her say my name. "Touch yourself like you did before, okay?"

I watch as her hand drifts beneath the covers and her fingers brush mine as they settle over her clit.

The change in her is instantaneous and electric. She is bucking against my hand and hers, and I can feel her opening wide for more than my fingers.

I have to pull away from her, over her protests, to grab for the last condom. The second was gone last night not long after the first.

She starts to roll over toward me.

"No, wait," I say. I open the condom and roll it on quickly, chucking the wrapper away from us.

When I return my fingers to her, she squirms eagerly against them.

I press my lower body tighter against her. "Put your leg up on mine," I whisper, sliding my hand down her thigh to her knee and helping guide her up and over.

Then I inch closer, rubbing my covered hard-on against her, letting her get used to the slightly different sensation, what will be a sharper angle of penetration.

She moans and slides herself against me, her foot working behind my calf, trying to draw me in closer. But we're not quite lined up right.

"I want to push in from behind," I say, my voice hoarse with need. "Just like I did with my fingers. Okay?"

"Yes," she says, drawing out the word.

Thank you, God. "Bend forward for me a little."

She shifts a few inches, bringing us into alignment.

Using my hand to help get the angle right, I press the head of my aching hard-on into her. It's tighter this way, and I don't want to get it wrong and hurt her.

She gasps.

I freeze. "Too much?"

"No . . . just . . . really good," she pants.

So maybe not just morning, but this position.

Now that I'm in, I thrust again, deeper this time, and she moves with me, so slick and welcoming I'm going to lose my mind in a matter of seconds.

But it doesn't matter because she's already rocking faster than I am, taking me all the way in.

"Your hand . . . touch yourself," I say through gritted teeth, trying to hold on.

I feel her touch herself and brush me where I'm plunging in and out of her, and she makes a soft surprised sound. Then the ripples start in her, clamping down hard on me.

I groan and push into her faster, the need to spill building up in me, like pressure in my lower back, until it breaks, sending splinters of pleasure through me.

When I return to myself, she's running her hand over my arm in a soothing manner.

"Wow," is her only comment, with a small self-deprecating laugh.

I kiss her flushed cheek. "Yeah, I think maybe that works."

She laughs, and I feel the contractions of it inside her. God. I don't want to leave her, but a condom leak is a complication we don't need.

I shift away from her reluctantly, and she makes a noise of protest.

"Back in a minute." Climbing over the covers, off the bed, and into the bathroom to deal with a condom is my least favorite Olympic event ever, but it has to be done.

While I'm in there washing my hands, clothes land in the doorway. My jeans, a shirt from my closet, boxers.

"Pancake time," Amanda says from outside in a determined cheerful voice. She's not allowing time or space for the inevitable argument to begin.

Except, is it so inevitable? The thought of watching her vanish down the road in a car hurts. I don't want her to go. But I want her to be safe, and that means staying away while my stalker problem is out there somewhere. What if Leon and the cops catch Sera right away, though? They might even have her already; stealth wasn't her strong suit. She tried to move into my condo, for fuck's sake.

So even if she's out there now, she probably won't be for long. And if Amanda wants to stay, is it that much of a danger? We have Leon, guards, people on our side. Plus, as Amanda has said to me over and over this week, she makes her own decisions. If I take that from her by unilaterally making a choice on her behalf, I'm doing exactly what she said, trying to control her. Which I don't want to do. It's what she's working so hard to get back.

So, maybe the real danger—and the unformed dread in my gut—is actually something else. Maybe it's believing that, even if there is trouble, even if there's risk, I'm still worth it to her. To anyone.

I want to be worth it. I want to be worthy of her. Which means maybe I need to act like it. By asking her if she wants to stay and respecting her decision. And by telling her the truth about how we began and hoping she won't change her mind.

"Amanda—"

"I'll be back," she calls from a distance. "I'm going to get clothes from my room."

"Wait." I grab a towel, wrap it around my waist, and hurry after her.

"You're not seriously worried about me going to my room alone, are you?" Still dressed in my shirt, she stops at the closed and locked adjoining door but doesn't turn around. "You checked it last night and there's a guard outside."

"No, I . . ."

Her shoulders slump. "After breakfast," she says. "Remember?"

"That's not it," I say quickly. "I just wanted to say . . . wanted to ask if . . ."

A knock sounds loudly on my hallway door, more like pounding, enough so that we both jump.

I frown. "Stay there," I say.

Amanda raises her eyebrows. "Because you're more bulletproof than I am?" she asks. "Also, I don't think she'd knock. We'd probably just see smoke curling in under the door."

She grimaces before I can say anything. "Sorry. Humor is my preferred defense mechanism."

"I've noticed," I say. Pulling my towel tighter around my waist, I edge toward the door. But a quick look out the peephole shows Leon and two Wescott uniformed police officers in the hall.

Thanks to my history, the sudden and unexpected appearance of cops signals trouble in my brain. But I throw back the bolt latch and open the door, hoping against hope that for the first time in my life, this is a good thing.

"What's going on?" I ask. "Did you find her?"

"Yeah," Leon says grimly. "We did."

But he doesn't look happy; in fact, he seems downright pissed. "These gentlemen would like to escort you to their place of business to answer a few questions."

Panic flickers in me. "Wait, what's going on?"

"Right now, they're asking you to come in as a courtesy," Leon says. "So get dressed and go before it's not a request." He looks at me in distaste, and my temper flares.

"What the hell, Leon?" I demand.

"Chase?" Amanda asks from where she stands by the other door, tugging at the hem of my/her shirt nervously.

Leon and the two cops bristle like they're going to leap at me.

"That's Amanda?" Leon asks, a frown carving his face into serious lines.

"Yeah, we were getting ready to go to breakfast," I say. "Can you just tell me what's going—"

"Tell *us*," she calls loudly. "Tell *us* what's going on."

But Leon ignores us. "Amanda, can you verify that you're unharmed and here by your own decision?" he asks in a raised voice.

Her face is one of shock and then pure, unadulterated fury. She snatches my jacket off the back of the chair, wraps it around her waist to cover herself, and then marches around the corner to stand next to me.

"What is going on?" she demands, angry like I've never seen her before. "I'm fine. I'm here by my own decision, and I've been here all week by my own decision. What the hell."

"My apologies," Leon says. "Recent developments"—his gaze cheats toward me—"have forced us to question what we know."

He shifts his full attention in my direction. "When is the last time you spoke to—"

"I haven't spoken to her, ever," I say firmly. "Except to tell her to leave me the hell alone and that I'm calling the police."

"Not the stalker," Leon says. "The publicist."

My stomach plummets. *Oh, shit. Shit, shit, shit.*

"That's who you found," I say weakly.

"And she had plenty to say about you," Leon says.

"Of course she did," Amanda spits. "He fired her."

"Did he?" Leon asks simply.

"Yes, Sunday afternoon. Before we ever even talked to each other," she says.

I try not to flinch at hearing the lie I told repeated with such conviction.

Leon's gaze meets mine steadily, and I know I'm fucked. He knows. Everything, and whatever Elise may have invented to make things worse for me. She told me if she was caught she'd take me down with her.

"I'll get dressed," I say, dread slowly weighing my limbs like concrete pouring through my veins.

"Good idea," Leon says.

"Wait, Chase—you didn't do anything wrong. He shouldn't have to do this," Amanda insists to Leon.

She looks to me for confirmation.

My mouth works without words coming out.

"Chase?" she asks. There's a hint of wariness in her voice suddenly, and I hate it. Hate that I caused it.

But I don't know what to say.

Leon gives me a disgusted look and then turns a gentler expression toward Amanda.

"Miss Grace, you've been given a misleading set of facts regarding your visit here," he says.

"I don't understand," she says, but she takes a step back from the door, and seeing her retreat kills something in me.

"It was a setup," he says.

I close my eyes. I should speak up, but how do you argue with the truth?

"You were told this was a charitable act, intended to draw positive media attention?" Leon presses.

"Yes," Amanda admits reluctantly.

"According to Miss Prescott, she and Mr. Henry have been secretly collaborating from the beginning to create the impression of a romantic relationship between the two of you. Without your consent or knowledge, as far as I know." Leon pauses. "He lied, Miss Grace."

I hear Amanda's sharp inhale. My eyes snap open against my will, and because of that, the stunned betrayal on her face will be etched into my memory forever.

31

Amanda

"Amanda," Chase begins in a voice gravelly with desperation, and if I had any doubt about what Leon was saying, it's gone now.

"No," I say softly. All the pieces are falling into place with a horrible smoothness, like the picture has been there all along, just waiting for me to open my eyes and *see* it.

The adjoining hotel rooms. Elise hadn't been a pissed-off ex lashing out; they were scheming and I played right into it. No wonder Chase was so willing to let me stay in the room next to his.

And was this why Chase loaned me his shirt on the first day? I warned him what it would look like and he . . . he said he didn't care. Of course he didn't. It was what he wanted in the first place.

I'm aware suddenly of how exposed I am, wrapped in Chase's jacket and wearing his shirt. Again. Like an idiot.

I fold my arms over myself as best as I can. "How much of it was real?" I ask him, surprised by the calm deadness in my voice instead of the shrill hysteria I'm feeling. "Any of it?" I don't care about the cameras or what happened in front of them; it's everything that happened privately that I'm concerned with.

His eyes widen. "Amanda, all of it. I went along with Elise's plan at first, but I stopped." His accent is stronger now. "You know I did. All the social media stuff—"

"You said you fired her," I say.

He tightens his grip on the towel around his waist. "I did!"

"When?"

His gaze darts away from me, and my heart falls. "Amanda, I never wanted to—"

"When did you fire her?" I repeat, enunciating each word carefully.

"I sent her a text on Monday night, late," he says finally.

Monday night. A whole day after he came to my house with apologies and claims of firing the person responsible for the worst moment I've had since escaping Jonathon Jakes's basement. And from the guilt in his expression, I know without even asking that it was also after I kissed him on Monday night. After he kissed me. He was still in contact with her. He only stopped it, theoretically, when he realized scheming was no longer necessary—I was willingly falling into their plan and his false assurances.

Trembling starts within me until I feel like my teeth are chattering from it. "The box with the flowers and the chain, was that you, too? More grist for the media mill?"

Chase looks horrified. "No!" He reaches for me, and I jerk away. Pain crosses his face, and in spite of everything, seeing it sets off a twinge in me. I hate myself for my weakness in that moment.

He holds his free hand up slowly. "I swear, I had no idea any of that stuff was going on until after it was already happening. And when I found out, I told Elise it had to stop. She was just doing it because she was pissed I stopped going along with her plan. I didn't even know Sera was here until I saw those pictures."

"Miss Prescott's version of events differs," Leon points out dryly. "The police caught her at the motel where they were searching for the Drummond woman."

And I realize that's why they're here. They're trying to figure out how much Chase had to do with the vandalism, with this crazy woman showing up here and making threats. Was he really desperate enough to participate in such a dangerous plan?

Suddenly, I'm not sure I want to know the answer to that question, in light of these new revelations.

"You better go with them," I say to Chase.

He rakes a hand through his hair in a heartbreakingly familiar gesture of frustration. "Amanda, please, I screwed up in the beginning, but I never wanted to hurt you, and I didn't have anything to do with the threats, I swear to you. And I was going to tell you everything this morning."

This morning. After we slept together.

He registers the mistake almost immediately. "Amanda, no," he says. "It didn't have anything to do with that. I wasn't waiting until . . . after. You have to believe me. You *know* me."

The worst part is, I want to think that I do. I still want us to be real, want the pleading in his eyes to be genuine.

But I can't trust that impulse. And I don't think I can trust him.

"No," I say, the word coming from what feels like a great distance. "I'm not sure I do."

His face pales, and he lurches back a step like I've slapped him.

Though it feels like I'm going to break into a thousand pieces or vomit or both, I make myself nod at Leon and the two officers in the hallway, who are scrupulously pretending not to hear any of this. And then I turn and walk with wooden limbs toward my room. I have to get dressed. I have to get out of here.

"Amanda," Chase says, but the fight has gone out of his voice.

"Chase. Leave it." The warning in Leon's tone is unmistakable.

I make myself face him then, even though I know I'll hate myself for it later. He's still dressed in nothing but a towel, his shoulders are slumped, and he looks defeated. His hair is rumpled from his hand and from sleeping next to me, and in spite of everything, I still want to run back to him and throw my arms around him.

Which only makes it all worse.

Hot tears fill my eyes, but I don't want to cry, truly cry, because if I start now, I'm not sure I'll be able to stop. "Bye, Chase."

It turns out, when forced to consider it, there are very few people you can call to ask for an immediate ride home in the middle of the day when you're sixty miles away.

Fewer still who will respond in the affirmative to me saying, "I messed up. I'm okay, but I need to come home now. Please. Don't ask me why. And don't tell anyone."

All my friends from school are gone or might as well be, for the strangers that we are now to each other. Mia would have gladly ditched class, but she would have peppered me with questions the whole way here—on the phone—and back. My mom would have cried before even starting the car. I wasn't sure if my dad would pick up until after I left a voicemail, which I didn't feel capable of doing.

After Chase left with the officers, Leon offered to have someone take me home. An hour of awkward silence and pity, and me pretending not to notice or care?

No, I wanted someone who knew what it was to make a mistake with the best of intentions. So, after I asked Leon to do

738 DAYS / 377

one last thing for me, even though it made my self-loathing reach new peaks, I made my call, packed up my stuff, and then went down to the hotel's service entrance to wait.

Our battered red Toyota Camry, the one my mom used to drive before she got the van, rumbles into the back parking lot less than an hour later and screeches to a halt on the blacktop.

I walk outside. Thankfully, all the photographers are still out front or maybe they followed Chase to the police station, I don't know.

Liza leans over the center console to push the balky passenger door open. "Hey," she says. I must have pulled her away from studying. Her dark hair is up in a messy knot, and she's wearing her thick-framed reading glasses and a serious expression, her forehead pinched with concern.

She is so familiar, so comfortingly Liza, and such a reminder of home that, suddenly, the tears that I've been working to hold back pour out.

She looks alarmed as I half-sit, half-fall into the car and close the door.

"Okay, okay," she says, putting the car in park and then reaching out awkwardly to pull me against her shoulder. Her sweater smells like the lilac body wash in the shower at home and the coffee shop where she studies when Mia's driving her crazy.

That just makes me cry harder. I don't know what's wrong with me. Well, I do, but I'm safe now, away from the source of pain. I should be feeling better, but instead, I just keep sobbing, like I'm hoping that the tears will leach all the hurt out of me and I won't feel anything.

"I know you don't want to talk about what happened," Liza says after a few moments.

"I don't," I manage between sobs and gasps for breath, feeling like a baby and yet unable to stop myself.

"Can you just tell me who I need to kill?" she asks.

That catches my attention.

I pull back from her shoulder and look up at my big sister, the one who is so painfully serious all the time.

And she nods, her mouth set in that prim straight line. She means it, in her Liza way.

I want to laugh, but I can't, not yet. "Chase," I say slowly, my voice rusty. "He lied, pretended to care about me to get media attention. He was working with his publicist even when he said he wasn't. It was all for his career. And I don't know if any of it was real."

But he says he loves me and I want to believe him anyway. And that hurts worse than anything else.

I can't make those words come out, though.

Liza blinks, the motion magnified by her glasses. "Well . . . ," she says, clearly struggling for words. "Well . . ."

I sit up, pulling away from her. "Liza, it's okay," I say wearily. "I know you liked him and—"

"Well, fuck that guy," she finally bursts out.

My mouth falls open, and I stare at her.

She raises an eyebrow at me. "What? Do you want to sue him? We could probably do that. Emotional damages." She waves a hand at me, then looks down at herself and her tear-spotted lavender sweater with a frown. "Dry cleaning, too."

I do laugh this time, though it emerges more like a painful hiccup. "I don't think he has the money for either, honestly."

She scowls and opens her mouth.

I cut her off. "Thank you for coming to get me," I say. My stomach twists with a fresh knot of anxiety. "You didn't tell Mom and Dad, right?"

She shakes her head. "I didn't say anything. They don't even know I'm here."

I let out a breath of relief. I have enough to deal with, without additional scrutiny. Easier that they don't know anything until I'm ready to tell them. If I'm ever ready. "Thanks."

Liza turns her attention to the gearshift, fidgeting with it as she puts it in drive. "Thank you for calling me," she says.

"I'm sorry I . . . I'm sorry I told Mom and Dad to have the memorial—"

"No apologies necessary," I say, sagging into my seat. "You were trying to do the right thing by them. That's all anyone could have done in that situation."

We sit there for a moment, nothing but the whir of the heater and the rattle of the engine in the silence.

"It will get better," she says in an unexpected hopeful, emotional statement.

"That's the really weird thing," I say, lifting my shoulder in a weary shrug. "I don't know if I want it to, if I care. I'm just so . . . tired." The word drags out of me like it's bearing the weight of everything that has happened in the last four years.

Liza gives me a severe look. "Okay, Amanda, listen to me. You're just feeling overwhelmed right now. But I have a very short and simple process for feeling better. Survival method for my extremely stressful torts class."

I roll my eyes. My sister is back in lecture mode. "Liza . . ."

She pushes a button, and our windows go down with a groan, letting in cool, crisp air. "Now," she says in a bossy voice, "you sit straight up in your chair—"

"And breathe in for four counts, hold it, and then out for eight," I interrupt. "Yeah, I know that one. But trust me, breathing isn't going to help."

She glares at me. "Are you ready to listen?"

I hold my hands up in surrender. "Fine."

"Extend your arm out the window."

I frown at her in confusion, but mimic her actions in reverse. Her left arm is out the window, so I put out my right.

"Now raise your arm at the elbow slowly and extend your middle finger as far as it will go and then on the count of three, say whatever expletive will make you feel better."

Still following her instructions, I gape at her. "Wait, what?"

"*Assholes!*" she shouts on my behalf and peels out of the

parking lot, and for a second, we're both laughing like crazy people, our middle fingers up at the world.

My heart is broken, my belief in myself hemorrhaging like a fatal tear in an artery, but my sister came for me. And I have to admit that flipping off the Wescott Inn, and the mistakes made within it, makes me feel incrementally better.

For a second.

32

Chase

I'm a fucking mess.

After eight hours of interrogation, the police had to let me go. Couldn't find enough to keep me. But my head is throbbing, the side of my face is bruised from an "accidental" brush with the frame of the squad car door, and from the sound of Karen's heavy footsteps behind me in the hotel hallway, I'm in for an explosion of epic, ear-blistering proportions as soon as the door closes behind us.

But none of that compares to the gnawing anxiety beneath my ribs.

My hand shakes getting the key card in the door, and Karen sighs.

But I ignore that and get inside as quickly as possible.

Even with my single-minded determination, it slows me a little to see the room just as we . . . I left it eight hours ago.

Minus Amanda.

I knew she wouldn't be here. But some part of me was still hoping, I guess.

The late-afternoon sun is slanting through a crack in the curtains that are drawn from the night before. Because Leon canceled housekeeping, the bed is unmade, the covers thrown back where Amanda left them when she got up this morning to toss clothes at me. It hurts my heart to see the two pillows pushed together on one side of the bed, the dents in them from our heads.

I would do anything, *anything*, to go back to that moment this morning.

But I can't.

"I don't understand what you were thinking," Karen says, far more quietly than I was expecting. It sounds almost like she's in shock. She moves deeper in the room, parking herself in front of the entertainment center and the mini-fridge. "If they could have found a solid connection between you and that crazy stalker bitch, you would have been done. Accessory to vandalism and stalking, assuming Amanda presses charges, which she should. The production company's insurance sure as hell will."

I find my jacket on the back of the dining room chair, where I hung it last night, even though the last time I saw it, Amanda had it wrapped around her.

I don't let myself replay the moment because I'm afraid it'll stop my heart.

Instead, I plunge my hands into the pockets, searching. But they're empty except for a receipt and a plastic knife. From breakfast in the car the other morning. The memory hurts.

What if I never see her again?

"I mean, I've known you to do stupid things, sometimes selfish ones, too," Karen says in wonder. "But never deliberately cruel like this."

I close my eyes. "It's complicated," I say.

"It better be."

The keys to the rental car might be in my suitcase, maybe. But as soon as I turn in that direction, I'm faced with the sight of my shirts, the ones Amanda borrowed, folded neatly on the sofa cushion. On top of them are her visitor credentials for the set, with the cord neatly tucked to the side, and her hotel room key.

It steals my breath and for a second, I'm just gasping for air.

She's gone, and she wanted nothing of me to go with her. Fuck. I have to fix this. I have to undo it.

"Chase?" Karen asks, alarmed.

"It didn't start out that way," I say, bending over, resting my hands on my knees. "It was supposed to be simple. No one gets hurt."

Karen gives a derisive snort. "That's what she said, right? Elise?"

"I didn't realize it wouldn't work. I didn't realize that I would feel—"

"So it was real. You fell in love."

"Yes!" I glare at her.

"And you still didn't tell Amanda the truth," Karen says in a resigned tone.

"I couldn't tell her. I knew she would hate me, and she might leave. And I—"

"Was a giant fucking coward. Again," Karen says flatly. "Ran away, maybe not literally this time, but close enough."

Sometimes having a brutally honest friend who knows you this well is not as much help as you'd want.

The tightness in my chest increases, and I duck my head to catch my breath.

Karen shifts her weight, inching closer to me. I can see only her legs with my head down.

"Are you okay?" she asks, and I can hear the frown in her voice.

"I'm fine." I just need the damn car keys.

I straighten up and push myself to cross the room to the

window and dig in my suitcase on the wooden luggage rack, spilling clothes, chargers, and shoes everywhere.

"What did I do with them? I just had them the other day."

"What are you looking for?" Karen asks, making no move to help me.

"The keys for the rental car." Which are nowhere to be found. "Damnit!" I shove the suitcase away from me, and the rack tips over, colliding hard with the wall and tearing a gash in the beige wallpaper.

"Where do you need to go?" she asks warily. "Your call time is in forty-five minutes."

"Amanda's not answering her phone." I tried a dozen times in the cab with Karen on the way over from the police station. "I need to talk to her."

Karen raises her eyebrows, the piercings giving her severe look even more intensity. "Chase, you need to leave her the hell alone," she says. "If you show up now, she's not going to open the door to you. She might even call the police and you'll enjoy a second visit with the local authorities."

Even if Amanda doesn't, her family might. And they would be right to.

I sag to the floor. "I fucked up."

"Yeah, you did."

"I have to *do* something." I look up at her, pleading silently for her to have answers. I can't take it back, I know that, but surely there's something that will make this better.

But Karen just shakes her head, her twin braids wobbling with the movement. "Some mistakes you only get to make once."

She sounds so tired and defeated, instead of pissed or disappointed, and that somehow only makes it all worse.

"Who asked you?" I demand, shoving myself to my feet. Anger is better. Fury is easier to handle than this other feeling, the one that tells me that Karen is right, that I've messed up one too many times and too badly with this girl.

I stalk out of the living area and into the bedroom, keeping my gaze focused on the nightstand drawers rather than the bed, which holds memories that I can't let myself think about right now. "What are you even doing here anyway?" I ask, searching the drawers in the nightstand. They hold a Bible and an out-dated phone book.

No keys.

I slam the drawers shut and head for the bathroom, the one place I haven't searched. "I could have called a cab from the police station."

I pause at the threshold and turn to face her, a very belated realization clicking in. "Wait, how did you know I was there?"

As soon as I walked out of the police department, she was in a taxi out front, waiting for me. At the time, I didn't question it, my mind too preoccupied with trying to reach Amanda.

Karen takes a deep breath and lets it out slowly, like she's holding some big secret that needs to be broken to me with care. "I'm here because Leon called me and asked me to come," she says.

"I'm fine," I snarl. "I don't need him to—"

"Oh, yeah, you're great," she says. "Clearly."

I glare at her. "That's not—"

"He called me because Amanda asked him to," she says grimly.

I can't move.

"Before she left. She said she was afraid if they released you, you'd do something dumb."

My mouth works but no sound comes out at first. "She was afraid of . . . Jesus, she's afraid I'll come after her?" Oh my God, how badly have I fucked this up?

"No, she was afraid *for* you, hon," Karen says with a frown. And the endearment, instead of her normal "dumbass," makes me panicky. It must be so much worse than I thought if she's resorting to kind names instead. "That you'd hit the bottle."

Suddenly, Karen's position in front of the mini-bar makes sense. Too much sense. Cracking open everything in the fridge sounds like a much better idea than a likely doomed-from-the-start mission that I can't even find the car keys to begin.

Except I had the hotel take out all the bottles before I even got here. My resolve was so strong then. Still, there are ways around that. Especially if I can find the stupid car keys.

Because even after Amanda learned exactly how I had lied to her, she was still watching out for me.

"You don't deserve her anyway, Chase," Karen says with a shrug, more a statement of fact than an insult toward me. "I can't believe I encouraged her to trust you. I thought . . ." Her mouth thins into a line. "But I was wrong."

"I know I don't," I choke out. "But what am I supposed to do?"

"You handed control over to someone else. Again. You sacrificed things that weren't yours to give, all for your career." She looks at me with distance in her expression, like she doesn't know me anymore. Maybe she doesn't. "But you got what you wanted, so I suggest you don't blow it. Go to work. Or else it was all for nothing anyway. You did the shittiest thing I've ever known you, or pretty much anyone, to do."

"Yeah, I know, but I—"

"Do you know?" Karen demands, folding her arms across her chest, the edges of her fish scales peeking out from the fake fur on her jacket cuffs. "You, the great actor, decided to throw just a little more icing on top of that shit cake that is her life. Why? Because *you* needed it. Because *you* wanted it."

I want to protest that it wasn't like that, but it was, maybe, a little.

"So you want to know what to do? Take some fucking responsibility. Go do your fucking job, the one that was supposedly worth all of this. If you throw away the results of what you did, then you're throwing away the pain you caused her, too, making it nothing."

I swallow hard over the lump in my throat. "Kare, I don't know if I can—"

"Chase, for the record, I don't care what you think you can or can't do right now," she says wearily. "I don't care if they find you passed out in a steaming heap of vomit tomorrow morning. Just like old times. But I'll tell you one thing you're going to do. You're going to leave that girl alone, the way you should have from the start."

With that, she walks away from the mini-fridge and toward the door to the hall, pausing only once to lift a set of keys—the keys with the bright yellow rental tag, the keys I tore the room apart looking for—off the center of the dining table and pocket them.

Then the door slams shut behind her, and I'm alone.

33

Amanda

By early evening, it's like I never left home. I'm camped out on my bed, with my class work spread out around me while my mom finishes cooking dinner downstairs and Mia complains loudly about setting the table.

Any reporters or photographers who might have been hovering in our front yard after those first pictures of Chase and me broke obviously decided Wescott was a richer hunting ground. They're gone now, the only signs of their former presence a few discarded coffee cups in the matted-down grass.

My mom, upon her return from the grocery store to find me in the kitchen with Liza, dropped the bags on the floor immediately—with no care for the eggs, it turns out—and hugged me so hard I felt my ribs creak. Clearly, I was forgiven for what I'd said on the phone.

When she got a good look at me, though, she suspected something was wrong. It's hard to hide from your mom, especially when your eyes are swollen and your nose is red from crying. But when I refused to answer her questions and she started to push, Liza jumped in with an amazing floor show of distraction, bringing up a series of my mom's favorite hot-button issues—suspected unfair grading (in Liza's civil procedure class), the dangerous chemicals in microwave popcorn (my dad's favorite snack), and the decline of handwritten thank-you notes as a common courtesy (Mia's THX texts to elderly relatives who barely know how to use their flip phones to make calls)—until I could escape to my room.

Mia, herself, though, was a harder sell.

After she returned from school, she walked past my room on the way to hers, stopping with an almost comedic lurch when she saw me.

"Why are you here?" she asked with narrowed eyes.

"I decided to come back," I told her, forcing a shrug. "That's all."

"What happened?"

"It just . . . it wasn't going to work," I said, avoiding her gaze. "You know, the lure of Hollywood life. He was going back, and I'm staying here."

Mia frowned at me, studying me for a long moment, until I was afraid I was going to break and either tell the whole awful story or cry or both.

"So you're just done. With him. With all of it. Just like that?" she asked, suspicion heavy in her voice. "Even after you spent the night with him?"

"Yep," I said, trying for casual. "Sad but true."

Which is an unfortunately accurate descriptor for the entire course of events.

I don't think Mia believed me, not entirely, but because I'm doing an okay job not being a total wreck, she and the rest of my family are willing to let it go. For the moment.

And really, I'm fine; I'm doing okay. It's been a whole ten

hours. Maybe Liza's flip-them-off-and-scream technique really does work. Or maybe I just cried so hard earlier I've got nothing left. An empty tank until I rehydrate.

I'm going to be okay. I've survived worse than this. I'm going to be okay. I'm just going to keep repeating that to myself until it feels true again.

At the moment, I'm trying to focus on homework between loads of my laundry, which requires ignoring the smell of Chase on my clothes—his deodorant, his soap, *him*—until it's obliterated by the fresh, nothing scent of our sensitive-skin laundry detergent and that teddy bear fabric softener that my mom started buying just because I liked the character on the box when I was five.

I haven't showered yet. I should. I can still feel his touch, his mouth on me.

But Wescott and Chase Henry are miles away, just sixty, though it might as well be a million. When I wash him off me, he'll be gone forever. And though it might make me the biggest doormat in the history of ever, I'm not ready to do that. Yet.

Even if his feelings weren't real, mine were.

Are. Mine *are.*

And that's an accomplishment I'm not ready to let go of at this exact moment. It's not enough, of course. It doesn't make up for what he did, the lies.

I shut my eyes, remembering the burn of humiliation. I think that's the worst part. Before I loved him, I *liked* him. If Chase had explained it to me and told me what he needed, I would have been all over the chance to help. We could have been just friends. Maybe.

That's what sets the rage to a slow, thick boil in my chest. All he had to do was ask. That's it. But he didn't. Why? Because it was more fun to trick me? Because he didn't know me well enough to realize I would say yes? Because he's completely brainless, spineless, and operated solely by Elise's hand on his penis?

I don't like any of those answers, and yet they might all very well be true.

Despair bubbles up in me, breaking up the contained broth of fury into something far less manageable. And it's not just directed at Chase, but myself. How could I have fallen for it? How could I have decided to trust someone like that? Even worse, after all of it, how can I still ache to see him?

I'm such a sucker.

A knock sounds on my open door, startling me out of my thoughts.

I look up to see my dad in the doorway. I didn't know he was home.

My shoulders tense automatically. If he's seeking me out, that means he's going to yell or demand answers I'm not ready to give.

That's our pattern: when he's not ignoring me, he's radiating stern disapproval. Gone is the patient father who used to teach us about changing flat tires and putting. This man looks like him but he's been made sharper and harder by everything that happened.

But instead of shouting, my dad hesitates in the doorway, looking uncomfortable. "Your mother asked me to come tell you dinner is ready," he says, rubbing at his beard with a faint roll of his eyes.

My mouth curves in a smile. For a brief moment, we're united in the absurdity of this premise. My mom, if she wanted to, could just shout up the stairs as she has a million times before. Or, better yet, give Mia the excuse to turn it up to eleven and bellow for me.

But evidently, my unexpected arrival home has triggered in my mom the desire to bring my dad and me together.

Not that it's going to work. "Liza has class, so we're eating now instead of waiting," my dad says, already turning away like I don't exist. It is, I suppose, the better of the two options.

Still . . .

"Okay," I say. Then before I can stop myself, I call after him, "Dad."

He stops, his posture stiff.

"I need to ask you something." I put my pencil down in the seam of my American government textbook, not sure how to formulate the question when I'm still afraid of the answer. "I know things have been hard the last couple of years, and I haven't always made them easier. Especially this week."

He doesn't say anything, a silent, slightly darker shadow in the already dark hallway, but he hasn't walked away. I have to take that as an encouraging sign.

"But someone . . . someone told me something recently, and I just want to know if it's true." Drawing my knees up to my chest, I swallow over the dryness in my throat and force the words out. "I've been thinking that you blame me for what happened, and that's why you're avoiding me. But then he . . . someone said maybe that wasn't it. Maybe it was something else. And I just need to know."

My dad is a statue, unmoving, on the edge of the hall. In the intervening silence, I lose my nerve and race to fill the gap with words. "It's okay if you blame me. I do."

He turns around slowly, a dumbstruck look on his face.

"Blame you? Why would I ever blame you?"

"Because it was a dumb mistake," I say, surprised, the words pouring out from the dark, secret place where I've held them for so long that they've worn grooves into me. "Because I didn't follow instructions."

Don't go anywhere with a stranger. Pretty basic kindergartner stuff, and I failed. Stranger danger was one of the first lessons we learned when we started walking to school. And I paid attention; I just didn't understand that "stranger" meant more than someone you'd never met before.

"Because I should have known something was off about his story about a dog," I continue, feeling the lump of unshed tears swell in my throat. "I walked by there every day, and I'd never seen one before." Then, against my will and despite desperate blinking on my part, the tears roll free. "Because I should have screamed."

"Amanda . . ."

"I didn't scream," I repeat, confessing the worst of my sins and unable to look at him while I do so. "I should have, but I didn't know until it was—"

"Amanda, no." My dad stalks toward me faster than I've seen him move in years, and I flinch automatically though he's never raised a hand against me, ever.

He kneels next to the side of my bed, resting his hand carefully on my foot. "You were a child," he says calmly and firmly, meeting my eyes without hesitation. "And we raised you to have a good heart. That's what you were listening to. You did nothing wrong. Nothing at all."

Then, I watch in shock as his face crumples.

"We should have looked harder. We knew you were taken somewhere on your way home, but we assumed there was a car. The police . . ." His voice breaks then, and he stops long enough to try to recover himself. "There were reports of a van and a man who no one recognized, parked near the high school." He wipes his eyes with the back of his hand.

"But we didn't know, and you were right there, the whole time, waiting for us." He looks up at me with raw misery in his expression. "Volunteers knocked on doors, in the beginning. We knocked at every house on your route home." He swallows hard.

"Daddy, it's okay—"

"When we found you, I went back to the list, the spreadsheet I made to make sure we covered every house, every person on your way home. And it was me. I knocked on his door, baby. I knocked and I talked to him, and I had no idea you were there. I am so sorry." My dad, the stern, distant figure I've learned to avoid, breaks into sobs, burying his face against the side of my bed. "I'm so sorry."

"It's not your fault. It was never your fault," he says, his face muffled against my comforter, his big hand clinging to my foot.

But it's not his fault, either. It seems maybe I'm not the only one blaming myself when I shouldn't be. Jakes is really the only person to blame, and that's clearer to me now more than ever.

I touch my dad's hand lightly with mine but have to shift my gaze to the ceiling to try to get my tears under control.

Because Chase was right.

He was so, so wrong, in so many respects, but he was right about this.

I can feel my heart breaking again, into even smaller pieces.

Because it's that contradiction in Chase, that mix of good and bad, that's going to make it so much harder to let him go.

34

Chase

"That's a wrap for Thursday," Max shouts. "Well, Thurs-riday." He glances up pointedly at the already brightening sky, and everyone else chuckles.

It's almost dawn. I haven't slept. Filming nights sucks.

It always does. But tonight is worse. And going back to my room, that won't be any better.

"Good work, everybody," Max says to a smattering of applause and some halfhearted cheers.

Shivering in Smitty's hoodie, I shuffle to my chair, where my coat is waiting. It's below freezing now, and there was a major discussion around 3:00 a.m. about our breath showing, clearly indicating it was colder than it should have been for late summer, when the events in the movie are supposed to be taking place. It would be taken out in post-production, but that's another expense.

Max wasn't happy. But I don't care. I didn't care when they were talking about it, didn't care when they finally decided.

In the end, I did what Karen told me. I showed up on time and did my job. Everyone had heard the basics of what had happened by the time I arrived. A set is pretty much like a small town. Gossip travels at lightning speed. Even faster when it involves scandal. There were plenty of stares and whispers among the crew, especially from those who'd met Amanda. People liked her. I'm guessing whatever respect I'd earned by being a professional instead of a screwup this week is long gone now.

Karen ignored me other than to give me direction on how to tilt my head so she could finish her work. Ron, the van driver, wouldn't look at me. Emily stayed quiet and made no attempt at conversation for the first time since I met her.

Now, my driving need to fix, to do, has vanished beneath a thick layer of despair and inevitability. I can't do anything, can't fix anything. This is just reality, and I have to live with choices I can't unmake.

I feel like I'm drowning.

Even the surprise phone call from Rick, my agent, the first one from him in months, didn't help. His voicemail was positive, excited, passing along word that everything—rumors that Amanda and I are being targeted by a stalker due to our new couple status—is generating highly visible attention in the media. And the casting agent for the Besson film contacted him to confirm I was coming next week because they "really want to see you."

Most of the cynical people in the business, it seems, have assumed Amanda's visit was a planned publicity stunt from the beginning—one she was in on. But the fact that it can't be proved either way only generates more and more speculation and discussion.

No one who knows the truth is talking, so I look savvier—if more heartless—than I am, which makes me ill. It hasn't been announced yet if Elise has been charged with accessory status, but it probably won't matter once the publicity agency's lawyers get involved. The truth, as always, is less important than whatever legal maneuvering can be managed. My guess is that George, my former publicist, and whoever else Elise has called in for help will work to keep this sanitized version of events spinning. It's better for them.

Nobody knows yet that Amanda's gone home. That I made that haunted look appear on her face.

The crowd outside the hotel tonight was so out of control that we didn't even try for a pickup out front.

I got what I wanted. My name is the one on everyone's tongue and Twitter feed right now, in a good way.

And I go home day after tomorrow. Actually, if it's Friday already, I've got a late flight tomorrow. Back to my life, the one I pulled from the wreckage of my previous mistakes. I won't have to crawl back to my dad in Texas, begging for a place to stay.

I saved my career.

And now, with that newly bright future in front of me again, I find the shine is empty. Just a handful of glitter and carefully placed lights, nothing real.

Acting is the only thing that has ever meant anything to me, the only time I felt like I belonged. And I would have done anything to keep going, to keep feeling that way. But now I've apparently found a line I'm not willing to cross, only after I've crossed it.

Amanda loves me . . . loved me. The real me. And I didn't, couldn't, step up to accept it. Because I was too self-involved to tell the truth and too afraid of losing her.

Forget Elise, Sera, Max, everyone. That's on me. I wasn't who I should have been, who she deserves.

Amanda, I'm so sorry.

"So that was fun, huh?" Adam asks as he drops into his chair, which is, unfortunately, next to mine.

I ignore him, focusing on making my numb fingers line up the zipper on my coat and pull it up.

"So I guess you're back in the headlines again. What's it feel like to relive the glory days for a few minutes?" He sighs, stretching his legs out in front of him. "I mean, don't get me wrong. It's a smart play. Maybe I just need to find some famous, damaged girl with a pretty face who'll let me—"

I turn and lash out with my foot, kicking over his chair with him in it. He hits the ground with the crack of wood and a satisfying thud.

But it's not enough to sate the blood thundering in my veins, demanding that he pay.

Wrapping my hand in the front of his shirt, I drag him up from the ground. Distantly, I hear gasps from the various cast and crew who are watching, but it doesn't really register.

He doesn't get to talk about her like that. Ever.

But as I draw back to hit him, I see the flicker of a smirk on his face and Amanda's words echo in my head: *He wants you to break.*

It sends a shock through me, to realize that she was right. I don't *need* to do this. It's letting him control me, just like everyone else. He's pushing my buttons to get a response, and if I hit him, I'm giving him exactly what he wants. The same way I caved to Elise, when she told me she knew better and I wanted the promised results so badly I didn't care if what she was suggesting felt wrong.

But I know better than that now.

I let go of Adam, dropping him onto his broken and splintered chair. Then with my heart pounding and my hands shaking from the excess adrenaline, I turn and walk away.

"Hey, fucker, come back here and finish it!" he bellows, and I hear him trying to scramble to his feet out of the wreckage.

It would be so much easier, more familiar, to turn around and hit him, but I keep going until I find Emily huddled under one of the heat lamps.

"Can you find out where Leon is?" I ask. I'm no longer cold, at least.

Her eyes are puffy from lack of sleep but still capable of projecting intense wariness. She nods quickly and points across set to where Max and Leon are deep in conversation.

"Oh." *Awesome. Max. I'm sure he has plenty to say to me.* "Thanks."

I hang back a few feet, waiting until Max finishes talking to Leon before I approach.

"Great work tonight, Chase," Max says, beaming at me as he passes.

I stare at him wordlessly. Tonight, of all nights, he chooses to praise me?

Then he leans forward and says in a confidential tone, "Look, I know I gave you a hard time about . . . you know, but with this extra attention . . ." He grins. "We're already getting calls about distribution."

Shame wells in me and I look away, studying the ground in the distance until he pats me on the shoulder and strolls away, whistling.

When he's finally out of hearing range, I risk glancing up at Leon, who's watching me with an impenetrable expression.

Swallowing my pride, I ask, "Have you heard anything from Amanda? I've tried to call—"

"No, I haven't and I don't expect to," Leon says. His bald head wrinkles with a frown. "You shouldn't, either."

"I just want to make sure she's okay." I stuff my hands in my coat pockets.

He looks at me incredulously. "Do you think she's okay?"

I shut my eyes. "No, of course not. That's not what I meant. I just—"

He pokes a finger in my shoulder, and I open my eyes.

"I'm not sure what you expect, son. But you're damn lucky that she's not going public with her side of this. She could destroy you." He shakes his head in disbelief. "All those people who are clapping you on the back now would turn on you so fast you'd feel the breeze. Better to leave well enough alone and pray she doesn't change her mind. You hear me?"

I clamp my jaw shut and give a tight nod. "Do you know anything more about Sera?" I don't like the idea of her out there, especially when I don't know if Amanda is safe and taking precautions. The chain Sera sent threw me, not just because of the message it carried, but because it was the first time she'd ever attempted contact with someone in my life instead of me directly.

Leon sighs. "They're getting closer. I don't think they were real motivated until this afternoon. Evidently, she knows about your little escapade with law enforcement here. Someone threw a lit book of matches in the open window of a squad car while the officer was inside a Starbucks grabbing coffee."

I grimace. Sounds about right.

"Then she smashed the windshield with a crowbar and ran." *Holy shit.* "That's new." Fire, yes. Direct violence, no.

"He lost her in a crowd. She's good at blending in when she wants to. And now that we've locked down security for you here and at the hotel, they're having a hard time drawing her out."

"You're sure she's still here for me? She won't bother Amanda?" I persist.

He shrugs. "I notified the PD in Springfield. Even offered to send Amanda home with an officer, but she wanted to wait for her sister."

Liza or Mia? I wonder which one came and how Amanda felt about it. I want her to tell me, to talk to me.

"That's all?" I ask Leon. It doesn't seem like enough.

"Miss Grace is not my responsibility. The people on this set are," he points out. "Don't worry about it. Just keep your head down and don't go making yourself a target. We'll take care of the whackjob. You just keep doing what you do." He jerks his head in a dismissive gesture toward the cameras.

Then he walks away, leaving me fuming with impotent fury. The thing is, if I do what everyone is telling me to now, I win. I'm the good little actor who played my role in the scheme and got everything I wanted.

But if I accept the rewards as my due, then there's no difference between me and Elise. Or Adam and me.

But at least the two of them are deliberate schemers. I just followed blindly, hating every second of it but doing nothing to stop it. That's worse.

I need to do something else. I need to *change*, or I'm going to end up back here, hating myself again in six months, a year. Or maybe I won't be that lucky.

A flicker of an idea, something Leon said, tickles the far reaches of my brain.

I can't do anything to take back what I've done. But maybe I can fix things going forward. Maybe I can still try to be the person I should have been all along.

If I follow through, it'll destroy everything I've done this week, every bit of career advancement gone. Forget the Besson audition, or any audition for a while after this. It might well land me back in Tillman on my knees, with a manure shovel in one hand and a groveling apology in the other.

Even worse, it's possible that Karen's right, and Amanda will hate me even more for making her humiliation greater and her pain worth nothing.

But just considering the idea makes me feel like I can breathe again, like I might be able to cough the water from my lungs and stop drowning. Which also makes me think it's possible Amanda might understand exactly what I'm doing.

Breaking free.

35

Amanda

"What are you doing?" Liza asks, sticking her head in my partially open door before I can pretend to be reading or doing anything other than staring into space.

Technically, I'm staring at the torn-out pages I swiped from Liza's discarded college brochures and taped to my walls years ago. All of them portray happy people in various stages of crossing the green open space of a quad. Sometimes they're lying on blankets with books. Others are obviously in the middle of a (staged) Frisbee game. One of them, my favorite, is taken at dusk with the sky turning pink behind an enormous chapel, and a pair of students holding hands are cast in silhouette.

I think I could do that now, be one of those students. Suddenly, it just seems more possible. Before, I'd stalled out on progress to the point of no advancement at all. But I just spent five days, give or take, away from home and once I got past the rough start, I was mostly okay.

I'm not done, I know, working through the issues from being taken. But now, it seems like maybe the light at the end of that endless tunnel could be sunshine instead of another fluorescent light illuminating the tracks disappearing into nothingness.

But when I should be celebrating that fact and trying harder to push forward and make decisions, part of me now just wants to sit on the tracks and stay in the darkness.

"Nothing," I say to Liza finally. I'm wallowing today, with self-indulgent abandon. But I've decided I'm allowed to for one day. Then, starting tomorrow, I'm going to figure out what comes next.

But that's tomorrow.

Liza frowns. "Are you going to get up?"

"It's only ten thirty in the morning," I point out. "And for what? Mom's not here." She fussed repeatedly last night about canceling her dentist appointment to stay home with me. But Dad, in a rare moment of solidarity that I hope will become more frequent, backed me on my ability to stay home by myself.

I've never broken up with anyone before, never had my heart shattered, but I'm inclined to think that solitude is one of the recovery requirements.

"You're hiding," Liza accuses.

"No, I'm brooding. There's a fine difference. Please note the chocolate-covered pretzels." I shake the foil bag that I dug out of the pantry this morning at six when I couldn't sleep anymore.

Liza rolls her eyes. "I have to leave for study group," she says. "I just wanted to make sure you were all right."

"I'm . . ." Empty, angry, lonely. Sad. "I'm here," I say finally. "I'll be better tomorrow."

"Do you still want me to keep this?" She pulls my phone from her pocket and holds it aloft.

My heart leaps, and I curl my hands into fists to keep from reaching for the phone. In the car on the way home, I shut it off and gave it to her before Chase might even have a chance to text or call. *If* he even would attempt it.

"Did you turn it on?" I ask.

She frowns. "You told me not to."

"Oh." In that moment, I'm kind of wishing I'd given it to Mia or held on to it myself. My resolve would have weakened and I would have powered it on to check for messages. Now, I have to ask for it from Liza, who, despite her best intentions, will totally judge me for it, in true big-sister style.

"Do you think—" I begin.

The garage door goes up then, with a distant rumble, and a second later, the kitchen door bangs open.

Liza and I exchange confused glances.

She leans back into the hall. "Mom?"

There's no answer but the sound of feet pounding through the kitchen and then up the stairs.

I tense.

"You aren't going to believe this," Mia crows breathlessly, pushing past Liza and throwing herself onto the foot of my bed.

"What are you doing here?" I ask, pulling my legs back before she crushes my kneecaps with her elbows in a further fit of enthusiasm.

"It's Friday. You're supposed to be in school," Liza says, folding her arms across her chest, my phone still in hand.

"It's just gym." Mia waves her hand dismissively. "Everyone knows that's optional." She frowns at me. "You have chocolate all over your face."

I swipe at it immediately with the back of my hand, guessing at its location.

Liza's mouth pinches tight in disapproval. "Gym is not optional. Mia, you can't just—"

"What aren't we going to believe?" I ask, to prevent the fight that's brewing.

"This." Mia holds up her phone and presses a button. On the screen is a video beneath a huge headline: "Chase Henry Speaks Out on Amanda Grace, #AMASE, and the Future."

"It's all over everywhere. As of twenty minutes ago. I came home as soon as I saw."

"I don't want to see it," I say automatically, my hand moving to cover my heart. Where it used to be, anyway.

"Yes, you do. Trust me." Mia pushes the play button and scrambles to the head of the bed to shove in next to me, taking most of my pillow for herself.

"I'm going to be late," Liza says, but she doesn't move.

The video loads slowly, and for a second, I think I'm going to be watching that spinny circle and holding my breath forever.

But then the dark screen clears, and I recognize the turn-around in front of the Wescott Inn immediately. The crowd is still there with their signs, but Chase is the center focus, standing in front of the glass doors with the barricade up in front of him, holding everyone back.

The image is slightly blurred until the video starts to play. There are other cameras, professional setups, closer in, but this is someone in the middle of the crowd, holding up a cell phone and recording it.

"Thanks for being here this morning. For letting me talk to y'all." His accent is back. He looks tired yet determined, and it makes my heart hurt. I want to reach through the screen and hold his hand.

"We love you, Chase," someone near the camera holder bellows.

"Shhhh," the camera holder hisses.

He looks up directly into the camera phone, and even with the distance, between us and between Chase and the lens, it's electric. He's staring straight into me, it seems, and I feel it like a kick to my ribs.

"I've been told not to do this by pretty much everyone I know," he says, his gaze steady and defiant. "But we all know how good I am at following directions." He pauses. "Actually, I've been better at it than you think. Not anymore, though."

People chuckle uneasily, not sure what he means or where this is going, given his reputation.

"I want to start by saying I owe all of you an apology but one person particularly." He stuffs his hands deep in his pockets, and in his pause, I hear the click-click of dozens of cameras. "There's been a lot of, um, speculation this week about certain, um, aspects of my personal life."

Liza makes a face. "He's 'um'-ing too much."

"Stop," I say. Because this is Chase as I know him, uncomfortable with the attention when he's not acting or reciting someone else's words. And I want to hear *him*. The real him, I hope.

"Told you you'd want to see it," Mia says with a grin, but she keeps her voice low.

"It was, as many of you suspected, a publicity stunt," Chase says, and the collective gasp from the assembly is loud.

"Oh my God," Mia squeals. "Here it comes."

"You've already seen this," Liza protests. "Let us hear." She leans closer so she can see the screen better.

"Shhhh." I wave my hands at both of them, my entire focus riveted on Mia's phone.

"—fake, at least, it was in the beginning," Chase continues. "It wasn't my idea, but I went along with it because I thought I needed it and I thought what I needed was more important than anything else. Than anyone else." He's looking at me again, and I want to turn myself inside out to escape the pain and I never want it to end, all at the same time.

"Then it turned into something more, and I didn't handle it right," he says, the confession dropping his head low for a moment. Then he straightens his shoulders. "I wasn't expecting to . . . feel what I felt, and when I did, I didn't know what to do, how to tell the truth. But what happened was more real to me than anything, and I don't regret that for a moment." His expression is fierce, and it tears at me.

The camera bobbles a bit as the girl holding it squeals under her breath.

He shakes his head. "All of that is personal and more than I'm willing to discuss, but I want to apologize to y'all for the lies. That was wrong. You should decide if you like what I do without being tricked into it."

I think I might be the only one to hear the faint tremor of uncertainty beneath the determination in his voice. He's putting himself out there, drawing a line in the sand, without knowing for sure if people will follow him across it. He's been told for so many years and by so many that he's only worth what they find valuable in him, what they can use.

Oh, Chase. I draw my knees up to my chest, hugging them to me. Hot tears roll down my cheeks to drip off my chin.

"And to Amanda Grace, I'd just like to say I'm so sorry." His voice cracks, and someone near the recording makes a soft "oh" sound. "I know you think I was pretending to be someone else. But I wasn't."

Mia's free hand finds mine and squeezes.

"I was trying to be a better version of myself, the person you make me want to be." His gaze catches "our" camera again, and I go still, watching his throat bob up with barely restrained emotion. "But I messed up. My fear got the better of me. I thought if I told you the truth, you'd leave, so instead I let you down in the worst way. That's completely unforgivable, I know. But when I said I loved you, I meant it."

The crowd explodes with noise, and he waits until they shush themselves into something resembling quiet before he continues.

"You told me once that we're all on our second or third or fourteenth chances. And I hope . . . I guess I'm still hoping for another one, even though I don't deserve it." His smile is tremulous and uncertain. "I still need to know your favorite color."

He runs a quick hand under his eyes, which makes the camera holder tremble again.

Then he shifts his gaze to the entire crowd, seeming to search for someone before nodding his head. "Thank you."

The screen freezes on him turning to go inside, and I want to push forward through it and chase after him.

But then the image goes dark and vanishes, and Mia lowers her phone to tuck it into the oversized pocket of her jacket.

Liza looks at her watch and sucks in a breath. "So late."

Mia takes advantage of her distraction and reaches up to snatch my phone from Liza's hand. "Give me that."

"Wait," I say.

Holding it away from both of us, she powers it on, and it sings to life. Almost immediately, it chirps with voicemails and texts.

"Chase . . . Mroczek?" She frowns. "Is that—"

"His real name," Liza and I say together.

"Huh. Probably a good thing he changed it, then," Mia mutters.

"Amelia," Liza says in warning. "Give me the phone."

Mia ignores her. "Well, Whatever His Name Is called you like twenty-seven times, and you have thirty-one new texts." Turning toward us, she lets her finger hover above the screen. "Should we find out what Mr. What's His Name has to say?"

"No," I say sharply even as a voice screams, *Yes!* inside my head.

"Why not?" Mia demands with a pout.

"Because it doesn't matter," I say wearily.

Liza hesitates. "What he said in the video *seemed* genuine," she admits. "Even with all the stammering."

"See?" Mia says.

"It's not up to you." Liza reaches over me to snatch the phone back from Mia, who's too busy scowling at me to see her coming.

"Hey!" Mia protests.

"She said no," Liza says. "So forget it. Just go back to school." Then she hesitates. "You okay?" she asks me with a cautious glance.

I nod, my chin rubbing against my pajama-covered knees. The fabric is damp from my tears. "Sure."

She gives me a considering look. "Maybe we need to take another drive when I get back from study group, try my stress-relieving technique again."

"What are you talking about?" Mia asks with a put-out expression.

"Nothing," Liza says firmly. "I'll see you tonight. *After* school."

But as soon as she's gone, the garage door's rumble signaling her departure, Mia resettles at the foot of my bed, reaching up to steal my bag of chocolate pretzels.

"So what's the plan?" she asks with her mouth full. "Hey, these are good." She examines the bag with new respect.

"What plan?" I ask, wiping away my tears with the back of my hand.

"Are you going to wait until Mom comes home and take the minivan to Wescott?" Mia crinkles her nose. "Ugh. Gross. No one wants to be seen rolling up in that. Oh!" She bounces a little, making the mattress shake. "I know. I have some cash saved. Maybe you could rent a car. Something, you know, star appropriate, like one of those Humvee limos or—"

"I'm not going to see him," I say quietly.

She stops bouncing, her expression the definition of crest-fallen. "What? Why not?"

I press the heels of my hands against my eyes, where a headache is beginning to throb. "It's not about him. Not entirely. It's about me. And yes, he apologized and told the truth, but that doesn't change anything." No matter how much I want it to.

Mia's mouth falls open. "Um, he just blew up his life for you," she says with a dramatic wave of her hand.

I shake my head. "I hope he didn't. I hope he did it for himself."

"And you don't want him back?"

"No! I mean, yes, I do. But it's *because* I do," I try to explain.

She raises one eyebrow. "Did you hit your head recently?"

I glare at her. "It's not about trusting him; it's about trusting me. He lied to me, and I believed him. I couldn't tell the difference." Just the memory of that makes my throat go dry and tight. "How am I ever supposed to believe him again?"

"Amma," she says with the air of someone taking great patience in the face of immense stupidity. "I met him. He cares about you. If he says he loves you, then—"

"You don't understand—"

She makes a frustrated noise. "I do, actually, and Chase Henry orchestrating a convenient rumor, which then happens to come true because he falls in fucking love with you, is not at all the same as a creepy bus driver who—"

I stiffen, every inch of me revolting at the comparison. "Amelia!"

"What—you're allowed to think it, but I can't say it?" she demands. "That's what this is about, isn't it?"

"Not everything is fixable," I say, avoiding the question.

"You're right," she says flatly. "Not when all you think about is being broken still. You're just scared. And that's bullshit. Because *everyone* is scared; they just don't have your excuse to quit."

I suck in a breath, jerking back from her.

She tosses my pretzels at me—my head, more like—then pushes herself off my bed and flees my room.

"That's not fair," I call after her. "Mia. Amelia!"

But she ignores me and thumps her way down the stairs, each clomp of her boots an indictment against me.

Damnit. I sag back against my pillows. I understand that *my* life over the last four years has been, for better or worse, holding theirs hostage.

And Mia's right—it's incredibly unjust. To her, to my parents, to Liza. But I don't know how to change, how to fix me. I want to trust Chase, but more than that, I *need* to trust myself again. And I don't know how to do that. I'm not sure it can be done.

The television clicks on in the family room, an ad for fast-food chicken blaring into existence, clearly indicating Mia's lack of interest in returning to school.

Which means I probably need to go down there and try to, I don't know, say something to her.

But I don't know what I'm supposed to say. Maybe leaving her alone to cool off is the better move. I have no idea.

As I'm sitting there, debating, the doorbell rings, and I straighten up, the loud, unexpected sound sending a jolt through me.

"I got it," Mia shouts, the habit a leftover from the days when we used to compete to see who could get the phone or the door first.

"No, Mia, don't!" I call. "It's probably reporters or a—"

"It's okay—it's just flowers!" She sounds excited, and I hear the noise of the deadbolt retracting. "Hey," she says in greeting to someone.

Flowers. From Chase? Is Chase *here*? I'm not sure I'm ready for that.

I scramble out of bed, but my foot gets caught in the covers, delaying me just a few extra seconds as I shake myself free.

Extra seconds that matter, as it turns out.

As I'm rushing out of my room and toward the stairs, I hear a thump from below and a surprised squeak from Mia.

When I peer over the railing toward the main floor, where Chase once stood facing off against my whole family, I see Mia and someone I don't recognize. The stranger is in a black base-ball cap and an oversized black jacket with her arm locked around Mia's neck.

An empty clipboard and a cheap grocery store vase of flow-ers are on the floor. The vase is tipped over on the blue and white rug, slowly staining it as water leaks out, and there's a heavy chemical smell in the air, familiar and yet out of place. I can't think of what it is, though, because Mia's face is so pale, her eyes huge in her face. As she pulls at the stranger's arm, the stranger's jacket sleeve moves, and I see the flash of shiny metal at Mia's neck. A knife.

"Amma," Mia whispers.

I freeze. This is everything I've ever feared. I can't move. Can't breathe.

Can't scream.

The stranger looks up, a too-bright grin flashing across her narrow face. Her familiar face, though I've only seen it in black-and-white security camera stills. "Amanda, right? I think we need to talk."

I'm in dancing-teacup flannel pajamas, and Chase's stalker, the one who sent me a box of rose petals and a chain, the one who burned a picture of us, is standing in the entryway of my house with a large kitchen knife pressed against the pulse in my sister's throat.

Adrenaline makes my ears buzz, and my lips go numb. I remember this feeling. This is danger, real danger. I felt it every time I heard Jakes's uneven steps on the stairs to the basement. I never knew when he would decide to kill me. He reminded me repeatedly that it would happen, sooner or later, when he was tired of me.

But it didn't.

And it doesn't have to happen today, either. Not for me or Mia. I have choices here, options. But I need to *move*.

And like that, air returns to my lungs, and I'm in motion.

"What do you want, Sera?" I ask, slowly walking down the staircase.

Her face brightens, revealing wrinkles by her mouth and her eyes. She's older than I thought, in her late thirties. "He mentioned me?"

Before I can say anything more, though, she shakes her head.

"It's not about what I want; it's about what you deserve." The seething hatred in her voice makes my knees wobbly, but I make myself keep going.

"You ruined him," Sera says. "Elise told me all about it. You *had* to just latch on to him and make this mess!" Her knife moves in a half-aborted gesture, and blood runs beneath the line of the blade.

Mia squeaks, tears rolling down her face.

I stop, three steps from the bottom. "Mia, stay still," I say quickly, trying to think. The nearest phone is the landline in the kitchen. There's no way I'm getting to that in front of Sera. But the front door is open. If someone will notice or just come up to the door . . . where are the reporters and photographers now that we need them?

"He can't even mention me publicly now and we've been waiting for years!" Sera shouts.

Okay, crazy. Definitely crazy. Think. Agree, agree. Keep him . . . her, keep her calm.

"You're right," I say.

Startled, she jerks her gaze to me.

"We should talk. Woman to woman, get this sorted out." It's complete bullshit, but I'm operating on experience now and it feels familiar in a horrible, reassuring way. I learned by hard experience that Jakes hated passive resistance the most, even more than screaming and crying. Which means that the few times I tried to reason with him, he felt the need to explain, to make me understand why I deserved to be taken. Why it was my fault: for being pretty, for walking by his house, for being alive.

It kept him from hurting me. Temporarily. But that was better than nothing.

"Glad you see it my way," Sera says, nodding approvingly as if I've passed some kind of test.

"I just need you to let Mia go. I don't feel like I have your full attention, otherwise. And you want me to have your attention, right?"

She narrows her eyes at me and points the tip of the knife in my direction. "Oh, no, no, I can't let her go. She'll call the police and then I'll have to explain to them all over again and they just won't listen. They never listen, and they keep confusing Chase."

"The bathroom just past the stairs," I say quickly. I don't want to put forth the idea that Mia is too much of a liability to be handled. "If you tie her up in there, no one will be able to see her and she won't be able to get out and call the police." Not to mention, tying her up will require that Sera find something to tie her up with and put down the knife to do so. Both of those might distract her long enough that I can dial 911 on the kitchen phone.

"Amma," Mia protests, fat tears wobbling down her face.

"Shut up," I say evenly, keeping my eyes on Sera. "Tie her up and then we can talk. I'm the one you want, aren't I?"

"Fine," she snaps. "But you tie her."

I move down the last few steps, barely feeling the wood beneath my feet but hearing every creak and every labored breath from Mia as she tries not to cry.

I can do this. I just need to get her away from Mia. After that . . . I'll deal with after, after.

I turn to lead the way toward the bathroom, certain with every cell in my body that I'm going to hear a sharp gasp and turn to see Mia sagging to the floor, her throat a gaping wound.

But her terrified whimpers and reluctant, stumbling footsteps tell me she's still alive. For the moment.

When I reach the doorway to the bathroom, I pivot to face the two of them.

Sera shoves Mia in the bathroom and steps back, waiting for me. For a half-second, I'm tempted to shove into her and hope for the best, but her knife is up, the edge dark with Mia's blood. If I die, I'm not sure what she'll do to Mia.

I turn on stiff legs and enter the bathroom ahead of Sera.

Mia is curled up in the tub near the faucet, one arm around

her waist and the other pressing her hand against her throat. A little red seeps through her fingers, but that's all. Her gaze is locked on Sera behind me.

As I approach the tub, I start to ask, "What do you want me to use for—"

Sera pushes past me to slash at the shower curtain.

Mia screams as strips of fabric and plastic land around her, and I'm paralyzed by indecision and fear. I could maybe run and make it out of the house, but I can't leave Mia behind and risk that Sera will take her anger out on a more convenient victim.

"There, ties. Ready, steady, go," Sera says, retreating to the doorway again. "I didn't bring any chains with me this time. Did you like my present, though?"

"It was very thoughtful," I manage, bending down to grab the end of a fabric strip with shaking hands and tear it free from the rest of the curtain.

Behind me, Sera laughs, and I shut my eyes for a second, convinced I'm going to feel the sharp point of the knife in my back at any second.

"You know, I've been thinking," she continues in that light, playful tone. "Instead of talking here, we should go for a drive. There's just not enough privacy around here. Too many nosy people interfering in our business." The harshness in her voice returns. She means Mia.

Get it together, Amanda.

"Sure, sounds good," I say, as dread pools in my stomach. If I go anywhere with her, the next time anyone will hear from me is when they find my bones in a trash bag in the woods.

"Amma, no," Mia whispers.

"So hurry up!" Sera stomps her feet, an impatient child eager to play with her toy. "Stop dragging it out."

I open my eyes and wrap the ragged fabric around Mia's wrists. Tight enough to pass inspection, should Sera check, but not so tight Mia can't get out on her own eventually.

"Just stay still. Keep pressure on your neck. You're going to be okay," I tell her quietly, hoping and praying I'm right. If I can just get Sera away . . .

Mia shakes her head at me, a quick jerk of her head, her lip quivering. Then her hand moves to her side, tapping her pocket once.

It takes me just a second to understand. Her phone. She still has her phone on her. The revelation is electricity in my veins.

All I need to do is get rid of Sera long enough for Mia to call.

As I loop the other end of the shower curtain strip over the faucet, I dare a quick glance over my shoulder at the mirror. Sera is behind me, at the threshold, but her focus is on my efforts at restraining my sister.

She's holding the knife lower now, tapping the flat of it against her leg, like it's a pencil and she's in a hurry to start the exam.

This is it. The best chance I'm going to get. My heartbeat is thunderingly loud in my chest, so much so that it feels like it'll give me away.

Keeping low, I spin and launch myself toward Sera, my hands aiming for her middle to shove her back.

"Amanda," Mia shrieks.

I expect to feel cold metal piercing my flesh, but instead, Sera clutches at my arms in surprise as she falls backward into the hall.

Twisting free of her, I leap back to make a grab for the door.

But before I can get it fully closed, she's up and reaching into the gap between the door and the frame.

She pushes the door against me, her knife coming in wildly, the tip of it slicing into my right forearm. The cut burns hot, and instinctively, I stumble back a step. That's enough for her to shove her shoulder and her face in. We're practically eye to eye, and I can feel her breath on my cheek.

If she gets both shoulders in, we're done. Mia's still tied, even though I can hear her working frantically at the knots I made. I won't be able to hold the door by myself, and then she'll kill us both.

But no, that's not going to happen. I *refuse* to let that happen.

With a bellow of rage that comes from deep inside me, I close my right hand into a fist, thumb on the outside just as Chase taught me, and drive it straight at her face with every bit of my weight.

My knuckles collide with her cheekbone with an impact that reverberates up my arm. But she falls back, clutching at her eye.

I shove my shoulder into the door, slamming it shut and locking it. Then I lodge my foot against the base of the door to keep it shut.

I'm panting, my legs are shaking so hard I don't think I can walk, and blood is dripping off my elbow, but I'm keeping this door closed no matter what.

Twisting my head so I can see Mia, I say, "9-1-1. Now." I'm bracing, expecting the thud of Sera's body against the door, her howl of frustration and rage.

But it's eerily silent out in the hall. For now.

Sobbing, Mia finally tugs free of the bonds around her wrists and fumbles her phone out of her pocket with a shaking hand. A few seconds later, I hear the reassuring beep of the numbers being dialed and then the beautiful sound of a connection going through and ringing on the other end.

"9-1-1, what's your emergency?" the operator asks in a crisp voice.

"Help us! Please!" Mia shouts.

That's when I smell smoke and look down to see the first curls of it drifting underneath the bathroom door.

36

Chase

My phone has been vibrating off and on all morning, ever since I stopped on my way back from set and announced to the waiting photographers, reporters, and fans outside the hotel that I would be making a statement in a couple hours.

It wasn't long before Max, Leon, Rick, even George, Elise's boss, were calling. I didn't listen to the messages, but I could easily imagine what they thought of the idea.

With the texts, I didn't have to imagine.

Don't do this. Call me.

You're being an idiot. Call me.

Call me. You're going to ruin everything.

All variations on the same theme.

But none of the messages, voice or text, was the right one, from the right person. So I ignored them all until after my statement, when it would be too late for any of them to do anything.

Standing out there, telling the truth, in my own words, was the most exhilarating and terrifying thing I've ever done.

Then I heard from Leon.

Now, forty-five minutes later, my phone is buzzing again insistently in the cup holder of my rental car.

I glance down at the screen. Karen.

I'm only about fifteen miles from my destination now. She can yell at me then.

But as soon as the call drops or goes to voicemail, she calls back immediately.

On the third attempt, worry worms its way into my gut.

Keeping one hand on the wheel, I reach for the phone with the other, answering it and hitting the speakerphone button. "Karen? What's wrong?"

"Where are you? Why aren't you answering your phone?" she demands.

I hesitate. No matter how I explain it, it's going to sound bad. I'm going to leave Amanda alone. I won't bother her; she's made it clear with her silence that's what she wants.

I told the truth this morning because it was the right thing to do, because it was what I needed to do for myself. But my whole reason for announcing that I would be making a statement instead of just doing it was to lure Sera out and keep her attention focused on me instead of Amanda.

But according to Leon, the last confirmed Sera sighting was still when she took a crowbar to the squad car. A whole day ago. She could be anywhere. Including somewhere near Amanda.

I hung up on Leon right then, grabbed my keys that I'd taken back from Karen, and headed straight for my crap-ass rental car.

"I'm busy," I say to Karen now. "Can you yell at me later?" Five minutes of research on my phone before I started driving gave me the name of the officer who found Amanda in Jakes's basement. Beckstrom. Even if no one else in the Springfield PD takes my concerns about Sera seriously, I'm betting she will.

Karen makes an impatient noise. "I hope that's your cagey

way of saying you're doing the dumbass thing and going to Springfield."

I frown, confused. "What?"

"Are you or are you not on your way to Amanda?" she demands.

"I'm going to the police in Springfield," I say cautiously.

"Skip the cops; go to her house."

I take my eyes off the road for a second to stare at the phone as if it will give some clue to Karen's bizarre behavior on this call. "Karen, I'm not just going to show up and—"

"They're already there," she says. "The cops."

A chill rises on my skin as the heavy weight of dread settles over me. "What?"

"It's all over television." She swallows audibly, and in the silence, in her reticence, I can hear genuine fear. "I guess the photographers and the reporters . . . they were going to try to get a reaction to your statement, but then they got this . . ."

"What, Karen? What did they get?" I demand, my hands tightening on the wheel.

"I don't know." Her voice grows more distant. "It's hard to tell, exactly."

"Karen!"

"I don't know, okay? They haven't said, but her house is on TV. It's live. Police, ambulances, everywhere."

"Ambulances?" I ask weakly.

"And fire trucks." She hesitates, then adds, "There was a fire at the house, Chase. They've got footage of it."

Oh, Jesus.

The smell of smoke, of wood burning, is thick in the air, even through the vents in my car. Normally, that's a happy scent, one of fond memories of bonfires in high school.

But not now, not this.

The front of Amanda's home is blackened, especially near the door. Firefighters are moving around inside. I catch flashes of yellow, their protective gear, through the front windows.

Two ambulances are backed in by the garage. Police cars block the lawn and part of the driveway, and yellow crime scene tape flaps in the breeze, tied to trees and the mailbox, to keep people back. Clusters of paparazzi and a few reporters with full camera setups are standing as close as possible to the tape line.

I'm sick with dread.

I jerk the wheel to the side of the road and shove the gearshift into park. Grabbing my phone, I bolt from the car, not even bothering with shutting the door.

But as soon as I reach the tape, a cop is in front of me, his hand up. "No."

"But I'm—"

"I don't care who you are." His glare tells me he knows exactly who I am and that pretty much anyone, including the devil himself, would have a better shot of getting through.

My pulse is rattling in my throat. I need to see Amanda, need to see that she's okay.

I move along the edge of the caution tape, looking for a chance to duck under, but there are too many cops blocking the way. I have no problem challenging them, but getting arrested before I find Amanda is the very definition of an impulse control problem.

"Fuck," I mutter.

I turn to the closest group of photographers, all of whom are focusing their cameras on the house and the ambulances.

"What happened?" I demand. "Did you see anything?"

The closest guy, with shaggy hair sticking up all over the place, lowers his camera with an annoyed look until he recognizes me. "Chase Henry," he says with a broad smile. "Well, all right, then."

"It's Chase Henry," someone else whispers.

"Get it, get it!" another voice yells.

Cameras start going off all around me.

I put my hand up. "I'll give you whatever pictures you want; just tell me what's going on."

"Don't know, mate." The shaggy-haired guy shrugs. "We got here and Emergency Services was already on it. Smoke was pouring out of the house, but they've got that down now."

"What about people? Have you seen Amanda? Have they said anything?" Multiple ambulances means multiple injuries. Or worse. The fact that ambulances haven't left yet makes me afraid there's no reason to hurry.

"No, sorry." And he almost looks like he means it, even as he snaps another photo of me.

With shaking hands, I lift my phone and hit her number again. But it goes straight to voicemail. Again.

Frustration and fear get the better of me then. "Amanda!" I shout toward the house. "Can you hear me?"

"Hey, Amanda!" someone else nearby yells.

"Amanda Grace, Chase is here!" the shaggy-haired paparazzo shouts.

They all take up the call, in various forms, shouting my name and hers until the noise is louder than the engines running on all the emergency vehicles.

The Australian looks at me and shrugs with a rueful grin. "Either way, it's a good story, mate."

After a moment, I see movement around the side of the garage, and I catch my breath.

It's Liza, the older sister. Her glasses are shoved up on her head, and her face is streaked with soot and tears. Most alarming, though, is the blood on her pale blue sweater, in a large splotch shaped like a handprint. Her arms are locked around her waist against the cold or shock or both, and she's peering out at us, like a rabbit cornered by wild dogs.

I press against the tape and wave wildly at her, not caring if I look like an idiot.

"Back up!" the cop shouts at me.

I ignore him. "Liza!"

"He's over here," my Australian friend shouts to Liza on my behalf, pointing at me with one hand and snapping pictures with the other the whole time.

Liza's gaze finds mine, and she jerks back in shock. Or anger—it's impossible to tell.

"Wait!" I shout as she disappears from view behind the garage. *Damnit.* "I just want to know if she's okay!" But there's no way she can hear my words now.

My heart sinks.

A moment later, though, there's movement on the same side of the garage.

It's not Liza.

Amanda's moving slowly, barefoot and splashed with soot. The right side of her shirt is covered in brownish-red blotches and splatter.

Blood.

The sleeve on that side is slashed and flapping open. Bright white bandages stand out against the pale skin of her wrist. Her eyes lock with mine, and her hand flies up to cover her mouth. Then she's running toward me.

I duck under the line over the nearest cop's protest—fuck that guy—and run for her.

She collides hard with me, her arms going around my neck as I wrap my arms around her waist and lift her up. Her feet are bare, and it's so cold out here.

Burying her face against my neck, she shivers, and I feel the heat of her tears against my skin.

"Are you okay?" I ask, my voice muffled in her hair.

"I'm fine," she says, but the words make her cough so hard her whole body shakes with it.

Carrying her over to the edge of the driveway, where at least the ground is dry, I set her down and shrug out of my coat to put it around her shoulders. I think the coughing is from the smoke, but it's still really cold out here.

When she catches her breath, her eyes are watering. "I . . . need stitches, I guess." She waves her left hand vaguely toward the bandages on her other arm. "But I wanted to answer their questions first."

"What happened?"

"Sera . . ." She coughs again. "She came to the house. Mia . . . Mia didn't realize and she opened the door. Sera had flowers. Gasoline in the vase, though. I think Mia thought she was a delivery person."

I grit my teeth. "I'm so sorry, Amanda. I'm so fucking sorry."

"She wanted me to leave with her, to talk. She had a knife. She cut Mia." Her face crumples, but she struggles against it and maintains her composure.

"Is Mia okay?"

Amanda nods slowly, dazed still. "Scared. Cut on her throat. She doesn't need stitches, but they want to take her in to check her out, and she won't go without me." She pauses. "Sera tried to set us on fire."

My eyes are watering fiercely. "Jesus, Amanda, I—"

"I stuffed wet towels under the door and kept most of the smoke out, and they got us out pretty fast because Mia was already on the phone with 9-1-1." She shakes her head. "They caught Sera because she stayed around to watch," she says, with a dry, painful-sounding laugh. "How messed up is that?"

I lean my forehead against hers, tears rolling down to join hers. "I'm so sorry. For this, for everything." I'll never be able to say it enough, so I'm going to say it as often as she'll let me in this moment. Because I don't know what, if anything, comes after.

She nods, and we stand there together, touching but barely, for a moment.

"I made a statement this morning," I begin, "and I—"

"I saw it," she says, her gaze on the ground.

I swallow nervously and wipe at my face. "You did?"

"Mia showed me, right before." She glances up then, a weary smile creasing through the dirt and soot. "It was good."

"Yeah?" I ask.

"Yeah."

I gnaw on my lower lip before releasing it to speak. "When they couldn't find Sera in Wescott after, I was worried. I was coming to talk to the police here, when Karen called and told me."

Amanda's forehead creases in a frown. "You shouldn't have taken the risk."

"That's not why I did it," I say softly. "I meant what I said. Every word of it."

"I know," she says. "But it was still a risk." She pokes me sharply in the shoulder.

"Had to do it. Some risks are worth taking." I reach up to push her hair back away from her face, but stop, not sure if it would be welcome. I want to touch her, want to pull her against me and feel her chest moving against mine and her heart beating.

"I did it, you know," she says after a moment. She sounds distant, almost thoughtful.

"Did what?" I ask cautiously.

"I fought back. Hit her." She holds up her right hand, displaying bruised and swollen knuckles. "Apparently, I have a mean right cross, according to the EMT." Her mouth curves in a small smile.

I suck in a breath at the sight of her hand. "You need X-rays," I say. "Trust me. Fractures aren't always so easy to—"

"I froze. But just for a second. I didn't need someone else to protect me, to tell me what to do, even an imaginary someone else," she says.

"You never did," I say quietly. "I told you, you're the bravest person I know."

She gives me another small smile. "I was scared as shit, though."

"I think that's normal," I say, trying not to choke on the laughter and pain that are both vying for preeminence. I am happy for her, even if it means she won't be part of my life. Even if it means she won't be mine. She'll be *hers* and that's more important.

But she doesn't seem to hear me. "I'm going to be okay," she says with the air of someone figuring something out for the first time. "Maybe not yet, but soon."

I risk touching her uninjured cheek gently with my thumb. "I never doubted it for a moment." *I will miss you so much.*

Amanda leans toward my touch and then pulls back with a faint frown, and my heart goes with her.

I swallow hard, bracing myself for the words I know are coming next. *I'm sorry. Good-bye. Thank you, but . . .*

But then she lifts herself up on her toes to kiss me, her mouth moving fiercely against mine. And it's not a farewell gesture, not unless those usually include tongue.

I wrap my arms carefully around her, not sure where all her sore spots are, and pull her close, tasting her, the smoke, the tears, what I thought I'd lost forever. I'm going to do whatever it takes to be a person who is worthy of her.

Distantly, I hear hoots and hollers from the watching crowd, and over Amanda's shoulder, I see her family has come around the side of the garage as well. None of them looks particularly thrilled, other than Mia, in a pale version of her normal enthusiasm, but no one is rushing over to pull us apart, either.

"So," Amanda says when she pulls away, breathless. "I heard there's this great pancake place not too far from here."

I stare at her.

"What?" she asks. "I mean, we can't go today, but later." When I'm still too stunned to say anything, she rolls her eyes in faux exasperation. "And yes, okay, fine, you can mix one of those horrible syrup concoctions for me. But no orange-caramel-whatever."

"Goji berry." I grin at her, my vision growing blurry. "I love you." I hear the wonder and amazement in my voice, not that I love her but because I didn't know it was possible to feel so much for one person.

Her hand finds mine and squeezes. "I love you, too. And my favorite color is purple."

EPILOGUE

Amanda

One year later

"Amma, come on—you're going to make us late!" Mia bellows from downstairs. Experiencing trauma at Sera's hands has not dampened her drama or her volume. "Either you're ready or you're not. Nothing in that closet is going to make a difference now."

Actually, Mia's wrong about that. I dig out the pair of strappy sandal heels that Karen sent to go with my dress.

"Be right there!" I shout toward my partially closed door.

Once I have the shoes on, I take a deep breath and one last look in the mirror next to my dresser. It's the boldest thing I've ever worn and that includes the last time I visited Chase in Los Angeles, as documented by the infamous V-neck photos. So, sue me—I wanted to entice my boyfriend. When you're squeezing in-person visits between weeks of Skype, while he visits his family in Texas (literally mending fences sometimes) and prepares for a role in a stage production of *Hamlet* in Los Angeles, you do what you can to blow his mind.

I'm aiming for that again tonight.

My shoulders are bare in the strapless dress with a black bodice that clings to, well, what little I have on top, making it look like more. The skirt is a light, floaty peach material with an artfully uneven hem. I love it. I've never felt more beautiful in my life.

Thanks to careful stitching at the time, the wound on my arm from Sera's knife has faded to a thin white line, barely noticeable. The thick scar on my left wrist, however, is as visible as ever. And tonight, for better or worse, I'm showing it off. The heavy black beaded bracelet, also a Karen pick, could just as easily go on my left wrist to hide it, but I'm not hiding anymore.

My pulse dances in an excited rhythm when I hear the front door open and a familiar voice downstairs.

Chase is here.

And in a couple of months, I'll be in California with him. I've already started to pack—okay, I'm a little excited. After a few months of taking gen eds at Springfield Community College, I'm ready for my second-semester start as a psychology major at Woodbury, which isn't far from Chase's apartment. But I'm living on my own in a dorm for at least a year. It's important to me to prove to myself that I can do it, and Chase understands that, probably better than anyone.

My parents are . . . mostly okay with it. It helps that Mia's pushing it, mainly because she wants to live there, too, once she graduates. And Liza has volunteered to come out and stay with me for a couple of weeks to help me get settled in my new room. The best part about that is, I *want* Liza and Mia to come, but I don't *need* them there to feel like I can do it.

Before I leave, I take an extra second to pull the closet door shut, feeling the moment as strongly as I did that day over a year ago when I tucked myself inside. Not anymore. Never again.

I walk out of my room without looking back. When I reach the landing at the top of the stairs, Chase glances up and his mouth falls open. "Wow," he says.

A ridiculously happy smile stretches the limits of my face. Okay, *now* I've never felt more beautiful in my life.

"Red-carpet worthy?" I tease, as I descend carefully in my heels.

"Definitely. Though, apparently, it's blue carpet tonight. Blue and gold are the Wescott town colors, so . . ." He shakes his head. "Wow," he says again, in that soft awed voice.

I laugh. He looks amazing, too, of course. He's wearing a dark, fitted suit and a white shirt, both of which make his eyes look an even more beautiful shade of dark blue. His blond hair is a little longer than when I saw him a few weeks ago and I can't wait to touch it. Can't wait to touch him. To hear him call my name in those soft, private moments in the dark.

"Come on," Mia says impatiently, a blur in bright blue satin as she darts out the door to the limo that will take the three of us to the premiere of *Coal City Nights* in Wescott. My parents and Liza, insisting that they won't want to stay for the after-party, have already gone ahead in a separate car. Mia will probably want to be out later than all of us.

Chase extends his elbow when I reach the bottom of the steps, as formal as our clothing. I love it. I take his arm, and he starts us toward the front door.

"Wait." He pauses with a frown. "It's cold out. Do you have a jacket . . . shawl thing?"

"A wrap?" I ask, amused.

"Yeah."

"Yes, it's upstairs."

He raises his eyebrows.

"I don't want to cover up this dress," I admit with a grin.

I'm finally feeling comfortable enough with myself, with all of who I am and what I've been through, thanks in part to Dr. Lundstrom. She's lucky number eight, a therapist I found through a fellow member of a sexual violence survivor's group I joined last year.

"I don't want you to, either," Chase says, watching me with a heated gaze as he moves to open the front door for me.

As I pass him, he leans forward and brushes his lips against my bare shoulder, and I go still. "I'm warning you, though: I don't have any extra shirts to give tonight," he murmurs against my skin.

With a delicious shiver, I turn to face him. "Bet I could talk you into it." With these heels, I'm a lot taller than normal, which brings my mouth within easy reach of a lot of interesting places, and I can't resist temptation.

I lean forward and press my mouth against his jaw, and he catches his breath sharply.

"Always," he says. "Always."